Henry Stephens Salt

The Life of James Thomson

Henry Stephens Salt

The Life of James Thomson

ISBN/EAN: 9783337416690

Printed in Europe, USA, Canada, Australia, Japan

Cover: Foto ©Raphael Reischuk / pixelio.de

More available books at **www.hansebooks.com**

THE LIFE

OF

JAMES THOMSON ("B.V.")

WITH A SELECTION FROM HIS LETTERS
AND A STUDY OF HIS WRITINGS

BY

H. S. SALT

AUTHOR OF "LITERARY SKETCHES," ETC.

LONDON
REEVES AND TURNER, 196 STRAND
AND
BERTRAM DOBELL, CHARING CROSS ROAD
1889

Ballantyne Press
BALLANTYNE, HANSON AND CO
EDINBURGH AND LONDON

PREFACE.

—•—

I COULD wish that the duty of writing this biography
had been entrusted to one who had enjoyed the advantage of personal acquaintance with James Thomson. As, however, no such biographer was forth-
coming, I have done my best to put together the
scattered records already published, and to collect
such further information as could still be obtained.
It has been my object to avoid all fancy portraiture,
and to give a clear and reliable narrative of the main
facts of Thomson's life, allowing his letters as much
as possible to tell their own tale, and quoting in many
cases the actual words of those who have recorded
their personal reminiscences.

I gratefully acknowledge the cordial help I have
received from a large number of Thomson's friends
and correspondents. To Mr. Bertram Dobell, in
particular, I owe my best thanks for his untiring
kindness and goodwill, and for the loan of numerous
letters and manuscript poems. Mr. Percy Holyoake
generously placed at my service his interesting collection of Thomson's papers, including the diaries

kept between 1874 and 1881, without which this
biography could hardly have been written. I am
indebted to Mrs. John Thomson, Mr. J. W. Barrs,
Mrs. Pelluet, Mr. W. M. Rossetti, Mrs. Greig, Mrs.
Bradlaugh Bonner, and Mrs. James Potterton for the
use of letters, notebooks, and other documents, and
for information about certain points in Thomson's
life and character.   For further assistance of various
kinds I have to thank Mr. John Grant, Mr. and Mrs.
T. R. Wright, Mr. George Meredith, Mr. William
Sharp, Mrs. George Duncan, Mr. Charles Duncan,
Mr. W. Weller, Mr. G. W. Foote, Mr. Charles Brad-
laugh, Mr. W. E. Jaques, Mr. G. J. Harney, Mr.
Byron Webber, Mr. A. A. Thomson, Mr. Thomas
Carson, Mrs. Birkmyre, Mr. C. A. Watts, the Rev.
C. M. Barnes, Dr. R. Garnett, Mr. F. Potterton.

The frontispiece is from a photograph taken in
1869, when Thomson was in his thirty-fifth year.

H. S. S.

CONTENTS.

— ◆ —

LIFE OF JAMES THOMSON.

CHAPTER I.

YOUTH.

JAMES THOMSON, the second poet of that name—one
who, in spite of his present comparative obscurity,
is perhaps destined to take rank hereafter among
the foremost writers of the age in which he lived—
was born at Port Glasgow on the 23rd of November
1834, of Scotch parentage on both sides. His father,
James Thomson, who was the son of a Scotch weaver,
and a native of Pitlochry, is said to have been a
clever man in many ways, with a strong talent for
mechanics. He was a sailor, and being devotedly
attached to his profession, attained a good position
in the merchant service; he is described by those
who knew him personally as a delightful companion, bright and cheerful in disposition, reading
and reciting well, fond of music, and singing a good
song in congenial society. On January 12, 1834, he
was married, in London, to Sarah Kennedy, a deeply
religious woman of the Irvingite faith, whose nature,
unlike that of her husband, seems to have been of a
somewhat melancholy cast; though she was a most

A

affectionate wife. and mother. Their family consisted of James, the eldest child ; a daughter born in 1836, or thereabouts, who died three years later ; and a second son, John, born in 1842. The religious training which James received in his childhood was of the strictest kind ; forty years later, he had still a vivid recollection of having to commit to memory what was known as the "Assembly's Shorter Catechism," and of the dismal feelings with which he looked forward to the longer task that was to follow.*

In 1840 an accident occurred which had an important influence on the boy's career. His father, who was the chief officer of the ship *Eliza Stewart* of Greenock, was entirely disabled by a paralytic stroke while on a distant voyage, and was rendered helpless for the rest of his life, the family being thus suddenly thrown into distressed circumstances. It has been said that their fall in the social scale was owing to intemperance on the part of the father ; but no direct evidence of such habits is discoverable, except that Thomson once told a friend, in after years, that intemperance ran in the family, and that "nearly all the members of it who 'had brains,' especially a gifted aunt of his, fell victims to its power." † However this may have been, the paralytic stroke was the immediate and direct cause of the misfortunes that followed ; and in 1842 we find the family residing at various addresses in the east of London, having now lost their former comfort and internal happiness. Through the kindness of friends, especially a Mr. James Boyd of Burgess Hill, an old

---

* *Memoir*, by Bertram Dobell, p. xvii.
† *Progress*, April 1884.

fellow-townsman of Mrs. Thomson's, an application
was made in August 1842 for the admission of James
to the Royal Caledonian Asylum, and on December 1
the boy was elected by vote, having been previously certified to be "in every particular in a good
state of health." Shortly after James's admission
to the Asylum his mother died—a blow which he
undoubtedly felt very severely, though he seldom
mentioned it—and his younger brother was taken to
Glasgow by an aunt. The father lived till 1853, but
as his health and mental powers were seriously
affected by his illness he could no longer take charge
of his sons; and thus it came about that James was
left practically without relatives, or at least without
any who were willing to help him. But he was not
friendless; for during the time he stayed at the
Asylum, and some years afterwards, he was a constant visitor at the house of Mr. William Gray, an
old friend of his parents, in whose family he regularly spent his holidays, and was treated with great
kindness and hospitality. In a letter written to his
sister-in-law, Mrs. John Thomson, in the last year
of his life, in answer to a request for some information concerning his parents and childhood, Thomson
has put on record the following reminiscences, though
for the most part he was extremely reticent, even
to his closest friends, on the subject of his family
relations :—

"I was just past eight years old and at the school when
mother died, so I can only give you very early impressions.
These are, that father and mother were very happy together
when he was at home, until, when I was about six, he
returned from his last voyage paralysed in the right side,
the result, as I understand, of a week of terrible storm,

during which time he was never able to change his drenched clothes. Before then I think he was a good husband and a kind father : her I always remember as a loving mother and wife. He may have been a bit gay, in the sense of liking a social song and glass, being, I believe, much better looking and more attractive in company than either of his sons. She was more serious, and pious too, following Irving from the Kirk when he was driven out. I remember well Irving's portrait under yellow gauze, and some books of his on the interpretation of prophecy, which I used to read for the imagery. The paralysis at first unhinged father's mind, and he had some fits of violence; more generally his temper was strange, disagreeable, not to be depended upon. I remember him taunting her with being his elder. Mother must have had a sad time of it for a year or so. His mental perturbations settled down into a permanent weakness of mind, not amounting to imbecility, but very, very different, I should say, from his former brightness and decision. Before I went to the School he used to take me to chapels where the members of the congregation ejaculated groaning responses to the minister's prayer, and to small meetings in a private room where the members detailed their spiritual experiences of the week. Good, bad, or indifferent, these were not the sort of things with which he had anything to do in his days of soundness. The right hand remained useless, but the leg had gradually grown strong enough to walk well, though with an awkward dragging pace.

I think mother, who was mystically inclined with Edward Irving, had also a cloud of melancholy overhanging her; first, perhaps, from the death of her favourite brother, John Parker Kennedy, drowned on the Goodwin Sands; then probably deepened by the death of my little sister, of whom I remember being devotedly fond, when she was about three and myself five, of measles caught from me. Had she or some one else lived, I might have been worth some-

thing; but, on the whole, I sincerely judge that it was well
for both to die when they did, and I would not, for my own
selfish comfort, call them back if I could. At first I would
doubtless have done so, but not for many years past.

"We had also good friends, mother and daughter, named
Smith, whom I knew still some years on in my schooldays,
and then lost sight of. Speaking generally, you know far
more of my family than I do, who have been Ishmael in
the desert from my childhood."

It has been generally assumed by those who have
written about Thomson, that the two most prominent
traits of his character were inherited from his parents,
the emotional and imaginative temperament being
traced to his mother, to his father the constitutional
dipsomania which was the cause, or at any rate the
aggravation, of the gloom of his closing years. One
can only speculate vaguely on such a subject as this;
since, where so little is positively known of either
parent, it would be rash to speak with certainty.
This much, however, may be confidently stated at
the outset, and will become more and more evident
as we follow the story of Thomson's life,—his nature
was a compound of two diverse and warring elements,
a light-hearted gaiety and rich sensuous capacity for
enjoyment being set side by side with a constitutional and ever-deepening melancholia. Much that
may seem incongruous and contradictory in the following narrative must be ascribed to this fact, in which,
too, may be found the explanation of the different
impressions made by Thomson's character on different
friends and acquaintances.

At the early period of which I am now speaking
the germ of melancholy was wholly imperceptible and
unsuspected. We cannot doubt that the sudden

break-up of his home life was a heavy grief which
left its mark on his character, but there is no ground
for regarding Thomson's boyhood as that of a mere
neglected orphan and "institution-child," or for supposing that the eight years he spent at the Caledonian Asylum were nothing but a time of solitude
or unhappiness.   Among his schoolfellows his especial "chum" was the late Mr. George Duncan,*
whose elder brother, Mr. Charles Duncan, remembers
Thomson, a fine, clever, high-spirited boy, taking the
lead among his companions both in the schoolroom
and the playground, and thoroughly popular with all
who knew him.   He was first clarionet in the school
band; and it is said that on one occasion, when the
boys had performed at an entertainment given at the
Chelsea Hospital, Jenny Lind, who was present, was
induced, at Thomson's request, to sing to the boys
by way of making them a fair return for their efforts
on her behalf.

On August 2, 1850, Thomson left the Caledonian
Asylum, and was admitted, as a monitor, at the
"Model School," Royal Military Asylum, Chelsea.
Owing to his powerful memory and great natural
abilities, he had made unusually rapid progress in
his studies; in mathematics especially he showed
that he possessed talents of no common order.   He
was now close upon sixteen years of age, and the
question of his future profession had been decided in
favour of a school-mastership in the army, for which
it was necessary first to qualify at Chelsea.   It had
been Thomson's own wish to obtain a clerkship in
some bank or mercantile office, but as he had no

---

* Late of Madras Educational Department: died 1886.

resources of his own, he was compelled to take the advice of his teachers at the Caledonian Asylum, and to enter the profession in which he could most quickly earn a livelihood. His schoolfellow, George Duncan, accompanied him to Chelsea, where he soon made other good friends, among whom he was known familiarly as "Jimmy;" the title of "little Thomson" was also applied to him in order to distinguish him from a taller namesake. At Chelsea, as at the Caledonian Asylum, he rapidly proved his superiority as a scholar; and stories are still related by his surviving schoolmates, how, when the other members of his class were anxious to throw a veil over their own deficiencies, they would beg Thomson to put forward "something stiff," in the form of a mathematical problem, to which he would opportunely invite the master's attention, and so occupy his time. His literary tastes were also very remarkable, both in their choice and scope, for a boy of his age; for he was already well versed in many of the masterpieces of Swift, Fielding, Smollett, Sterne, De Foe, De Quincey, and other favourite authors. It was about the time of his admission to the Chelsea military school that he became a reader of Shelley. "I and a chum," he wrote in a letter of 1874, "used to read and hugely admire Byron when I was about fifteen; but a year or so later, when I was about sixteen, I fell under the dominion of Shelley, to whom I have been loyal ever since." This intense love of reading was retained by Thomson to the end of his life, and we shall more than once have occasion to note how eager he was to induce others to take a like pleasure in good literature.

The following account of Thomson in his youth is

given by Mrs. Greig,* who, as Miss Agnes Gray, had known him intimately when he used to spend his holidays at her father's house between 1842 and 1852 :—

" Being several years younger than James, I cannot re-collect much about him as a boy, but I remember we always thought him wonderfully clever, very nice-looking, and very gentle, grave, and kind. He was always most willing to attend to our whims, but my eldest sister was his especial favourite. Her will seemed always law to him. She was gay as he was grave, but whatever Helen said or did won approbation from him. . . . Previous to going (to Ireland) he earnestly requested that my sister might be allowed to correspond with him, a request which my parents thought it wiser to refuse. I was allowed, however, to do so, and although his letters came few and far between, I always welcomed and appreciated them. He used to endea-vour to guide my tastes and give me good advice as to the books I should read, sending me Charlotte Brontë's ' Life and Letters,' Mrs. Browning's ' Aurora Leigh,' some poems by Robert Browning, and a few other books."†

The departure for Ireland, referred to in the above passage, marks the next stage—and a very important one, as it happened—in Thomson's career. Before a student was enlisted as an army-schoolmaster, it was customary for him to serve for twelve or eighteen months as an assistant-teacher, in order to gain some practical knowledge of his profession ; Thomson was accordingly sent from Chelsea, on August 5, 1851, to the garrison of Ballincollig, a village lying about five miles from Cork, amidst picturesque scenery.

---

* *Memoir*, by Bertram Dobell, p. 10.
† Some of these letters are given in Chapter II.

His position here was that of a pupil and master in one—his duties consisting in teaching in the regimental school under the direction and supervision of the regular garrison-master, whose name was Joseph Barnes. Mr. Barnes was a self-educated man, of strong native sense and kindly disposition, with whom Thomson soon became a favourite, and in whose family he was treated, as he has himself recorded, " with great and rare kindness." Both Mr. and Mrs. Barnes felt the warmest affection and admiration for their brilliant and accomplished young assistant, who, at the early age of seventeen, was already qualified to discharge the duties of a teacher; and " Co" (for " Precocious ") was the pet name by which he was known in their house; while Thomson, on his part, never forgot the kind treatment he experienced at their hands. It is said that at one time, when Mrs. Barnes was ill, and Mr. Barnes happened to be absent from home, Thomson taught in the schoolroom at Ballincollig, holding Mrs. Barnes's child on one arm, and with his disengaged hand writing on the blackboard. As late as 1862, ten years after he left Ballincollig, we find him addressing a series of six sonnets, not meant for publication, to these friends of his youth, and speaking with grateful recollection of Mr. Barnes as " a man of genial heart and liberal mind," and of Mrs. Barnes as the " second mother of my orphaned youth."

> My dear, dear Friends, my heart yearns forth to you,
> In very many of its lonely hours ;
> Not sweetlier comes the balm of evening dew
> To all-day-drooping in fierce sunlight flowers,
> Than to this weary withered heart of mine
> The tender memories, the moonlight dreams,

Which make your home an ever-sacred shrine,
    And show your features lit with heavenly gleams.
I have with some most noble friends been blest,
    I wage no quarrel with my human kin,—
Knowing my misery comes from my own breast,
    At war with Fate by chance, and God by sin :
But of all living friends you claim in me
The love most sanctified by memory.

It was at Ballincollig, in 1851, that Thomson first became acquainted with Mr. Charles Bradlaugh, and formed a close friendship with him which lasted for more than twenty-three years. Mr. Bradlaugh, who was Thomson's senior by one or two years, had enlisted in the army about the time when Thomson was sent to Ballincollig ; and the two young men, in spite of their marked diversity of temperament—the iconoclast and the idealist, the man of action and the man of thought—were soon intimately associated. They read together, and talked together, and sometimes, when Mr. Bradlaugh was on picket duty, Thomson would walk up and down with him, on a fine summer's night, discussing in a friendly way the various subjects, social, political, or religious, in which they were both interested. Their opinions at this time differed very considerably, but there was no attempt, on one side or the other, to effect anything in the nature of a conversion ; each was content to state his own views, without any thought of urging them on the acceptance of his companion.

We now come to a most important incident in Thomson's life, about which much has necessarily been written, though there is unfortunately a great lack of detailed information. It was at Mrs. Barnes's house that he first met the beautiful young girl whose love he won, and whose sudden death was the heaviest

calamity he ever endured. In the sonnets addressed
to Mr. and Mrs. Barnes he thus alludes to his early
love and bereavement :—

> Indeed you set me in a happy place,
>   Dear for itself and dearer much for you,
> And dearest still for one life-crowning grace—
>   Dearest, though infinitely saddest too :
> For there my own Good Angel took my hand,
>   And filled my soul with glory of her eyes,
> And led me through the love-lit Faërie Land
>   Which joins our common world to Paradise.
> How soon, how soon, God called her from my side,
>   Back to her own celestial sphere of day !
> And ever since she ceased to be my Guide,
>   I reel and stumble on life's solemn way ;
> Ah, ever since her eyes withdrew their light,
>   I wander lost in blackest stormy night.

This girl, the object of Thomson's devoted attach-
ment, was the daughter of the armourer-sergeant of
a regiment then stationed in the garrison at Ballincollig; her name was Matilda Weller, and she was
somewhat younger than Thomson himself, being about
fourteen at the time of which I speak. She was
afterwards described by Mrs. Barnes as resembling
Eva St. Clair in " Uncle Tom's Cabin," so that the
following passage from that novel may be taken as
giving at least a general idea of her appearance and
bearing :—

" Her form was the perfection of childish beauty, without its usual chubbiness and squareness of outline. There
was about it an undulating and aerial grace, such as one
might dream of for some mythic and allegorical being.
Her face was remarkable, less for its perfect beauty of
feature than for a singular and dreamy earnestness of
expression, which made the ideal start when they looked
at her, and by which the dullest and most literal were

impressed, without knowing why. The shape of her head
and the turn of her neck and bust were peculiarly noble,
and the long golden-brown hair that floated like a cloud
around it, the deep spiritual gravity of her violet-blue eyes,
shaded by heavy fringes of golden-brown, all marked her
out from other children, and made every one turn and
look after her, as she glided hither and thither. . . . Always
dressed in white, she seemed to move like a shadow
through all sorts of places without contracting spot or
stain." *

Such was Matilda Weller, as she lived in Mr.
Barnes's recollection; and it is a noticeable fact that
a very similar picture is given of her by Thomson
himself in the autobiographical poem entitled "Vane's
Story":—

> For thought retraced the long sad years
> Of pallid smiles and frozen tears
> Back to a certain festal night,
> A whirl and blaze of swift delight,
> When we together danced, we too !
> I live it all again ! . . . Do you
> Remember how I broke down quite
> In the mere polka? . . . Dressed in white,
> A loose pink sash around your waist,
> Low shoes across the instep laced,
> Your moon-white shoulders glancing through
> Long yellow ringlets dancing too,
> You were an Angel then ; as clean
> From earthly dust-speck, as serene
> And lovely and above my love,
> As now in your far world above.

There are many other passages in Thomson's
writings where his early love is idealised in various

---

* Quoted in Mr. Dobell's *Memoir*. A daguerreotype, taken
about 1850, now in the possession of Mr. William Weller,
confirms the general correctness of the description.

forms; in "The Fadeless Bower," for instance, we have a poetical description of the scene where the young lovers first plighted their troth. When one considers their extreme youth at the time (Thomson could only have been in his eighteenth year) it may seem strange that there should have been any actual engagement between them; but it must be remembered, on the other hand, that Thomson's nature was an altogether exceptional one, and that both in feeling and experience he was far in advance of his years. The story has sometimes been regarded as an exaggeration, or even a myth; but there is evidence in existence which proves beyond all doubt that the facts as above narrated are substantially correct.

On January 16, 1853, Thomson returned from Ballincollig, to the "Normal School" at Chelsea, as routine demanded a further course of study before he could be appointed to the post which, as a matter of fact, he was already quite capable of filling. His prospects at this time looked brighter than at any other period of his life, before or after. He had already acquired a considerable stock of knowledge, and no slight experience of the world; he had made many excellent friends; he had won the love of a beautiful girl; and he was about to receive an appointment which would at least enable him to earn a competent living. His rich and genial nature, no less than his rare intellectual faculties, seemed to mark him out at this opening period of his career as one eminently qualified to be happy, prosperous, and beloved.

A few months later the blow had fallen. In July 1853 a letter reached him at Chelsea with the news

of Matilda's illness; the next day he learned that
she was dead.* This was a crisis in his fate on
which, as far as is known, he uttered no word in his
after-life, even to his most intimate associates; but
those who knew the depth and intensity of his nature
could feel how great his grief must have been. He was
not unacquainted with death; for, as we have seen,
he had lost his only sister when he was a child of five
years, and his mother when he was eight; but this was
a still deeper and more fatal wound. It is said that
Mr. Barnes received a letter from a friend at Chelsea,
asking him what could be amiss with Thomson, as
he had not tasted food for three days; another
account records that he "lay about in the windows"
of the Military Training College in silent grief and
solitude. There can be no doubt whatever not only
that his sorrow was overwhelming at the time, but
that it left its traces on his whole subsequent career.
To what extent this early bereavement can be considered the *cause* of his later pessimism and unhappiness, is a more subtle question, which it is easier
to raise than to decide. Thomson himself seems on
rare occasions to have expressed, in confidence, to
one or two friends a belief that all his calamities
were due to this source; † and such is the purport of some pathetic autobiographical stanzas (not
intended for publication) which he wrote in 1878
under the title of "I had a Love;" in which he
speculates fondly on what might have been if the
hand of death had been averted. The following
stanza is expressive of this mood :—

---

* She died at Cahir, Tipperary, July 19, 1853.
† Note the reference to this point in the letter quoted on p. 4.

You would have kept me from the desert sands
   Bestrewn with bleaching bones,
And led me through the friendly fertile lands,
   And changed my weary moans
To hymns of triumph and enraptured love,
And made our earth as rich as Heaven above.

On the other hand, there are equally noticeable passages in which Thomson more philosophically regards his own unhappiness as the inevitable result of his destiny; and it is contended with great force by some of those who knew him that, being the victim of an inherited melancholia, he would in any case have seen his life grow dark around him as time went on.* The parallel between Thomson's case and that of his literary sponsor, Novalis, is a singularly close one; so close, indeed, that the remarks made by Carlyle on the effects of Novalis's bereavement may be quoted as exactly applicable to Thomson :—

"That the whole philosophical and moral existence of such a man should have been shaped and determined by the death of a young girl, almost a child, specially distinguished, so far as is shown, by nothing save her beauty, which at any rate must have been very short-lived—will doubtless seem to every one a singular concatenation. We cannot but think that some result precisely similar in moral effect might have been attained by many different means; nay, that by one means or another, it would not have failed to be attained. . . . We do not say that he continued

---

* *Cf.* Mr. Foote's article on Thomson in *Progress*, April 1884 :—" I do not agree with Mr. Dobell in regarding this bereavement as the *cause* of his life-long misery. She was, I hold, merely the peg on which he hung his raiment of sorrow; without her, another object might have served the same purpose. He carried with him his proper curse, constitutional melancholia."

the same as if this young maiden had not been; but surely it appears unjust to represent him as so altogether pliant in the hands of Accident; a mere pipe for fortune to play tunes on; and which sounded a mystic, deep, almost unearthly melody, simply because a young woman was beautiful and mortal." *

But while we fully recognise the force of this reasoning, we are compelled to believe, at the same time, that it was the death of this young girl that, above all other single circumstances, fostered and developed the malady to which Thomson was perhaps predisposed, and that in this limited sense, at least, it was a cause of his subsequent despondency. Nor need we be much surprised at the fact that some of his early friends noticed no change in his outward demeanour, and found him no less gay a comrade than heretofore, for he was by nature extremely reticent on all personal subjects, and on this particular point it was to be expected that he would set a special guard upon his lips. "His wounds," says Mr. Dobell, speaking of a period later by more than twenty years, " were not the less painful because he did not exhibit them in public, and of their deep and permanent character I once had a striking proof. We were talking together lightly and cheerfully enough, when a casual remark which I made chanced to recall the memory of his lost love. Well do I remember the effect upon him, how his voice changed, and how tears started to his eyes!" It would, I think, be as unfair to Thomson to assume that he was only lightly and transiently affected by the sudden death of the girl he loved, as to make the contrary mistake of attributing

* " Miscellaneous Essays."

to him the weakness of allowing his whole life to be wrecked by his bereavement. " Young Love," so he wrote in one of his " phantasies" more than twenty years later, " tendered them the apple of his Mother, golden and rose-red from her divine warm hand ; but it turned to dust and ashes on their lips ; for the bitterness of death they can never find peace ; they moan their frustrate lives."

So Thomson, burying in his heart the grief which he felt none the less acutely, lived out the rest of his time at the Chelsea Military School ; and was still regarded by his comrades as a genial, lovable, thoroughly genuine character, though even now possessed of a certain pride and *hauteur*, and capable at times of showing strong resentment against any injury or slight. He was a Radical ; and his keen, eager intellect was apt to make him impatient of the restraints imposed by authority. He doubtless felt, what indeed was true enough, that his further stay at the Asylum was wholly unnecessary ; and he is said to have made the governor of the school indignant by asking to be excused the remainder of his course, though his request seems to have been partly granted by the shortening of the required term. His namesake and fellow-student at Chelsea, Mr. A. A. Thomson, remembers " Jimmy " as a high-spirited, pleasure-loving companion, finding matter for merriment under the most unpromising conditions, and so far from being a pessimist in those days, that he was wont to laugh at the philosophy of " old Schopenhauer." It must not be supposed from his impatience of the ordinary scholastic routine that he was idle at this time ; on the contrary, it is probable that he did much hard reading during this second stay at Chelsea

B

—all the more, perhaps, since his mind needed a distraction from the remembrance of his calamity. "He had," it has been well remarked, "the Scotch square-headedness. He was strong in brain and of well-knit frame, a hard thinker, and a good endurer. His early life was that of stiff head-work—in which he excelled—and none too much luxury." * His self-taught mastery of languages remains to be spoken of in the next chapter ; but we may feel sure that his literary tastes were pretty well formed before he left Chelsea, and he had already become acquainted with the reading-room at the British Museum, which he frequented so much in later life. Reticent though he was at this time—to such an extent that it is said "you might talk to him for half-an-hour and he would only smile on you,"—he was nevertheless a good speaker, and took a prominent part in the School Debating Society and in all literary and social discussion.

His religious views had been considerably modified since the time when he was grounded in Presbyterian theology ; for, while still retaining the chief tenets of the faith in which he had been brought up, he had now entered into a dubious and transitional stage of thought, from which he did not altogether emerge till several years later. On August 7, 1854, about the time of the commencement of the Crimean war, Thomson was finally enlisted as an army school-master, being then just under twenty years of age.

---

* Mr. G. G. Flaws' essay on Thomson, *Secular Review,* June 24, 1882.

CHAPTER II.

ARMY SCHOOLMASTER.

THE first post to which Thomson was appointed was in connection with a South Devon Militia Regiment, at Plymouth—a difficult and trying position, among a dull, rough set of men, for which he was hardly suited, his finer qualities being entirely thrown away. From 1855 to 1856 he was at Aldershot with the Rifle Brigade; and here, though successful enough with his educational duties, he was unfortunate in not winning the favour of the commanding officer —not, as it appears, from any fault or failing on his part, beyond the fact that his high spirit was not sufficiently amenable to the imperious and exacting manner of the officer in question. An army schoolmaster, it should here be mentioned, is regarded as a soldier, and not as a civilian; he wears the uniform of the regiment to which he is attached, and is obliged to conform to the regular military discipline; his position, however, is, to a certain extent, undefined, inasmuch as his treatment depends a good deal on the personal feeling of his superiors, who have it in their power to be either courteous or supercilious as the case may be. The routine of school-work consisted in teaching the children in the morning, and the soldiers in the afternoon; at times, too,

the schoolmaster was liable to be asked to give
extra tuition to some more zealous or more backward
pupil, a service which Thomson was always willing
and prompt to perform. That he felt any keen interest in his profession, it would be rash to assert;
for the daily drudgery of the schoolroom could not
have been congenial to his swift and subtle intellect
and imaginative temperament; while, good comrade
though he was, there must have been times when he
longed for some more sympathetic society than that
of the camp and barrack-room. Nevertheless, there
is no reason to doubt that he discharged his duties
as a schoolmaster successfully and conscientiously;
and he certainly possessed two qualities which are
of the utmost value to a teacher—a methodical and
painstaking habit, and the power of simple and lucid
expression. A friend, whose daughter received some
lessons in modern languages from Thomson many
years after he had left the army, was struck by
the admirable method in which he conveyed the
instruction.

In the summer of 1856 Thomson was removed
from Aldershot, and having been sent to Ireland,
was afterwards attached to the 55th Foot, with which
regiment he remained as long as he continued to
serve in the army. For the next four years he
was stationed either at Dublin or the Curragh camp;
and it was while he was at the former place, in 1856,
that he made the acquaintance of Mr. John Grant,
also an army schoolmaster, with whom he was on
terms of intimacy during nearly all the rest of his
life. Mr. Grant had been a fellow-student with
Thomson at Chelsea in 1854, but, being his junior
by some years, had not then been brought into

contact with him; he had also heard anecdotes from
Mr. Barnes of Thomson's intellectual prowess and
originality of character, so that his interest was
already awakened before they had actually met. The
records of Thomson's army life are very scanty, like
those of his youth; but by means of the reminiscences of one or two intimate friends, a few letters
which have fortunately been preserved, and some of
the early poems, we are able to form a fairly clear
notion of him as he then was.

The popularity which he had enjoyed among his
comrades at Chelsea did not desert him in the army,
and he was generally liked and respected by those
who knew him. He took considerable interest in
various social movements for the recreation or instruction of the soldiers, would give lectures on
subjects with which he was familiar, and act as
showman during the exhibition of a magic-lantern, a
part which he performed to the full satisfaction of
his audience. He was also a good athlete, being
strong and hardy in frame; and was known as a
skilful rower and a powerful walker, often trudging
with his friend Grant to and fro between Dublin and
the Curragh camp, and other long distances. Nor
was his love of reading diminished by the demands
of his educational duties, which fortunately left him
leisure in the evenings for the self-instruction to
which he still devoted himself with characteristic
vigour and industry. He had dropped the study of
mathematics, in spite of his great talent in that direction, after leaving Chelsea; but being by nature an
excellent linguist, he set to work to acquire a knowledge of modern languages, beginning with German
soon after 1854. His method of learning was of the

severest and most rigorous kind, with no attempt
at gilding the educational pill; first the grammar as
a preparatory step, then one of the authors whom he
wished to read, no matter how hard the style and
idiom, to be puzzled out with no other assistance
than that of a dictionary.* On this system he taught
himself German, French, Italian, and a fair amount
of Spanish; also a little Latin and Greek, though he
does not seem to have spent much time on the latter.
Meantime he was still adding diligently to his knowledge of English literature; and it was about 1856
that he began to be a serious student of Robert
Browning, with whose earlier works, as well as
those of George Meredith, he had become acquainted
—by a sort of unerring literary instinct which always
led him to what was most vital and vigorous—even
before he left the military school. By this time he
had himself felt strongly the instinct towards authorship, and had written many poems; these, however, with one or two exceptions, he subsequently
destroyed.

Yet, happy and contented as Thomson might have
seemed at this period to a casual observer, or even
to those associates who knew him only as the quick-
witted and genial comrade, and not as the idealist
and bereaved lover, there is ample proof that he was
already experiencing a mood of deep dissatisfaction and
despondency. In some unpublished stanzas written
at Dublin on his twenty-third birthday (November
23, 1857) he seems to be divided between the torpor

---

* "His way of teaching himself Italian was simple; he
went to hear an Italian opera, bought a book of the words,
and studied each word down to its origin."—*Obituary notice
by P. B. Marston, Athenæum, June* 10, 1882.

of his grief in the past and the lingering hope of yet effecting something in the future :—

> Oh, for the flushed excitement of keen strife !
>   For mountains, gulfs, and torrents in my way,
> With perils, anguish, fear, and strugglings rife !
>   For friends and foes, for love and hate in fray—
> And not this lone base flat of torpid life !
>   I fret 'neath gnat-stings, an ignoble prey,
> While others with a sword-hilt in their grasp
> Have warm rich blood to feed their latest gasp.

So weary did he feel, at times, of the monotony of his profession, and so eagerly did he crave for a more active life, that he even discussed with his friend John Grant a plan of deserting from the army and going to sea. Reasons that may partly account for this state of feeling will readily suggest themselves to readers of the foregoing narrative ; the loss of love, followed, or perhaps preceded, by the loss of religious faith—without, as yet, the substitution of any philosophic conviction *—was in itself a terrible ordeal for a man of Thomson's intense sensibility, who above all things yearned for a rich, full life of domestic love and external action, for some certitude to lean upon, whether in the present or in a future existence. But now a fatal melancholy was beginning little by little to creep over his nature, which had seemed at first, and still seemed to outward observation, to be altogether joyous and light-hearted ; already his mind had begun to ponder those pessimistic thoughts which were afterwards summed up in the burden of his greatest and most sombre poem—" Dead Love, dead Faith, dead Hope." But, in addition to these de-

---

* On the question of Thomson's religious opinions, see pp. 295, 296.

spondent promptings, another and still more fatal
tendency was now manifesting itself—a tendency
which, in the opinion of those who had the best
means of judging, was inherited and constitutional
in its origin, though doubtless it was aroused and
accentuated by circumstances of grief and disappointment.   Intemperance, the bane of Thomson's later
career, was unknown to him up to about 1855; but
from that date onward he gradually became liable to
its power; not in the sense that it became an ordinary
habit of his life—his true nature, as witnessed by his
friends and expressed in his writings, is a proof to
the contrary—but rather a periodic disease, against
which he struggled hard, and often for many months
successfully, but never so as to shake it off altogether.

Thomson's friendship with his old schoolfellow
George Duncan had continued unbroken when they
both left Chelsea, and after his friend's marriage, in
1855, he regularly spent his holidays at Mr. and Mrs.
Duncan's house, until their departure to India in
1860.   "It was like coming," writes Mrs. Duncan,
in some interesting reminiscences of Thomson, "to a
brother and sister, for he was dearer to us than a
friend.   Often afterwards did we talk of him and his
great talents, and how he dreamed away the time,
always happy and contented with his Shelley.   When
a student, he would just glance over a subject, or
read it over once, and yet know it perfectly.   He
had a great fund of humour, and would often say
witty things.   Once my husband said to him, 'Jimmy,
do you know what it is to have a button off the
collar of your shirt?'   'No, George,' was the reply,
'for I don't know what it is to have one *on.*'   Another
time they were walking in Dublin, by the Law Courts,

I think. The pillars outside are fluted, and Thomson, seeing a begging musician playing in the front, remarked quietly, ' You see, George, those pillars are *doubly* fluted.' He had also frequent fits of melancholy years ago ; these my husband said were caused by his brooding over the death of a young and lovely girl, whom he loved most devotedly ; in fact, more as a saint than a mortal. A correspondence was kept up, and the friendship also, after we went out to India ; and if we wanted anything done in England, ' Jimmy ' was always the one to do it."

Another friend with whom Thomson was intimate during his stay in Ireland, and with whom he afterwards corresponded, was Mr. James Potterton, also an army schoolmaster. They had studied German together at the Curragh camp, and Thomson's letters sometimes enclosed copies of his translations from Heine, on which he invited his friend's criticism and advice ; at other times were cast in the form of verse —of a free, familiar, doggerel style—in which the writer opens his heart on the subject of his army life, the gossip of the camp, the drudgery of the school-room, and the philosophy which rendered it all endurable. Here is a specimen which may throw light on the feelings with which Thomson regarded his educational profession :—

And if now and then a curse (too intense for this light verse)
Should be gathering in one's spirit when he thinks of how he
    lives,
With a constant tug and strain—knowing well it's all in
    vain—
Pumping muddy information into unretentive sieves :
Let him stifle back the curse, which but makes the matter
    worse,
And by tugging on in silence earn his wages if he can ;

For the blessed eve and night are his own yet, and he might
Fix sound bottoms in these sieves too, were he not so weak
    a man.

These lines were written at Dublin in May 1858,
at which time Thomson was just about to move from
the Ship Street to the Richmond Barracks.   A couple
of months later we come to the first of a very interesting series of letters (or, rather, the first of those
preserved, for some earlier ones must have been lost)
addressed to Miss Agnes Gray, whose reminiscences
of Thomson's school-days have already been quoted.
I give these letters almost in full, as they are not
only good specimens of Thomson's admirable style
of letter-writing, but also afford us a glimpse into
his life as "dominie," and throw light indirectly on
many points in his character—his love of literature,
and eagerness to encourage other students ; his taste
for music and dancing ; his precise, methodical habit
of mind, which shows itself not only in the lucidity
of expression, but in the clear, bold penmanship ; and
his sympathy with the poor and suffering.   It will
be noted that he had already become an inveterate
smoker.

To Miss Agnes Gray.

RICHMOND BARRACKS, DUBLIN,
July 16, 1858.

DEAR AGNES,—You are graciously pleased to laugh at
me again concerning my many apologies for delay in writing:
it seems to me, however, that a young lady who can find
no better excuse for a three or four months' silence than
chronic laziness, should be well occupied in considering
and repenting her own deplorable condition.   I feared that
my evil criticisms on your poetry had given you offence.

But I think I may safely promise—should you favour me with any more specimens—to be less stingy of my invaluable praise to each successive one ; for you will be writing better and better year by year.

Woe is me ! that I could not join your delightful "forest trip," which I trust you enjoyed even beyond your expectations. Pray let me partake of your pleasure by giving me a long description of it. You will thus, too, increase your own pleasure in the recollection by making that recollection more vivid ; not to speak of the excellent exercise which will be afforded your descriptive powers.

By the bye, your humble servant has spent since (six?) weeks in another Barracks since he had the honour of writing you last, and is now attached to the 55th Foot. Whither this noble corps will be sent no one just now ventures to guess. Lately, vague rumours were afloat of its speedy transportation to India. Probably, however, a tender Government would preserve the precious dominie at home, even when banishing his regiment.

One of our class died out there not long since,—a thin wiry fellow who promised to endure all climates with the sallow tenacity of parchment. We have also heard lately of the sudden death of a fine friend of ours, Damerow, Bandmaster of the 17th Lancers. He was the best talker and actor I ever knew, and a red-hot Republican, who had shared in all sorts of revolutions and escaped half the police of Europe ; beginning his career as a Berlin Guardsman, and getting to England at length with a sixty-two times *viséd* passport. He told us how on his first arrival (having been hounded like a wild beast from Paris to Havre) he stood at the Tower stairs, with the precious passport in his hand, waiting for the official who should demand it, and perhaps—after keeping him a few hours more or less—graciously sign it. He burst into tears when he was made to comprehend that he was in a country so superhumanly free that passports were unknown, and everybody might

go where he pleased. Poor fellow, I met him for the first
time in a fever of high spirits, consequent on hearing—a
false report—that King Bomba was in deadly peril, and
the streets of Naples were running blood ! It did one
good to hear his imprecations upon Louis Napoleon. He
was Adjutant of a Rifle Corps (Jäger's) in the Bavarian
upset ; and proposed for remedy of the revolutionists'
dearth of finances a march upon Frankfort and seizure of
the Rothschild there, with a "Money or your Life ! "

With regard to the Piano, I shall be indeed rejoiced to
hear you playing some fine day, but, for myself, I am utterly
innocent of the art.

With kind love to Father and Mother and all,—I remain
your sincere friend,

JAS. THOMSON.

To the Same.

RICHMOND BARRACKS, *April* 8, 1859.

DEAR AGNES,—I have just been re-reading your last
letter, which plunged me deep into Christmas-jollities again.
We, also, over here have had our dancing parties and the
other common and pleasant vanities. As you are now—
according to your own statement—past your majority, one
must, I suppose, be very sedate with you. But you ought
to let a poor fellow, bewildered in his Addition, know who
lent or gave you the four precious years by which you have
gained upon him in age.

I of course thoroughly despise your unprovoked assault
upon smoking. I have experience both in smoking and
non-smoking, and so am entitled to pronounce which is
the better. But you have no right to speak upon the
question until you shall have smoked some scores of cigars
and hundreds of pipes. To you ladies it may be even the
fox's sour grapes—for I am told that abroad, where the
ladies are graciously permitted by their lords to smoke,

they are very fond of it; and I am also told that never does a lady look more charming than when, reclining luxuriously, she inhales and exhales the fragrant ether from nargileh or cigarette. It seems to me that the greater portion of the much speaking and writing against Tobacco is blank nonsense. I think tobacco considerably less hurtful to us than our tea and coffee; and I think it is truly beneficial to men engaged in the fierce toil and struggle of modern business. But you might as well lecture me on crinoline or any other feminine absurdity, as I you on the "divine" weed, as old Spenser sagely calls it.

I don't know whether the Parliamentary confusion (which you are doubtlessly much interested in and well acquainted with) has anything to do with it; but the War-Office is unusually late this year in determining what to do with regiments. We don't know whether we have to stay here or be removed. If removed, it will almost certainly be to England. But we may be kept to control the wild Irish during the General Election. I suppose Mr. Gray is intensely disgusted with the whole Parliament in the Reform business.

I have been searching my poor brain for something to say, but find it quite empty. I want a little inspiration from your friend Mr. Greig, the magnificent laugher. I must try to write soon, some fine day when in the humour for scribbling gossip and nonsense. It's a hard case when one cannot find even anything foolish to say! The smoking must stupefy one's head after all; or perhaps one might improve by practice in writing against it?

I shall be glad to hear that David is well, and also all the rest of you. Poor Mr. Barnes's house has been full of sickness ever since Christmas. Did I tell you that I a second time stood god-father to one of his sons? I am getting quite an important and paternal character. Double god-father is almost as respectable as a married man, one would think.

To the Same.

RICHMOND BARRACKS, DUBLIN,
May 14, 1859.

DEAR AGNES,—I remember promising in my last (even more stupid than usual) epistle to write again soon. Admire my remembrance of promises and my rapidity in setting about to perform them! At Easter I ran up for a few days to Belfast on a visit to an old schoolmate and fellow-dominie. In the hope of adding to your geographical knowledge, let me trouble you with a few words about this great capital of Ulster. People who have seen it call it a fine city : for my part, I can scarcely pretend to have seen it, though I looked at it about a week. In Christian countries one expects rain from a canopy of heavy clouds, and hopes for clear skies after; but the Belfast firmament managed to persist in a sulky darkness day after day, while still keeping nearly all its rain in store to spite and spoil future good weather. East and north-east winds, also, trailed the thick and smutty factory smoke continually about us. The streets of the city are very wide, and so far good, but the houses are not remarkable, and two parallel rows of common buildings— even though half a mile apart—would scarcely make a grand street. We went once to the theatre : it looks outside like a Methodist chapel very far gone in decay, inside like a grandfather of theatres, very sick and dismal. For a long time the dress circle numbered two occupants ; of whom one half was asleep, and the other fidgety and nervous, feeling himself a forlorn hope. When the cornet-player absconded (and he stopped away about half the evening) only four-fifths of the orchestra was left. However, the musicians were a most manly set ; far too independent to be subject to their leader ; each one played in his own tune and time to his own sole satisfaction. Officers who came lounging in the boxes after Mess, smoked tranquil cigars and kept their fine countenances ostentatiously turned from the stage.

You doubtlessly know that Belfast stands on Belfast Lough, which is fed by the Laggan. We had a row up this river, and in three or four miles found one branch fastened with a lock and the other with a weir. Yet even in getting thus far we stuck fast twice (to the charming consternation of the ladies), for river and lough are choked with mud. In the Lough, however, they have managed to make a pretty fair island, called Queen's Island, out of a mud-bank. On this is a conservatory and some starving infant trees. In the conservatory we stayed some time, perhaps secretly hoping that it would force the growth of our whiskers and moustachios. A fountain therein they could not afford to keep playing for more than two or three minutes, and this by special request. The place, of course, was full of aquariums. Are you infected with the mania for these toys yet? It is imperative that a lady, to be a lady nowadays, have two or three glass cases enriched with various specimens of wormy sea-vegetation, water-snails, tadpoles, sticklebacks, and similar rare luxuries ; all dimly discoverable through the slimy dusk of green water. I had no opportunity of going through one of the great factories, as I should have much liked to do. Neither would the weather permit us a trip to the Giant's Causeway. To finish with Belfast—the most conspicuous object near it is a strangely profiled hill called Cave Hill. Whenever this old gentleman wears his " night-cap " of cloud or mist, bad weather is in the ascendant; and—judging by what I saw of him—the disreputable old sluggard is not ashamed of appearing in it for weeks together.

I take the liberty of sending you by this post two volumes of verse which fell into my hands some time back. The author, Robert Browning, is about the strongest and manliest of our living poets. His wife (*née* Elizabeth Barrett Barrett, to adopt the style of wedding-cards) is beyond all com-

parison the greatest of English poetesses—*those whose works are published*, I mean. I happen to have her last book, and will send it to you some day. You will probably not care for these poems at first; but they are worth your study, and you may find, as I did, that they improve much with longer acquaintance. If I might school you a bit, I should order you always to look up in a dictionary what words you don't understand, and always to puzzle over difficult passages until they become either perfectly clear or thoroughly hopeless. No lazy reading will ever master a masterly writer. Should you care enough for Browning to wish thoroughly to comprehend him, I shall of course be happy to render you what little assistance may be in my power towards the clearing up of obscurities. The final poem, you will perceive, is addressed to his wife. To the best of my remembrance he used not to write so large a proportion of love-poetry aforetime : his marriage must do its best to excuse the poor fellow for his present extravagance in that article. My notion was that your poets, though always fluttering about Love like moths about a rushlight, generally took good care not to singe seriously their precious selves. This unfortunate Mr. Browning, however, seems to have flung himself headlong into the flame, determined to get burnt up—wings and all.

I have lately heard from John. He is in Manchester now with an Uncle John who is a station-master (Railway) there. My brother is a clerk in the service of the same company. He is well, and seems to like well his situation. Cousin Charles from Glasgow has also written, and we have agreed to correspond regularly.

How are all your studies and accomplishments progressing? Have you mastered French, German, and Italian yet? You must play the piano for us some day after the style of Miss Arabella Goddard. Perhaps you have heard that young lady? I heard and saw her some time back, and for two or even three full days continued in love with her pure face and splendid music. She seldom practises any of the modern namby-pamby songs and flashy dances, but is devoted to the great and solid pieces of such masters as Mozart, Beethoven, Mendelssohn, &c. There is an excellent example for you! If your gentleman of the magnificent laughter is as riant as ever, you may perhaps be so kind as to send me a few of his jolliest cachinnations in your next for the amusement of a dull evening. As it is now very late, and I am considerably tired, you are now—supposing you to have toiled so far—about to have the pleasure of ending this.

To the Same.

CURRAGH CAMP, KILDARE,
June 27, 1859.

DEAR AGNES,—Your kind letter would have been answered ere now, had we not when it arrived been in daily expectation of a move. The move has come, and we are now fairly settled in this Camp. Imagine an undulating sea of grass, here and there rising into hillocks, and spotted with patches of flowerless furze. In the midst, on a slightly elevated ridge, stretches for about a mile the Camp, consisting of ten squares of dingy red huts—each square holding a regiment—with a somewhat irregular accompaniment of canteens, wash-houses, hospitals, huts for the staff, &c. The squares are lettered from A to K, my much ill-used initial, the J, being considered unworthy of a place. In the centre of a line, chosen probably as about the highest spot, stand the Church, the Chapel (Roman Catholic), and the Clock-tower : at the extremities are the white tents of Artillery and Dragoons. It is a fine place for freedom and expanse, and in itself much pleasanter than Aldershot, though I could wish to be there for the sake of its nearness to London. Aldershot is set amidst dark heath, the Curragh amidst green grass ; and the difference is like that

C

between cloudy and sunshiny weather. It is good to get out here from a town. The sky is seen, not in patches, but broad, complete, and sea-like ; the distance where low blue hills float in the horizon is also sea-like, and the uncorrupted air sweeps over us broad and free as an ocean. Last night, for instance, it blew a stiffish gale. Well, the gusts came with a broad rush and sway against the broad school-hut as billows come against a ship's side. The rattling of the windows, the creaking of the window-cords, the sound as of sails flapping, might have made a squeamish stomach sea-sick. I almost fancied that my hut had got under weigh ; and hoped that if so it would drift down the Irish Sea, through the Channel, and up the Thames to London. What a pity it held its anchor fast ! I have very good quarters for the Camp, better probably than most of the officers. Two rooms, one of them papered, forming the end of the school-hut, are something to boast of for an habitation.

The Camp is now about full. Between two and three miles off is the village of Newbridge, a cavalry station. Here and there together the troops must number nearly ten thousand men. So that with the assistance of those in Dublin we ought to be able to get up a good "Field-day" or Review for Her Majesty, should she come over, as is expected. Lord Seaton, the Commander-in-Chief for Ireland, is here, with all sorts of generals, staff-officers, and aides-de-camp. I wish you could have seen the whole division the other day as they marched past before the great man. The Horse-Artillery careering as if their guns were cabs and carriages ; the more sober Foot-Artillery and Military Train ; the Scots Greys with their bearskins like mounted Guardsmen ; the Royal Dragoons, brass-helmeted ; the 5th or Irish Lancers looking splendid, like the chivalry of old, with lances erect, and each topped with its red-and-white pennon ; then regiment after regiment of infantry, including a battalion of the Fusilier

Guards ; each corps marching past to the music of its own band, the Fusiliers having their bagpipes. Then there were aides-de-camp and regimental field-officers galloping about in all directions, swift and brilliant as butterflies : mere butterflies, perhaps, many of them, but very pleasant and exciting to look at.

What do you mean by that strange description of Helen, with its mocking conclusion, " I rather think it would be strange if true"? If you wrote it to bewilder me, you have almost succeeded. I picture Miss Helen as an extremely fashionable and pretty young lady, accustomed to London Tavern Balls and similar aristocratic assemblies ; rather coquettish because she has so many admirers, and loving fun no less than when we used to romp at Blind-man's Buff together. Which is the correct portrait—yours or mine ? However, to revenge myself for your mystification in this matter, I am going to ill-use your last epistle. Do you know that, good as it is, it is shamefully careless in spelling and punctuation, and not quite so correct as it ought to be in grammatical construction. Most of these errors are evidently not of ignorance but of carelessness. Will you pardon my thus assuming the schoolmaster over you ; and consider that I am a dried up, pedantic, finical old dominie, fit for nothing else but school drudgery ?

By the bye, I did not *l*end but *s*end the rhyme books, and trust that you will oblige me by not troubling me with them again. A nomadic soldier can't afford to carry about many books with him ; they are more bother than they are worth. Besides, there are large libraries now at almost every military station ; each having enough good books (amidst much heavy lumber sacred to the moths) to satisfy a moderate man for the year or so of his probable stay. But you need not fear to try my patience with as many questions as you please.

To the Same.

CAMP, CURRAGH, *January* 6, 1860.

DEAR AGNES,—I suppose you have taken up your new quarters by this time. I hope you have had a merry Christmas, and will have many more of them in many happy New Years.

How have I offended you by irreverent allusions to our Future Abode? By saying that you will go to heaven? that I shall go thither? that we shall meet there? that you will play the harp there? that I shall hear your harp-playing there? that your said harp-playing there will afford a criterion of your pianoforte-playing here? that I shall be able to apply this criterion there? By which, or by all, have I shocked you? One might almost imagine that our Present Abode is a subject of meditation even more solemn than our Future : but, then, one could not be a young lady with no care in her head. I beseech pardon.

Miss Helen shocks me. Twenty-four pounds sterling a year scarcely sufficient to keep her in dress! I think that teachers in Ragged Schools should go clothed in rags, humbling themselves in sympathy with their scholars, and thus winning their confidence. How can tattered fustian and cotton believe that silk and lace have any affection for them? She might as well clothe her lessons in French phrases as herself in French finery, when appealing to the hearts and minds of the poor little ignorant beggars. However, I give up the scheme on account of the sweetheart. I suppose she will soon be married, for after profound calculation I have discovered that she is three or four months over twenty. Is my arithmetic correct? As for you, most venerable of women! you will be eighteen next month, will you not? I wish the world would stand still a while, and not bring on grey hairs at this alarming rate.

My good friends Mr. and Mrs. Barnes expect to go to

London soon, he as Garrison Schoolmaster there. Please ask Mr. and Mrs. Gray whether I may give the Barneses a note of introduction to you all. They are really good people. Mr. B. is clever, intelligent, full of fun and humour, honest, kindly, and genial. I am bound to confess that his conversation is dashed with that roughness to which we unfortunates, knocked about hither and thither into involuntary intimacy with each other in the Army, get, and must get, pretty well used. Civilians cherished in the shadow of quiet and retired homes think this coarse and evil; but most frequently it is quite apart from harm.

Mrs. Barnes I like even better. She is very reserved at first, but quite motherly and womanly when one gets to know her well. Both have treated me with great and rare kindness.

You say that you "may study German in a few more years." Indolent and procrastinating. Give one hour a day to it regularly. "You have no partiality for it." Did you ever have partiality for grammar, arithmetic, &c.? The language is becoming an essential in education; and it has the best modern literature in Europe. I shall throw overboard all my belief in your ability and intelligence, if you turn listless and unaspiring at this time of your life. Are you going to turn out anything, or are you going to be a commonplace nothing? You deserve a good scolding.

To the Same.

(*Fragment—undated.*)

As I, like you, detest crossing, I trench upon another sheet. As I am on the subject of books, it may be worth while to remark that if Mr. Gray still takes in periodicals as of old, he cannot get a better and cheaper one than the

Cornhill Magazine. It is a monthly, costs only a shilling, is edited by Thackeray, and the writing is first-rate.

Our present Regimental Rumour says that we shall soon go to Aldershot (which will be London for me), and then to Australia—Melbourne. I shall return to England abounding in nuggets in that case. The sooner we go the better. I am eager to be in the position of the Jacobite in the gude old Scotch song :—

> " He turned him right and round about
>   Upon the Irish shore ;
> He gave his bridle-rein a shake,
>   With adieu for evermore,
>   My dear,
>   Adieu for evermore ! "

The difference will be, that he was going to, and I shall be escaping from banishment.

Pray write soon and comfort my dolefulness.—Your sincere friend, JAMES THOMSON.

Thomson's expectation of being sent to Melbourne was not realised ; but at the beginning of June 1860 his regiment was transferred from the Curragh Camp to Aldershot. In the following verses, addressed to his friend Mr. Potterton on the last day of May, he describes the relief with which he looked forward to the prospect of a change :—

O the hurry and the racket and the tumult and the din,
     The turning out and packing up and all,
When the jolly news arrives that " the Route " 's coming in,
     As sure as our pay is small.

O it's then the Barrack-square it puts on the very air
     Of Balaclava town ;
With everything and nothing all a-scatter everywhere,
     And everybody running up and down.

O it's then we're on the loose, and the swiping grows profuse,
    And we drink rivers, lakes, and seas :
For giving up a post is like giving up the ghost—
    You may "go off" how you please.

There's a proverb I have heard—which it seems to me absurd—
    That "Rolling stones gather no moss" :
Which means, as I'm a soldier, that the rolling stones don't
      moulder,
    And that I count no loss.

When you've worn a coat a year, it begins to look so queer,
    That you'd better get a new :
When you've stood one place a year, it becomes so dull and
      drear,
    That you'd better change it too.

Well, all the things are packed, and corded, nailed, and
      stacked,
    And they trudge away in the vans :
So the Barracks being bare, we are left as free as air
    And as light as our old soup-cans.

Then the girls they come and sigh, and they vow and they cry—
    For cunning are the dears :—
As if they never swore to the fellows here before
    That *we* shouldn't dry their tears !

But at length it all is over and the parting moment come,
    And all spry for the march we form :
Then the trumpets flash through the thunders of the drum—
    And we vanish right off in the storm.

"We start," he adds in a postscript, "on Monday or Tuesday, going in two vessels from Dublin to Portsmouth, thence to Aldershot. Packing up has commenced ; no more school ; no more Mess ; no more nothing. Woe unto my friends, for sorely shall I sponge upon them in these days. Have you heard of George Duncan's mishaps ? The ship in which he with his family had secured an uncommonly cheap and comfortable berth, got on to the Arklow sands, and poor George was in considerable danger. The ship is done for, or materially injured. He must go out alone now, and by the overland route. . . . As I have other letters to write this evening, I let you off with this brief infliction."

While Thomson was at Aldershot, in 1860, he paid a visit to his old friends the Grays, whom he had not seen for several years. The following is the account given by Mrs. Greig : *——

" At last he wrote saying that he was to have a fortnight's holiday, and would pay us a visit. We were all excitement at his coming. I had previously informed him in one of my letters that Helen had become a Ragged-School teacher, and in reply he said he could not imagine a creature so bright, and in his remembrance so beautiful, being arrayed in sombre habiliments and acting such a character. When he arrived, Helen met him in the most demure manner possible, and kept up the deception, or rather tried to do so, for he was not to be deceived. Two days after his arrival, when he was sitting reading, she suddenly sent something flying at his head, at which he started up, saying, 'Ah ! I have just been quietly waiting for this ! You have been acting a part which does not become you, but you have now resumed your true character, and are the Helen of old.' During this visit we thought him much altered in appearance and manners ; indeed we were somewhat disappointed. He was by no means so manly-looking as when he left London, and was painfully silent and depressed. He went from us with the intention of again going to Aldershot; but from that day until Mr. Maccall mentioned him to us, we never once heard of him. Ever

---

* *Memoir* by Bertram Dobell, p. xxii.

since we have felt greatly puzzled to account for his singular conduct."

It is difficult to suggest any adequate cause for Thomson's dejection during this visit, or for his failure to keep up a friendship which had long been very dear to him. That he was not ungrateful or forgetful of the kindness which the Grays had shown him, is proved by some remarks which he made in a letter to his sister-in-law written in the last year of his life, in which he speaks of their services to him after his mother's death. Mr. William Maccall's essays on Thomson * bear witness to the same grateful recollection. "It was at their house," he says, "and as the playmate of their children, that James Thomson spent his happiest days. Those days he seemed in his letters to me never tired of recalling. I often pressed him to renew his relations with the hospitable friends of his childhood, who were as willing as in the past to welcome him. But his constitutional shyness, or some other cause, hindered him from gratifying a desire which evidently stirred his being very deeply." It is possible that Thomson's discontinuance of his visits to Mr. Gray's house after 1860 was due to a revival of his early affection for Miss Helen Gray, with whom, it will be remembered, he had earnestly desired to correspond, and who was now engaged to be married. It is known that he still treasured many years afterwards a purse which she had worked and given to him ; and it is noticeable that among his early poems there is one named " Meeting Again," which is dated September 1860, and may perhaps refer to this occasion. It may be,

---

* "James Thomson, Laureate of Pessimism."

however, that Thomson's conduct was merely an instance of that eccentric tendency to sudden fancies and changes to which many poets have been prone, and from which he was by no means exempt.

Thomson's regiment, the 55th Foot, remained at Aldershot about a year. Here are a few extracts from his letters to Mr. James Potterton during this period :—

Aldershot, October 11, 1860. Why are you not here, O my friend, to partake with me of the German feast, which we prepared so laboriously on the green Curragh? We would plunge headlong into Latin this winter, and emerge Ciceronic next summer. My friends are away, and the heart is taken out of me. What fun in finding some exquisite German sentence, when there is no one whom I can bore with it? Alleleu! . . . You old matter-of-fact! Of course I sent that ditty to Bradlaugh as a chaff, and called it the "Reformer's Hymn"! Do you remember one beautiful day in March, when you, Bob, and I went strolling over the Curragh between eleven and one? The larks we heard that day for the first time; it was the first (and almost the last) fine day this year. The long quiet sheep-studded glen, beginning out by the little police-barrack? The lady and gentleman we saw at archery in the hollow beneath our square? I found the other day some verses * made that evening, and have finished them into the trifle which I herewith send you. The day is marked with a white stone in the calendar of my memory. You will understand that I am so poor in letter-worthiness that I have to take refuge in doggerel. . . . We will try to meet at Christmas. I write in haste, not for want of time, but because of a most restive mood which is leaping, kicking, doing "caprioles, lavoltas, and demivolts," with

---

* The punning stanzas entitled "Arch Archery."

such infernal agility that the rider, Common-sense, must infallibly soon be thrown.

Aldershot, November 21, 1860. Lectured last night on English History as showman of certain magic-lantern slides. They were pretty well done, and I knew a little of the subjects; so the speech came rather trippingly from the tongue. With practice of a preliminary hundred or so, I might become able to give a not intolerable lecture. But who would willingly undergo such practice, even if it made perfect? * News none. Have just scrawled to Mr. Barnes, and am going to devote a special P.S. to your most affectionate regards.

Aldershot, March 22, 1861. You know of course that Le Mar has got the Chelsea berth, to the exclusion of unworthy me. Grant has failed to get the Hibernian one, being too late in his application. . . . I have been reading fairly in my noble Schiller, but have attempted no translation. How are you prospering with yours and the Reineke? I wish I had a fellow-Christian to read with in the evenings; for the Mess strongly attracts a poor solitary, and plays the deuce with his studies. Having nothing original to write about, I send you some more Heine, to put you in my debt for something.

In the spring or summer of the following year

---

* An amusing story is told, illustrative of Thomson's eccentric and uncertain temper, how the officers of his regiment, having heard of the success of his magic-lantern entertainments, organised one on a grander scale at which he was to have the honour of lecturing to themselves and their families. When the time came and the company had assembled, Thomson, for some unexplained reason,—perhaps from dislike of being patronised,—limited his duties as lecturer to a bare enumeration of the scenes exhibited, omitting altogether the comments which had delighted his previous audiences, so that the whole performance passed off in a few minutes, and was a complete fiasco.

(1861) Thomson accompanied his regiment to Jersey, whence the following letter was written to Mr. James Potterton :—

Fort Regent, Jersey, July 24, 1861.   You have, I doubt not, execrated me,—yea, many times,—for not writing. Did Alec Thomson tell you, as I desired him, how I have been looking out for your appearance in this beautiful isle? Are you coming this autumn, or not?   I shall be very glad if you do.   There is good sea-bathing very handy. Leave the great Babylon, the Queen of Abominations ; fly from her, and seek Revelations in the remote Patmos. So when you return, you shall be able to confound Cumming and outthunder the Boanerges Spurgeon.   This would be a jolly station for two congenial Normals * ; for one by himself it is not so good.   I have none with whom to ramble on the Saturdays—a sad want, were it not that nearly every Saturday has been wet.   Still I have had one or two good expeditions.   I have at length left the Mess, and mess with our good friends the Egans, who would be glad to see you also.   Grant has not written for five weeks.   Mr. Barnes I write to now and then.   Have you heard that his house was broken into, and about £8's worth of property stolen?   You people of property must be on your guard.   Neither Duncan nor Jones the Only has written.   We begin at French next month, and intend to fasten to it like a bull-dog.

Thomson seems to have spent a pleasant, uneventful year in Jersey, where he made the acquaintance, among others, of Mr. G. J. Harney, then editor of the *Jersey Independent*, to which journal he contributed some translations from Heine, and Mr. Byron Webber, who was acting as sub-editor, both of whom remember him as quiet, cultivated, unassuming, and reticent.

---

* A reference to the " Normal School" at Chelsea.

The numerous letters written by Thomson to Mr. Bradlaugh between 1852 and 1862, many of which were from Jersey, have unfortunately been destroyed; and the same fate has overtaken those addressed to Mr. and Mrs. Barnes. While he stayed in Jersey, Thomson wrote a great part of a narrative poem entitled "Ronald and Helen," * in which are many fine descriptions of the coast scenery. In a letter to his sister-in-law, written many years later, he thus alludes to Jersey :—"You are right in thinking it a very pretty place, with very fine cows (they are all tethered as they graze in the lush valley-bottoms), and with delightful lanes, fringed with rich ferns, whereon the apple-blossom falls in warm flakes like a shower of summer snow. It has also the most wonderful magic-working mists I ever saw anywhere." A small note-book, dated 1861–1862, contains similar evidence of Thomson's enjoyment of this sojourn in Jersey. In May 1862 his regiment returned to Portsmouth.

These years of service in the army, however unsuitable the life may have been in many respects to one who was becoming more and more conscious of his poetic calling, had at least brought Thomson one great advantage which he might otherwise have missed. Had he settled down at once to a city clerkship, he would have seen but little of natural scenery and open-air life ; but now, by his wanderings to and fro between Devonshire, Ireland, Aldershot, and the Channel Isles, he had found opportunities for becoming intimate with Nature in many of her wildest aspects—with seas and skies, hills and plains,

---

* See Chapter VIII.

lakes, rivers, and forests. It would be difficult to exaggerate the importance of this influence on his poetical style; for idealist and dreamer though he was in this early period, he was nevertheless gifted with very keen powers of observation, and was laying by the material, at this time, for much that is splendid and picturesque in his poetry. Of the many poems that he wrote before he left the army, some ten or twelve found publication in *Tait's Edinburgh Magazine* between 1858 and 1860, under the signature " *Crepusculus*," his first published piece being " The Fadeless Bower," which appeared in *Tait* in July 1858. The prevailing characteristics of these early poems are their intense ideality and passionate reverence for beauty and love; some, however, are pensive and melancholy in tone, while a few, such as " The Doom of a City" and the " Mater Tenebrarum," are distinctly pessimistic.* In 1858 and 1859 Thomson also contributed some prose essays to the *London Investigator*, a paper edited by his friend Mr. Bradlaugh, chief among which were his " Notes on Emerson" and " A Few Words about Burns." It was in the *London Investigator* that he first used the signature of " B. V.," by which he was afterwards so well known to the readers of the *National Reformer*. " Bysshe Vanolis" (it was thus appended in full to one early contribution) was a *nom-de-plume* adopted out of reverence for Shelley and Novalis, Vanolis being an anagram of the latter name. From 1860 Thomson became a contributor both in verse and prose to the *National Reformer*, which was established by Mr. Bradlaugh in that year; but this subject may

---

* See Chapter IX.

be fittingly reserved for the next chapter. It is sufficient to note here that Thomson's attention was now fully turned to literature, and that in no case would he have been likely to remain much longer in the army, though, as it happened, his departure was accelerated by an unforeseen incident.

In 1862, when his regiment was at Portsmouth, it chanced that Thomson went on a visit to a fellow-schoolmaster at Aldershot, and in the course of a stroll in the neighbourhood of the camp, one of the party, out of bravado or for a wager, swam out to a boat which was moored on a pond where bathing was prohibited. An officer demanded the names of those present, and on this being refused, further altercation followed, with the result that a court-martial was held on the recalcitrant schoolmasters. No real blame seems to have attached to Thomson, but he paid the penalty of being one of the incriminated party, and was discharged from the service on October 30, 1862. His life in the army, as we have seen, had not been altogether a congenial one, but it had also its proportion of pleasure and good companionship; and looking back on it afterwards, through an interval of twelve or fifteen years, he could say to a friend, that "it had comprised some of his happiest days." *

---

* G. W. Foote, *Progress*, April 1884.

CHAPTER III.

LIFE IN LONDON.

When Thomson left the army, his position might have been a somewhat precarious one, but for the ready assistance and welcome hospitality of his friend Mr. Bradlaugh, who not only obtained him a clerkship in a solicitor's office of which he was then acting as manager, but also offered him a home in his own family, an offer which Thomson willingly accepted. He lived in Mr. Bradlaugh's house at Tottenham for several years, during which time their intimacy was very close and affectionate, Thomson being regarded and treated in every way as one of the family, and being beloved by every member of the household. Nor indeed was this any exception to the general rule of his life ; for one of the most signal proofs of the lovableness of his nature was his power of attracting the interest and friendship of all those with whom he came in contact. Few women were insensible to his quick natural sympathy, delicate tact, and chivalrous purity of heart ; with children he was always and instantaneously a favourite. He had soon gained the complete confidence and affection of Mr. Bradlaugh's children, one of whom, in some delightful reminiscences of this friendship, has given us a good insight into the sunnier and brighter aspect of Thomson's character as he then appeared, "trim and neat, with a smile on eye and lip; a genial, merry friend and companion." The following passage is quoted from her account : *—

"He lived in our house for some years, and was beloved by every one in it. He came when I was about five or six years old, and my earliest recollection of him is of sitting on his knee and asking him to make an 'ugly face' for me. First he refused; and when, after renewed and vehement entreaties, he complied, I was so terrified that I incontinently fled upstairs.

"My sister was his 'Sunday baby;' on Sunday afternoons she was installed in state on his knee, whilst my brother and I sat more humbly at his feet, to listen with breathless interest whilst he told us wonderful tales of brave knights and fair ladies, boundless seas, high mountains, and wide-stretching prairies. Sometimes the summons to tea would break off our story at a vital point, and then the next Sunday afternoon we would clamour for the end. We of course thought he first read his tales out of books, as we did ours, and it was greatly to our surprise when he laughed and said he had forgotten it, he must tell us a new one. As we grew a little older he told us the stories of the operas, whistling or singing some of the airs to us. I have never seen 'Fidelio,' yet he told us the story of it so dramatically that the scenes could hardly be impressed more vividly upon my memory if I had seen them acted instead of merely listening to his description.

"On Sunday mornings he mostly took us for long walks. We lived at Park then, and he would take us to Edmonton to see Charles Lamb's grave, or Enfield, or Chingford, or if—as occasionally happened—my father came too, our

---

* "Childish Recollections of James Thomson," by Mrs. Bradlaugh Bonner, in *Our Corner*, Aug. and Sept. 1886.

walk was across the Tottenham Marshes, to give our old favourite, Bruin, a swim.

"Nearly all our fairy-tale books we owed to Mr. Thomson. Amongst those he gave us were 'The Arabian Nights' Tales,' 'The Magic Ring,' 'Undine,' and 'Don Quixote;' there were many others, but I regret to say that in 1870 a mistaken spirit of self-sacrifice prompted us to give them away. La Motte Fouqué's 'Magic Ring' was given me in 1868, when I was between ten and eleven. When I opened it I found written on the outer side of the fly-leaf, 'Hypatia Bradlaugh, Yuletide, 1868;' on the inner side, much to my delight, were the following verses, written expressly for me and all my own, as, with childish vanity, I took care to explain to every one;—

'L'ENVOY.

'When the sixties are outrun,
  And the seventies nearly done,
  Or the eighties just begun;
  May some young and happy man,
  Wiser, kinder, nobler than
  He who tenders this one, bring
  You the real Magic Ring.

'This one may have pleasant powers;
  Charming idle girlish hours
  With its tales from faerie bowers;
  Tinting hopeful maiden dreams
  With its soft romantic gleams;
  Breathing love of love and truth,
  Valour, innocence and ruth.

'But may that one bless the life
  Of the woman and the wife
  Through our dull world's care and strife;
  Year by year with rich increase,
  Give you love, and joy, and peace;
  And at last the good death bring,
  Sweet as sleep: your Magic Ring.

'Wednesday, December 23, 1868.'

"Shortly afterwards Mr. Thomson happened to see on a bookstall a perfect second-hand copy of 'Undine.' In the middle of the top of the title-page was already written the name 'Lilah.' He bought the book, bracketed the names 'Alice,' 'Hypatia,' with the unknown Lilah's, and wrote these verses under the title :—

> ' Who was Lilah ?   I am sure
> She was young and sweet and pure ;
> With the forehead wise men love,—
> Here a lucid dawn above
> Broad curved brows, and twilight there,
> Under the deep dusk of hair.
>
> ' And her eyes ?   I cannot say
> Whether brown, or blue, or grey :
> I have seen them brown, and blue,
> And a soft green grey—the hue
> Shakespeare loved (and he was wise),
> ' Grey as glass ' were Silvia's eyes.
>
> ' So to Lilah's name above
> I will add two names I love,
> Linking with the bracket curls
> Three sweet names of three sweet girls.
> Sunday of Saint Valentine,
> Eighteen hundred sixty nine.'

"He took us to the Monday Popular Concerts when they were much less 'popular' than they are to-day, and taught us to understand somewhat of the beautiful music interpreted by that unrivalled quartette, Joachim, Strauss, Ries, and Piatti. He gave us the scores of 'Don Giovanni' and 'Le Nozze di Figaro,' and took me to see 'Il Barbiere di Seviglia'—my first opera. The memory of that evening remains with me as one of perfect happiness and delight, although, of course, maturer opera-goers would be inclined to look on it with scorn. We started in good time from Turner Street (Commercial Road), and walked to Covent Garden ; there we waited a long time on the

stone steps, and then went up and up, until at length I
found myself very high up in the world indeed, with all
the theatre at my feet, as it seemed to me.   Marimon took
the part of *Rosina*, and so great was the pleasure she gave
me that evening, that I have had great difficulty since in
divesting myself of the notion that she must be in the first
rank of singers.   Between the acts Mr. Thomson explained
the scenes to come, and all the while kept his finger on the
line then being sung on the English side of his Italian
and English 'book of the words,' so that I was never at
a loss to understand what was going on on the stage.   Mr.
Thomson seemed to share my enjoyment fully, but his
pleasure must have been derived in great part from seeing
mine.   He also first took us to see the pictures in the
National Gallery, the wonders of the old Polytechnic, and
to many other places."

But though this happier side of Thomson's nature
is well worthy of attention, it must not be forgotten
that the gloomy side existed also, however little he
might let it appear in his manner or conversation.
The very capacity for enjoyment which he possessed
in so large a degree implied a corresponding capacity
for suffering ; for, as one of his critics has truly remarked, "it is a fallacy to believe that it is men
constitutionally sombre, habitually sad, who are the
supreme sufferers ; the supreme sufferers are the men
who have a profound relish of existence."   Such relish
Thomson certainly possessed, but it is equally certain
that at the commencement of his London life his views
had already settled down from a vague mood of alternate despondency and hopefulness into a state of confirmed pessimism, this change in his internal convic-
tions being almost contemporaneous with the change
in his profession and manner of living.   It was not

without a severe struggle and much pain of heart that
Thomson had broken away from his early religious
belief; but, having once done so, he was far too
honest and fearless a thinker to take refuge in any
half-way-house of intellectual sophistry, however comfortable to his feelings such a sojourn might have
been; he was determined to look what he considered
the facts of existence fairly in the face, at whatever
cost to his own mental happiness. A fuller consideration of his pessimistic creed must be deferred
to a later chapter, but it may here be said briefly that
the belief in a stern immitigable Destiny was now
the cardinal tenet of his philosophy, and that this
belief produced in him a uniform mood of passionless resignation, more rarely a state of agonised
despair.

But necessitarian and pessimist though he was,
Thomson had not lost any of his native energy and
power of strenuous application, and the first ten or
twelve years of his London life were marked by the
production of his best, most varied, and most characteristic work. His methodical ways and clearness
of mind made him an excellent man of business;
while his strongly democratic opinions and keen sympathy with every kind of free-thought caused him to
take a close interest in the secular movement of which
the *National Reformer* was the chief organ. His part,
however, was more that of a brilliant free-lance than
of a recognised leader; for his intense individuality,
coupled with his almost cynical disbelief in the possibility of any real progress, must always have prevented
his giving himself heart and soul to a "cause." He
worked, as he himself avowed, on the side of liberty
and free-thought, not because he believed in the ulti-

mate triumph of those principles, but simply because
he was prompted thereto by a natural instinct and
inclination. His hatred of all fuss and sham, and
his impatience of the occasional " clap-trap " and false
sentiment not wholly separable from any popular
movement, made him at times a sarcastic critic of
his own party no less than of his adversaries. He
was, however, strongly in sympathy with all genuine
revolutionary efforts, and was even Secretary for some
time to the Polish Committee in London—witness his
beautiful and stirring lines on " A Polish Insurgent "
written in 1863.

Under the signature of " B. V." he now contributed
frequently to the *National Reformer;* and a large proportion of his most spirited writings, both in verse
and prose, may be found in the columns of that
journal between 1862 and 1874. That his chance of
literary fame was jeopardised, or at any rate retarded,
not only by the heterodoxy of his views and the
startling frankness with which they were expressed,
but also by the very fact of his connection with the
Secular party, can hardly admit of doubt. But it
should be remembered, on the other hand, that, together with the drawback of this position, he secured
an important advantage—the opportunity of giving
the freest possible play to his own powers, without
being compelled to adapt his writings to suit the
popular prejudices. " For me," he says in one of
his letters, with reference to the *National Reformer,*
" its supreme merit consists in the fact that I can
say in it what I like how I like ; and I know not
another periodical in Britain which would grant me
the same liberty or license." If, therefore, Thomson
was a loser as regards literary interests, from his

Secular connections, he was intellectually a gainer, in being able, though a poor man, to follow un- molested the bent of his own genius; and English literature thus received a valuable addition in an age when virility of thought is not too common, in the works of a poet who refused to be cramped by any conventional formula, and was not afraid to express the utmost conclusions to which his speculations led him.

It has been well said of Thomson that "in time to come the critic of these years will look back won- deringly upon the figure of the somewhat solitary poet who belonged to no special community or brother- hood in art."* Both in his life and literary work there was a remarkable individuality and apartness. He was possessed of none of the advantages usually enjoyed by the poet, artist, and man of letters—a liberal education, cultured ease, and immunity from the petty cares and ever-present anxiety of earning one's daily bread; on the contrary, his higher education was wholly self-acquired in the face of constant poverty and the drudgery of an uncongenial profession. He was a poet, endowed with a poet's wide sympathy and lofty aspiration; but he was at the same time a battler and a struggler with all that is meanest and most harassing in commonplace life; and indifferent though he was to fame, in the ordinary sense, he could not but repine inwardly at the thraldom of a lot which checked and thwarted his noblest endeavours. But his soldier's training, which showed itself in his methodical habits and conciseness of literary style, now stood him in good stead, enabling him to bear

---

* P. B. Marston, in *Athenæum*, June 10, 1882.

with stern and silent endurance whatever fate might
have in store :——

> Over me pass the days and months and years
>   Like squadrons and battalions of the foe
> Trampling with thoughtless thrusts and alien jeers
>   Over a wounded soldier lying low ;
> He grips his teeth, or flings them words of scorn
> To mar their triumph ; but the while, outworn,
>   Inwardly craves for death to end his woe.*

Many of the poems and essays written during these
years and published in the *National Reformer* are full
of autobiographical interest to those who read them
aright.   Two of them in especial, " Vane's Story "
and " A Lady of Sorrow," contain, in poetry and prose
respectively, an idealised version of the story of the
poet's life and the secret of his pessimistic creed ;
while in both of these, as in many other writings,
he reverts fondly to the memory of his lost love,
transfigured now into the guardian spirit with whom,
in his great loneliness in the midst of the gloomy
city, he holds rapt and sacred communion.   The experiences of London life (it should be remembered
that Thomson had known London from childhood,
and had learnt its lessons well) contributed largely
to the construction and imagery of these poems and
prose-phantasies, so profoundly gloomy in tone and
so intensely pessimistic in doctrine ; while insomnia,
a curse from which he suffered acutely at various
periods of his life, was undoubtedly productive
of a great part of his suffering.   The references
in his poems to sleepless hours should by no means
be overlooked by those who would understand his

* " To our Ladies of Death," 1861.

pessimism ; for such lines as the following, from the " City of Dreadful Night," were founded on the experience of many previous years :—

> The City is of Night, but not of Sleep ;
>   There sweet sleep is not for the weary brain ;
> The pitiless hours like years and ages creep,
>   A night seems termless hell . . .

Yet, during these very years, this same pessimist, in some rare moment of rapturous joy and spiritual exaltation, could sing strains of such pure unalloyed happiness as has been felt and expressed by few other poets :—

> Let my voice ring out and over the earth,
>   Through all the grief and strife,
> With a golden joy in a silver mirth :
>   Thank God for Life !
>
> Let my voice swell out through the great abyss
>   To the azure dome above,
> With a chord of faith in the harp of bliss :
>   Thank God for Love ! *

From 1862 to 1869 there is little actual record of Thomson's doings. In October 1866 he ceased to be an inmate of Mr. Bradlaugh's house, and took lodgings for himself in the Pimlico district, first in Denbigh Street, then at 69 Warwick Street, a house occupied by two maiden ladies named Spurway, and afterwards at 240 Vauxhall Bridge Road, where he stayed from 1869 till 1872. In November 1869 there is an entry in a fragmentary diary with reference to his poem of " Sunday up the River," which appeared in *Fraser's Magazine* for October of

---

* " Sunday up the River," 1865.

that year. This was one of the few occasions on which Thomson's poetry gained admission into any but secular periodicals—his "only production in reputable society," as he called it—the acceptance in this case being partly due to the favourable judgment of Charles Kingsley. Thomson thus recorded the event in his diary :—

October 1869.—"Up the River ; an Idyll of Cockaigne," accepted by Froude for *Fraser's Magazine*, appears.

November 19.—Breakfasted with Froude, who has just returned from Ireland, and is alone at present. Found him very cordial and homely, so that I was quite at my ease. Found an early opportunity to tell him about my having written a good deal for the *N. R.* Had thought this might shock him, but he took this quite as a matter of course. Lent me Spinoza in French (Emile Saisset's trans., with Introduction and Life,) and four vols. of Tieck's "Phantasms." Spent more than two hours with him in quite frank chat.

That this year, 1869, had been, for some reason or other which cannot now be conjectured, a more than usually unhappy one for Thomson, may be gathered from the following entry :—

Sunday, November 4, 1869.—Burned all my old papers, manuscripts, and letters, save the book MSS. which have been already in great part printed. It took me five hours to burn them, guarding against chimney on fire, and keeping them thoroughly burning. I was sad and stupid—scarcely looked into any ; had I begun reading them, I might never have finished their destruction. All the letters ; those which I had kept for twenty years, those which I had kept for more than sixteen. I felt myself like one who, having climbed half-way up a long rope (35 on the 23rd inst.), cuts

off all beneath his feet ; he must climb on, and can never
touch the old earth again without a fatal fall. The
memories treasured in the letters can never, at least in
great part, be revived in my life again, nor in the lives of
the friends yet living who wrote them. But after this
terrible year, I could do no less than consume the past.
I can now better face the future, come in what guise it
may.

It is a relief to turn from these despondent mus-
ings and forebodings to Thomson's correspondence
with the Bradlaughs, with whom he still maintained
most cordial relations, though not living in their
family.*

To Mrs. Bradlaugh.

240 VAUXHALL BRIDGE ROAD, PIMLICO, S.W.,
November 16, 1869.

DEAR MRS. BRADLAUGH,—As Grant tells me you want
a copy of last month's *Fraser*, I have great pleasure in
forwarding you one. You will find the article, "Suggestions on Academical Organisation," very interesting, as also
Bonamy Price's Reply to the Article on Currency, July
1869—I would also commend as worthy the most careful
study the paper on Professor Tyndall's "Theory of Comets."

I was surprised to find in the Magazine a lot of verses
which I remember being offered to Mr. B. three or four
years ago for the *N. R.*, and which he wisely refused.
The Editor of *Fraser* must have been very soft when he
accepted them. He was having his holiday in Ireland at
the time, and perhaps had taken too much punch when he
happened to read them.

Having at last had my noble portrait taken, I enclose

---

* These letters are reprinted from *Our Corner*, August and
September 1886.

the least bad copy I can pick out. With love to all,—
Yours faithfully,

JAMES THOMSON.

P.S.—The portrait would have doubtless had a much
more benevolent expression but for the fact that I had to
wait a full hour while a lady was having her beautiful baby
taken. Baby had four expositions (I think they call them),
Mamma making wonderful efforts to secure its steadfastness, and the photographic artist making the most comical
whistlings and chirpings, with the notion that these would
conduce to the same great end. I am happy to believe
that baby winked or started or spoiled the business somehow through all four expositions. The artist at length,
ashamed to keep me waiting any longer, told Mamma that
the gentleman below must be done before they had another
try at triumphant baby. You will doubtless discover all the
amiability of that hour in my expression.

To Miss Hypatia Bradlaugh.

240 VAUXHALL BRIDGE ROAD, LONDON, S.W.,
July 5, 1871.

MY DEAR HYPATIA,—This is exactly how the case stood,
to the best of my recollection.

Yourself, Alice, and I, with two or three more who were
very vague people and apt to change into other persons,
had been roaming about for a long day in a country place
something like Jersey. We had dinner at an inn, and were
very jolly. Roaming farther, I found myself upon the top
of a sandy sort of a cliff looking down upon a sandy beach,
and you girls just pulling to land in a boat. You were
nearly touching land among a group of boatmen when your
boat settled quietly down by the stern, and I saw your
heads go quietly under water. I cried out, "The girls are
in the water!" but saw the boatman pulling you out. I

wanted to get to you, but couldn't attempt to run down the cliff. Presently, however, a tall Guardsman stepped lightly down on business of his own, and his example gave me courage. I found it as easy to run down a concave slope as a fly finds it to walk on the ceiling. When I reached the shore, you and Alice and another girl were all nestled rosy and cosy in a kind of caboose or bathing-machine, muffled or sunk up to your necks in a heap of boatman's guernseys or some such garments. You said that you were none the worse for your ducking save a few bruises. I said that you must have something to restore you. You all agreed to this; and one proposed dinner with ale (although we had just had a dinner before), another tea. It was resolved that you should have a meat-tea, and I went off to be your waiter. I went up by an easy path to the inn, and entered a room. I found a pale, tall, old-fashioned, semi-genteel lady there, dressed and with her bonnet on, and I said, "Can you serve——" She cut me short in a very mild and cutting manner, saying, "If you want to be served, the servant is in the next room. *I* am a teetotaller, sir, and don't serve." Here she opened the door. and said to the girl in the next room, "Serve this gentleman, and give him a copy of the *Independent*" (which I understood to be a teetotal publication). "Well," said I, " ma'am, it seems funny to me that you should boast of your teetotalism and yet keep a public-house;" for I was rather nettled by her ways. The girl nudged my elbow from behind as a hint to go on with my scolding; the mistress spit fire at the girl for liking to see her insulted. I then told Mary that I only wanted to be served with tea, a good meat-tea for three or four, when I heard a knock at the door and a voice crying out cruelly, "It is quite eight o'clock, sir; eight o'clock. Are you sure you are awake?" So I had to leave you there in the caboose or bathing-machine, buried in guernseys, waiting for your dinner-tea; and had to be awake and get up myself. Was it not a sad case? I hope you

won't starve.   I hope all the people at home won't suffer
too much from anxiety.

This remarkable adventure of ours this morning put me
in mind that I have not written to you for an age.   So I
resolved to write this very day.

How are you enjoying this delightful summer?   Are
your chilblains very bad?   Do you often slide on the pond?
Or is the country all one pond, and do you go to school by
boat?   I had to get up this morning and throw coats on
my bed, being awakened by the cold.   It is raining this
moment as hard as it can, and has been raining for I don't
know how many days.   June chilled us to the bone, July
is drowning us.

When Mr. Grant last wrote to me, he had been foolish
enough to get up early to work in his garden, and had just
managed to lose his purse with more than two pounds in
it.   That was a nice fat worm for some other early bird.
Moral: Never get up early if you can help it, and never
have two pounds in your purse.

As I am sure to be interrupted again in a few minutes
(for I am really writing this at the office, in spite of the
humbugging heading), I may as well finish it up while I
can.

I hope you will let me hear from you soon, if only to
tell me whether you suffered much from your dip, what sort
of a tea you were served with, and how you got out of the
caboose and home.

Love to all and best wishes.—Yours affectionately,

JAMES THOMSON.

240 VAUXHALL BRIDGE ROAD, LONDON, S.W.,
October 28, 1871.

DEAR MRS. BRADLAUGH,—This morning I sent by book-
post Thalberg's arrangement of " Home, sweet Home," as
desired by Alice.   The price is only one-half what appears
marked.   I had my sister-in-law in town for three or four

days the week before last. She is a quaint little creature, whom I feel inclined to like. Unfortunately I couldn't have any quiet chat with her, as she had come to meet her mother and friends, who had been having a month in the Isle of Wight, and the said friends consisted of one widow, two old maids, and one young maid. Fancy me going to Drury Lane with five of them under my charge! I did it with the utmost coolness and self-possession, I can assure you. Sister-in-law is not very strong, and I think brother is not very strong either.

I spent an evening at Turner Street last week with Hypatia. Mr. B. came in before I left, looking better, I think, than I had ever seen him since I came to London. He appeared as though he could have supped off a creature the size of me, and not have been troubled with indigestion if he had eaten it all.

I saw Austin last evening. His wife has a regular engagement now at Sadler's Wells, and has been very well spoken of in the London daily papers under the name of Miss Alice Austin. Curiously enough, the manager's wife acts in her maiden name, and this is Emma Austin. I thought this was Mrs. Bayston at first.

Yesterday I got a letter from Grant. He says that he has written twice to you without an answer. A pretty creature you are to grumble about people not writing to you, when you never reply if they do. And you have no writing at all to do except in the way of letters, while some persons I know have to write morning, noon, and night, till pen and ink make them feel sea-sick.

Hoping you are all well, with love and best wishes,— Yours truly,   JAMES THOMSON.

240 VAUXHALL BRIDGE ROAD, LONDON, S.W.,
January 3, 1872.

DEAR MRS. BRADLAUGH,—I hope you have all spent a pleasant Christmas, and will have a happy New Year, and

many of them.   I was very sorry that I could not come to
you, this being the first Christmas I have not passed with
you since I came to London.   But we were late at business on the Saturday, and had a Board meeting on the
Wednesday.   I spent the day very quietly at Jaques'; and
as for Tuesday, it was so wet and filthy that I didn't know
what to do with myself.

I haven't a word of news about anybody or anything.
Grant has not written for several weeks; it is true that I
only answered his last letter the other day.

I hope you have more seasonable weather down there
than we have in London.   Abominable, mild, muggy,
drizzling, slushy days and nights make it miserable to go
about.   I have in consequence been enjoying a thick cold
in my head, and an extremely promising sore throat.—
Yours truly,

JAMES THOMSON.

The above letters contain references to several
of Thomson's best friends.   Mr. Grant was the
old army comrade already mentioned, with whom he
still kept up his intimacy.   Mr. Jaques had made
Thomson's acquaintance through being engaged in
the same office; his name often occurs in the
diaries of a later date, and Thomson frequently spent
Sundays at his house.   Mr. Austin Holyoake was a
sub-editor of the *National Reformer*, which was printed
at his offices in Johnson's Court, and being thus associated with Thomson in journalistic work, he soon became one of his dearest and most valued friends.   Of
his younger brother, John, who was now married,
Thomson saw but little, their only meetings being on
such occasions as that referred to above, when his
brother and sister-in-law paid short visits to London.
The two brothers had been parted early in life

through the sudden breaking up of their home, and while the one had lived chiefly in Ireland or London, the other had been engaged in business in Scotland and the north of England, so that their paths lay far apart. To his sister-in-law, whom he first saw in 1867, Thomson took a strong liking, and was inclined to open his heart about his own concerns more than he usually did to his correspondents. Here are some extracts from two letters written to her in 1872 :—

To Mrs. John Thomson.

240 VAUXHALL BRIDGE ROAD, S.W.,
January 1, 1872.

I hadn't time to write more to you the other day, and since then I have been so stupid (even much more stupid than usual) with a thick cold in the head that I have been afraid to write, lest you should be forced to judge that either I had gone out of my mind or my mind had gone out of me—the one case being about as bad as the other, I suppose. As an additional pleasantness I have had a sore throat, which indeed suffered me to eat (with suffering), but would not allow me to smoke. This deprivation proved so heavy a calamity that I have sometimes caught myself pondering whether life is really worth having when one cannot smoke in the long dull evenings. If you are not a smoker yourself you can scarcely imagine the anguish, but try to think how you would feel if you were not permitted for a whole twelvemonth to go shopping, or even to peep into the windows where dresses and bonnets are enshrined for the ardent adoration of the fair sex. However, having been able to smoke this evening, I feel bound to write, although still (as you will have discovered long before reaching this line) prodigiously stupid.

E

What made you, O wilful little woman, send unto me
gold-rimmed eyeglasses? Did you think they would give
my nose and the rest of my countenance an air of respectability and dignity, and even perhaps make me look rather
venerable? But it was kind of you to write on Christmas
day itself, though how you could compose your mind to the
task, if you dined at home and were burthened with the
anxiety of how the sacred pudding would turn out, baffles
my comprehension. I hope it turned out better than the
similar work of a friend of mine, who told me that when a
young private soldier it came to his turn to be cook for the
company on Christmas Day. He managed to make the
precious thing pretty well, he asserts; but forgetting that
puddings are in the habit of swelling with monstrous self-
importance as they approach the state of perfection which
fits them for the festive board, he did tie up that poor
creature in its cloth as if he wanted to strangle it in its very
infancy. The consequence was that the pudding, after
short struggles, succeeded in bursting its bonds asunder,
and my friend, to his great astonishment, found that he had
succeeded in producing a sort of rich plum-pudding broth.
When his comrades came to cast eyes on this wonderful
mess, they looked much more ready to devour him than it,
and I believe they never trusted to his uncontrolled genius
for a pudding again.

You think I have left Mr. B., and wonder what I am about,
and I often wonder myself. Mr. B. gave up city business
altogether more than eighteen months ago, in order to
devote himself solely to the great business of illuminating
the benighted intellect of this nation on social, political,
and religious matters. For some time after he left I did
nothing, an occupation which would suit me exceedingly
well, and for which I have fine natural talents that I have
taken care to cultivate to the best of my abilities. That
is, would suit me extremely well on a fortune, or in a semi-
tropical climate, but here, without money, it is a luxury too

etherial for my taste. Afterwards I did some work in a
printing office, reading proofs, revising, &c. ; and as to this
I will only say that if ever you have the misfortune to be
condemned to penal servitude, and they offer to commute
the sentence for such work in a printing office, you had
far better stick to the penal servitude. I then became
Secretary *pro tem.* to one of the thousand companies which
came into being last year, and in some very hard commercial campaigning have already had two companies killed
under me. I am at present astride a third, which may
carry me out safely or may not : it has received three or
four shot and sabre wounds already, but seems tough and
tenacious of life. By the bye, our slain companies brought
no one down but the riders ; our friendly foes the share-
holding public having received all their money back. As
I was nearly thirty when I came to London, I could not
go through the regular course in any business, and have
had to seize whatever honest chance offered. Perhaps
some fine day I shall turn up a trump and win a good
stake ; it is much more probable that I shan't. In the
meantime, having no one to look to but myself, I quietly
take things as they come, and quietly let things go as they
go, fortifying myself with that saying of the philosopher
that it matters not in this vale of tears whether we wipe
our eyes with a silk or cotton handkerchief, or blink through
tortoiseshell or gold-rimmed eyeglasses. Perhaps the said
philosopher had himself the silk handkerchief and gold-
rimmed glasses, or perhaps he did not use a handkerchief nor wear eyeglasses, and was thus enabled to be so
philosophical on the subject. Not that I need to wipe my
eyes in this vale of tears, for I always find the prospect
either much too sad or much too comical for weeping.

To the Same.

240 VAUXHALL BRIDGE ROAD,
March 13, 1872.

What has kept me so long from answering your last
kind letter I really don't know.   Very likely my intense
sympathy with the Prince of Wales in his illness, and my
frantic joy at his recovery, made me incapable of thinking
of anything else.   Now that he is safe and on the Continent, I can attend a little to the ordinary affairs of life.

Were you dazzled by the blazing descriptions of our
Metropolitan Thanksgiving, you other poor provincials?
As for me, I kept out of it all as well as I could.   It drove
me from the Strand and Fleet Street to the Embankment
for a week or so in going to and coming from the City ;
for time was lost, clothes were in danger, and even limbs
were not safe, with carpenters, painters, roughs, *badauds*,
noise, hurry, and confusion in full possession of the route.
On the solemn and sublime day itself I went to a concert
far away from the multitude, and in the evening stopped
at home reading a moral French novel.   So much for my
part in the Thanksgiving.   But I promise you that when
I hear that yourself and John are quite well and hearty, he
about half as stout as the Tichborne claimant, and you
devouring chops and beefsteaks with alacrity, I will have
private rejoicings and an illumination of my own lamp and
fire in celebration of the happy news.

So you are rather glad that I am no longer with B.,
exposed to the contagion of his dreadful heresies.   To tell
you the truth, I don't think that there's a pin to choose
between his opinions as to things in general and my own ;
only while he considers his opinions of the utmost importance, and is unwearied in the profitable task of trying to
convert the world to them, I care very little for mine, and
don't believe the world capable of being benefited much
by having any opinion whatever preached to it.   But you

must not blame him or anybody for my wicked opinions,
which I have arrived at by the mere force of my own evil
nature, influenced very little by the opinions of others.
The Sunday-school views of this life and dissolving views
of a life hereafter proved quite unsatisfactory to this philosopher many years ago.

It may occur to the reader to inquire why, if
Thomson was so often in pecuniary straits, he did
not turn his literary talent to account as a journalist.
As a matter of fact, a chance of this sort had been
offered him a few years earlier, for in 1864 he had
written two or three articles for the *Daily Telegraph.**
But Thomson's spirit was too uncompromising, and
his individuality too distinct, to allow him any chance
of permanent success on the ordinary lines of journalism ; he could not, and would not, write " to order ; "
and poor though he was, he valued his own intellectual liberty above any prize the world could offer
him. " Luckily," he says in one of his essays, " I
am an author thoroughly unknown, and writing for a
periodical of the deepest disrepute ; " and elsewhere
he imagines his Muse saying to him : " Of all children, you are the most difficult to please ; I shall never
make anything of you ; you will never reflect any
credit on me. Poor you shall be always, and obscure,
unvalued, and without value ; better had it been for
me if, many years ago, I had taken interest in some
one else." So unwilling was he to accommodate his
writings to the temper of his readers that one of
his articles was found to be too audacious even for
the *National Reformer*. At a later period (to be

* An article by Thomson, on Middle Class Education,
appeared in the *Telegraph* for July 19, 1864.

mentioned in due course) he was able to get re-
munerative literary work more on his own terms ;
but at that time he was hampered by other and less
creditable disqualifications.

In 1872 began Thomson's correspondence with
Mr. W. M. Rossetti, to whom, as a well-known critic
holding liberal views, he had sent a copy of his
narrative poem " Weddah and Om-el-Bonain." The
following is Mr. Rossetti's account of their first
meeting and his impressions of Thomson :—

" Towards February 1872 I received by post the numbers
of the *National Reformer* containing the poem of ' Weddah
and Om-el-Bonain,' signed ' B. V.' I knew at the time
nothing of any sort about B. V. I read the poem, and
thought it excellent. I remember that same evening my
brother called upon me and saw the poem lying about, and
asked me about it. I replied that it was certainly a work
of very unusual value. My brother looked at it, and said,
' Yes, I see you are right. One ought to know something
about the author.' I wrote to B. V. at the office of the
National Reformer, expressing my high opinion of the
poem, and referring to my brother's as well, and Thomson
then replied to me. Soon afterwards I called at his
lodgings (in Vauxhall Bridge Road) to leave him a copy of
my edition of Shelley, but did not find him in.

" At some time (I hardly know when, but certainly think
it must have been before Thomson announced, in April 1872,
his expectation of going to the Rocky Mountains) * I asked
him to call on me if his convenience allowed. He came
one evening, when the only person at home with me was
my elder sister (authoress of ' A Shadow of Dante '). I
saw him partly alone, and partly in my sister's company.

---

* Thomson's letters show that it was in April 1873, just
after his visit to America.

Thomson was a rather small man,—say hardly five feet six in height,—with sufficiently regular features, bright eyes, and at that time a cheerful, pleasant manner. There was (but only, I think, in later years) a rather peculiar expression in his mouth; something of a permanently pained expression, along with a settled half-smile, caustic but not cynical, not 'put on,' but adopted as part of his attitude towards the world. I had expected to find him rather of the type of the intellectual working-man, but did not find this to be the fact; he seemed to me more of the 'city-clerk,' or minor man of business with literary tastes. His manners were good, free from nervousness, pretension, or self-assertion. He talked extremely well, and without, I think, any symptom of defective education, except that his *h's* were sometimes less aspirated than they should be. Not that he *dropped* his *h's*, and he certainly never inserted them where they ought not to come. There was no trace of the Scotchman in his pronunciation. We passed a pleasant evening, and I can recollect that my sister, who was an intense religious devotee, received an agreeable impression from his conversation—which shows that he knew when to keep his strong opinions to himself.

"As Thomson's opinions on religious, political, and other subjects did not, in essentials, differ much from mine, he was under no restriction in saying what he liked. However, he never said in my presence anything against religion which could be considered offensive in manner or tending to ribaldry. His talks with me may have been principally on literary matters: he was quite as ready to listen as to talk, and his conversation was in no degree pragmatic or controversial. I never saw him out of temper, vehement, or noticeably gloomy; his demeanour mostly (so far as I saw it) was that of a man of habitually low spirits, who did not allow these to affect his manner in society or the tone of his conversation.

"The whole of my personal acquaintance with Thomson

may have amounted to some half-dozen interviews. I
don't remember what may have been the last date when I
met him ; probably not later than 1876 or 1877. He and
I were always on the best terms ; and we had occasion to
correspond every now and then up to I dare say a couple
of years preceding his death."

His correspondence with Mr. W. M. Rossetti, which
deals largely with the subject of the text of Shelley,*
contains some of Thomson's best and most characteristic letters, the three first of which may bring this
chapter to a conclusion.

240 VAUXHALL BRIDGE ROAD, S.W.,
February 8, 1872.

DEAR SIR,—Mr. Bradlaugh has forwarded me your letter
of the 4th inst., and I know not how to thank you for your
very generous expression of approval of the "Weddah and
Om-el-Bonain." In sending you this piece I had indeed
some slight hope of obtaining the verdict of so distinguished
and competent a judge, but I chiefly intended it as a sort
of apology for my very inadequate notice in the *National
Reformer* last March of your popular edition of Shelley,
written at the request of my friend Mr. Bradlaugh when I
had no leisure for anything like a fair attempt to examine
and discuss that work properly. Feeling not at all contented
with such treatment of Shelley and yourself, I was anxious
to show that your too off-hand critic was nevertheless a
genuine lover of the poet to whom you have devoted so
much worthy labour, and a serious student of poetry.

To clear up your doubt, permit me to state that no living

---

* Some of the correspondence, chiefly relating to Thomson's
suggested emendations of faulty passages in Shelley's text, was
included in the volume of his Shelley studies privately printed
in 1884.

writer can have much less reputation than myself, who am simply known to some readers of the *National Reformer* as B. V., the author of many pieces and scraps in prose and verse which have appeared in that periodical during the last seven years or so. And I am bound in honesty to confess that some of those pieces were among the most wicked and blasphemous which even Mr. Bradlaugh ever published. The only production in reputable society which I can cite in my favour is "Sunday up the River; an Idyll of Cockaigne," which Mr. Froude inserted in *Fraser's Magazine* for October 1869, and which he and Mr. Kingsley thought very good. The "Weddah and Om-el-Bonain" Mr Froude rejected, finding the story beautiful, and the treatment excellent in arrangement and conception, but deficient in melody of versification, in smoothness and sweetness, much less finished in style than the "Idyll." Both pieces have been refused by four or five of our chief magazines to which they were sent.

I hope that you will pardon me for saying so much about myself, as I have only done so because your letter seemed to indicate a desire to know something on the subject.

The praise of two such men as yourself and your brother, however much kindliness may have tempered your judgment, is very valuable to me, and I am truly grateful for the generous promptitude and cordiality with which you have rendered it to an obscure stranger.

While to the public I wish to remain anonymous as a writer, I have no wish to shroud myself from persons I esteem, and am happy to sign myself your obliged and faithful servant,

JAMES THOMSON.

240 VAUXHALL BRIDGE ROAD, S.W.,
March 2, 1872.

DEAR SIR,—I have to thank you for your very kind letter of the 25th ult., and for your too-liberal offer of a copy of your complete edition of Shelley. While I do not like to refuse the honour of this gift from you, I must really protest against your attacking me suddenly with so valuable a present on such insignificant and unintentional provocation. It is one among the works of our higher literature which during the last three or four years I have put off reading, waiting for more settled leisure to study them as they ought to be studied. I will do my best to profit by it, and should any notes occur to me which I can think worth your attention, will submit them to you frankly.

I regret that you have been put to the trouble of procuring the number of *Fraser*, which I could not offer to send you, having no copy left. Your judgment on the relative merits of the "Idyll" and "Weddah" confirms my own. I was aware that the former as a piece of pure pleasantness was more smooth and easy in style than the latter, but I knew also that the latter in its style as dictated by the nature of the story was honestly wrought out to the best of my ability, and was comparatively a serious bit of work. By the bye, the "Idyll" as I wrote it had two more joints to its tail, ending thus after some points to mark the transition :—

What time is it, dear, now?
We are in the year now
Of the New Creation One million, two or three.
But where are we now, love?
We are, as I trow, love,
In the Heaven of Heavens upon the Crystal Sea.

And may mortal sinners
Care for carnal dinners
In your Heaven of Heavens, New Era millions three?
Oh. if their boat gets stranding
Upon some Richmond landing
They're thirsty as the desert and hungry as the sea!

These two stanzas, though of little worth in themselves, had the merit in my eyes of bringing back the piece at last to the sober realities of pleasant Cockaigne ; but Mr. Froude and (as he informed me) Mr. Kingsley were so strongly in favour of its evanishing in the sentimental infinite that I submitted to them, not without reluctance. Whether you will agree with those gentlemen or with myself on this point, I of course cannot divine.

I have a parcel of leaves of the *National Reformer* containing most of my contributions to that paper, kept by me for the purpose of reference, which I shall of course be happy to send you if you care to turn them over, glancing into any that may seem not without interest. They would give you a much more ample and accurate knowledge of me than you can have gathered from two select poems, and would probably enough considerably lower me in your opinion ; but I have not the slightest wish to seem to you at all better than I am, and would indeed (if I know myself) rather be under than over estimated. You will also, I trust, understand that I have not the least desire to abuse your kindness by asking you or expecting you to read a single line of my writing or express any opinion thereon, except as your own good pleasure may move you. Your criticism, whether favourable or adverse, would be very highly valued by me, but I cannot doubt that you have literary matters much more important than anything of mine to occupy your leisure.

Hoping that you will find in the nature of our correspondence an excuse for my again writing to you so much about myself,—I am, dear Sir, yours very respectfully,

JAMES THOMSON.

240 VAUXHALL BRIDGE ROAD, S.W.,
April 10, 1872.

DEAR SIR,—I have to thank you for the copy of your complete edition of Shelley's Poetical Works, which I found on reaching home last evening, and especially for the inscription therein with which you have honoured me.

Turning over the leaves, I find so many places where your
hand has been at work improving on improvement that I
cannot but regret so much trouble taken on my account,
while rejoicing in your persistent passion for accuracy and
perfection thus evidenced. That your name (which may
well live in its own right) must be linked enduringly in our
literature with that of Shelley, by virtue of the standard
text of his poems, is already my conviction.

I will do my poor best towards reading these noble
volumes worthily; and welcome so fair an occasion for
studying once more, and with such excellent assistance,
the poet who fascinated me in my youth, and of whom my
reverence remains undiminished and my estimate scarcely
altered after twenty long years.—I am, dear Sir, yours
truly,

JAMES THOMSON.

CHAPTER IV.

IN the spring of 1872 Thomson's residence in London
was interrupted by a visit to America, undertaken in
the service of the "Champion Gold and Silver Mines
Company," of which he was then Secretary. Towards
the end of April he received instructions from the
directors to proceed at once to Colorado, in order to
undertake the correspondence at the mines, and send
home weekly reports on the condition and prospects
of the Company's property; he accordingly started
from London on April 27, and arrived at Central
City, Colorado, on May 15. During the seven months
that he stayed among the Rocky Mountains, "the
big vertebræ of this longish backbone of America,"
as he calls them, he kept two diaries, in one of which
are entered the details of his business transactions,
in the other his private jottings, with descriptions of
scenery, records of expeditions, and notes of racy
American anecdotes heard during his travels. After
ten years spent in London, this recurrence to a free,
healthy, open-air life, with long walks and rides across
mountain-tracks—"rough jaunts," to quote his own
phrase—and plenty of bathing, fishing, and out-door
recreation, must have been a novel and welcome
experience; while the insight, now for the first time

obtained, into the grandest natural scenery of mid-ocean and snow-mountains was not lost on the observant eye of the poet.   Soon after his arrival in Colorado he addressed the following letter to Mrs. Bradlaugh :—

Post-Office, Central City, Colorado, U.S.A.,
May 31, 1872.

I wrote you a note the day I left London, telling you that business gave me no choice of time or vessel.

I left London 27th April, reached New York 8th May, stayed there one night, and got out here on the 15th, having been detained a little on the road at Lancaster (Pennsylvania), St. Louis, Kansas City, Golden City.

It is rather dull here, among hills all ugly with much mining, and I haven't been able to get about much yet. There are some fine places in the region. The stores here, however, are well stocked, though everything is very dear to our notions ; and the people are very quiet, keen, and civil.

You would like to be here for the beautiful climbing : it would just suit you.   Don't you envy me my yesterday's walk ?   Early in the morning I rode (on horseback too, but the pace was a walk most of the way) with a friend over to Idaho, and in the afternoon, as he and the horses belonged there, I walked back the same road.   The first three miles ascend 1800 feet up a fine winding cañon (pronounce canyon) or ravine, with a brook dancing all the way down.   The next three miles are partly level, but manage to descend nearly 1200 feet to Central City.   I was pretty well " milked " at the last half-mile of the cañon, but on reaching the Divide at the top felt as light and buoyant as a balloon with a large reserve of air.   This thin atmosphere (we are always over 8000 feet high) dilates your lungs by making them work for breath.   I can assure you if you could only have a few months of running up and down these foothills and the Rocky Mountains you would get back as light and frolicsome as a sylph.

A few days after I reached here I got a letter from George [his mother's brother] dated New York, 16th May. I have just received another from him dated Denver, 29th. So he and the Williamsons have got out safely, but they are more than a fortnight after me. The Williamsons go to Dr. Hitchman's ranche or farm; George is not quite settled yet. I heartily hope that he will soon find a good opening. He is sure to do well when he does, for out here they like a man who can work.

I may mention that there seems no more need of revolvers out here now than in any respectable English place. If a man gets into a low drinking and gaming saloon, he may likely enough get into rows, but the same is the case in England. Most people here are respectable and prudent; the time of the roughs is past.

As for myself, I feel just about as much at home here as among the people in England.

There seems little drinking, except a glass at night, among the decent people. Never any liquor on the dinner-table; only water, milk, tea, or coffee.

The women, as you may guess or reckon, are a rather small minority here. They seem very respectable as far as I have observed. As a rule they are slender, and dress lightly, with hats and bright scarves, so that they all look girlish till you get close to them.

They are more French than English in taste, I fancy, and some of them would be very graceful if the absurd boots did not make them hobble broken-backed with their Dolly Varden bunches behind. They incline to leanness, which one fears must grow somewhat scraggy with age, just as our fine women grow rather corpulent.

But in our coach from Golden City to this place was a New England lass of seventeen or eighteen, really charming, with a bloom upon her face, brighter than apple, softer than peach, and with a finely developed figure. If this is how New England lasses mean to grow now, I would advise Old England lasses (such as Alice and Hypatia) to get as beautiful as possible without delay, for they will have formidable rivals over the ocean.

It takes such a long time to write, even when the writing is nonsense, that I must put off telling you everything until I can do so by word of mouth. I have a good deal of business, writing and interviewing, and I have got to detest the pen more than I ever liked it.

How keenly he appreciated the grandeur of the mountain scenery, and how minutely he observed what he saw, is shown by many entries in his diary, of which the following may be taken as specimens :—

Tuesday, June 11, 1872.—Walked as far as head of Virginia Cañon. Near the Divide, with a snow-covered triple mountain right opposite, found a little unenclosed cemetery on the stony slope, not unpathetic in the solitude. Thin grass and weeds are the only growth just there. To the S.W., under the afternoon sun, a gentle hill shining green with the cottonwood aspens and darker firs, ridging eastward into promontory brown and sombre with thin firs. In front, down the cañon, beyond Idaho, the ridges of hills and mountains swelling obliquely from left to right, the right being S.W. They were dark green with brown patches, and the highest bore some thin sprinkling of snow. Immense cloud-shadows, black and irregular, lay upon them. They swell obliquely through one rounded mountain into two high sharp scalped peaks, with many foldings and dells. Behind were white clouds massed and in round islets, and the blue sky. . . . Turning back towards Central, green slopes and gulch with shanties and mills. Right and left firs and cottonwoods. These are the small bright green firs which turn yellow and russet in needle and apple, and then, seen with sun behind them, look like withered ferns similarly seen, burning gold and red. Beyond, a long massy hill-wall, brown and dark green with pines. Beyond still, a high sharp mountain on right, brown and dark green. Leftwards, a keen steep range, accentuated and abrupt in outline, with white gleaming precipices on the highest left.

Thursday, June 13, 1872.—Heavyish rain last night. Clouds this morning; no dust. Started for Idaho soon after nine. Half-way from Missouri City to Divide, front and rear saw white clouds seething over the crests of the hills and overlapping far down. The right-hand hills from Central clear with strange pale-green stony gleams. Some rain and hail-drops, then the sun breaking out in blue, high overhead. Two or three kinds pretty yellow flowers by the wayside. White convolvulus-like flowers, but with dull brownish centre-boss, on wrinkle-leaved bush, so inter-wreathed with a bush of smooth light-green finely-serrated leaves, that it was difficult at first to know which owned the flowers. . . . At Idaho between eleven and twelve. Very wet afternoon.

Friday, June 14, 1872.—Lovely bright morning. Every-thing so green after the rain. Idaho, with its hills and booming brown creek under the large sky, about as beautiful a place as I ever saw. Walked up the cañon, catching up coach, keeping behind it, and then up a long way ahead. Fine piney bluff on right soon after leaving Idaho. The hills and mountains never the same for five minutes together in form, colour, or expression; the shadows shifting, the forms varying, the lights changing, the colours running through a hundred different shades. Enjoyed my walk very much, and thought with a certain vigour as I used to think.

During the week ending July 20, Thomson had a short but sharp attack of "mountain fever," which he describes as "a kind of crisis in the process of

F

acclimatisation out here, which the doctor and others tell me most persons pass through who stay for any length of time." "Felt at death's door," he writes, "Wednesday and Thursday: down and up with a steep run, for I managed (though with great difficulty) to dress and walk about a little on Sunday. Illness very expensive out here, besides the lonesomeness, every little common service and thing having to be paid for. Some fellows kind in calling and watching."

The fullest and most graphic account of the place of Thomson's sojourn is that given in a long letter to Mr. W. M. Rossetti :—

CENTRAL CITY, COLORADO, U.S.A.,
August 5, 1872.

DEAR SIR,— Your letter of the 28th April reached me here about a fortnight since, having been forwarded by a friend. I cannot say anything about the Shelley notes now, as the only books I could find room for in my portmanteau were the Globe Shakespeare and Pickering's diamond Dante (with Cary's version squeezed in for the notes and general assistance). But I hope on my return to resume the attentive reading of your Shelley, and to send you any remarks upon it which may occur to me and seem worth sending. Your liberal reception of the few already sent would encourage me to proceed, even were I not impelled by so strong an interest in the subject.

Mr. Bradlaugh promised to forward you a copy of the *National Reformer* containing a piece of verse called "In the Room" which I left behind me. I learn that it appeared in the issue for May 19, but don't know whether you received a copy or not.

From the close of your letter I gather that you somewhat misapprehended what I said about my business trip. When

I wrote to the effect that I was going in search of the Heathen Chinee in the Rocky Mountains, I did not mean to convey that I was about to start for China. I believed that John Chinaman had already swarmed thus far east from California, and was alluding to the popular poem by Bret Harte, a writer who seems to me capable of doing really excellent work, and some of whose poems and sketches I am very fond of. As to the Chinese, they have not got here yet, with the exception of four or five who are male laundresses (the proper masculine for this feminine noun I am quite ignorant of), and whom I never see.

I have been out here since the 15th May, having left London on the 27th April, but have seen very little of the country as yet, business confining me to this place. I am hoping to have some trips around shortly. Every village out here is termed a city: this Central with Blackhawk and Nevada, the three virtually forming one straggling town, numbers between four and five thousand people. Of these the great majority are miners, perhaps a thousand being Cornishmen, who earn from $3 to $4 a day wages, and much more when they take leases or work by contract. The stores are well stocked, but nearly everything is very dear. The working miner can get most of the mere necessaries of life almost as cheap as at home; the comforts and little luxuries are so priced that I find living here twice or three times as expensive. A small glass of English beer costs twenty-five cents, or say a shilling currency. To get your boots blacked (I always clean my own) you pay twenty-five cents, but then they get a " Dolly Varden shine," and are wrought upon by a " Boot Artist." A "tonsorialist" very naturally charges seventy-five cents or three shillings for cutting your hair ; &c., &c., &c. We have churches, chapels, schools, and a new large hotel, in which a very polite dancing party assembled the other evening. This week we are to have a concert, and also a lecture on the Darwinian Theory, admission one dollar. We have a theatre, in which we

now and then have actors. The old rough days, with their
perils and excitement, are quite over; the "City" is civilised
enough to be dull and commonplace, while not yet civilised
enough to be sociable and pleasant. There are no beggars,
and petty larceny is almost unknown; storekeepers extort
your money blandly and quietly, and the large larceny of
selling mines at preposterous prices makes the people
despise all larceny that is petty. You might as well carry a
revolver between Euston Square and Somerset House as
here. I brought one under persuasion, and have never
taken it out of the bag.

This Central City is the headquarters of gold-mining in
Colorado Territory, but it has been very dull for some time
past, the working of most of the large mines having been
suspended, in some cases through want of capital, in others
through litigation (mines are wonderful breeders of lawsuits),
and in others because the ores are not rich enough to pay
the enormous charges for haulage and reduction and smelt-
ing out here, though they would be of immense value in an
old country. However, a railroad connecting with the whole
east is now within ten miles of us, and is being pushed on
rapidly, so things are likely to improve ere long.

The houses, chiefly of wood, and some of them pretty
enough in themselves, though spoiled by their surroundings,
are huddled and scattered along the bottom and slopes of
a winding ravine, intermingled with prospect-holes, primitive
log-huts, mill-sheds, of which many are idle, fragments of
machinery that proved useless from the first, heaps of stones
and poor ores, and all sorts of rubbish. No one has ever
cleared up anything here: the streets and roads are usually
many inches deep in dust, which the rare heavy rains and the
more frequent turning on of some foul sluice make mud which
is verily abominable unto one who cleaneth his own boots.
Men dig a shaft, shallow or deep, and leave it gaping for
any one to tumble into. Trees are cut down, and the stumps
all left to make night-wandering safe and agreeable. The

hills surrounding us have been flayed of their grass and
scalped of their timber; and they are scarred and gashed
and ulcerated all over from past mining operations; so
ferociously does little man scratch at the breasts of his great
calm mother when he thinks that jewels are there hidden.
The streams running down the ravines, or, as they say here,
the creeks running down the gulches, are thick with pollution from the washing of dirt and ores. We are 8300 feet
above the level of the sea, and 3000 feet above Denver,
which lies about forty miles eastward. The highest peaks of
the Rocky Mountains hereabout are 14,000 feet; we are
among the foothills. To get out of the city in any direction
one must climb for a considerable distance. These foothills
are distributed remarkably amongst the snowy ranges of the
mountains, curtain beyond curtain, fold within fold, twisting
and heaving inextricably. Those immediately around the
city are of flat tame curves, as if crouching to their abject
mercenary doom; but beyond there are keen crests and
daring serrated contours, green with firs and cottonwood-
aspens or nobly dark with pines; and one massy range ends
in a promontory whose scarped precipitous upper flank gleams
grand and savage in its stony nakedness, like the gleaming
of set white teeth in some swart Titanic barbarian. Some
of the loftier hillsides are as smooth meadows; but their
grass at this season can scarcely be distinguished through
the multitudinous flames and broad blaze of countless
species of wild-flowers, nearly all of the most positive intense
colours, scarlet, crimson, purple, azure, yellow, white. Few
of them remind me of English flowers, and the people here
(if I may judge by the few I have asked) don't seem to
know their names. From these higher hills one gets magnificent views : vast billowy land seas, with dense woods and
deep ravines and exquisite emerald dells, whereon and where-
over sleep and sweep immense shadows, and of all shades
even at noonday, from bright green to solid black ; beyond,
a crescent of the mountains, some with broad fields or deep

furrows of snow, some sheathed wholly with this white splendour; eastward toward the plains, what the keenest eye cannot distinguish from a distant sea-line, faint or dark blue, level to the horizon, with pale streaks like the shadows of clouds and long shoals and the haze of evaporation. The sky is wonderfully pure, azure or deep burning blue; the clouds are large and white; however hot the sun, there are cool fresh breezes on these hills. There are few birds, and they scarcely sing. Butterflies abound, some of them almost as brilliant as the flowers. Crickets keep up a continual song like the whistling of the wind through reeds; and one species take long jumps and short rapid flights, making such a rattle with some bodily machinery that one can scarcely believe it comes from so small a creature.

The nights are always cool, and mosquitoes there are none. Snakes or any other vermin I have not heard of. One would have to go some distance now to find any wild animals such as bears and cougars.

I don't think that I have been out a single night, however cool and clear with moon and stars, without seeing frequent lightnings play up from behind the surrounding hills. Almost every day we have a slight shower. On the day of my arrival we had a hailstorm with thunder as we drove up the cañon, the largest stones being quite as big as good-sized walnuts. Our horses were so nervous that we had to unhitch and hold them. A few days after they had snow, thunder and lightning all together among the same hills. Occasional waterspouts sweep away bridges and destroy roads for miles. I have seen from here a terrible storm raging over the plains, dead-silent through remoteness: white lightnings momentarily surging up, veiling the stars, making the lower clouds ghostly, striking pale reflections from clouds at the zenith; and these broad sheets of white light were seamed and riven by intense darting lines of forked lightning, zigzag, vertical, transverse, oblique.

We have no dew here at night; one can lie out in a

blanket between earth and sky with perfect safety and comfort.

Six miles from us is Idaho, the pleasantest place I have yet seen in the mountains. Going to it you ascend about a thousand feet in three miles to the Divide (and climbing on foot tests your wind in this thin pure air), and then descend about 1800 feet in three miles, winding down Virginia Cañon, whose hill-walls range from six to twelve hundred feet in height, and are still well wooded with firs and pines. The roadway is good, wild-flowers abound, and a clear rill runs down with you all the way.

Idaho, which its boldly prophetic inhabitants call the Saratoga of the West, and which is just now full of visitors, lies comfortably at large on the level floor of a broad and long valley. The houses are of wood, shingle-roofed, most of them neat, many of them pretty. The hills around rise to the height of a thousand feet ; and as little mining has been attempted on them, they are delightfully green, and their timber has not been felled. Between them, southwards, you see the scalped heads of two mountains (until lately covered with snow) reckoned about 11,000 feet high, with a lower rounded height between ; these are the Old Chief, the Squaw, and the Pappoose. Westwards also you glimpse snowy mountains. A stream, rapid and broad in summer after the rains and melting of the snows, runs from west to east through the midst of the village the whole length of the valley. Excellent trout have been caught in it. Two creeks join it from the south in this valley. There is a hot-water spring impregnated with soda and sulphur, which feeds private and swimming baths. There is a cold spring chemically allied to it, which people drink with faith or hope, and which to me tastes like seltzer-water bewitched. There are beautiful walks and rides in all directions. I reckon that this village of Idaho or Idaho Springs will indeed ere long be one of the fashionable holiday resorts of America. Gray's Peak, over 14,000 feet, is within twenty-four miles of it. A good horse-trail goes right up to the scalped crest of Old Chief, a distance of about eight miles.

I have chatted with the man who first struck Virginia Cañon and found the Idaho Creek (South Clear Creek) through the dense woods which filled the valley, and caught fine trout for himself and fellow-prospectors. This was in '59. Men used to make marvellous sums by mining and gold-washing then, and pay marvellous prices for the necessaries of life. For some years existence was pretty rough, though never perhaps half so wild as in California during the early days of its gold-fever.

I was told in Idaho (by a Justice of the Peace too) of a couple of men who were on terms of shoot at sight, of whom one tried to avoid and the other sought a meeting. At length the latter attained his desire, and in the " difficulty " which ensued was shot by the other, who was tried, but got off clear as the evidence was not considered perfect. The dead man had $64 odd in his pockets, so it was resolved to give him a decent burial. They stopped the funeral procession at a store, drank to his salvation out of his own money, and also took a bottle of whisky with them to the burial-place, that they might be not altogether without comfort when they had finally deposited him in the earth. Both deserved shooting, said the Justice of the Peace philosophically ; and himself was one of the funeral party.

In a tobacconist's here among specimens of ore is an object labelled " Burr from the pine-tree on which Pennsyltuck was hanged." Pennsyltuck was so called because Pennsylvania and Kentucky somehow shared the honour of raising him. He was a bad lot, so bad that the citizens at length determined to promptly relieve him and themselves of his noxious existence. Accordingly, without any tedious legal preliminaries, they took him forth and hanged him on a pine-tree, and there left him. As the night was very cold, some one suggested that it was doubtful whether

Pennsyltuck met his death by strangulation or freezing. As the citizens, on cool reflection, thought it wise to discourage Lynch-law, they generally agreed to consider that he had been frozen to death.

As to the drinking, one anecdote (true or not) will suffice. An officer sent out to cater for some division of the army in the West returned with six waggon-loads of whisky and one of provisions. The commanding officer, having overhauled the stock, cried out, "What the hell shall we do with all these provisions?"

I did not intend to inflict all this nonsense upon you, but having begun to write, it seemed queer to send a mere note five or six thousand miles and not say something about this country; so, having leisure, I let my pen run away with me. Fortunately you are not in any way called upon to read what I was not called upon to write.

I may be here for two or three months yet for all I know.—I am, dear Sir, yours truly,

JAMES THOMSON.

The following letters to Mrs. Bradlaugh show the domestic and social side of Thomson's Colorado life :—

CENTRAL CITY, COLORADO, U.S.A.,
August 7, 1872.

DEAR MRS. BRADLAUGH,—I wrote to you about a fortnight after arriving here, and presume that you got my letter in due time; that is to say, from seventeen to twenty days after date. Grant tells me that he sent you my letter to him, so you know pretty well how I found this place.

I just drop a line now to let you know that I am alive and well. I had a little while since a short attack of what is called mountain fever, but am now quite right again. Most people pass through it in getting used to the climate. One Englishman here had it the very day he arrived.

I have of late been much confined to this city, and am

longing to have some trips about the country. This is a town one would only resign himself to live in on condition of making plenty of money, but the country all around is as pleasant for travelling at this season as one could wish.

We are not at all sociable here, but we did have a social dance last week, the first to which I have been in America. The party was very pleasant and polite, and I danced freely for the first time since the Old City Road Hall of Science days. The go-ahead Yanks are not content with our old-world quadrille figures, and they have invented a multitude of new figures for themselves. Fortunately they have a fashion that the leader of the band sings out what is to be done, not merely at the beginning of each quadrille, but of each new movement in each quadrille. I soon managed to get on pretty well. In setting to partners and promenading we modestly took the ladies by their hands, instead of seizing them in your gross fashion round the waist.

Twice as many quadrilles were danced as all the round dances put together. Polka was done as with you. Schottische ditto, but only the first part. Redowa ditto. Waltz old-fashioned style. No Galop, Varsoviana, or Mazurka. We had a Valse Quadrille somewhat like our Valse Cotillon, if I remember rightly. We also had a Sicilian Circle, pleasant and comical; and we wound up with the "Home Sweet Home" Quadrille, doing the grand chain to this popular air played very slowly (and joining in chorus) three or four times in the course thereof.

I have given you the foregoing elaborate notes, because they relate to a subject which I know must be profoundly interesting to yourself and the girls. If I can only attend a few more such here, I may distinguish myself on my return by introducing dances fresh from the Rocky Mountains into London. I may be here for two or three months longer for aught I know.—Yours truly,

JAMES THOMSON.

September 23, 1872.

DEAR MRS. BRADLAUGH,—It gave me great pleasure to receive yesterday the letters from yourself, Alice, and Hypatia. It is very good of you all to remember that letters from home are particularly pleasant to an exile. I am glad that you enjoyed so much your trip to Cowes, and feel sure that the schooling in Paris will be of great value to the girls (whom I perhaps ought to call young ladies now), though it is naturally very painful for you to part with them. I wonder whether any of our sex will be allowed to correspond with them or to visit them while they are the schoolmates of Mdlle. Arago? If yes, I shall certainly correspond, and even hope to visit. Pray enlighten me on this important point.

The date of my return is still quite uncertain; it may be very shortly, or may be months hence. The business is as unsettled as when I first came out.

George I have not heard from for a long time—I wrote to him the other day. I am very glad to learn that he is so pleased with his ranche. Perhaps I shall meet him this week at the great Agricultural Fair of Denver, which people from all the surrounding districts attend.

Mdlle. Alice is respectfully informed that I have heard of no dangerous snakes in Colorado, or at any rate in this part of it. She is further informed that the people here are not barbarians, but quite civilised, with schools, churches, chapels, music-halls, dancing-parties, lawyers, newspapers, constables, fashionable milliners, and the other characteristics of polite life. Thus we had a picnic to James Peak last Wednesday. Three charming young ladies in an open carriage, which you may call a buggy if you like, with a gentleman to drive them. Three more of us men on horseback—I am a famous horseman by this time. Lunch of tongue, eggs, sardines, bottled beer, &c., &c. Climb up last mile or two with the most charming of the charming girls on my arm. Ride home by moonlight through pine

woods and among mountains.   James Peak is more than
13.000 feet high, or 5000 above us here in Central.

We have now a young matron in our house, where four
of us held a bachelors' mess.   But one of these bachelors
(not the present writer) persuaded his betrothed in England to get married to him out here, and out she came
the other day, and married they were here in this happy
mansion, in the evening, by the Episcopal clergyman.   We
had elegant bridesmaids and a gorgeous supper, worthy to
be mentioned with that never-to-be-forgotten breakfast for
the wedding of the Grants.

Let me hope that the above facts will convince Alice,
although she *is* going to Paris, that we are not barbarians
out here.   Moreover, we have had other dancing-parties, and
the sound of the piano is heard every day in our house.

The worst of my life here is, that I have not enough to
do, and yet am confined a good deal to this place.   You
will be happy to learn that I am quite clever at cleaning
boots, practising regularly on my own, and that I have
even made some way in the noble arts of sawing and
chopping wood.   Our fire fuel is delivered in four-feet
logs as thick as my leg.

I still manage to have my bath, having cleverly devised
a six-inch ledge to an eighteen-inch tin pan.

Kind love to all, including Mr. B., to whom, by the bye,
I have not written yet.   Shameful! but one can't write in
this country.

Hoping all this nonsense won't injure your health,—
Yours faithfully,

JAMES THOMSON.

P.S.—My little trip was to the Middle Park, over the
mountain range.   Five men of us on horseback, with two
boys, mule, and pony.   Two days' ride each way, two days
there.   Plenty cold provisions, trout, and grouse.   Camping
of nights in buffalo robes and blankets—delightful; but
weather too English.

By the time the last letter was written the approach
of winter had begun to make itself felt at Central
City. "First snow here of the season," is the entry
in the diary for September 24. "Felt it drifting
in on me in bed, with rough flaws of wind. Up at
7.30 ; bath. Snow over hills and houses in patches.
Walked top of our hill before breakfast. Keen N.W.
wind. Afterwards bright midday, but keen." At
this time Thomson had no information as to the intended date of his return, though he had already
convinced himself, and informed the directors, of the
unsoundness of the Company's speculations and the
uselessness of his making a prolonged stay. The
negotiations he had been carrying on as the Company's representative had not been concluded without
much discussion and the exhibition of some hostility
by the parties with whom he had to deal ; mention
is made in the diary, for instance, of a person bearing
the ominous name of Stalker, who "had been to the
bank drunk, swearing that he would not give way an
inch, and saying that he only wanted a shot-gun and
the other parties in reach, and he would soon find
the best way of settling the matter." The matter,
however, in spite of Mr. Stalker's intentions, was
finally settled without bloodshed ; and on December
28 Thomson started for Denver and Chicago on
his way home, arriving in London towards the end
of January 1873. The expenses incurred during his
journey and stay at Central City were of course de-
frayed by the Company ; but of a considerable sum
of money, which he contended was due to him as
salary, only a small part was paid, the engagement
having apparently been made by word of mouth, and
without the formal sanction of the directors. In

spite of this disappointment—a serious one for a poor man—Thomson's American trip was one of his most satisfactory and agreeable experiences, and one which he always remembered with pleasure. The following passages of a letter * written to a friend in England sum up his opinion of the Americans as a nation, and bear testimony to his own enjoyment of travelling :—

I think we must forgive the Americans a good deal of vulgarity and arrogance for some generations yet. They are intoxicated with their vast country and its vaster prospects. Besides, we of the old country have sent them for years past, and are still sending them, our half-starved and ignorant millions. The Americans of the War of Independence were really a British race, and related to the old country as a Greek colony to its mother city or state. But the Americans of to-day are only a nation in that they instinctively adore their Union. All the heterogeneous ingredients are seething in the cauldron with plenty of scum and air-bubbles atop. In a century or two they may get stewed down into homogeneity—a really wholesome and dainty dish, not to be set before a king though, I fancy. I resisted the impression of the mere material vastitude as long as possible, but found its influence growing on me week by week ; for it implies such vast possibilities of moral and intellectual expansion. They are starting over here with all our experience and culture at their command, without any of the obsolete burdens and impediments which in the course of a thousand years have become inseparable from our institutions, and with a country which will want more labour and more people for many generations to come.

I am quite well again. Though never, perhaps, very

---

* Published in the *Secular Review*, July 15, 1882.

strong, and rarely so well as to feel mere existence a delight (as to a really healthy person it must be; no inferior condition, in my opinion, deserves the name of health), I am seldom what we call unwell. When travelling about I always find myself immensely better than when confined to one place. With money, I believe I should never have a home, but be always going to and fro on the earth, and walking up and down in it, like him of whom I am one of the children.

After Thomson's return to London from Colorado he again stayed in the Vauxhall Bridge Road, a few doors from his former lodgings, the number of the house being now 230 instead of 240. The following letters were written at this time :—

To Miss Hypatia Bradlaugh.

230 VAUXHALL BRIDGE ROAD, LONDON, S.W.,
February 28, 1873.

DEAR HYPATIA,—I ought to have answered your pleasant letter long ago, but all sorts of business and other worries have made me quite neglect friendly correspondence. However, mamma's letter, which I got last evening, aroused my conscience, and I resolve to write at once, if only a few lines. The newspapers sent would, I thought, prove to you by the handwriting of the address that I was still alive, and by the postmark that I was in London.

Very glad to hear that you are getting so much better, and hope that you will be quite well soon. The riding I dare say has done you much good. You on ponyback and myself on horseback would make a pretty pair of equestrians, I guess.

I enjoyed my visit to America very much, and should like to be sent out there again. If I were only about twenty years old, or if, old as I am, I had a good trade, I would certainly emigrate and become a citizen of the free and enlightened Republic. But for mere clerks and accountants and *sich*, they have more out there than they want.

I don't know when I shall be able to give you a call at Midhurst. I should very much like do so. Perhaps I shall have little or nothing to do for my Company after next month, and then I may be able to manage a short visit.—Yours faithfully,

JAMES THOMSON.

To Mr. W. M. Rossetti.

April 2, 1873.

DEAR SIR,—Although I returned from my American trip about two months since, I have been so unsettled and occupied with a thousand nothings that I have scarcely looked at a book since my return.

I have at length managed to go pretty carefully through "The Witch of Atlas" and "Epipsychidion," and herewith I send you a few notes thereon, which you must take for what they are worth. Although they are naturally very much like the notes of a reader for the press, whose special business it is to hunt out faults and ignore merits, you may be assured that I duly appreciate the great improvements you have made in the text.

While agreeing with you in ranking "The Witch of Atlas" very high, I cannot agree with you in preferring it to the "Epipsychidion." It has always seemed to me that Shelley never soared higher than in this poem, which I find full of supreme inspiration. It is his *Vita Nuova*, tender and fervid and noble as Dante's ; and his premature death has deprived us of the befitting *Divina Commedia* which should have followed.

I am considerably ashamed to speak of anything of my own in this connection ; but, as I believe my little piece " In the Room" was sent to you, I take the liberty of forwarding a corrected copy, that, having it at all, you may have it as I wrote it.—Yours very respectfully,

JAMES THOMSON.

April 22, 1873.

DEAR SIR,—Please accept my thanks for the kind invitation with which you have honoured me. I shall be very glad to make your personal acquaintance, and will call upon you at Euston Square next Friday evening about eight o'clock, unless you inform me in the meanwhile that that time will not suit you.

As we are likely to meet soon, I will not here discuss one or two matters mentioned in your letter, which can be much more easily settled by word of mouth than by writing.

Permit me, however, to take this opportunity of making a few remarks by way of apology, which I feel may be needed for such notes as I am sending you on Shelley.

1. I never until reading your edition saw any notes on the text, save those of Mr. Garnett in the "Relics," and am still quite ignorant of whatever critical comments and discussions have been published, except such as are indicated in your notes. Nor have I ever known personally any reader of Shelley with whom to compare notions on the subject; in fact, I have only come across two people in my life who gave signs of real intelligent interest in the poetry of Shelley, or indeed in any really great poetry, as poetry. I am thus only too likely to vex you with discussion of points long since settled, and with such wrong-headed notions as are the *fungi* of seclusion.

2. Having been used for many years to read his works in editions obviously corrupt, I have naturally taken many more and much greater liberties in guessing at true readings than I should have dreamed of doing had the editions been decently correct. The certainty of numerous errors made the text throughout uncertain.

G

3. On the other hand, I have naturally come to love by usage and old association, certain readings in which I divined no error, in which there was nothing manifestly wrong; and am thus reluctant to yield them for others, which I might have recognised as decidedly superior had the opportunity been offered at first of choosing between these and those.

4. Knowing that you intend the utmost attainable accuracy, I make notes on many points, and some of these very minute, merely to indicate faint doubts, or shadows of doubts, and not with the least idea of shaking the text where authoritative—I, irresponsible, challenge and challenge freely : with you (as I never forget) rests the responsibility of vigilantly guarding intact all that can be guarded.

Explanations too large for notes so small ! Let me conclude by cordially congratulating you that your good work must save generations of students of Shelley from countless perplexities and errors into which so many of us have hitherto inevitably fallen.—Yours truly,

JAMES THOMSON.

Thomson's stay in London was a very short one, for in the following July he obtained, through Mr. Bradlaugh's assistance, the post of special correspondent to the *New York World* in Spain, where the Carlists were then in insurrection against a Republican Government. In a letter of July 20 he thus refers to his new engagement :—" I am called on suddenly to start for Spain as correspondent of the *New York World* by the representative of that journal here. It is rather sharp irony of fact that one like me should be attached to Carlist headquarters, full of clericalism and legitimacy. It is my first experiment as a correspondent for a journal." Thomson started from London on July 22, and his Carlist

passport is dated July 30, 1873. Our knowledge of
his adventures in Spain is chiefly derived from the
account which he published two and a half years
later in the pages of the *Secularist*,* under the title
of "Carlist Reminiscences."

Having crossed the French and Spanish frontier
on August 1, about twenty miles from Bayonne, at
which place, the scene of the Carlist junta, he had
already passed some days, he made his way, with a
party of volunteers and correspondents, through the
mountains of Navarre, until they joined the royal
army at Lacunza on August 6. After this he was
nearly a month at headquarters, with many opportunities of seeing and some of conversing with Don
Carlos and his staff. "I cannot say," he writes,
"that he shone in conversation, except by his frank
kindliness. His utterance was thick and slow, and
he did not give sign of either ability or energy. On
the whole he seemed to me an amiable man of somewhat phlegmatic temperament, who would be much
happier as a country gentleman with his wife and
three children, than leading the advance-guard or
forlorn-hope of the Restoration." It had been expected that the Carlists would make a bold, and perhaps a successful, dash on Madrid; but there was a
long and disappointing delay, and for a long time, as
Thomson remarks, it was chiefly "*Vivas* and bell-
ringing," as they loitered in the friendly district of
the Basques.

In the meanwhile our business appeared to be rather a
military promenade than serious warfare. . . . The common

---

* March and April 1876.

routine for some days was healthy if unexciting. Your
assistente or attendant, a young fellow waiting for a rifle,
called you early in the morning with the concise " *Tocau* "
(equal to *Tocado !*—"It has sounded !"), and you jumped up
in the dawn, dusk, or dark. You washed and dressed as
you would, and ere you had finished he brought you a cup
of very thick chocolate, with two or three fingers of bread,
and a glass of water to drink after as a preventive of bile.
We marched till about noon, with a halt of some minutes
about ten for a bite and a sup, for which we reserved from
the previous evening's meal. As we approached our noonday halting-place, the *assistentes* (bat-men or bow-men, as
they would be called in the English service) were hurried
off to buy up anything to be got in the way of eggs, milk,
vegetables, fruit : it was a race organised by keenly com-
petitive stomachs. . . . The assistants prepared the midday meal, which we called breakfast, as best they might,
generally with what utensils they could seize and secure
amidst a fierce scramble, and with a strictly limited share
of a fire of wood on a stone floor. . . . Two of us who
had been in the States used to plead for some maize, but
our masterful servants shook their heads and said it was
only good for the beasts. . . . Breakfast over, came a smoke,
with a cup of coffee and a glass of *anisau* (spirit tinctured
with anise) or *agua ardiente* (an inferior white brandy), if
we were in luck. Then we all disposed ourselves for
the siesta ; on a bed, on the floor, or in the open air if
we could find grass and shade, or even if we could find
shade without grass. At about four or five we resumed
our march, reaching our resting-place at nightfall. Then
came the bother about billets ; one attendant looked to the
horses, and the other set about the solemn and sacred
work of preparing dinner. . . . After dinner, if not very
late, we went to some neighbouring quarters, or other men
came to ours, for a chat and smoke, and perchance a glass
If the resting-place was largish, we had decent beds in cur-

tained alcoves ; if not, we had matresses on the floor ; and in either case we slept the sleep of the just.

On August 14 the Carlist army entered, Puente de la Reyna, where they were entertained with a bull-fight and other performances. On the 19th and following days Thomson was a witness of some desultory fighting in and about Estella, resulting in the capture of the town by the Carlists ; and on the 30th he was at Viana, on the Ebro, where, with his fellow-correspondents, he saw and enjoyed a contest "more like a frolic of schoolboys than a serious fight." Here his "Reminiscences" break off rather abruptly, with a warm tribute of admiration to the gallantry and loyal devotion of the Carlists in general and of the Basque nation in particular.

Early in September, as we learn from a pencilled note-book, Thomson was prostrated by a sunstroke, being laid up for three days at Alsasua, and again for ten days at San Esteban. In the meanwhile the London agent of the *New York World*, from whom he had received his appointment and instructions, had already written him a letter, dated August 4, requesting him to make arrangements for returning to London in about ten days' time, and to correspond during those ten days with greater frequency than he had hitherto done. On September 3 Thomson received the expected letter of recall, from which it appears that he had only contributed three letters to the *New York World* during the month he had then spent in Spain, with which the agents of that journal were naturally dissatisfied. He arrived in London on September 23 after an absence of two months ; and in consequence of his failure to supply a larger amount of information, the salary of £5 per week, which had been guaranteed him when he started, was withheld by the proprietors of the *New York World.* Thomson, on his part, asserted that he wrote to the best of his opportunities and abilities, "in circumstances which (especially at first) were very disadvantageous." "I sent word," he adds, "of every event of even the slightest importance which came to my knowledge; and it was not my fault that during my stay the important combats and movements which had been expected did not take place." Thus Thomson's journey to Spain, like his journey to America, resulted in considerable pecuniary disappointment. In the second case, however, it certainly seems that the loss was mainly due to his own remissness, and not, as on the former occasion, to the fault of others.

On the day after his arrival in London, Thomson addressed the following letter to his sister-in-law :—

230 VAUXHALL BRIDGE ROAD,
September 24, 1873.

MY DEAR JULIA,—This is to inform you that I arrived home, or at least *chez moi*, last night. You will be a little sorry, perhaps, to learn that in that dreadful war in Spain I have got wounded with a cold in the left eye. It is not yet extracted, but the doctors hope that it will not prove fatal. I have to wear a green shade or blinker, which scarcely sets off to advantage my great personal beauty; in fact, I doubt whether the features of Apollo himself could struggle successfully with a green eye-shade. The funniest thing is, that my right eye, being unaccustomed to independent action, continually wants to shut itself up in sympathy with the left (just as a young piano-player finds that his two hands want to do the same thing while he wants them to do things which are very different), so that in the streets I am in constant danger of becoming an inverted sleep-walker—eyes shut awake instead of eyes open asleep.

I have another fearful wound, but this also the faculty do not consider fatal. My horse and I used to have a daily contest as to whether he should be bridled or not. Although every morning the result proved to him that he must bear the bridle, he had such a bad memory, or was so incurably stubborn, that he always renewed the struggle on the next. In one of these ever-recurring battles he managed, or I mismanaged, to knock my thumb against something which cut and flayed it a little. Such are my war-wounds—worse than fell to the lot of most warriors in Spain. You must therefore imagine your poor brother with a white linen bandage round his right thumb, and a verdant shade over his left eye—an affecting picture. You must be hard-hearted indeed if you do not weep and mourn for him.

CHAPTER V.

"THE CITY OF DREADFUL NIGHT."

TOWARDS the close of 1873 Thomson's position and
prospects were far from satisfactory. Not only had
he made no profit by his journey to Spain, but he
returned from that country in extremely depressed
spirits and in a wretched state of health, with a severe
cold in his left eye which for some weeks incapa-
citated him for reading and writing or any sort of
business; while, to add to his troubles, he was unable to get the promise of any employment at home.
He thus wrote on November 24 to Miss Alice
Bradlaugh, from his old address in the Vauxhall
Bridge Road :—" My eye is quite well again, thank
you. I only want now some good employment for
it and its fellow. The time was very tedious during
the weeks it remained bad, as I could hardly read,
write, smoke, or do anything but lounge indoors
unoccupied. Mr. Girard (of the *New York World*)
has now no work for an assistant, and I have not
managed to get hold of anything in the City yet, though,
of course, I have been making every effort." After
some time Thomson succeeded in obtaining a secretaryship to another commercial company, but this also
collapsed after a few months. His old friend and
schoolmate, George Duncan, who had returned from

Madras on a visit in 1873, and had met Thomson
in London after an absence of thirteen years, was
much concerned by the change he observed in him
towards the end of this year and the beginning of
the next. We find him, however, in November able
to interest himself once more in literary matters, and
resuming his Shelley correspondence with Mr. W. M.
Rossetti.

230 VAUXHALL BRIDGE ROAD, S.W.,
November 12, 1873.

DEAR SIR,—Towards the end of July last I sent you rough
notes on the "Minor Poems and Fragments," excepting
the "Triumph of Life." On this I herewith enclose some
remarks. It is a poem which has always been a particular
favourite of mine, and suggests questions which nothing less
than an essay could indicate. Here I touch only on the
text. It has been pure pleasure to follow again the unique
terza rima ; liquid, sinuous, continuous, a full-flowing river
of music and light.

I think with a piece left unfinished like this you might
venture upon obvious metrical rectifications, which do not
affect the sense, just as you have ventured upon obvious
grammatical ditto.

I hope you enjoyed your Italian holiday. I thoroughly
enjoyed Navarre, but was recalled too soon, because Re-
publicans and Monarchists wouldn't kill each other whole-
sale, the unfeeling wretches!—Yours truly,

JAMES THOMSON.

The New Year—the first two weeks of which were
spent with the Bradlaughs at Midhurst, "a pleasant
fortnight," as he records in his diary—was destined
to be in many ways an important one to Thomson,
and especially by the publication of the "City of
Dreadful Night." The diaries which, with the occa-

sional omission of a few weeks, he kept from this time
to within eight months of his death, have fortunately
been preserved, with the single exception of that for
1875. They are very characteristic of his observant
nature and methodical habits, containing, amidst a
variety of matter, concise daily notes of his literary
work as projected or completed; books read; letters
received and answered; friends visited, or seen at his
own lodgings; the direction of his afternoon stroll;
the place and nature of his meals; and the manner
of spending the evening. An account is kept of the
sums received in payment of literary work (after
1875), and of the expense incurred for lodging,
clothes, &c. A special feature of the diaries is the
regularity with which the state of the weather is recorded, no aspects of sky-scenery, bright or gloomy,
being lost upon the senses and spirits of this dweller
in his own city of darkness. The ordinary routine
of Thomson's London life has been thus described
by Mr. Dobell:—"In London he lodged in one
narrow room, which was bedroom and sitting-room
in one, and where he could hardly help feeling a
sense of poverty and isolation. A morning spent at
the British Museum, an afternoon walk through the
streets, and an evening passed in reading or writing:
such was the usual course of his daily life in London.
Visits to or from his few London friends sometimes
varied the monotony of his existence; and now and
then he would go to a concert, or to the Italian Opera,
for he was passionately fond of music." On the
whole, the impression conveyed by the diaries is, that
Thomson, as regards outward circumstances, led a
far less solitary and friendless life than has usually
been supposed; for in London, as in the army, his

genial and gentle disposition never failed to win him
good and faithful friends.   At the time of which I
am now writing, his Sundays were usually spent at
the house of his friend Mr. Jaques ; he was fond of
going to the Monday Popular Concerts with his old
comrade John Grant ; he would sometimes, but more
rarely, go for a day's expedition into the country ;
and there were few days on which he was left
altogether without some friendly society, one of his
most frequent visitors in 1874 and thereabouts being
Fred Hollett, a former fellow-lodger, whose name
often occurs in the diaries of this date.   The statements subsequently made to the effect that it was
during " a period of friendlessness and suffering, and
whilst actually trudging through London at night,
that he wrote his ' City of Dreadful Night,' " * are
decidedly exaggerated and misleading ; though the
mental suffering which Thomson endured was in all
verity grievous enough.

At the beginning of 1874 he was putting the
finishing touches to his great poem, previous to its
appearance in the *National Reformer*.   The following
letter addressed to Mr. W. M. Rossetti at this time
is an instance of how Thomson could jest grimly on
the humorous side of very serious subjects :—

243 VAUXHALL BRIDGE ROAD,
January 30, 1874.

DEAR SIR,—I am much obliged to you for your generous
determination to bring my work into notice, but, should you
refer to me at all, would prefer to be mentioned simply as
B. V.

---

* *Manchester City News*, June 17, 1882.

I write just now principally to ask a favour. Though knowing about nothing of art, I have long been profoundly impressed by the "Melancholy" of Dürer, and my sole engraving is a copy of that work signed Johan Wiricx, 1602, which, I am glad to find, Scott describes as admirable. Wishing to bring this great figure into a poem, and rapidly enumerating the accessories which help to identify it, I find myself bothered by the animal prone at her feet. Ruskin in one place terms this a wolf, and in another a sleeping wolfhound. Scott does not characterise it, I think.

For myself, I have been used to consider it probably a sheep, and as dead, not sleeping; in fact, a creature awaiting dissection, and suggesting anatomy as among the pursuits of the labouring and studious Titaness.

Can you, who are an art-adept, resolve the question, and tranquillise my agitated mind?

Hoping that your Blake and all other work is proceeding well,—I remain, yours truly,

JAMES THOMSON.

My animal stanza runs thus :—

Words cannot picture her ; but all men know
  That solemn sketch the pure sad artist wrought
Three centuries and three-score years ago,
  With phantasies of his peculiar thought :
The instruments of carpentry and science
Scattered about her feet, in strange alliance
  With the poor creature for dissection brought.

Must I, as Ruskin dictates, change this last into,

With the keen wolfhound sleeping undistraught—

(a villanous makeshift)?

"Wet, coldish morning," writes Thomson in his diary for April 4. "Not up till past one o'clock.

Wet all day. Then wrote away at Whitman, finishing in a fashion draught of biographical sketch, as well as going through last 'two parts of ' City of Night.' Walked with Fred before and after dinner. Walked self after tea. Imagination deeply stirred."

The "City of Dreadful Night," the poem referred to in the above letter and extract was, as Thomson has himself described it, " the outcome of a good deal of sleepless hypochondria suffered at various periods." " About half of it," he says, " not the first half as it now stands, was written in 1870 ; and then it was not touched till 1873, when I roughly finished it, licking the whole into shape at the beginning of this present year." It was the crown and consummation of his pessimistic poetry ; the fullest and most powerful expression of that gloomy mood which for many weary years had been gradually gaining the ascendency in his mind. The seeds of pessimistic thought, at first latent in his nature, had been quickened and ripened by a long course of calamity and error, and the fruit was now apparent in the spirit of deliberate, measured, relentless despondency which inspired the " City of Dreadful Night." It has been called an opium poem, and on the strength of this assertion some writers have spoken of Thomson as an habitual opium - eater. This, I believe, is a mistake ; for though there is some evidence that he had now and then taken opium, both before and after he left the army, it seems certain that he did this only by way of an occasional experiment, and that the practice never obtained a hold on him. There is, moreover, a solidity of grasp and firmness of outline about the " City of Dreadful Night " which does not seem to warrant the idea that it owed any part of its origin to the use of opium.

In March 1874 the "City of Dreadful Night" began to appear in the *National Reformer*, and ran through four numbers.* It at once attracted more attention than any of Thomson's other writings, being recognised as a very remarkable work, not only by Secularists, but in wider literary circles, and receiving notices from the *Spectator* and the *Academy.. ,* The latter article, which was very favourable, caused quite a series of applications to be made at the office of the *National Reformer* for the numbers containing the poem by the unknown " B. V. ;" these, however, were already out of print, so that for the six years that elapsed before the "City of Dreadful Night" was published in book form persons who wished to read it had to take a good deal of preliminary trouble. Emerson and Long-fellow, among others, expressed a desire to see it, when its fame had reached America a few months later. Several critics praised the poem very highly ; among these were Mr. W. M. Rossetti, to whom Thomson had sent a copy, and the blind poet, Philip Bourke Marston. " I hope "—thus the latter wrote to Thomson in 1875—"when your poems come out, I may have an opportunity of expressing publicly the deep admiration I have for your work, which seems to me powerful, beautiful, and masterly, and full of deep and beautiful sympathy with the sad race of men. Few poems in these days have more impressed me." But the most gratifying encourage-

---

* The dates of these were March 22, April 12 and 26, May 17, 1874.

ment which Thomson received was the letter addressed
to him by George Eliot, to whom he had sent a copy
of the "City of Dreadful Night."

George Eliot to B. V.

THE PRIORY, 21 NORTH BANK, REGENT'S PARK,
May 30, 1874.

DEAR POET,—I cannot rest satisfied without telling you
that my mind responds with admiration to the distinct
vision and grand utterance in the poem which you have
been so good as to send me.

Also, I trust that an intellect informed by so much
passionate energy as yours will soon give us more heroic
strains with a wider embrace of human fellowship in them—
such as will be to the labourers of the world what the odes
of Tyrtæus were to the Spartans, thrilling them with the
sublimity of the social order and the courage of resistance
to all that would dissolve it. To accept life and write much
fine poetry is to take a very large share in the quantum
of human good, and seems to draw with it necessarily some
recognition, affectionate and even joyful, of the manifold
willing labours which have made such a lot possible.—Yours
sincerely,   M. E. LEWES.

The following letters were written by Thomson in
reply :—

60 TACHBROOK STREET, S.W.,
June 18, 1874.

DEAR MADAM,—Having been absent for several days,
I am only now able to thank you for your very kind letter,
for your generous expression of praise, and for your yet
more generous trust, though this, I fear, will prove to be
misplaced.

I have no Byronic quarrel with my fellows, whom I find

all alike crushed under the iron yoke of Fate, and few of whom I can deem worse than myself, while so many are far better, and I certainly have an affectionate and even joyful recognition of the willing labours of those who have striven to alleviate our lot, though I cannot see that all their efforts have availed much against the primal curse of our existence. Has the world been the better or the worse for the life of even such a man as Jesus? I cannot judge; but I fear on the whole considerably the worse. None the less I can love and revere his memory. A physician saves a life, and he does well; yet perchance it were better for the patient himself and for others that he now died. But it is not for me to introduce such thoughts to you.

I ventured to send you a copy of the verses (as I ventured to send another to Mr. Carlyle) because I have always read, whether rightly or wrongly, through all the manifold beauty and delightfulness of your works, a character and an intellectual destiny akin to that grand and awful Melancholy of Albrecht Dürer which dominates the City of my poem.

I cannot conclude without expressing to you my gratitude for many hours of exquisite enjoyment.—I am, Madam, with profound respect, yours sincerely,

JAMES THOMSON (B. V.).

60 TACHBROOK STREET, S.W.,
June 20, 1874.

DEAR MADAM,—In my note of Thursday I omitted to qualify, as I intended, the general statements by the distinct admission of what, however, is in all likelihood quite obvious—that the poem in question was the outcome of much sleepless hypochondria. I am aware that the truth of midnight does not exclude the truth of noonday, though one's nature may lead him to dwell in the former rather than the latter. Pray pardon me for troubling you on so small a matter.—Yours very respectfully,

JAMES THOMSON.

We must now turn back for a while to the brighter and more playful side of Thomson's character, as shown in his letters to his two friends, Alice and Hypatia Bradlaugh, to whom, during his recent visit to Midhurst, he had given the nicknames of Fatima and Lina. "After all your Parisian experience," he wrote in November 1873, "I think you ought to write me in French. It would be good practice. I was obliged to talk French (in my terrible fashion) while in Spain. You would have laughed to hear me sometimes; still more at my Spanish." It was accordingly agreed that the correspondence should henceforth be carried on in French.

> 240 VAUXHALL BRIDGE ROAD.
> *Février* 21, 1874.

MES CHÈRES PETITES FILLES,—Je vous dois mille remercîments pour vos bonnes lettres, et je vous aurais écrit plus tôt si je n'aurais pas été très affairé depuis l'Election. Je vous remercie pour les fleurs cueillés par Mlle. Fatima et envoyées par Mlle. Lina; la senteur des violettes était charmante. Mais pourquoi donc Lina, n'écrit elle pas en Francais? Elle le peut faire assez bien, pourtant. Peut-être parcequ'elle ne se portait pas bien ce jour-là. J'espere que cette méchante migraine ne la tourmente pas encore.

M. Austin Holyoake reste chez lui, et je suis occupé tous les jours en lui aidant comme je le puis, à faire ses comptes, etc. Il est très faible, mais je ne crois pas que sa santé est pis, quoique elle n'est guère mieux, à cause de son séjour en ville. L'autre jour un médecin éminent est venu le voir et l'a très soigneusement examiné. Vous apprendrez avec regrette qu'il ne donna pas d'espoir de guérison. On ne peut pas faire pour lui, a-t-il dit, que de procurer qu'il meure le plus lentement et avec le moins de

H

souffrance possible. C'est un mot triste pour sa famille et
ses amis.

Dimanche dernier j'ai diné chez M. J——. Le soir on
a fait de la musique et nous avons dansé gaiment, Madame
J—— et moi ; elle portait les pantoufles de Monsieur,
parceque ses bottines la gênaient. Elle n'est point bégeule,
cette bonne dame là.

Je crains beaucoup que vous ne sortez pas pour fumer
tous les soirs, comme vous avez fait jadis, quand j'étais
aussi heureux d'être chez vous.   Moi, je garde toujours
mon brûle-gueule, et je fume avec une régularité religieuse ;
mais c'est tout autre chose, et infiniment moins gai, que de
fumer seul chez soi au lieu de fumer en se promenant avec
deux jeunes filles, bonnes, jolies, spirituelles et charmantes.

Comme vous rirez de mon pauvre baragouinage français !
détestable, misérable, atroce, honteux, etc. ! (Voilà que
je fais comme Fatima quand elle écrivait des exercises, en
y mettant tous les adjectifs possibles.)   Moi, je m'en ris,
et sans gêne, moi-même.   Ecrivez-moi bientôt, je vous
prie.—Votre très-humble et très-respectueux serviteur,

JACQUES THOMSON.

230 VAUXHALL BRIDGE ROAD,
Mars 10, 1874.

MA CHÈRE FATIMA,—Je serai enchanté d'aller avec vous
et Mlle. Lina chez tante Eliza dimanche prochain, et je
ferai un grand effort sur moi-même—mais un effort vraiment
effroyable et héröique—à fin d'arriver à la grande Salle dans
la Vieille Rue à onze heures le matin (s'il fait beau temps
ce jour-là, bien entendu) ; quelle heure matinale pour le
dimanche !

Si j'ai montré votre lettre à M. Grant, c'était parce qu'elle
était si bonne et si spirituelle.   Je ne crois pas que vous
en êtes vraiment fâchée, quoique vous dîtes.   Mais ne vous
avisez pas de montrer la mienne à personne ; ça serait
cruel.

Je ne puis pas écrire plus loin, je suis tout gelé de froid.
Je vous baise la main, à vous et à votre confrère (c'est à
dire, votre con-sœur) dans le secrétariat. Adieu !

JACQUES THOMSON.

The illness of his dear friend Austin Holyoake,
mentioned in the above letters, was a constant grief
and anxiety to Thomson during the first three months
of this year; "Austin's, in and out," and "Austin's,
all week," being frequent entries in his diary. The
death of his friend on April 10 was a severe blow
to him, though the loss had long been foreseen. The
funeral took place on the 17th, at Highgate Cemetery,
Thomson being one of those who stood round the
grave—the very grave which he himself was destined
afterwards to share. On the day after Austin
Holyoake's death Thomson had said farewell to
another of his most intimate companions. "With
Grant," he notes in his diary, "to see George
Duncan for last time, he starting for Madras on
Monday." Five years later Mr. Duncan was again
in London for a short visit, but owing to an error
as to Thomson's whereabouts the friends did not
then meet, and never afterwards found another
opportunity.

These losses were in some measure mitigated by the
acquisition of new friends, mostly owing to the publication of the "City of Dreadful Night. Thomson's
correspondence with Mr. Bertram Dobell began in this
manner, and resulted in a friendship which continued
to the end of his life.

James Thomson to Bertram Dobell.

17 JOHNSON'S COURT, FLEET STREET, E.C.,
April 9, 1874.

DEAR SIR,—I have just received from Mr. Bradlaugh your note about myself, and hasten to thank you heartily for your very generous expression of approval of my writings. While I have neither tried nor cared to win any popular applause, the occasional approbation of an intelligent and sympathetic reader cheers me on a somewhat lonely path.

You must not blame Mr. Bradlaugh for the delay in continuing my current contribution to his paper. He is my very dear friend, and always anxious to strain a point in my favour; but as an editor he must try to suit his public, and the great majority of these care nothing for most of what I write. As for this "City of Dreadful Night," it is so alien from common thought and feeling that I knew well (as stated in the Proem) that scarcely any readers would care for it, and Mr. B. tells me that he has received three or four letters energetically protesting against its publication in the *N. R.*, yours, I think, being the only one praising it. Moreover, we must not forget that there is probably no other periodical in the kingdom which would accept such writings, even were their literary merits far greater than they are.

I address from the office of the *N. R.*, because I am just now rather unsettled, and not sure what will be my private address for some time to come. While preferring to remain anonymous for the public, I have no reason to hide my name from such correspondents as yourself.—I am, dear Sir, yours truly,

JAMES THOMSON (B. V.).

To the Same.

60 TACHBROOK STREET,
June 24, 1874.

DEAR SIR,—I have found out what set some people calling for my CITY. I had a letter from Rossetti the day before yesterday in which he asked me whether I had seen a notice in the *Academy*, treating my poem with distinguished respect. He himself writes in that paper, but had nothing to do with the notice in question, nor does he know who wrote it. Yesterday I got the number (that for June 6). The paragraph leads off the notes on magazine articles, coming under the head of "Notes and News," and certainly does me more than justice, especially as compared with Leopardi. They also quote complete the twentieth section about the Sphinx and the Angel. But I daresay you are in the way of getting to see the paper. . . .

I have just written to the editor of the *Academy*, thanking him and his critic, and saying that it seems to me a very brave act, on the part of a respectable English periodical, to spontaneously call attention to an atheistical writing (less remote than, say, Lucretius), treating it simply and fairly on its literary merits, without obloquy or protesting cant.—Yours truly,

JAMES THOMSON.

On asking Thomson why he did not bring out his poems in book form, and on learning that he was unable to do so because he had not the means of paying for the publication, Mr. Dobell, who for more than ten years had been a reader and admirer of " B. V.'s " writings in the *National Reformer*, and was fully convinced of the writer's genius, generously determined to take the risk on himself. The following extracts from Thomson's letters have reference to this proposal, and to its enforced abandonment; after

which there ensued a long and disappointing search
for a publisher who should be willing to accept the responsibility of bringing out such heterodox works :—

May 18, 1874.—I duly received your letter with estimate
for printing and binding, and yesterday I had the opportunity of talking over the matter with Mr. Bradlaugh. He
thinks with you that the experiment is worth trying. I still
fear that you will be disappointed in your expectation of
even a very moderate success. However, if you wish to
make a venture, and would prefer to make it with something
of mine, I am quite willing so far as I am concerned,
though if you suffer any loss through your association with
me I shall much regret it.

Your proposed terms, of profits, if any after repayment of
your expenses, to be divided equally between us, I accept
as fair; in fact, as you may remember, I suggested the
same in our conversation. All I ask in addition is, that a
few copies shall be reserved for me, as there are friends to
whom I should like to present them.

October 17, 1874.—I say again, as I have said from the
first, that it will be more than imprudent on your part, and
will certainly cause regret to me, if you at all strain your
resources in order to publish the poems. I regret much
that business has not gone so well with you of late as you
expected, and I do hope you will take good heed ere risk-
ing funds on a venture which is not at all necessary, and
which it seems to me is at least as likely to fail as succeed.

On April 13 Thomson had left his lodgings in the
Vauxhall Bridge Road and moved to a Mrs. Baxter's,
at 60 Tachbrook Street, Pimlico, where he remained
for the next eighteen months. The following extracts are from his letters to his sister-in-law :—

April 18, 1874.—Please note that I have changed my
address, moving, however, but a very short distance, as this

neighbourhood suits me. I do not yet know whether I shall stay here long; but the house is nice and clean, and the landlady seems a very decent body. As inscrutable destiny decides that I am to lodge with married women and old maids alternately, I am with a family woman this time, though I have really not yet learnt whether the husband is dead or living.

Friendly regards to your parents; much love to their lazy little daughter and their son-in-law who is so assiduous, being of the race of the Thomsons. I guess that *we* are all lineally descended from my namesake, the childless architect of the Castle of Indolence. As for *you*, your ancestor must have been a Bruce who, having watched the spider make a couple of attempts, yawned and thought the animal very stupid to exert itself so much, and fell fast asleep before it could make a third, and never awoke until all the wars were over, and Bannockburn was an ancient tradition.

July 27, 1874.—You cruel little woman, to call longing for holidays "insane"! As for me, I am always "insanely" longing for holidays in hot weather. As soon as the glass reaches 70° in the shade, my pure conscience finds work of any kind very sinful, and thorough *idlesse* the only way to sanctification and beatification. And yet I have to work: this is a wicked world, and also "a mad world, my masters," as the old playwright has it.

As to Lilian in Bulwer Lytton's "Strange Story," I know nothing at all of that lay-figure. When I was even younger than you are still I read some of that book-wright's romances, and became enduringly convinced that he was one of the most thorough and hollow humbugs of the age; false and flashy in everything; with pinchbeck poetry, pinchbeck philosophy, pinchbeck learning, pinchbeck sentiment; stealing whatever good thing he could lay his hands on, and making it a bad thing as he uttered it. So you won't persuade me to think of you in connection with his Lilian of "A Strange Story." No; but if you keep very very good, and write me many many nice letters, I may think of you in connection with the lady of Shelley's "Sensitive Plant," or her to whom he sent "Lines with a Guitar." Read these poems (if you haven't them, may I send them to you?), and then you will see how you are thought of by,—Your lazy brother,   JAMES THOMSON.

The next letter refers to a complaint on the part of his youthful correspondent that "Tachbrook" was an ugly name :—

60 TACHBROOK STREET, LONDON, S.W.,
Mai 7, 1874.

MA CHÈRE LINA,—Pourquoi, donc, n'écrivez-vous pas en Français ? Que vous êtes oisive ! Savez-vous que vous êtes aussi très-impertinente de vous moquer du nom de la rue dans laquelle je demeure ? *Brook* est toujours un très joli mot avec nous autres Anglais ; et quant à *Tach*, quand quelqu'un jeune et beau vous dira tout bas à l'oreille, " Tâche de me voir toute seule ce soir dans le petit sentier, ô ma bien aimée ! " (soit dans les environs de West Cowes ou de quelqu' autre ville) je parie que vous ne trouverez pas le mot *Tâche* ni baroque ni déplaisant. . . .

Il a fait assez froid ce mois de vous glacer après les jours caniculaires desquels vous vous plaigniez en Avril. Probablement il ne faut point beaucoup de chaleur de rendre toute languissante une petite fillette si paresseuse qu'elle s'abandonne sans effort à oublier notre belle langue française !

Moi, je suis pour le present à cheval sur un *si*, c'est a dire sur une compagnie anonyme ; mais je crains beaucoup qu'elle ne sera tuée sous moi, comme toutes les autres, et cela très prochainement.

60 TACHBROOK STREET, S.W.
June 5, 1874.

MY DEAR FATIMA, MY DEAR LINA,—MY DEAR LINA, MY DEAR FATIMA,—I don't know which to address. One *did* write me a nice long letter in French; but then she followed it with two telegrams in mere English.—Ah, but the other hasn't written in French at all. That truly is shameful; but do you know, Sir, that you are writing in English yourself? So I am ! ! ! The fact is that the day is too hot for French; I find that the genders are melted into one, and the accents have all evanesced. Now, although I may freely "confound" the genders colloquially, I am not going to do so in writing; therefore, avaunt French !

I am heart-broken that I did not see you before you left. I did mean coming on the Sunday, but it was hot then too, and so I got lazy.

To console you for not seeing me I send you two gentlemen.* A Serious Man and an Attic Philosopher (I mean the *cove under the tiles*). I don't know which either or both of you prefer, so I send both addressed to both. (I tossed up several times to settle the question, but got tired of the ties.) The Serious Man will remind you of that desperate boarding-school life you led in Paris : which of you gained the Vicomte Moréal ? Did Hypatia object to him because he was a poet ? or did she ignore his verses on the ground that they were quite innocent of poetry ? . . .

I don't think I shall take the trouble to read a note in English from either of you any more. So write in French, my good little children. Does Dora still remember your second grandfather?—Yours (3 P.M.) deliquescent,

JAMES THOMSON.

P.S.—I hope really you will like the two books I send, else I would not send them. I enjoyed them much myself a few centuries ago, in the days when I was young.

I find that the writing is very bad; but then I have bad ink and a bad pen. I could get better ink and pen with exertion, but exertion is strictly forbidden in the " Castle of

---

* " L'homme Serieux " and " Le Philosophe sous les Toits."

Indolence" of James Thomson on the afternoon of 5th June 1874—Oaks Day.

A visit of his brother and sister-in-law to London is recorded in the diary for September 1874. During this same summer he had begun to correspond with Mr. William Maccall, to whom he had once been introduced at Mr. Bradlaugh's office. The correspondence originated in Thomson's discovery that Mr. Maccall was an old friend of the Grays, with whom he had himself been so intimate in his youth, though he had not visited them since 1860. Mr. Charles Watts, who acted as sub-editor of the *National Reformer*, and Mr. G. W. Foote, another friend whose acquaintance Thomson made about this time, are referred to in the following letter :—

To Mrs. Bradlaugh.

60 TACHBROOK STREET, S.W.,
November 29, 1874.

MY DEAR MRS. BRADLAUGH,—I have rather less than more news to send you than you have to send me. Grant and I go to the concerts on Monday evenings, and that is my only dissipation just now, except that I have had a couple of suburban strolls with young Foote. Grant, as you say, does not look well, and I fear that he is not so. The redoubtable Kenneth I haven't yet seen, not having called at the barracks since that tall grenadier returned to town.

I am sorry indeed for poor Hypatia with her teeth and headaches. She must be very careful in pronouncing the most Germanic of the Germanic words, else they will certainly twist and tug out what sound teeth she has left. As for the German round-about sentences, as they give people who are well the headache, they ought, on the homœopathic system, to cure those who have it. We shall see how they affect her. By the bye, it seems that I frightened *les chères petites enfants* by saying that the grammar would do for the first year or two of their studies. I meant to speak, not of the grammar, but of the dictionary : when they get on a certain way in the language, they will want one with more idioms in it. If they want full directions for acquiring German, they had better refer to Hans Breitmann (whose book I believe their papa gave them), who has an excellent poem on the subject :—

> " Willst dou learn die Deutsche Sprache ?
> Denn set it on your card,
> Dat all the nouns have shenders,
> Und de shenders all are hard."

There is to be an amateur performance for the benefit of the Secular or some such club at the King's Cross Theatre on the 15th December, Tuesday. Mr. and Mrs. Watts, Othello and Desdemona ; Mr. Foote and Mrs. Holyoake, Iago and Emilia. I saw a sort of first rehearsal the other evening, but only a few persons were there, and they had different acting editions of the drama ; so I soon came away.

I should be very glad to come to see you all at Christmas, but I fear that I must put off my visit until after B.'s return from America. Besides the writing, there is a good deal to do at the office. The responsibility of the acting editorship weigheth heavily on Watts' shoulders as yet ; Atlas with the world on his back was nothing to him.

With love to all, and hoping you are well,—Yours truly,
JAMES THOMSON.

To Mr. Bertram Dobell.

60 TACHBROOK STREET, S.W.,
November 16, 1874.

DEAR SIR,—Many thanks for the books, which I shall look through as I have leisure. I should have called on you ere this had I been less occupied. Now that the weather is cold, I do my writing and reading more in the evenings, and two of these are taken up by Johnson's Court, while a third (the Monday) I dedicate to St. James's Hall. Let me know freely when you want any or all of your books back, and I will send them at once.

If you like chamber music, and can spare the time, I shall be happy to meet you any Monday at St. James's Hall. I usually go with a friend [Mr. Grant], another melomaniac. You get Orchestra ticket, Piccadilly entrance, and get to Orchestra from Piccadilly Place, a narrow passage a few steps farther on. Be careful not to fall into the abomination of the Christy Minstrels, who are in the Minor Hall! Concert commences at eight. I usually get there about seven, as the doors are open, and one can sit and read or chat while waiting. In the Orchestra you can easily see whether a friend is present, and get beside him.— Yours truly,

JAMES THOMSON.

On Thomson's birthday, November 23, 1874, there is the following significant and pathetic entry.—" Forty years old to-day. Cold ; third day of fog. Congenial natal weather. No marvel one is obscure, dismal, bewildered, and melancholy." The year which was just drawing to its close had been a memorable one in Thomson's lifetime, as having witnessed the publication of his most characteristic poem ; but it had also deprived him of two of his most valued friends, while to himself it was the beginning of a downward course of deepening poverty, diminishing vigour, ill-health, disappointment, and despondency.

The diary for 1875 is unfortunately lost, the chief available record for this period being the letters to Mr. Dobell, which are in great measure concerned with Thomson's vain attempts to secure the publication of a volume of his poems. In the early months of this year he was in severe pecuniary straits, and his troubles were increased in the summer by the severance of his long connection with the *National Reformer*, in which so many of his best writings, both in verse and prose, had been published during the preceding twelve or fourteen years. The following extracts, taken from his letters to Mr. Dobell, will explain the course of events :—

January 18, 1875.—I'm still on the staff of the noble *N. R.*, but have been crowded out of late. C. B. and Ajax * take up much room, and we wanted to bring in other things. I'm always willing to give way, especially when doing so saves me from writing nonsense. I resume in next week's number.

April 17, 1875.—Your former note came too late for me to let you know that I am always late on Wednesdays. On that night the *N. R.* goes to press ; I am not done with it till about nine, Watts till about eleven ; so he and I, with a few others, generally spend an hour or two together after nine, waiting for the first proof.

May 18, 1875.—You may tell any one you like my name, as the *N. R.* people and B. haven't in the least respected the anonymity. I shall put my name to the volume if published. As to my position, I don't want strangers to

---

* Mrs. Besant.

know that I am somewhat hard up; it's none of their business. They may know that I help and contribute in the *N. R.* for aught I care. I don't do any more "Jottings,"* simply two or three columns on one or two topics of the day, a sermon or religious meeting, or any nonsense of the sort. Philip Bourke Marston has been at the office wanting a copy of the "City," and Miss Mathilde Blind has been asking B. for loan of all my pieces, in order to draw attention to them in some German periodical.

July 9, 1875.—I have since been reflecting on the matter, [a conditional offer of publication], and am inclined to take a reasonable number of copies, should they make this an essential condition, as it is so important to me to procure publication. I believe that a good many would be disposed of through advertisement in the *N. R.* I am quite off this now, B. having taken the first opportunity of terminating our connection, which I myself had only submitted to for some time past because it afforded me mere subsistence. So I must get other engagements at once, and a published volume would be of immense service to me. Of course B. could not refuse my advertisement, nor do I suppose that he would charge for it even now, seeing that he had all the verses for nothing; but I should send it to the office in the ordinary way of business.

August 24, 1875.—Foote and George Jacob Holyoake hope to start a good Secular weekly, price twopence, soon, with a guarantee fund to secure its existence for three years. Mr. H. will not be able to do much work on it, but his name is very influential with many old Secularists who don't like B's hammer-and-tongs style. Some good writers would contribute, *gratis* at first; it being understood that

---

* The "Jottings," occasional notes in the *National Reformer*, were written by Thomson, under the signature "X," from the middle of 1874 to the date of this extract. They are full of characteristic humour and pungency.

all shall be paid as early as possible. I go in for this new paper thoroughly of course, not caring to be gagged at the pleasure of Mr. B.

This rupture of an intimate friendship of more than twenty years' standing is a subject on which it would be profitless and painful to dwell. I will therefore merely say that it is not to be supposed that the blame rested wholly on one side or the other; or, indeed, that there was necessarily any blame to be adjusted at all. The striking dissimilarity of character between the two friends would in itself be sufficient to account for their final disagreement, when each had gradually settled down to a separate course of his own, and when new interests were arising to accentuate their differences. Mr. Bradlaugh, who had certainly shown much kindness to Thomson at one period, was naturally annoyed at the increasing irregularities and want of self-government which marked the conduct of his friend; while Thomson, on his part, strongly resented certain features of Mr. Bradlaugh's later policy; so that the breach which ensued, deplorable as it was between two such old friends, was probably inevitable. After their parting in 1875, Thomson never met Mr. Bradlaugh again, except once or twice for the formal discussion of some details of business; and there is no doubt that the cessation of his friendship and correspondence with Mr. Bradlaugh's family was a great grief to him. "Evening party at Hall of Science," he enters in his diary for January 27, 1876. "Alice and Hypatia there with C. B. First time of seeing the girls that I could not speak."

CHAPTER VI.

"SEVEN SONGLESS YEARS."

For seven years after the publication of the "City of Dreadful Night"—"seven songless years," as he himself described them—Thomson ceased to produce poetry, his writing, with the rare exception of an occasional lyric or political piece, being now altogether critical and journalistic.. As he had no longer any secretaryship in the City from which he could gain a livelihood, he was henceforth dependent altogether on his literary work, and the *National Reformer* having now failed him, he was forced to look afield for fresh employment. It was for this reason he was so anxious to issue a volume of his poems, hoping that a wider reputation would bring him more opportunities of obtaining work ; in this attempt he was for several years unsuccessful, but he was fortunate in finding two journals to which he could contribute freely, and from one of which he received most substantial remuneration. The establishment of the *Secularist*, a weekly paper which commenced on January 1, 1876, has already been alluded to, and is further mentioned in a letter to Mr. W. M. Rossetti.

12 Gower Street, W. C.,
December 21, 1875.

Dear Sir,—I believe a prospectus was sent you some time ago of the *Secularist*, a Liberal weekly Review, price twopence, edited by G. J. Holyoake and G. W. Foote, of which the first number will appear on the 1st January. I shall be one of the regular contributors. Would it be troubling you too much to ask you to send a note of this for insertion in the *Academy?* The *Secularist* will be advertised in that paper next Saturday.

Mr. Holyoake has always differed from Mr. Bradlaugh in maintaining that Secularism is a practical rule of life, and as such quite distinct from Atheism and all other merely speculative systems; and many of us are at one with Mr. Holyoake on this matter.—Yours truly,

JAMES THOMSON.

The joint-editorship of the *Secularist* continued only for a few weeks, for differences soon arose between the two editors, and on February 26 Mr. G. J. Holyoake's withdrawal was announced, and the paper was thenceforth conducted by Mr. Foote, until, in June 1877, it was merged in the *Secular Review.* During the eighteen months that it lasted, Thomson contributed largely to the pages of the *Secularist* under the old signature of "B. V." His writings ranged over a wide variety of subjects, religious, social, and literary; a few of his poems, written at an earlier date, were also included, and many of his translations from Heine, as well as a series of essays on that author, to whom he was devotedly attached. He also (perhaps rather unwisely) took a prominent part in the wordy warfare which raged for some time between the adherents of the *National Reformer* and the *Secularist.*

The other journal to which Thomson became a contributor was *Cope's Tobacco Plant,* a monthly periodical, edited, on behalf of a well-known firm of Liverpool tobacco-merchants, by Mr. John Fraser, to

1

whom Thomson had obtained an introduction through Mr. William Maccall. The fact of *Cope's Tobacco Plant* being primarily a trade-advertising sheet is apt to give a wrong impression as to its literary value, for in reality it contained many articles of a high order, being, as Thomson himself described it, "one of the most daring and original publications of the day," a periodical "which actually loves literature, though it has to make this subordinate to the Herb Divine." To one whose love of literature was almost equalled by his love of smoking, the task of writing for the *Tobacco Plant* was a thoroughly congenial one; it, moreover, offered him two great advantages, both of which he could hardly have obtained elsewhere—a regular source of income, and a medium by which he could give independent form to his views, for he was allowed by Mr. Fraser to have almost his own way with the purely literary matter of the *Tobacco Plant.* "My work on it," he wrote a few years later, is chiefly of the hack order; the 'Tobacco Legislation,' signed 'Sigvat,' the last two or three 'Mixtures,' * (former Mixer having lately died); sometimes a literary article signed 'J. T.,' the 'Smoke-Room Table' notices of *English Men of Letters.* The editor is an admirable one to have dealings with; payment is fair and regular; I have not to violate my conscience by writing what I don't believe, for I *do* believe in Tobacco, the sole article necessary to salvation in the Cope creed. On the whole one earns a little money in this way not more wearisomely and rather more honourably than in any other just now

---

* "Cope's Mixture" was the name given to a column or so of miscellaneous notes in each number of the *Tobacco Plant.*

open to me." From his first contribution in September 1875 until the discontinuance of the *Tobacco Plant* in 1881, Thomson wrote for it pretty regularly, and always spoke of the connection with pleasure and gratitude.

At the beginning of 1876 we thus find Thomson entering on a fresh period of his life, and in addition to being engaged on new work, he was now settled in new lodgings in another quarter of London.

To Mr. Bertram Dobell.

35 Alfred Street, Gower Street, W.C.,
December 15, 1875.

Dear Sir,—I have delayed answering your letter partly because I have been busy and unsettled, partly because I wished to consult about the publication by subscription suggested by Mr. Bullen and yourself. All things considered, I would rather wait unpublished than adopt this mode; but I thank you none the less for your kind offer in connection with it.

You will note changed address at top. I only moved on Monday, and don't know that I shall stay here, but at any rate I shall settle in this neighbourhood for a time, as I want to be near Foote for the *Secularist* business, and also near the British Museum for the Reading-Room. . . . Wishing you heartily a merry Christmas and a happy New Year,—I am, yours truly,

James Thomson.

In these lodgings at 35 Alfred Street (or 7 Huntley Street, as the house was afterwards renamed) Thomson stayed till a few weeks before his death, and was treated with much kindness and consideration by the housekeeper, Miss Scott, who did all that it was in her power to do for his health and

comfort. Mr. Foote, with whom Thomson was
closely associated at this time, was living at 12
Gower Street, the house of Mr. T. R. Wright, who
had married the widow of Mr. Austin Holyoake.
Thomson was thus within immediate reach of his
most intimate friends; indeed during the last six
years of his life he was less a visitor than an inmate of the Wrights' house, being regarded with the
deepest esteem and affection by Mr. and Mrs. Wright
and their family.   The course of his life for the next
few years was quiet and uneventful, the entries in
the diary relating chiefly to his work for the *Tobacco
Plant*; frequent walks with Mr. Foote or Mr. Percy
Holyoake, the son of his old friend Austin; and
pleasant evenings with the Wrights, when the time
was spent in music, billiards, or conversation.   On
Sundays he was usually with the Wrights, or with
his old friend Mr. Jaques; but he had now lost sight
to a great extent of his earlier set of friends and
old army comrades.   For several years he seems to
have been only twice out of London, these occasions
being his attendance at the stormy Conference of
the Secular Society at Leeds on June 4, 1876, and a
four days' visit on Secular affairs to Leicester in the
following September, when he was accompanied by
Mr. Foote.   Few letters written at this period have
been preserved, except some to Mr. Dobell concerning literary matters and the proposed publication of a
volume.

To Mr. Bertram Dobell.

35 ALFRED STREET, GOWER STREET, W.C.,
Sunday, January 9, 1876.

DEAR SIR,—I have been half a dozen times on the point of replying to your last, but something or other has hitherto prevented me. First, accept my sincere thanks for your kind offer, which fortunately I need not take advantage of. I have, of course, still ground to make up, but the *Secularist* and *Tobacco Plant* keep me going for the present.

With regard to Mr. Bullen's criticisms on "Our Ladies of Death,"—criticisms which really flatter me, as any man's work is really praised by such examination,—I must hold myself right. The only English Dictionary I have by me is a school one, but as such little likely to venture on neologisms; moreover, it is very good of its kind, being Reid's of Edinburgh. This gives Sombre, Sombrous, dark, gloomy; Tenēbrous, Tenēbrious, dark, gloomy, obscure (and, of course, Tenebrious implies Tenebriously); Ruth, pity, sorrow; Ruthful, merciful, sorrowful; Ruthfully, sadly, sorrowfully. The huge Worcester Webster, into which I looked a day or two after your letter came, agrees as to tenebrious and ruth; I forgot to look in it for sombrous. But as to ruth, I used it in the common sense of pity, not that of sadness and sorrow. When I wrote—

> " My life but bold
> In jest and laugh to parry hateful ruth,"

I meant to parry the pity of others, not to parry my own sadness, which, indeed, jest and laugh must intensify instead of parrying. My thought was much like that of Beatrice, " The Cenci," Act v. sc. 3 :—

> "Shall the light multitude
> Fling at their choice curses *or faded pity*,
> Sad funeral flowers to deck a living corpse,
> Upon us as we pass, to pass away ?"

*

And from the light, indifferent multitude, as you must know, curses are even less unwelcome than pity when we are profoundly suffering.   I looked into the Dictionaries, not knowing whether their authority would sustain or condemn me, as I am used to trust in careful writing to my own sense of what is right; this, naturally, having been modified and formed by reading of good authors.   Even had the Dictionaries condemned me, I should in these cases have been apt to assert my own correctness; in many others I should be ready to yield without contest.   In the " City of Dreadful Night " I used tenebrous instead of tenebrious; just as good writers use, as it happens to suit them, either funeral or funereal, sulphurous or sulphureous (Shelley often in " Hellas "), &c.   You will think that I have troubled you with very many words on a very little matter.   As it is now just 11 P.M., and I have much to do to-morrow, I will conclude in pity for myself if not in ruth for you.—With best wishes, yours truly,   JAMES THOMSON.

The following extracts are from the same correspondence :—

June 22, 1877.—I find it hopeless to attempt publishing before, at earliest, winter coming on.   I hope to stir in the matter September or October.

I will call on you one of these evenings with your two books.   Will you forward by book-post a copy of Garth Wilkinson's " Human Body and its Connection with Man " to Mr. John Frazer?   He writes that he will be glad of it.   I will settle for book and postage when I see you, and he will settle with me.

I shall probably do an article or two for Watts and Foote on your " Alger's Eastern Poetry : " it would form a good introduction to a series on Omar Kháyyám which I have in my heart to accomplish some day.   Note my new address (7 Huntley Street).   It is the same house as before, only they have renamed and renumbered the street.

February 12, 1878.—I expected to give you a call long ere this; but Fraser put off answering my inquiries as to the Christmas or New Year card—the Pilgrimage after Chaucer, as misinterpreted by Stothard—and other matters, and when at length he did write seemed so urgent about the Pilgrimage that I put on full steam, spinning out from seventy to a hundred lines a day, for the thing had to be done in rhyme (a long way) after Chaucer too. I have called at ——'s about poems. He told me that trade was so depressed that they are withholding several works ready for publication. If the damned Dizzy suspense be over, and trade improved, will be happy to see me on the subject in June, when they make their arrangements for works or chief works to be brought out in the following season, which, as you doubtless know, begins with November. There would be no fair chance for a volume now. So I must wait once more.

November 18, 1878.—I am very sorry but scarcely surprised that things are not very flourishing with you just now. You are correct in supposing that it is ditto with me. With the natural depression of trade infinitely aggravated during the past two years by the infernal impolicy of our Jewish-Jingo misgovernment, it cannot be well with anybody but arm-manufacturers, Exchange speculators, and Hebrew adventurers; and things seem likely to grow much worse before they grow better. . . . The "Improvisations"* I shall be delighted to see. It is so scarce that I have never yet been able to come across it, and have never seen any mention of it save that by Rossetti in his supplementary chapter (a very fine one) to the "Life of Blake." It is not even in the British Museum, having been printed for private circulation only, if I remember aright. I should think it would be a real treasure to any of Wilkinson's few admirers; for, as you know, the fewer the devotees of any man or thing, the more enthusiastic.

---

* "Improvisations from the Spirit," by Dr. Garth Wilkinson.

December 23, 1878.—Just lately, and in these days, I am
pretty busy for Fraser; and well for me that it is so, for I
have not earned a penny save from him the whole year.
There is more work to do on the Tobacco Duties; and also
verse and prose for the Christmas card, but not so much as
last year, nor offering such genial opportunities and associations as "Chaucer's Canterbury Pilgrims." The subject this
time is the "Pursuit of Diva Nicotina," in imitation of Sir
Noel Paton's "Pursuit of Pleasure." Paton is a good painter
and poet too, but of the ascetic-pietistic school, or with
strong leanings to it.

The indefinite postponement of the publication of
his poems was a very serious misfortune to Thomson
for more than one reason; for it interposed a ruinous
delay in the realisation of his literary prospects, at
a time when a little encouragement and a lightening
of the load of his poverty would have been an inestimable boon, and thus disheartened him for all
further creative effort. That most of the publishers
to whom he applied should have candidly told him
that they were not disposed to become responsible for his volume was indeed no matter for surprise or dissatisfaction; for, as he himself wrote
in reference to this subject, "verse by an unknown
man is always a drug in the market, and when it is
atheistic it is a virulently poisonous drug, with which
respectable publishers would rather have nothing to
do." But he had good reason to complain of other
and less justifiable delays, caused by the inconsiderate
vacillation of certain publishers who held out promises
which they afterwards declined to perform. "This
is bad treatment; four months and more lost," he
writes in his diary in February 1877, when he found
himself once again cut adrift.

In July 1879, through Mr. Foote's introduction, Thomson became engaged in a correspondence with Mr. George Meredith, for whose genius he had long felt and expressed the utmost respect and admiration ; and he had now the great satisfaction of learning that his own writings were held in high esteem by one whose good opinion he probably valued above that of any living critic. " I am glad," wrote Mr. Meredith, " to be in personal communication with you. The pleasant things you have written of me could not be other than agreeable to a writer. I saw that you had the rare deep love of literature ; rare at all times, and in our present congestion of matter almost extinguished ; which led you to recognise any effort to produce the worthiest. But when a friend unmasked your initials, I was flattered. For I had read the 'City of Dreadful Night,' and to be praised by the author of that poem would strike all men able to form a judgment upon eminent work as a distinction." It was apparently about this same time, or perhaps a little earlier, that Thomson became personally acquainted with Philip Bourke Marston, with whom he had already corresponded from 1875, and the acquaintance soon ripened into a warm friendship. There was a natural bond of union between the two poets in the similarity of their destiny, each of them being gifted with an extreme sensibility, a strong love of action, and a full capacity for enjoyment ; while each had been bereaved in early manhood, and was spending the remainder of a disappointed life in a " city of darkness " of his own.

In the meantime, on January 1, 1879, there had been started, under Mr. Foote's editorship, a monthly magazine named *The Liberal*, to which Thomson

was an occasional contributor, one of his papers
being a series of articles on Dr. Garth Wilkinson's
"Improvisations from the Spirit," under the title of " A
Strange Book." Towards the end of the year, however, disagreements which had gradually been arising
between Thomson and Mr. Foote became so acute as
to prevent their further intimacy; after which rupture
the *Tobacco Plant* was for some time the only paper
for which Thomson wrote, and the sole quarter to
which he could now look for the earning of his livelihood. Thus ended his connection with Secularist
journalism, a connection that had extended over a
period of some fifteen or sixteen years.

To Mr. Bertram Dobell.

7 HUNTLEY STREET, GOWER STREET, W.C.,
Sunday, October 19, 1879.

DEAR SIR,—I can still but barely manage to keep head
over water—sometimes sinking under for a bit. You see
what I do for Cope. I have not succeeded in getting any
other work except on *The Liberal*, and this is of small value.
I thank you for keeping the Whitman for me : I sold it
with other books when hard up. In the meantime I have
the latest 2 vol. edition in hand from Fraser, who has
requested some articles on him, when Tobacco Legislation,
&c., will allow. I mean to begin him now in the evenings
at home, as the Legislation can be done only in the
Museum. He may occupy such intervals in the paper as
did the Wilson and Hogg, both done by request : the
" Richard Feverel " was on my own suggestion. George
Meredith, to whom I sent a copy, wrote me a very flattering.
because very high-minded, letter. He has seen the "City,"
and though by no means sanguine with such a public as
ours, he thinks it should float a volume. The admira-

tion of so many excellent literary judges really surprises me.

All this about myself because I have nothing else to write about, going nowhere and seeing no one.—Yours truly,

JAMES THOMSON.

The following extracts are taken from Thomson's diary for 1879 :—

Wednesday, Jan. 1.—Morning dull and mild. Aftn. wet & mild. Night, sharp sleety hail or icy sleet. Morng. Letter from Fraser. Cigars, P.O.O. and Proofs. Morng. & evg. (till 10.15), Proofs. Aftn. posted Proofs, lre. & formal receipt, with thanks, &c. Not a bad beginning of the year. Wrote all morng. without fire, so mild.

Wednesday, Jan. 8.—Bitter easterly. Some sun. Morng. & evg. Fair copy *Memorial;* then Blue Book & Financ^l Ref^m Alm^k, 1879. Aftn., Walk about Soho. (Coal scuttle ; after three years !) Moon keen as crystal, sky pale & cloudless, stars few and dim, ground like iron, wind like a razor.

Sat., Jan. 11.—(To Wm. Maccall.) How is one to discover or invent a *phrenometer* or *psychometer* by which to regulate one's writings to the capacities of the average " intelligent reader " !

Monday, Feb. 17.—Fog morng. Some sun midday. Wet evg. Cool. N.W. Morng., Up late, dawdled. (Poor strange cat in back coal-cellar and under kitchen since Saty. morng.) Aftn., Stroll Oxford S^t; also before dinner. Evg., Reading Erasme : *Eloge de la Folie* (Biblio : Nationale). Slight bilious indigestion. Listless & sleepy. Beer early for early bed.

Ash Wednesday, Feb. 26.—Cold. N.E. wind ; glum ; snow in the air, slight powder falling. Morng., To B. M. Shut. Did my Commination Service alone ; cursing the idiots who close such a place on such a day. Stroll before dinner. Aftn., Gower St. Evg., Writing bit *Men of Letters*. Reading Goldsmith. Coals (1) full.

Friday, *Feb.* 28.—The dull rheumatic pains shoulders & right arm continue ; slight, but I rather fear after father.

Sunday, *March* 2.—Queer dream morng. Condemned to death for sort of manslaughter on one who deserved it for wronging another. No remorse, no fear, some perplexity as to chance of commut^n to imprisonment for life. Some trouble on awaking to make sure it had been a dream.

Thursday, *June* 19.—Trousselle handed me old silver tankard (which I left with poor Mrs. B.), & a note from Alice.

Tuesday, *July* 1.—Heavy rain with gale, almost incessant till 4 P.M. Brief clear up, then shower, then clear. At 9 (dusk) great ragged rack to N. sweeping from W., across very pale blue skimmed-milk sky, & beneath it the brick-dust-yellow rift ominous of storm. 1st of July, & no summer yet !

Thursday, *Aug.* 14.—Have got into bad way of waking two or three hours before I want to get up (before 5 or 6), & being unable to sleep afterwards. Hence I arise weary at last ; and am very drowsy after tea, when I want to read or write. This morng. awoke at 5.40 ; this evg. had to lie down, & slept from 6.30 to 8.30, losing two good hours.

Saturday, *Sept.* 6.—Dim, dreamy, misty, brooding day. Red beamless sun. Very languid. Morng., B. M. After, stroll with G. W. F. ; met in coffee-house. Evg., dawdled and strolled.

Saturday, *Nov.* 1.—*Athenæum* ; openg. article on Egoist. The first critique on any of George Meredith's books I have ever come across, in which the writer showed thorough knowledge of his works, and anything like an adequate apprec. of his wonderful genius.

Saturday, *Nov.* 8.—*Athenæum*, adv^t of Egoist : cordial praise from *Athen^m*, *Pall Mall*, *Spect^r*, *Exam^r*. At length! Encour^s! A man of wonderful genius & a splendid writer may hope to obtn. something like recog^n after working hard for thirty years, dating from his majority!

Thursday, Nov. 27.—Cold but fine: 10 P.M. thaw yet cold; moon high in orange halo of immense high thin pale or dim grey cloud, drifting from the east.

Friday, Nov. 28.—Pretty fair day, cold. Moon thick yellow halo; immense rack of pale grey cloud, united, but with large curves, sailing from east.

Saturday, Nov. 29.—Fair, cold, N.E. Moon clear in deep azure or turquoise, not transparent.

Friday, Dec. 5.—Cold, slight snow; fine morng., livid day. Snowing pretty heavily at night (9 P.M.). Morng. B. M. Readg. for *Raleigh*. Aftn., Adeline (French). Evg. Thackeray (Trollope's). (Picked just twenty-one sticks out of my grate—fire laid by charewoman Lizzie; the rest being quite enough to light the fire! The prodigal poor!)

Sunday, Dec. 14. Mr. R—— yesterday; lre. from mother to live with his cousin, a lonely widow & religious. He in consternation: I won't stop; I'll be back in a fortnight. And to-morrow is Sunday! (despair).

Christmas Day.—Black fog midday, and until night. Morng. (late) answ^s Fraser's with receipt. Dined Gower S^t. Billiards, &c. Evg. Home 12.20 or so. Bed past one.

Wednesday, Dec. 31.—Saw Old Year out and New Year in at Mitchell's; with Wrights, &c. Cards, whist, and Vingt-un.

Mention of ill-health occurs rather frequently in the diaries of this period, and it is certain that during the course of these "songless years" a decided change for the worse was taking place in Thomson's condition, and that his constitution, strong and hardy though it was at the outset, was gradually giving way under the terrible strain to which it had so long been subjected. If a decline of this sort, which under the circumstances must sooner or later have been inevitable, is to be traced back and ascribed to any particular time, we should probably be justified in regarding the visit to Spain in 1873 as the date of the commencement of disquieting symptoms. In February 1876, when he already had reason to be concerned about his health, he was further shaken by a very severe fall, which kept him indoors for some days, and threatened rather serious consequences. In the autumn of the following year he was troubled a good deal by insomnia; "my old friend, insomnia," he calls it in the diary. In 1879 the signs of failing health were still more frequent and unmistakable; for, in addition to the symptoms recorded in the above extracts (it will be seen from the entry for February 28 that he was apprehensive of a paralytic stroke, as in the case of his father), we find him suffering from a "queer catching pain" in the back and a painful constriction at the chest, "over and about the heart," and other similar ailments. With this decrease of physical strength he had lost somewhat of his mental nerve, promptitude, and vigour—even the handwriting, once so characteristic in its extreme regularity and firmness of outline, had now begun to show traces of increasing debility.

That this change was due in great measure to his fits of intemperance is, I suppose, beyond doubt; at the same time it must in justice be noted that these excesses were periodic, not habitual — a recurrent disease against which his true nature struggled, albeit unsuccessfully, with loathing and detestation. "He was not," writes one who knew him intimately during these very years, "a toper; on the contrary, he was

a remarkably temperate man, both in eating and drinking. His intemperate fits came on periodically, like other forms of madness; and naturally as he grew older and weaker they lasted longer, and the lucid intervals became shorter. The fits were invariably preceded by several days of melancholy, which deepened and deepened until it became intolerable. Then he flew to the alcohol, so naturally and unconsciously that when he returned to sanity he could seldom remember the circumstances of his collapse." *
"After the fit had spent itself," says another friend, "would come a dreary week of feebleness and self-abhorrence, then returning health would bring back the normal Thomson, and a few months of work would be the prelude to another attack. No mortal ever strove against an overpowering disease more grimly than Thomson, and when friends were to be pained by his succumbing to the mania, it was always combated and repulsed to the last moment. His absolute abandonment during these attacks was sufficient to attest their nature, and no more pregnant illustration of the metamorphosis he underwent could well be found than the remark made by his landlord's children on one such occasion. Thomson was naturally very loving with children, and children invariably returned his affection. Once, when he came back to his rooms in Huntley Street in the fulness of the change wrought by his excesses, the children went to the door to admit him, but closed it again and went to their father, telling him that "Mr. Thomson's wicked brother was at the door;" and for some time they could not recognise "their Mr. Thomson"

---

* G. W. Foote's article in *Progress*, April, 1884.

in the figure of the dipsomaniac claiming his name."

During the years that followed the publication of the "City of Dreadful Night," Thomson's pessimistic creed remained unaltered—darker it could hardly have become than in that poem. It will be shown in a later chapter that his pessimism, as advanced in his writings, is the expression of a mood rather than of a philosophy; yet he seems on rare occasions to have alluded to it in private conversation as a fixed and deliberate conviction. An instance of this sort is recorded by Mr. Foote :*—

"Thomson's life inclined him to a pessimistic view of nature, yet it must not be supposed that his philosophy was merely a matter of temperament. He was little of a cynic and less of a misanthrope, and you could not have inferred his philosophy from his ordinary conversation. He was naturally chary of talking about his ideas, even to his intimate friends, but when he broke through his customary reticence he spoke with the quiet gravity of intense conviction. I well remember the first time he ever conversed with me on the subject. It was a still summer's evening, and we sat together on the Thames Embankment at Chelsea. We smoked and chatted for a long time, and growing more and more communicative under the influence of that tender sunset, we gradually sank into the depths. I found his pessimism as stubborn as adamant. It was not a mood, but a philosophy, the settled conviction of a keen spectator of the great drama of life. He admitted that he had no special reason to scorn his fellows : on the contrary, he had met many good friends, who had treated him 'better than he deserved.' But all that was beside the question. He denied the reality of progress in

* *Progress*, June 1884.

the world ; there was revolution, but no forward movement ;
the balance of good and evil remained through all changes
unchanged ; and eventually the human race, with all its
hopes and fears, its virtues and crimes, its triumphs and
failures, would be swept into oblivion. In conclusion he
quoted Shakespeare, a very rare thing with him ; and he
rose from his seat with Prospero's matchless words upon
his lips."

We can well believe that these pessimistic convic-
tions were in great part the result of some constitutional tendency to melancholia ; though in studying
the development of Thomson's unhappiness, it is impossible to distinguish with any certainty between
consequence and cause. "What," asks the writer
of the passage just quoted, "could the fulfilment of
one dream have availed against this curse ? It
haunted him like a fiend. It stayed for no invitation and consulted no convenience. It often left
him free and happy in untoward circumstances, and
beckoned him forth to bondage and misery as he sat
at the feast or glowed with pleasure in the revel."
Yet there were many hours when his mind recurred
fondly to this "one dream," in the belief that its
realisation might have averted his subsequent misfortunes and errors. On three consecutive evenings
in September 1878 he was engaged in writing the
singularly interesting autobiographical stanzas already
alluded to, commencing "I had a Love." "Actually
got writing verses again !" he notes in his diary,
"but hard and harsh ; more truth than poetry." It
was one of Thomson's last injunctions that these
verses should not be published, since he considered
them to be merely a rough draft, though written with
all the solemnity of one who was "like a man making

K

his will at the gates of Death." But while penning
these lines he felt that the fresh creative impulse
arisen within him might be the throes, not of death,
but of "some new birth that gives the lethal illusion "—from which we see that even at this date the
spark of hope was not wholly and utterly extinguished.
And if his pessimism had failed to obliterate the
memory of his own love, as little had it affected his
intense sympathy and pity for all suffering humanity.
"He sympathised," says Mr. Foote, "with all self-
sacrifice, all lofty aspiration, and in particular with
all suffering. This last emotion was often betrayed
by a look rather than expressed in words. I vividly
remember being with him once on a popular holiday
at the Alexandra Palace. We were seated on the
grass, watching the shifting groups of happy forms,
and exchanging appreciative or satirical remarks.
Suddenly I observed my companion's gaze fixed on
a youth who limped by with a pleasant smile on his
face, but too obviously beyond hope of ever sharing
in the full enjoyment of life. Thomson's eye followed
him until he passed out of sight, and the next moment
our eyes met. I shall never forget the gentle sadness
of that look, its beautiful sympathy that transcended
speech and made all words poor."

Meanwhile Thomson still continued to exhibit all
his old gaiety and sprightliness in congenial society,
and his powers of conversation are described by all
who knew him as being singularly brilliant. Here
is a graphic account of his appearance and manner
at the period with which we are now concerned :—

"His personal appearance told in his favour. He was of
the medium height, well built, and active. He possessed
that striking characteristic sometimes found in mixed races—

black hair and beard, and grey-blue eyes. The eyes were
fine and wonderfully expressive. They were full of shifting
light, soft grey in some moods, and deep blue in others.
They contained depth within depth; and when he was
moved by strong passion they widened and flashed with
magnetic power. When not suffering from depression he
was the life of the company. He was the most brill'ant
talker I ever met, and at home in all societies; a fine companion in a day's walk, and a shining figure at the festive
table or in the social drawing-room. But you enjoyed his
conversation most when you sat with him alone, taking
occasional draughts of our national beverage, and constantly
burning the divine weed." *

Thomson remained to the last an inveterate smoker,
a constant worshipper at the shrine of the tobacco-
saint whose martyrdom and apotheosis he so humor-
ously described in verse.† It was his habit, as he has
told us in his " Stray Whiffs from an Old Smoker "
(the first article he contributed to the _Tobacco Plant_),
to smoke during the intervals of his literary work,
but not when actually writing. " There are some,"
he says, " who can smoke with enjoyment and profit
when writing : this I cannot do, when the writing
requires reflection ; for either the thought is distracted
by the smoke, or the fire goes out in the interest
of the thought. But how delightful and inspiring
are a few whiffs in the pausing spaces, when the
brain teems with new ideas gradually assuming form,
and the palate yearns for the tobacco savour with a
thirst as keen as the water-thirst of the desert."

But the charm in which Thomson found the surest
consolation for the sorrow and trials of his life was

---

* G. W. Foote, in _Progress_, April 1882.
† " Pilgrimage to St. Nicotine of the Holy Herb," cf. p. 259.

the charm of music. In one of his " Jottings " in the
National Reformer in 1874 he had declared that the
Monday Popular Concerts at St. James's Hall had for
some years yielded him more pure delight than all the
other public entertainments of London put together.
" There Beethoven," he added, " is King of Kings and
Lord of Lords ; on his forehead broods the frown of
thunder, but his smile is so ravishing and sweet that
naught can compare with it save the tenderness in
sternness of Dante the Divine ; with Handel and Bach,
Mozart and Haydn, Weber and Mendelssohn, throned
high but less loftily around him ; with Hummel and
Dussek, Tartini and Scarlatti, Spohr, Chopin, Hiller,
and their peers, as satraps of provinces ; and lastly, at
his very feet, that notable and but recently discovered
pair of shoes, Schubert and Schumann—whereof the
former is indeed lovely, but too large and lax, while
the latter, with its stiff embroidery, is of such shape
and size that I for one cannot yet wear it with
pleasure." The same worship of Beethoven as the
supreme musician is expressed in " He heard Her
Sing," a poem full of sustained melody which gives
proof in every line of Thomson's passionate love of
music—

And first with colossal Beethoven, the gentlest spirit sublime
Of the harmonies interwoven, Eternity woven with Time ;
Of the melodies slowly and slowly dissolving away through
    the soul,
While it dissolves with them wholly and our being is lost in
    the Whole ;
As gentle as Dante the Poet, for only the lulls of the stress
Of the mightiest spirits can know it, this ineffable gentleness.

Such was the course of Thomson's life, and such
were the alleviations which made life endurable, during

the period of his journalistic and critical work for the *Secularist*, *Liberal*, and *Tobacco Plant*. The "seven songless years" did not reach their final termination till the autumn of 1881; but the publication of the long-projected volumes, which took place before that date, is an event that demands the commencement of a new chapter.

CHAPTER VII.

BETWEEN LEICESTER AND LONDON.

It was in 1880, after six years of disappointment and delay, that Thomson had the satisfaction of seeing the issue of his first volume of poems. The publication, thus at last secured, was due to the untiring zeal and energy of his friend Mr. Dobell, who, by a fortunate application to Messrs. Reeves & Turner, succeeded in making the arrangement that the book should be forthwith published at his and their joint expense. The following is the note in Thomson's diary for March 4:—"Dobell having arranged with Mr. Reeves for publication of a small tentative volume (six full sheets = 192 pages; exclusive of Title-pages, Dedication, and Contents), Reeves put it at once to press with Messrs. Ballantyne, Hanson & Co., Edinbro'. On Thursday, 4th March 1880, I got first proof of 16 pp. Volume to be entitled "The City of Dreadful Night, and other Poems."

To Mr. W. M. Rossetti.

7 Huntley Street, Gower Street, W.C.,
March 6, 1880.

Dear Sir,—I enclose a very brief Shelley article, not because it has any intrinsic worth (which it has not), but because you are interested in anything, however minute, relating to him. Also, as a bit of fun, another on the *Burns* of Principal Shairp, with which you may sympathise, as you have no doubt seen that extraordinary Professor of Poetry's lecture on Shelley in *Fraser.* What a shameless nudity he would have discerned in Adam and Eve in Paradise!

At length I have actually in the press a small tentative volume, " The City of Dreadful Night, and other Poems. By James Thomson (B. V.)." " Weddah " I reserve to lead off another, should the success of the present be sufficient to encourage another. I was bound to start with the " City," it being already better known than any other, and having been noticed in the *Academy* and *Spectator* (hostile) as well as by yourself, and also mentioned in the *Athenæum* and *Notes and Queries.* Before I sent you (and you alone) the " Weddah," none of my pieces had been sent to any one : I allowed them to drift away in the obscure unpoetical world of the *National Reformer,* pretty careless as to their fate, for I did not then look forward to literature as a profession.

The *Tobacco Plant* has requested some articles on Walt Whitman, and I have already sent on the first. When the publication (which is sometimes long delayed) is far enough advanced I shall take the liberty of asking you for the latest news of him—his health and general condition. I will send you the articles when they appear.

Hoping that yourself and family are well,—Yours truly,

JAMES THOMSON.

To the Same.

7 HUNTLEY STREET, GOWER STREET, W.C.,
Wednesday, April 7, 1880.

DEAR SIR,—Herewith a copy of my first little book, which you must please accept as having done more both in public and in private than any one else to prepare the

way for it.   If it fails, the failure will have to be charged
to its own demerits, not to the default of excellent intro-
ductions.

The first batch of copies came yesterday (from Edinburgh),
and Reeves advertises in Saturday's papers, as the electoral
storm will have pretty nearly blown itself out by the end
of this week.

I was not aware that you get the *Tobacco Plant;* would
have sent it you myself had I thought you would care
for it.

I had proof of first Whitman article, but it is not in this
month's number, of which a copy reached me this morning.
Thank you for the details as to health and condition ; I
will write you again for information when the articles are
near the end.   You saw Ruskin's order for five sets of
W.'s volumes, with the characteristic note?—Yours truly,

JAMES THOMSON.

Whitman wrote to Fraser of the *Plant* that he never
smokes; but added that he likes to carry good cigars for
his friends.

This volume, which, as may be seen from the
above letter, was published early in April, gained on
the whole a very encouraging reception, the most
notable feature of which was the article headed " A
New Poet," which appeared in the *Fortnightly Review.*
That considerable hostility should be manifested
in some quarters against a writer of such unpopular
connections and unorthodox opinions was, of course,
to be expected, and Thomson was not a man who
would allow himself to be greatly troubled by such
adverse criticism.   " The reviewers "—so George
Meredith had written to him in 1879—" are not
likely to give you satisfaction.   But read them, nevertheless, if they come in your way.   The humour of

a situation that allots the pulpit to them, and (for having presumed to make an appearance) the part of Devil to you, will not fail of consolation. My inclination is to believe that you will find free-thoughted men enough to support you." This forecast was fully verified by the result; for many of Thomson's critics recognised that his volume, in spite of its novelty of tone, was the work of a true poet. George Meredith himself wrote as follows.

Box Hill, Dorking,
April 27, 1880.

DEAR SIR,—I will not delay any longer to write to you on the subject of your book, though I am not yet in a condition to do justice either to the critic or the poet, for, owing to the attack I suffered under last year, I have been pensioned off all work of any worth of late; and in writing to you about this admirable and priceless book of verse I have wished to be competent to express my feeling for your merit, and as much as possible the praise of such rarely equalled good work. My friends could tell you that I am a critic hard to please. They say that irony lurks in my eulogy. I am not in truth frequently satisfied by verse. Well, I have gone through your volume, and partly a second time, and I have not found the line I would propose to recast. I have found many pages that no other English poet could have written. Nowhere is the verse feeble, nowhere is the expression insufficient; the majesty of the line has always its full colouring, and marches under a banner. And you accomplish this effect with the utmost sobriety, with absolute self-mastery. I have not time at present to speak of the City of Melencolia. There is a massive impressiveness in it that goes beyond Dürer, and takes it into upper regions where poetry is the sublimation of the mind of man, the voice of our highest. What might have been said contra poet, I am glad that you should have forestalled and answered in "Philosophy"—very wise writing. I am in love with the dear London lass who helped you to the "Idyll of Cockaigne." You give a zest and new attraction to Hampstead Heath. . . .—Yours very faithfully,

GEORGE MEREDITH.

Nor was it only in a literary sense that the book was well received; for its financial success was sufficient to warrant the preparation of a second volume. "Arranging and preparing materials," writes Thomson in the diary on August 17, "for another vol. as requested by Dobell and Reeves. R., unasked, handed me cheque for £10 on a/c of first vol., which he reckons has already paid its expenses, & of whose profitable success both he and D. feel sure. Other publishers all firm that *no* vol. of verse, however good, can now pay its expenses, unless bearing one of three or four famous or popular names. Yet this vol. by an unknown writer, & burdened with the heavy dead weight of the sombre & atheistical & generally incomprehensible 'City of Dreadful Night,' *has* paid its expenses." Thomson might well feel gratified at this prosperous result, after the mortification of so many disappointments and rebuffs; but it is sad to think what invaluable poetical work he may have been prevented from accomplishing, owing to the long discouragement of this six-years' delay. Already a more hopeful tone is observable in the diary for 1880, though he did not actually recommence the writing of poetry until the following year.

On June 29 he had his first meeting with Mr. George Meredith, who had invited him to spend a day with him at Dorking. "Last Tuesday," writes

Thomson in a letter dated July 1, "I spent with Meredith; a real red-letter day in all respects. He is one of those personalities who need fear no comparisons with their best writings." Thomson's friendship and correspondence with Philip Marston were also fully maintained during this period; while through the kindness of such friends as Mr. W. M. Rossetti and Miss Mathilde Blind he had made many other literary acquaintances. Meantime his intimacy with the Wrights continued as close as ever, and it was at their house that he still spent most of his spare hours; he also walked frequently with Mr. Percy Holyoake, who, during the last few years of Thomson's life, was one of his most constant companions. "Splendid weather all week since Sunday," is the entry on August 14. "Several times to Regent's Park; never before found it so beautiful." In the autumn, however, we again find mention of ill-health, as in the following letter to Mr. Dobell :—

7 HUNTLEY STREET, GOWER STREET, W.C.,
Saturday, October 9, 1880.

DEAR SIR,—Yours with *Westminster Review* notice to hand. I have been going through the notices, marking what shall be printed on fly-leaf. I am engaged to dine with Mr. Reeves to-morrow, but have written not to wait or alter his hours for me, because if it is as wet as to-day I shall scarcely venture. The bitter nor'-easter of Saturday night gave me a chill that kept me in all Sunday (this is why I didn't give you a call). Since then we have had but one decent day, and I have had hints of rheumatism. As an agreeable addition, I have now a slight cold in the left eye, the eye which kept me from reading, writing, and smoking, five long weeks some years ago. So I must be careful.

I hope to be at Museum all the mornings next week

(you can always see me there by inquiring), but at home all the evenings from tea-time, say 4.30 or 5—unless I cannot go to Mr. Reeves's to-morrow, and so call one evening in the Strand.—Yours truly,

JAMES THOMSON.

In October 1880 appeared Thomson's second volume of verse, entitled "Vane's Story, Weddah and Om-el-Bonain, and other Poems," which was also well received in literary circles. High praise was especially awarded to the narrative poem "Weddah and Om-el-Bonain," for which Mr. W. M. Rossetti had expressed his admiration eight years before—a judgment which was now endorsed by the opinions of Mr. Meredith and Mr. Swinburne, the latter of whom characterised the poem as marked by "forthright triumphant power." A volume of Thomson's prose writings was already projected at this time.

To Mr. W. M. Rossetti.

7 HUNTLEY STREET, GOWER STREET, W.C.,
Wednesday, December 15, 1880.

DEAR SIR,—I am much obliged to you for sending me Mr. Swinburne's remarks on the "Weddah." When you next write to him will you please say that I count the value of such generous praise from such a poet simply inestimable. It immensely surpasses the most sanguine expectations I could have cherished had I known that he was going to give out any opinion at all on the poem.

I am also very much gratified by Mrs. Rossetti's sympathy with "Vane's Story," a piece too wild and capricious for most minds to follow. It is in fact a piece of pure phantasy, wherein I threw the reins on the neck of Pegasus and let him go whither he would. Hence I purposely made the title equivocal to the ear. Writing simply for my own pleasure, I enjoyed the writing.

My own intention, as you will readily believe, was to start the volume with " Weddah." But the publishers represented that many would be deterred by such an out-of-the-way title, that there would be all sorts of blundering and confusion in the orders, and that people in general are shy of asking for a book whose title they don't exactly know how to pronounce. As these appeared valid business arguments, I reluctantly yielded the first place to the fantastic " Vane," keeping, however, " Weddah " on the title-page.

I have been very unwell for a considerable time, and have only just now been able to resume and finish what was nearly completed before my illness, the preparation of a volume of prose requested by the publishers. It contains merely reprints, mostly from the *National Reformer;* but careful revision was required, and there was, and still is, some difficulty in the selection. However, I hope the first half of the matter will be in the hands of the printers by about Monday, and the other within a week after. But you need not mention the subject until we are further advanced.

I hope you have all been keeping well.

Pray tender my respects to Mrs. Rossetti, and kiss for me the miraculous little lady who at four and a half could listen to several pages of the " City of Dreadful Night."—Yours truly, JAMES THOMSON.

Thomson spent Christmas at the house of Mr. Wright, with whom, a few days later, he attended the funeral of George Eliot at Highgate Cemetery. It was agreed, early in 1881, that Thomson should produce a critical study of George Eliot's writings, to be published by Messrs. Reeves & Turner ; but the work proceeded very slowly, and was abandoned after two or three months in favour of a book on Heine—a project which also fell through. These matters are referred

to in the following extracts from the letters to Mr.
Dobell :—

January 5, 1881.—With Mr. Wright and Percy I went
to George Eliot's funeral.   It was wretched tramping through
the slush, and then standing in the rain for about three-
quarters of an hour, with nothing to see but dripping
umbrellas.   I was disappointed by there being any chapel
service at all   At the grave old Dr. Sadler mumbled something, of which only two or three words could be distinguished by us only a couple of yards behind him.

January 10, 1881.—As you mean to call to-morrow with
the *N. R.* volume for 1865, I will keep in all the morning
for you.   We can talk more to the purpose about your
proposals as to Geo. Eliot and Heine in half an hour than
we could write in half a month.   I may say at once that I
am willing to attempt both ; the former, as you suggest,
without my usual signature (unless such a hurried essay to
catch the moment as it flies contents me better and much
better than it is likely to do), and for a stated sum ; the
latter to be done more deliberately, with my name and on
such terms as may best suit us both.

February 2, 1881.—Geo. Eliot is starting slowly ; I shall
doubtless get on better, as to speed, when I have fairly
plunged into it.   I have been interrupted by an Address in
colloquial rhyme for the opening of the New Hall of the
Leicester Secular Society Club and Institute, on Sunday
March 6.   Mrs. Theodore Wright is to deliver it.   The
Committee is very pleased with it.   There are good men in
Leicester who have done liberal service, and I was most
hospitably entertained there in the *Secularist* time, so I
could not refuse their invitation to furnish an Address and
be present on the occasion.

On Saturday, March 5, Thomson travelled with
Mr. and Mrs. Wright to Leicester, in which neigh-

bourhood he stayed till Wednesday of the following
week, being present on the Sunday at the opening
of the Secular Hall, and enjoying the hospitality of
several Leicester friends.

Saturday, March 5.—Aftn. with Mr. and Mrs. T. R. W.
to Leicester by 3.30 train. Mr. Michael Wright met us
and took us home.

Sunday, March 6.—Three services. Heavy crush after.
Overflow service in Club Room, evg. Mrs. W. after quad-
ruple recit^n Address (very nicely printed, and not sold
until after her morn^g delivery) was repeat^g it and listen^g to
speeches all night. I slept the sleep of the just.

Monday.—M. Wright drove us to Quorn, with Miss
Holyoake. Factories—Floods—Remains Abbey—Wood-
house—Beacon Hill and Budden Wood. Ev^g *soirée.*

Tuesday. — To Gimson's House and Factory. Dinner
party at M. W.'s. Prosperity to New Hall in champagne.
Mr. Barrs drove us to his place, round by Braunstone
Wood (nightingales in summer) and ruins Kirby Castle.
His sister. Nice place & grounds.

Wed^y — Train at 12.20 to London. Very pleasant
visit. All of us *plus* Adeline and Percy *must* go in
summer.

After his return to London from this short holiday,
Thomson was occupied for some weeks in correcting
the proof-sheets of his volume of prose essays, which
was published in the spring of this year. The monotony, however, of his London life was soon again
broken by another and longer visit to Leicester,
where he was the guest of Mr. J. W. Barrs, whose
acquaintance he had recently made, and who quickly
became one of his trustiest and most intimate friends.
" To Leicester," he writes on June 4, " with the
Wrights and Adeline. Myself kept out of town

seven weeks—one week at Quorndon with Phil
Wright and brothers; three days in Leicester with
Mr. Michael Wright; one day with Mr. Gimson;
all the other five and a half weeks with the Barrs
at Forest Edge, Kirby Muxloe, four miles out of
Leicester. Unbounded hospitality; splendid holiday." There are several letters written during this
visit, and dated from Leicester or Quorndon.

To Mr. Bertram Dobell.

C/O MR. J. W. BARRS, FOREST EDGE, KIRBY MUXLOE,
NEAR LEICESTER, *Monday, June* 21, 1881.

DEAR SIR,—When you called at my place last Tuesday,
they might have told you that I was not only out, but out
of town. I came down to Leicester with the Wrights
and Adeline the Saturday before Whit-Sunday. Percy was
already down, and had been a fortnight, so I thought he
would return soon, and did not bother about letters. But
he found this place so pleasant that he prolonged his stay
till last Friday. I had a note from him yesterday, enclos-
ing yours and another, in which he tells me that he called
in passing, as arranged, on Mr. Reeves in the Strand and
told him of my whereabouts.

We are here four miles from Leicester, with railway station
a few minutes off, in a pleasant villa, surrounded by shrub-
bery, lawn, meadow, and kitchen garden. Host and hostess
(sister) are kindness itself, as are all other Leicester friends.
We lead the most healthy of lives, save for strong tempta-
tions to over-feeding on excellent fare, and host's evil and
powerfully contagious habit of sitting up till about 2 A.M.
smoking and reading or chatting. I now leave him to his
own wicked devices at midnight, or as soon after as possible.
Despite the showery weather we have had good drives and
walks (country all green and well-wooded), jolly little pic-
nics, and lawn-tennis *ad infinitum*. (*N.B.*—Lawn-tennis

even more than lady's fine pen responsible for the uncouth-
ness of this scrawl.) In brief, we have been so busy with
enjoyment that this is the first note I have accomplished
(or begun) in the seventeen days. I say *we*, because
Adeline is still here. She leaves about end of week, and I
shall then spend a week at Quorndon, where three of Mr.
Wright's sons live managing the factories there. Thence I
return here for two or three days, and perhaps shall have
two or three with old Mr. Wright in Leicester before
homing. You see I mean to have a good holiday before
setting to work again. . . .

Hoping that yourself and family are all well, and with
friendly regards to Mr. Reeves and his,—Yours truly,

JAMES THOMSON.

To Miss Barrs.

QUORNDON, NEAR LOUGHBOROUGH,
June 25, 1881.

DEAR MISS BARRS,—Raining hard since six in the
morning (not that *I* was up to see it begin), despite the
fair promise of yesterday and the steady rise of the glass
during the last two days. General despair as to hay un-
mown, or mown and lying unstacked. Special despair of
B. V. (Beautiful Virtue, mind !), who has to scrawl instead
of rambling, while the Wrights are engaged in the factory
till one.

Phil Wright having all his things in the other sleeping
chamber, I have the honour of sleeping in the wonderful
bedstead which Mr. and Mrs. Noah used in the ark some
short time ago. Under the beneficent protection of the
good angel with the scanty wings and the ample nose, and
sustained by a flawless conscience, I slept the sleep of the
just.

James Wright and wife were in town (Leicester) yesterday, and I stayed dinner in Regent Street, James coming

L

by same train to Quorn. Phil awaited us with boat. In the evening we were again on the river, which is not only of fair breadth, but really very pretty about here, and I renewed my friendly acquaintance with the water-rats, from whose charming society I have for several years been debarred by the force of circumstances I was unable to control. The W.'s have fishing rights opposite factory, and not only pike, perch, tench, and so on, are to be caught (they tell me), but also trout. Unfortunately I am no more a fisher of fish than of men (including women), but if others bring good trout to table, I am resolved, at whatever sacrifice, to bear my part of the burden of eating them. . . .

I must not inflict any more of my pluvial *ennui* upon you just now, as I am about writing for the first time to my good landlady, who is a credit to her sex, and who may be getting anxious about her model lodger.

To Mr. W. M. Rossetti.

C/o J. W. BARRS, ESQ., FOREST EDGE, KIRBY MUXLOE,
NEAR LEICESTER, *Thursday, July* 7, 1881.

DEAR SIR,—I have been in this district among very good friends for a month past, and the above will be my address till about the end of next week. I meant to send you a copy of the prose volume before leaving London, but have to confess that several things pressing drove the intention out of my head. I have written asking Mr. Reeves to send copies to yourself and two other friends equally neglected (one my sister-in-law), but do not know, as I do not know in your case, whether the target of the missive is in or out of town.

We had a most pleasant visit to Belvoir Castle (about twenty-five miles' drive from Leicester through Melton-Mowbray) just before the weather made its sudden leap from blazing July to the autumnal equinox.—I am, dear Sir, yours truly,   JAMES THOMSON.

To Mr. Percy Holyoake.

FOREST EDGE,
Wednesday, July 6, 1881.

DEAR PERCY,—Thanks for forwarding the book. I have written this morning to say why it was not sent by myself. This morning is wet and gusty, after three splendid blazing days. Saturday we drove *viâ* Melton to Belvoir; Sunday and morning of Monday in grounds and Castle, Monday afternoon drove back. Cousin Dick can tell you all about the shady alleys and arbours, and all the sunny terraces and slopes, from the pit of despair to declaration covert and fix-the-day secret bower. The subject is too young and tender for my rusty old pen. . . .

Adeline and yourself will be glad to learn that the tennis-court is being beaten flat after the rain. With a good rolling it will be in first-rate condition. Certain terrible omens this morning make us think that the duel has been fought with happily fatal result to the man who hasn't written as he was bound to do if able. Before midnight, lightnings ; afterwards, myself locked out of the house by a base conspiracy; after midnight, storms of rain ; at 1.30 Jack wet through, ringing for admission after an hour in the spinney, not listening to the nightingale, but vainly waiting for the rain to cease ; at breakfast, as already recorded, no letter for Dick ; then the brass tray in the hall fell down, knocking over candlestick and candle (meaning Dick's hopes extinguished); then a heap of books fell down in breakfast-room without apparent cause (meaning that Dick is quite floored). These last ominous incidents painfully remind me of my father's sword in our ancestral hall falling with a clash to the ground when any fearful catastrophe is about to happen to our ancient House. . . .   J. T.

The visit to Belvoir Castle alluded to in these letters was afterwards celebrated by Thomson in the stanzas headed "At Belvoir," which were published among his posthumous poems. It will be noted that even at this late period of his life he still retained, under favourable conditions, his natural vivacity, high spirits, and brilliant conversational powers. "Whatever," says Mr. Barrs, "has been said or written of his charm of manner and conversation has not and cannot give a just representation of them. Few men have known so delightful a friend, and his hilarity could equal his sombreness when in congenial company. One could hardly say more to any one who knows the 'City of Dreadful Night.' The poem, 'At Belvoir,' recalls three days of incessant mirth and midsummer pleasure, Thomson being chief jester."

"Home at length from Forest Edge," writes Thomson in his diary on July 23. "Seven weeks' holiday, most of it thoroughly enjoyable. Made fair progress in lawn-tennis. Man could not have kinder hosts." The following letters were written from his old lodgings in Huntley Street to his hostess at Forest Edge :—

To Miss Barrs.

7 HUNTLEY STREET, GOWER STREET, W.C.,
Saturday, August 6, 1881.

DEAR MISS BARRS, — Thanks for h'chief, and more for note. You will think me, not unjustly, a bore for writing so soon ; but I happen to be at home to-day with nothing particular to do, and rather unwell inside. I had to run about a good deal yesterday, and find that temperature was registered 84° in shade. My real Museum work recommences Monday.

I have been clearing off some arrears of correspondence. Finding when I called at Reeves' (my publisher) that

George Meredith had been there lately and inquiring after me, I took occasion to write him a note on Thursday about a little matter I had before lazily thought of writing about. My conscience, which, as you have doubtless perceived already, is always my only law, forbade me conclude without putting in some lines to the following effect (words pretty exact):

"I found a man in Leicester who has all the works of yourself and Browning, and appreciates them. Need I say that I gave him the grasp of friendship. I preached you to the dearest little Lady [What impudence! you cry], and fairly fascinated her with Lucy and Mrs. Berry.* Richard she heartily admired in the headlong imperiousness of his love, and you will be as grieved as I was to learn that she could not be brought to even the faintest moral reprobation of his unscrupulous fibbing (as in the cases of going to hear the popular preacher, and introducing to his uncle 'Miss Lœtitia Thomson'); while she exulted heartlessly in the tremendous threshing of poor faithful Benson. Such are women, even the best! But neither she nor any other women, and scarcely any man, will ever forgive you the cruel cruel ending."

Such is the judgment your own wicked judgment has brought upon you. As I have no reply this morning, Mr. M. may be off holiday-making (people have the queerest infatuation for holidays in these times: they ought to know that work is much pleasanter as well as nobler than idleness—see my moral essays on "Indolence" and "A National Reformer in the Dog-days"); but even if he is now in vacation (*i.e.*, emptiness!) your punishment can be delayed only for a month or two. Therefore tremble in the meantime. Should he demand your name in order to publicly denounce you, of course I shall feel

---

* The references are to George Meredith's "Richard Feverel."

conscientiously bound to give it. And if he has not yet
gone off, or having been off has returned, I may have to
spend a day with him ;—and then what a terrible tale I
shall have to tell by word of mouth ! . . .

7 HUNTLEY STREET, GOWER STREET, LONDON, W.C.,
Thursday, September 15, 1881.

DEAR MISS BARRS,—Pray thank brother Jack for letter
received this morning. . . . Jack kindly asks me to come
down to pay a last tribute of respect to Mr. W.'s memory.
I shall certainly do so if I can manage it, when I learn that
the end is come. I would promise it absolutely, but I have
a lot of work to do between now and Christmas ; too much
already, I fear, and I may have some more. Last night I
received proof of Part I. of certain notes on the structure of
Shelley's " Prometheus Unbound," which I had sent to the
Athenæum by way of an introduction, in the hope of getting
some occasional employment on that paper. Ask Jack
whether he read the " Reminiscences of George Borrow,"
by Theodore Watts, in the last two numbers of the *Athenæum*.
I found the second part very interesting, Borrow being an
old special favourite of mine.

Tuesday I spent with George Meredith at Box Hill ; a
quiet, pleasant day, cloudy but rainless, with some sunshine
and blue sky in the afternoon. We had a fine stroll over
Mickleham Downs, really parklike, with noble yew-trees
and many a mountain-ash (*rowan*, we Scots call it) glowing
with thick clusters of red berries,—but you have some at
Forest Edge. . . . We had some good long chat, in which
you may be sure that Forest Edge and its inmates, as well
as certain Leicester people, figured. M. read me an unpublished poem of considerable length, which, so far as I
can judge by a single hearing (not like reading at one's
leisure), is very fine, and ought to be understood even by
that laziest and haziest of animals, the general reader. He
says that having suspended work on a novel, poems began

to spring up in his mind, and I am glad that he thinks of bringing out a new collection.

Jack tells me that he has all "Omar Kháyyám," four hundred lines, by heart. Tell him from me that he is a prodigy, and profoundly impresses me with a sense of my own ineptitude. For, long as I have read "Omar," I don't think I could repeat half a dozen verses without book. . . .

Friendly regards to all friends there from all friends here. With best wishes, yours truly,

JAMES THOMSON.

Thomson's prose volume, entitled "Essays and Phantasies," which had been issued in April of this year, had not achieved the same measure of success as the preceding volumes of poetry, though here and there a critic recognised that his prose style bore the marks of genius no less surely than his verse. On the whole, he had certainly no reason to be dissatisfied with the reception accorded to the three volumes he had now published, but the necessity of obtaining some regular literary occupation was now becoming more urgent, as *Cope's Tobacco Plant*, which for over five years had been his pecuniary mainstay, was discontinued early in 1881, a loss which he felt very severely. Through Mr. Meredith's introduction he had an interview in October with Mr. John Morley, who was then editor of the *Pall Mall Gazette* and the *Fortnightly Review*, and an excellent chance of journalistic and literary work seemed to be thus opened to him. But, unfortunately, by this time, when he was at length offered the sort of writing which he had for years been vainly desiring, he had passed the point when he could be depended on for the punctual and regular execution of any given piece of work, so that his hopes of forming a con-

nection with a daily journal were of necessity doomed
to disappointment.   He was therefore compelled to
turn his attention to magazine articles and other
branches of literature, in which, being able to choose
his own time and manner of writing, he met with
more success.   He was a good deal occupied this
summer with two essays on Robert Browning's
poems, one of which was printed by the Browning
Society, the other in the *Gentleman's Magazine.*   " As
my longish Heine work is just now interrupted by a
bit of shortish Browning "—so he wrote in August
to Forest Edge—" I have half a mind to punish you
by the infliction of my presence for a fortnight.   But
then you are too careless, I fear, to have sets of
Cardinal Newman, Carlyle, and Ruskin, which may
be needed for comparison or contrast."

To Mrs. John Thomson.

7 HUNTLEY STREET, GOWER STREET,
October 18, 1881.

I enjoyed myself immensely at Forest Edge, near Leicester,
and came back several years younger than I went down.
They kept me there and in the neighbourhood seven weeks,
and then I could only get away with extreme difficulty, and
on a pledge to go again at Christmas ; and they began
urging me to come down before I was back three weeks,
saying that I could get all the books I wanted down there,
which was nearly true, and could work there as well as here,
which was very far from true, the society and recreations
being much too tempting.   I have very rarely met with
such liberal kindness even from old friends, and I have
had three or four as good as a man could wish ; and the
Leicester people knew very little of me personally, welcom-

ing me for the sake of my beautiful and pious books and
articles.

These books have brought me a little money directly,
which I scarcely hoped for, as two of them are in verse and
all three of them are full of the most unpopular heresies.
What I did hope for they now seem about bringing me;
that is, enough reputation to secure work which was denied
to the mere anonymous heterodox journalist. We shall
soon see.

I enclose prospectus new Browning Society. They, or
rather Furnivall, not only made me a member, but put me
on Committee, and set me down for a paper on January 27,
without my consent or knowledge. True, they sent me a
proof of the first issue, in which I might have cancelled my
name for Committee and paper, but I was then at Leicester,
and my people taking it for an ordinary circular, did not
think it worth sending on. So my protest when I returned
was too late, and behold me engaged. Miss Hickey, the
Hon. Sec., told me on Sunday that they have now fifty-nine
members; all doubtless highly respectable people barring
myself, so I shall be in good company.

Behold full measure, pressed down, heaped up, and over-
flowing, in magnanimous contrast to your stingy scribbles.

SAINT JAMES.

There is no entry in Thomson's diary later than
October 1881, the few remaining months of his life
being spent chiefly at Leicester. After his return to
London in July he had received more than one pressing invitation to pay a second visit to Forest Edge;
but for some time he was detained by stress of work.
In November, however, we find him again among his
hospitable Leicester friends.

To Mr. Percy Holyoake.

FOREST EDGE, LEICESTER,
Wednesday, November 16, 1881.

DEAR PERCY,—Here begin the Chronicles of the Edge of the Forest.

First and foremost, the Princess not only graciously deigned to accept your chivalric portrait, which I tendered with all due obeisance on the morning of the holy Sabbath, but was pleased to declare that she would have considered your conduct quite unworthy of the noble names you inherit, in the vernacular decidedly mean, had you not sent it. Her Highness went so far as to announce that in so sad a case of dereliction of duty she would no longer have regarded you as De Rohan of the Silver Tankard, but as Hollyhock of the Pewter Pot—a doom too dreadful to contemplate. So you see that, as usual, I was right.

As for my poor self, although I had another sleepless night on Saturday, I was already rather better on Sunday, and could eat and drink, and even smoke a little. The wicked T—— and B—— played lawn-tennis all the day, which was wonderfully bright and warm. We others walked a little and palavered immeasurably. We surveyed the grievous ravage wrought in the Royal demesnes by the late gale. Two trees blown down, a full pear-tree stripped, &c., &c.

On Monday, after a good night, consequent on the pious and jolly manner in which we had spent the Lord's Day, *I was first down.* This annoyed Her Royal Highness, who on the following morning directed Lizzie not to ring the bell; so I slept on in sweet security, and H.R.H. stole the victory she could not fairly win. But as she was not down until twenty minutes after the hour I should have been ready at had the bell been rung, the real triumph clearly rested with me. This morning I was first down again, despite the fact that Jack, that unholy Pilgrim of the Night, kept me up till half-past one in company with the naughty French *Nana*.

The poor Princess is suffering sorely, but not continuously, from a certain side tooth. When it is very bad she resolves to have it out; when it relents, she postpones the dreaded operation. The present decision is to undergo it shortly after to-morrow, whose evening brings a festive dance. How long this decision will hold who can tell? for it hath been written or sung by some veracious royalty or other *souvent femme varie*.

Our farm now comprises two cows and a calf and four little pigs. The mother sow lieth dead, to our great sorrow. Perhaps my arrival was too much for her, for she took cold and inflammation the very day thereof. . . .

Here endeth the first chapter of these Chronicles of small beer.—Yours truly,

JAMES THOMSON.

To Mr. Bertram Dobell.

FOREST EDGE, KIRBY MUXLOE, NR. LEICESTER,
Thursday, December 1, 1881.

DEAR SIR,—You see I am down here, drawn by urgent invitations, and glad of the change, as I was not feeling well in London, although of course the country here is very different in November and December from what it was in June and July. The home comfort itself.

You asked about the *Pall Mall Gazette*. Morley don't find an opening for me there at present, but he has accepted a piece of two hundred lines blank verse, "A Voice from the Nile," which I did down here and sent for the *Fortnightly*. He says that he likes it very much; can't promise positively for January number, but will try. The "Deliverer" duly appeared in November. I am doing now another which I shall offer him, and have planned yet another. As the *Gentleman's* proof of the "Ring and the Book" came and was returned yesterday fortnight, I presume it is in this month.   My host found that it had not arrived last evening. . . .

Please remember me to Mr. Reeves, and tell him my little literary news, and say that I will write him soon.

As the *Athenæum* printed the fifth and last instalment of my Shelley notes on the 19th November, I am about writing to offer articles on any books in my scope.

My photos reached me (*i.e.*, six of them) on Wednesday, November 23, which made me forty-seven, a month after the sitting.   Percy Holyoake has one for you, and one for Mr. Reeves.   They are very poorly done though they took so long, but friends say a good likeness.—Yours truly,

JAMES THOMSON.

Early in 1882 Thomson was back at his lodgings in Huntley Street; but after three weeks of ill-health and wretchedness he was only too glad to return once more to Forest Edge.   The following letter, a pencilled note, was evidently written after a period of great depression :—

To Mr. Percy Holyoake.

7 HUNTLEY STREET,
Monday, February 6, 1882.

DEAR PERCY,—Will you let me know whether the arrangement for Leicester holds ?   A really pious Sabbath has restored me to my mind, such as it is.   Of course I am still weak and nervous in body, and if I am to go will be grateful for help in packing, &c.   I write because my clothes are so fluffy that I don't think I shall have the courage to enter No. 12.

I will ask all the news when I see you.—Yours truly,

B. V.

If anything could have permanently restored Thomson's failing health and energies at this time, the

kindness of his friends in Leicester and London
would have done so. Mr. Barrs's house, like Mr.
Wright's, was scarcely less than a home to him, and
in addition to the encouragement of pleasant society,
every facility was given him at Forest Edge for the
pursuance of his literary studies. His prospects were
in some ways more reassuring than they had been
for some years past, for he had lately obtained an
entry to the *Fortnightly Review*, the *Cornhill*, and
other magazines, and was also contributing occasionally to the *Athenæum* and the *Weekly Dispatch*. He
still entertained the idea of writing a book on Heine,
and was also meditating the possibility of issuing a
third volume of poems. But his great need was that
of some definite occupation on which he might reckon
as a reliable source of income ; and this, owing to
his recent failure in journalism, he was unable to
command. The following extracts from letters to
Mr. Dobell give an insight into his literary plans
and difficulties in this the last year of his life :—

Forest Edge, near Leicester, December 31, 1881.—I wrote
to Mr. Reeves a few days before Christmas, telling him about
all my doings, and I daresay he has told you. Since then
the time has been chiefly spent in distractions with guests
here, so that I have even yet about half a day's work on
the fair copy Browning Notes to do. I still hold to the
Heine booklet, and hope to set hard to work on it when I
come back.

March 10, 1882.—Your March catalogue coming to
hand this morning reminds me that I ought to let you and
Mr. Reeves know how I am getting on, though I have very
little to tell. You are no doubt aware that one small sketch,
"The Sleeper," has appeared in this month's *Cornhill.*

Leslie Stephen writes in very friendly fashion, which encourages me to send him with fair hope any other piece not over long, and of the proper tone, that may come into my head.

Kegan Paul wrote me a fortnight ago for permission to include one or two short bits in a volume of extracts from living English poets, "in which only those really worth the name, and whose writings appear to be of permanent value, will be incorporated." The choice of extracts naturally to be with his editors. Of course I gave willing permission, and I assumed that yourself and Reeves would agree.

The Rev. —— has also written, wanting to include extracts in a collection of Social and Domestic Poems! Again assuming your concurrence, I have given permission. He will name books, author, and publishers. There are some queer clergymen in these latter days. . . .

Altogether, before and since Christmas, I have done about sixteen hundred lines down here, fit, I think, for inclusion in a volume when opportunity offers. Just now I want to do, if I can, two or three pieces of about one hundred lines or fewer, as bait for *Cornhill* or other magazines. So much for my news.

March 28, 1882.—I have been taking poetical stock with result set forth on other leaf. There seems to be enough in hand, half old and half new, for another volume. I understood from Mr. Reeves that, with Forman's Keats, and half a dozen other works, his hands are quite full for this season. Being, as usual, since the *Tobacco Plant* was cut down and uprooted, in sad want of cash, I should be very glad to sell the whole copyright right out, but suppose it would be impossible to get anything for it. You may have noticed a little skit of mine, "Law *v.* Gospel," in this week's *Dispatch*. Yesterday I sent another on the Prince Leopold grant. If the *Dispatch* will take such things, it will help a little.

It will be observed that towards the close of 1881

Thomson had resumed the writing of poetry, after a
silence of seven long years. The cause of this revival
of the poetic instinct must be sought in the success
achieved by the publication of his two volumes of
verse ; still more, perhaps, in the cheering influence
of the society of his Leicester friends. To his friendship with his host and hostess of Forest Edge is to
be ascribed the fact that Thomson's later poems were
mostly written in a tone of unwonted hopefulness
and confidence, as if there had at last dawned on
this weary dweller in the city of darkness a new and
unexpected light. "When, at the end of February,"
writes Mr. William Maccall,* "I received my last
letter from him, he appeared to have escaped for a
time from the dungeons and despairs of the Inquisi-
tion, and to be gladdened for an instant by the sun.
He was living at some hospitable abode in Leicester-
shire, and seemed to be almost hopeful and happy,
and half ashamed to be, for the first time since boyhood, happy and hopeful." In several poems we
find him actually reverting to the ideal and rapturous
melodies of his youthful period, striking much the
same note in "Richard Forest," "At Belvoir," and
"He heard Her Sing" as that which he had struck
more than twenty years before in the poems contributed to *Tait*. To those who love the man and his
work, there is something very pathetic in this sudden
and unlooked-for outburst of supremely beautiful song,
from one who was already nearing the end of a life in
which he had found little but sorrow and disappointment, reminding one of the "sudden resurrection

---

* "A Nirvana Trilogy ; Three Essays on the Career of
James Thomson."

glad" of the disused and neglected Fountain, which forms the subject of a piece of allegorical autobiography in his own "Vane's Story." In the stanzas, "At Belvoir," written in January 1882, Thomson could say—

> For though we are in winter now,
> My heart is in full summer.

Yet, looking at these lines with the knowledge of after-events, we can see that the warmth he then felt within him was nothing more than that "Indian summer" which may at times be observed in the life of man as in the life of Nature—that "last brief resurrection of summer," as a great writer has called it, "a resurrection that has no root in the past, nor steady hold upon the future, like the lambent and fitful gleams from an expiring lamp." That Thomson himself in his heart felt his new hopes to be as illusory as those which had preceded, might be gathered from those terribly pessimistic poems, "Insomnia" and "The Poet to his Muse," which were composed about this same time. He has also left a more explicit record of his own feelings in the following hitherto unpublished stanzas :—

TO H. A. B.

ON MY FORTY-SEVENTH BIRTHDAY :

Wednesday, November 23, 1881.

I.

When one is forty years and seven,
Is seven and forty sad years old,
He looks not onward for his Heaven,
The future is too blank and cold,

Its pale flowers smell of graveyard mould ;
He looks back to his lifeful past ;
  If age is silver, youth is gold ;—
Could youth but last, could youth but last !

2.

He turns back toward his youthful past
  A-throb with life and love and hope,
Whose long-dead joys in memory last,
  Whose shining days had ample scope ;
  He turns and lingers on the slope
Whose dusk leads down to sightless death ;—
  The sun once crowned that darkening cope,
And song once thrilled this weary breath.

3.

Ah, he plods wearily to death,
  Adown the gloaming into night,
But other lives breathe joyous breath
  In morning's boundless golden light ;
  Their feet are swift, their eyes are bright,
Their hearts beat rhythms of hope and love,
  Their being is a pure delight
In earth below and heaven above.

4.

And *you* have hope and joy and love,
  And you have youth's abounding life,
Whose crystal currents flow above
  The stones and sands of care and strife.
  May all your years with joys be rife,
May you grow calmly to your prime,
  A maiden sweet, a cherished wife,
A happy mother in due time.

5.

All good you wish me, past my prime,
  I wish with better hope to you,
And richer blessings than old Time
  And Fate or Fortune found my due :

M

> For you are kind and good and true,
> And so when *you* are forty-seven
> May spouse and children in your view
> Make Home the happiest life-long Heaven.

Too late was, in fact, the fatal word which was to be written against the brighter prospects and happier circumstances that seemed to be arising on Thomson's path. And the end which he himself felt to be at hand was foreboded by his more intimate friends and acquaintances, who could read in his changed appearance the story of broken health and failing vitality. "He looked," writes one who knew him at this time,* "like a veteran scarred in the fierce affrays of life's war and worn by the strain of its forced marches. His close-knit form, short and sturdy, might have endured any amount of mere roughings, if its owner had thought it worth a care. It is rare to find so squarely massive a head, combining mathematical power with high imagination in so marked a degree. Hence the grim logic of fact that gives such weird force to all his poetry. You could see the shadow that 'tremendous fate' had cast over that naturally buoyant nature. It had eaten great furrows into his broad brow, and cut tear-tracks downwards from his wistful eyes, so plaintive and brimful of unspeakable tenderness as they opened wide, when in serious talk. . . . I am far from saying that Thomson did not find any happiness in life. His wit and broad fun vied with his varied information and gift of happy talk in making him a prince of good fellows ; and he least of all would be suspected of harbouring the worm in his jovial heart. But these were the glints of sunshine that made life

* G. G. Flaws in *Secular Review*, July 1, 1882.

tolerable ; the ever-smouldering fire of unassuageable grief and inextinguishable despair burned the core out of that great heart when the curtain of night hid the play-acting scenes of the day."

How far this tragedy of a lifetime, which was now drawing to an end, was due to innate constitutional tendencies, and how far to the stress of external circumstances which might conceivably have been averted, is a question which scarcely admits of any confident conclusion, and which each reader of Thomson's life and writings will settle for himself. The following is the opinion of Mr. George Meredith, who is probably better qualified than any other man to understand the subtle complexities of such a character as Thomson's.

"I had full admiration of his nature and his powers. Few men have been endowed with so brave a heart. He did me the honour to visit me twice, when I was unaware of the extent of the tragic affliction overclouding him, but could see that he was badly weighted. I have now the conviction that the taking away of poverty from his burdens would in all likelihood have saved him, to enrich our literature ; for his verse was a pure well. He had, almost past example in my experience, the thrill of the worship of moral valiancy as well as of sensuous beauty ; his narrative poem 'Weddah and Om-el-Bonain' stands to witness what great things he would have done in the exhibition of nobility at war with evil conditions.

"He probably had, as most of us have had, his heavy suffering on the soft side. But he inherited the tendency to the thing which slew him. And it is my opinion that, in consideration of his high and singularly elective mind, he might have worked clear of it to throw it off, if circumstances had been smoother and brighter about him. For thus he would have been saved from drudgery, have had time to labour at conceptions that needed time for the maturing and definition even before the evolvement of them.   He would have had what was also much needed in his case, a more spacious home, a more companioned life, more than merely visiting friends, good and true to him though they were.   A domestic centre of any gracious kind would have sheathed his over-active, sensational imaginativeness, to give it rest, and enabled him to feel the delight of drawing it forth bright and keen of edge.

" We will hope for a better fate to befall men of genius. Nothing is to be said against the public in his case.   But I could wish that there were some Fund for the endowing of our wide Literary University with the means of aid to young authors who have put forth flowers of promise, as Thomson did when he was yet to be rescued."

On the 4th of May, having lately returned from Leicester to London, Thomson wrote a short note to Mr. Dobell (the last letter of the series) from his old address at Huntley Street, where he reported himself as staying for a few days until he could get another lodging, his own room, from which he had been so long absent, being now let.   Then ensued four terrible weeks of intemperance, homelessness, and desperation.   " Let it not be misread," says one of his friends, " as a harshness, or as a lightly tripped-off phrase, when I give out that, in all verity to me, his later life was a slow suicide, perceived and ac- quiesced in deliberately by himself." *   True or not true of Thomson's later life in general, this descrip- tion is certainly not an exaggeration as regards these last few weeks, when even his faithful friends in Gower Street lost all control over him, and were at

---

* G. G. Flaws in *Secular Review*, July 1, 1882.

length ignorant even of his whereabouts. His reck-lessness is explained by the fact that his visit to Leicester had ended in a fit of intemperance, and that he had returned to London in bitter remorse and despondency. It was on June 1, at Philip Marston's rooms in the Euston Road, at the very time when Mr. Percy Holyoake was searching for Thomson in vain, that the final catastrophe took place, an account of which has been written by Mr. William Sharp:—

"For a few weeks his record is almost a blank. When the direst straits were reached, he so far reconquered his control that he felt himself able to visit one whose sympathy and regard had withstood all tests. Thomson found Philip Marston alone: the latter soon realised that his friend was mentally distraught, and endured a harrowing experience, into the narration of which I do not care to enter. I arrived in the late afternoon, and found Marston in a state of nervous perturbation. Thomson was lying down on the bed in the adjoining room: stooping, I caught his whispered words to the effect that he was dying; upon which I lit a match, and in the sudden glare beheld his white face on the blood-stained pillow. He had burst one or more blood-vessels, and the hæmorrhage was dreadful. Some time had to elapse before anything could be done, but ultimately, with the help of a friend who came in opportunely, poor Thomson was carried downstairs, and having been placed in a cab, was driven to the adjoining University Hospital." *

From the moment of Thomson's admission to the hospital, the physicians gave no hope of saving his life; but the next day, when Mr. Sharp, accompanied by Philip Marston, visited him in the ward, he was not only conscious, but expectant of a speedy recovery. He

---

* "Memoir of P. B. Marston," by W. Sharp, pp. 27, 28. Prefixed to Marston's "For a Song's Sake, and other Stories."

asked for writing materials in order to write a letter which seemed to cause him anxiety. At the moment when his friends were going away he sat up in his bed, with a look of great animation on his features, and expressed his fixed resolve to leave the hospital on the following Monday "even if he left it in his coffin"—a conviction which was strangely verified by the result. He died on the evening of Saturday, June 3, 1882, from utter exhaustion consequent on internal bleeding, and his body was removed from the hospital on the day he had mentioned. The similarity of scene and circumstance between Thomson's death and that of Edgar Poe has not escaped observation.

He was buried on June 8, at Highgate Cemetery, in the very grave where, eight years before, his friend Austin Holyoake had been laid to rest; and with him was buried a locket, with a tress of yellow hair—his one memento of his lost love. Among those present at the funeral were his brother, Mr. John Thomson, Mr. T. R. Wright, Mr. Percy Holyoake, Mr. Bertram Dobell, Mr. J. W. Barrs and Miss Barrs, Philip Marston, and other friends. An adaptation of the Secularist Burial Service written by Austin Holyoake was read by Mr. Wright, who afterwards paid a just and faithful tribute to Thomson's memory in the following address :—

"As we stand around the grave of the last, but not the least, of England's poets, it is impossible not to think of the words of his great predecessor : 'We are such stuff as dreams are made of, and our little life is rounded with a sleep.' Of no one could this be more truly said than of our departed friend. Like all of us, his life was a strange mixture of dreams and realities; like many of us, the dreams were far better than the reality; like few of us, his dreams will be enduring, for they have been given to the world, and form a rich contribution to our national literature. As we look forward and think of the thousands who will study with admiration and delight the productions of his genius, we may well believe that many among them will envy us who have enjoyed the privilege of his personal friendship; and they would envy us still more could they but know, as we do, his genial and kindly character. Though he was the poet of dreadful night, and still more dread despair, neither the one nor the other was seen in his daily life. He was the pleasantest companion one could have, either in the fields and lanes which he loved so well, or by the fireside. . . . He was the soul of good company, and his laugh was always the heartiest, either at his own quaint fancies or those which he heard from others. Even those who knew him best must sometimes have been struck with the contrast between the tone of many of his poems and the merry mood which was habitual with him in society; while a casual acquaintance who heard him discourse so cheerily, as he so well knew how to do, of what he had seen in distant lands and read in many languages, would scarcely have believed that he was the same man whose pessimism was commented on in reviews. Not that all his writings were of this sombre tone, for some of his higher pieces are as bright and cheerful as a ray of sunshine across a bed of flowers, but I think there can be no doubt that the deepest strings of his heart were attuned to melancholy—only, like many earnest minds, he found it easier to confide to paper, and thus to the world at large, than to his most intimate friends, those feelings which lay deepest within him. The cause of this dark shade over a naturally bright temperament some of us can partly understand. He had sorrows in early life which blighted his hopes and cast a gloom over his whole career, and which, though never spoken of, were, I believe, never forgotten. This consideration may well make us think gently of his failings, and they were not many, while his virtues would take long to recount. He was brave, honest as the day, hating anything paltry or mean, high-spirited and proud, yet withal modest and retiring, almost to a fault; ever willing to do a kindness, and never so happy as when giving pleasure to others. Hardly any one knew but loved him; he constantly made new friends without losing old ones, and he had no more enemies than any man must have who was so frank and fearless in expressing what he believed to be right. What more can I say? 'Take him for all in all, we ne'er shall look upon his like again.'

"We now commit his body to the earth, and I cannot but deeply regret that he himself did not know its destination, for I am sure that even in his last moments it would have given him pleasure to know that his ashes would mingle with those of his old friend and fellow-worker in the great cause of the redemption of humanity from the bondage of superstition. The days of the singer have ended; but his songs remain. As we leave him here at rest, let us not think of the frail earthen vessel now lost to our sight, but of the rich mental treasure it contained, which is still left to us, and which we shall all cherish in our memories until our dreams too are over, and we sink into that deep sleep which knows no awakening."

Thus ended the life of one who, whatever his failings, impressed all those who knew him intimately, and many who only knew him in part, as not only the most brilliantly gifted, but without exception the noblest, gentlest, most lovable man with whom they had ever come in contact. The extraordinary charm of his manner and conversation is attested by the united record of many independent witnesses—there was a grace, a glamour, an attractiveness about his personality which has been possessed in equal measure

by no poet since the time of Shelley. We see in him
the high, heroic spirit, filled with intense natural love
of all physical and moral beauty, but met at every
point by the corruption and contagion of an artificial
mode of life; thwarted and hampered by the development of inherited infirmities and the weight of external
misfortunes, until he is involved in a Nessus-robe of
doubt and failure and despair; yet all the while by
sheer strength and courage of intellect looking his
destiny in the face, and maintaining to the last his
gentleness towards others and his constancy to
himself.

> Live out your whole free life while yet on earth ;
>   Seize the quick Present, prize your one sure boon ;
> Though brief, each day a golden sun has birth ;
>   Though dim, the night is gemmed with stars and moon.
>
> Love out your cordial love, hate out your hate ;
>   Be strong to grasp a foe, to clasp a friend :
> Your wants true laws are ; thirst and hunger sate :
>   Feel you have been yourselves when comes the end.

In these lines (for his thoughts are faithfully
reflected in his writings) we have the key to a correct
understanding of the main tenor of Thomson's life.
It is a life which, in spite of all its errors and short-
comings, great and undeniable though they were, is
no fitting subject for commonplace blame or cheap
pity, still less for unnecessary extenuation or apology ;
it asks nothing more than to be narrated and read in
a spirit of sympathy and candour. The study of
such a character may well set us meditating on those
mysterious conditions of modern society under which
a genial and sunny soul may be thus overclouded
by the deepest gloom of pessimism ; but to deplore
Thomson's pessimistic philosophy and unorthodox

views, while admitting the beauty of his poetry and
the lovableness of his nature (as if a man's opinions
were not an essential and inseparable part of his
personality), is inevitably to miss the true purport
of his life, and even the literary significance of his
writings.   Pessimism may not be the wisest and
healthiest view of human existence; but it is a view
which must be taken into serious account by all
thoughtful men, not least by those who hold a contrary persuasion; it deserves an attentive hearing,
if only as a protest against the slipshod thought of
a too easy-going optimism which sometimes passes
muster as profound philosophy.   We see in Thomson
an example of a man who, though naturally inclined to
unalloyed happiness and full sympathy with all heroic
effort, could not, in his more prevalent mood, feel any
real confidence in the truth of what he wished to be
true, or the success of what he wished to be successful; he refused to be led astray by false hopes, and
preferred, sternly and sorrowfully, to tread the path
which his own intellect indicated, with no more cheering watchword than the refrain of his great poem—
" Dead Faith, dead Love, dead Hope."   So much the
worse perhaps for him; but the better for us, who
can find in his life and writings what is unfortunately
less common in our literature than it should be—the
absolutely faithful expression of an absolutely genuine
character.

CHAPTER VIII.

THE POEMS.

EARLY IDEAL POEMS; FANTASTIC POEMS; ARTISTIC AND NARRATIVE POEMS.

ALMOST any method that a critic may adopt for the arrangement and exposition of a poet's writings must of necessity appear to a great extent artificial and unsatisfactory. Perhaps, in the case of a poet like Thomson, a direct chronological survey of his works would be at once the simplest and most suggestive; nevertheless, as there is also much advantage in being able to take a connected view of pieces of a kindred nature, I have not scrupled, in the following classification, to break the chronological order just so far as was necessary to enable me to draw together into groups those poems which seem to be inspired by a similar thought or treated in a similar fashion. The "City of Dreadful Night," and a few other poems of a more directly didactic and pessimistic cast, may fairly claim a place to themselves, as being perhaps the most notable and characteristic production of Thomson's genius; it will be convenient also to keep the late poems of 1881 and 1882 apart from the rest, as their peculiarity of tone, no less than their difference of date, affords a distinct line of demarcation.

I. *Early Ideal Poems.*—Starting from the time

when Thomson was trying to find in poetry a relief
from the crushing misfortune of his early bereavement, we commence with a class of poems all more
or less pervaded by a hallowed and chastened tone of
pathos and resignation and a belief in the mysterious
but overruling providence of God. It is true that
there are others, written in the same period, which
must be classed rather with those that breathe a
defiant and pessimistic spirit; but on the whole the
milder tone is largely predominant in the poems
written before 1862. In "Tasso to Leonora" (1856)
and "Bertram to the Lady Geraldine" (1857) the
poet's regretful love, instead of dwelling on the
mournful remembrances of the past, takes the form
of a lover's idealised passion for a mistress who,
though placed high above him by the circumstances
of life, may yet be his in a spiritualised sense or in
a future existence. "Tasso to Leonora," which appeared in *Tait's Edinburgh Magazine*, but was not
included by Thomson in his published volumes of
verse, is one of the earliest and least valuable of the
poems, its chief interest lying in the fact that the
picture of Tasso, appealing from his dungeon-life to
Leonora, who is throned above all his "soaring
hopes," seems to be meant to be typical of the
writer's own position. In spite of the wretchedness
of his fate, and the insuperable gulf that divides him
from Leonora, he persists in regarding this actual life
as a mere false show in which they both must play
their parts—she the part of a distant, stately queen,
he that of a forlorn prisoner—until the time when, the
farce being over, love shall unite them for an eternity
of blissful joy. The ideality of tone that runs through
the whole poem is very marked, space and time being

treated as unreal and transitory phenomena, in contrast with the enduring reality of love : —

> Yes—as Love is truer far
> Than all other things, so are
> Life and Death, the World and Time,
> Mere false shows in some great Mime,
> By dreadful mystery sublime.

In the following stanzas a belief in a future life is somewhat hesitatingly expressed :—

> But you cannot scorn me, Dear,
> Though I sink in doubt and fear?
> You know too, this mad Mime done,
> We shall evermore be one?

> Cling, cling fast to this dear faith,
> Rock of life in sea of death :
> Our mazed web of doom is wrought
> Under God's directing thought.

The poem is by no means without its fine passages, but as a whole it does not make a very favourable impression, some of the sentiments being rather overstrained and affected, and the style not quite free from youthful mannerisms and artistic blemishes.

"Bertram to the Lady Geraldine" (1857) is a great advance in every way on "Tasso to Leonora," exhibiting the same phase of thought in a more striking form and with far finer literary execution. Like Mrs. Browning's "Lady Geraldine's Courtship," in which the origin of the title must of course be sought, "Bertram to the Lady Geraldine" is a poetic rhapsody, instinct with passionate feeling which finds utterance in language of the richest and most rapturous melody. It is a poet-lover's expression of spiritualised affec-

tion for his ideal of perfect purity and perfect loveliness ; and through the outer meaning of the words,
which purport to be spoken by one who has lately
met in a ballroom a lady of peerless beauty—a
" Presence " whom he intuitively greets as the
" fulfilment of his heart's great need,"—it is easy to
discern an inner personal significance, an idealised
record, in fact, of Thomson's own great life-passion.

> Thou wert the farther from me, as so near ;
>   Veiled awful, at a distance dim and great,
> In that supernal spiritual sphere
>   To which Love lifts, that he may isolate
> The truest lovers from their union here :
>   Hence their eternal Bridal, consecrate
> By perfect reverence ; for the Loved must be
> An ever-new Delight and Mystery.
>
> Did aught of these tempestuous agitations
>   In irrepressible gust or lightning-burst
> Perturb thy heaven of starry contemplations
>   In depths of moonlit quietude immerst ?
> I long for answer ; but no meditations
>   Can realise those memories, all disperst
> In such wild seething mists of joy, hope, fear :—
> Oh that the question now could reach thine ear !

The description of the meeting in the ballroom,
and of the glories of the dance (a subject on which
Thomson is rather fond of dwelling), is given with
much splendour of imagery and profusion of poetic
metaphor, the *ottava rima* being a metre which he
always uses with good effect.   In the lover's instant
recognition of the Lady Geraldine as the one pre-
destined partner of his soul, giving him henceforth
an object for devotion and perseverance in life, we
are reminded of Mr. Browning's " Christina ; " while

the confident idealism of the following stanza contrasts strangely with the later utterances of its author :—

> But time is very brief :—Shall we away
>   Into the great calm Night besprinkled o'er
> With silver throbbing stars ?   My Dearest, say !
>   And yet, so rich in years is evermore
> That hurry were mean thrift : we well can stay,
>   Who long have stayed, some few brief time-lives more ;
> Being so certain from this hour sublime
> Of coming Union, perfect, beyond Time.

In " The Fadeless Bower " (1858) we have one of the most beautiful of Thomson's early poems, more pensive and pathetic in tone than the two already mentioned, but, like them, full of a young man's tender dreams and regretful imaginings. It is a " Vision of the Long-ago," a reminiscence of that crowning moment of his life, when in a " fadeless bower "—a place and scene fixed for ever in his memory—he had confessed his love, and learnt that he was himself loved in return.

> I have this moment told my love ;
>   Kneeling, I clasp her hands in mine :
> She does not speak, she does not move ;
>   The silent answer is divine.
> The flood of rapture swells till breath
> Is almost tranced in deathless death.

With the idealising tendency that distinguishes all the early poems, he imagines that supreme moment eternalised—there they remain for ever unchanged, they two, and the bower, and a young seraph from heaven, who has glided down through the night to be a witness of their vow.   In the following stanza we

catch an echo from Keats's " Ode on a Grecian
Urn " :—

> O happy bud, for ever young,
>   For ever just about to blow !
> O happy love, upon whose tongue
>   The Yes doth ever trembling grow !
> O happiest Twain, whose deathless bower
> Embalms you in life's crowning hour !

The poem closes with a contrast between the dark
reality of the present and the bright vision of the
past, and with an expression of trust in a futurity of
existence.

Somewhat akin, on the one side, to " The Fadeless
Bower " and " Tasso to Leonora," and on the other to
" Vane's Story " and the more mature poems, is " The
Deliverer," written in 1859, and published in the
Fortnightly Review for November 1881. The story,
which is told in elegiac stanzas of much strength
and beauty, is put into the mouth of a fevered
sufferer who recounts his imaginary imprisonment in
a dungeon, his prayer to God for release, and his
consequent deliverance. The Deliverer is the same
Lady of Love whom we meet in " Vane's Story " and
several of the prose phantasies, described in a similar
way as a spiritual visitant :—

> Oh bliss ! I saw Her thro' the sevenfold veil ;—
>   A mighty Seraph shining ruby-clear,
> Clothed in majestic wings of golden mail ;
>   A sun within the midnight atmosphere.
>
> But still her countenance I scarce could scan,
>   For living glories of the golden hair,
> And rapture of the eyes cerulean,
>   As solemn summer heavens burning bare.

The description of the safe escape of the prisoner

through the massive barriers of the dungeon, and through a mysterious "wall-veil," a curtain of jet-black air, is evidently typical of a mental release from the thraldom of despondent thought, a transition from the darkest of all moods to that sense of faith and hopefulness which pervades the majority of Thomson's early writings.

In "A Happy Poet" (1857) and "The Lord of the Castle of Indolence" (1859) the object seems to have been to draw a picture of the ideal poet and the ideal philosopher. Both poems are written in a distinctly optimistic vein, and are steeped to the full in that natural tranquillity and rich sensuous repose with which Thomson was largely endowed; they have both the "native hue of resolution," untainted for the time by "the pale cast of thought." "A Happy Poet" is the expression of the delight of a youthful bard in the exuberance of rich life around him, and the sympathy which he feels with every phase of nature and every emotion of man—a sympathy which finds utterance in the natural and inalienable instinct of song :—

> I sing, I sing, rejoicing in the singing,
>   And men all love me for my songs so sweet,
> Even as they love the rapturous lark upspringing
>   And singing loud his joy the sun to greet ;
> O happiest lot, to win all love and blessing
> For that whose own delight is past expressing !

It will be noted that this conception of the poet's function differs vitally from Thomson's later defini-tions of art and literature as "the refuge of the miserable;" indeed there are passages of the "City of Dreadful Night" which are the very antipodes of the sentiments here expressed. Regarded from a

literary point of view, the forty or fifty stanzas of
" A Happy Poet" are very beautiful and melodious,
but perhaps a little too diffuse.

"The Lord of the Castle of Indolence," on the
other hand, for which "A Happy Poet" might be
regarded as a first sketch, is, of all Thomson's early
poems, the one which shows the greatest grasp, concentration, and self-control ; it is difficult to realise
that such strong, weighty, vigorous stanzas, full of
mastery and confidence, yet at the same time highly
idealistic in tone, were the work of a youth of
five-and-twenty ; and we are fain to regret that Thomson so seldom used the Spenserian metre, which is
here wielded with such signal success.   The poem,
which consists of only twelve stanzas, is a description of an ideally perfect and well-balanced character,
a "right royal king," who takes life wisely and con-
tentedly, diffusing beneficence and cheerfulness on all
around him.

> While others fumed and schemed and toiled in vain
> To mould the world according to their mood, ,
> He did by might of perfect faith refrain
> From any part in such disturbance rude.
> The world, he said, indeed is very good,
> Its Maker surely wiser far than we ;
> Feed soul and flesh upon its bounteous food,
> Nor fret because of ill ; All-good is He,
> And worketh not in years, but in Eternity.

> Thus could he laugh those great and generous laughs
> Which made us love ourselves, the world, and him ;
> And while they rang we felt as one who quaffs
> Some potent wine-cup dowered to the brim,
> And straightway all things seem to reel and swim,—
> Suns, moons, earth, stars sweep through the vast profound
> Wrapt in a golden mist-light warm and dim,

Rolled in a volume of triumphant sound ;
So in that laughter's joy the whole world carolled round.

The best explanation of the meaning of this very characteristic poem is to be sought in Thomson's prose essay on "Indolence," and especially in the part which deals with the third class of idlers there described—"idlers by grace," as they are happily designated, possessed of "this perfect endowment of grace in indolence." "These," he says, "ride no hobbies, neither are they ridden, nor doth black care sit behind them; they are always all that they are, and seek not to be more or otherwise; the infinitesimal Present they dilate into scope for full firm life, while we, who can find in it no standing-place, straddle and totter with one foot on the Past that recedes, and the other on the Future that advances." We find, therefore, that Thomson often expresses admiration for the *sans souci* doctrines that are embodied in the "Lord of the Castle of Indolence;" and it may be surmised that in this sketch he is partly depicting the indolent side of his own character, which might have been fully developed under more favourable conditions. The title, however, of the poem seems also to indicate a reference to his namesake and prototype, the author of the true "Castle of Indolence," "Jamie Thomson," as he elsewhere calls him, "of most peaceful and blessed memory."

Last, but not least, in this group of Thomson's early and idealistic writings, there remains to be mentioned the poem on "Shelley," written in 1861, but not printed until 1884, when it was privately issued by Mr. Bertram Dobell, together with some prose essays on the same subject. It is written in Chaucer's seven-line stanza, consisting of a quatrain,

an odd line, and a couplet, and is cast into the form
of a vision—a style of narration which Shelley himself adopted in several of his poems.   The narrator,
lying on "a grassy slope of shore," during a moonlight night, sees in a trance the universe, where a
great drama is evolving of which he becomes the
witness.   He sees the stars, the "infinite armies of
the Lord," speeding on their course, yet our "earth-
speck" still continues to be the centre of his interest,
until he hears the solemn voice of Raphael proclaim-
ing that the world's iniquity now demands its destruction, unless some heavenly spirit will consent
to go down to chant "the changeless truths eternal"
to the erring tribes of men.   This mission is undertaken by "a fervent spirit, beautiful and bright"
(Shelley is not mentioned by name in the poem), and
the date of the events having been fixed by a reference to the rise and fall of Napoleon, the voice
of the poet-prophet is described, as heard by the
narrator :—

> A voice of right amidst a world gone wrong,
>   A voice of hope amidst a world's despair,
> A voice instinct with such melodious song
>   As hardly until then had thrilled the air
>   Of this gross underworld wherein we fare
> With heavenly inspirations, too divine
> For souls besotted with earth's sensuous wine.
>
>   .   .   .   .
>
> But ever and anon in its swift sweetness
>   The voice was heard to lisp and hesitate,
> Or quiver absently from its completeness,
>   As one in foreign realms who must translate
>   Old thoughts into new language—Ah, how great
> The difference between our rugged tongue
> And that in which its hymns before were sung !

With the return of the spirit to Raphael, full of

despondency at the supposed failure of his enterprise, and with the declaration of the great Archangel that "where holy love and truth contend with evil" there can be no failure, the vision concludes. In several ways this poem is a remarkable one. Though not altogether free from the mannerism of Thomson's early style, it is full of high imaginative power and splendid outbursts of poetry, reminding the reader, in several of its passages, of one of the grandest of Shelley's lyrics, the "Ode to Liberty." It presents, moreover, one of the truest estimates of Shelley's genius ever given by later writers.

(2.) *Fantastic Poems.*—The next group of Thomson's poems, that of which "Vane's Story" is the most notable example, may perhaps, in default of any fully adequate title, be called the fantastic. In the place of the idealism and richness of tone which marked the earlier writings, we now note the prevalence of a half-serious, half-humorous mood, accompanied by more maturity of thought and more boldness of speculation, but expressed with less verbal ornament and less deliberate elaboration of style. This change in literary method corresponds with the change in the actual circumstances of Thomson's life and in the tendency of his opinions; he having now become a London secularist instead of an army schoolmaster, and a confirmed atheist instead of a waverer on the border-land of belief and scepticism. Accordingly in "Vane's Story," and the other poems of the same class, we see him entirely emancipated from every trace of conventionality both in thought and style, and playing fantastically with his own views of life, now grave, now gay, as the case may be, and sometimes both at once.

"Vane's Story" (1864), which is the earliest of
Thomson's three masterpieces, and disputes with
"Weddah and Om-el-Bonain" for the honour of
being second only to the "City of Dreadful Night,"
is at once fantastic, speculative, and autobiographical, dealing freely with natural and supernatural elements, yet offering at the same time, as Mr.
Dobell remarks in his *Memoir*, as candid and complete an autobiography as was ever written. The
name Vane, as a pseudonym for the poet himself,
appears also in the Introduction to the prose work,
"A Lady of Sorrow," which was written about the
same date as the poem ; and the story which he tells,
though professing to relate the incidents of a single
night, in reality gives the concentrated experience of
many sorrowful years. As he lies on his couch at
sunset, musing in a drowsy state between sleep and
consciousness, he is visited by a vision of Her, his
"Rose of Heaven," in the spiritual form already
described in "The Deliverer," and again to be described, ten years later, in the prose fantasy, "The
Fair of St. Sylvester," between which and "Vane's
Story" much resemblance may be traced. She chides
him, half playfully, half sorrowfully, for his failure to
win fame as a poet, and expresses bitter grief at his
despondency and scepticism, he meantime replying
to her complaints and expostulations in words to
which it is difficult to do justice by quotation, but
which should be read carefully by those who wish to
understand his character and philosophy.

> No, I have worked life after life
> Of sorrow, sufferance, and strife,
> So many ages, that I ask
> To rest one lifetime from the task,

To spend these years (forlorn of thee)
Sequestered in passivity ;
Observing all things God has made,
And of no ugliest truth afraid,
But having leisure time enough
To look at both sides of the stuff.

Such is the tenor of his answer to the supposed reproach that in the loneliness of his despondency he is
shunning "the tumult of the strife ; " while scarcely
less interesting in personal reference, and far more
beautiful in poetic form, is the next portion of the
poem, in which Vane is represented as asking questions
about the world of spirits, and receiving a greeting
from Shelley, " the burning Seraph of the Throne."
Shelley, it should be remembered, is, even more than
Heine, the presiding genius of " Vane's Story ; " to
him the poem is dedicated ; and it is he who is appointed to be the guide to the throne of Demiurgos,
where the lovers' prayer for their final reunion is to be
offered. The prayer itself, with its singular mixture
of artless simplicity and exquisite melody, seems to
be conceived and written in the very spirit of Shelley's
own poems.

The second half of " Vane's Story " is chiefly devoted to the subject of the dance, to which Vane
suddenly determines to take his celestial partner, to
the great surprise of his friends and acquaintances
there assembled. To their amazed inquiries as to the
cause of his unusual vigour and animation an answer
is given in the singularly pathetic and beautiful
allegory of the Fountain, one of the most splendid
passages that Thomson ever wrote, and not unworthy
to be set beside Shelley's " Sensitive Plant," to which
it is in many points akin.

> There was a Fountain long ago,
> A fountain of perpetual flow,
> Whose purest springlets had their birth
> Deep in the bosom of the earth.
> The joyous wavering silvery shaft
> To all the beams of morning laughed,
> Its steadfast murmurous crystal column
> Was loved by all the moonbeams solemn ;
> From morn to eve it fell again,
> A singing many-jewelled rain,
> From eve to morn it charmed the hours
> With whispering dew and diamond showers ;
> Crowned many a day with sunbows bright,
> With moonbows halo'd many a night ;
> And so kept full its marble urn
> All fringed with fronds of greenest fern,
> O'er which with timeless love intent
> A pure white marble Goddess leant. . . .

It may be gathered, even from these few opening lines, that the Fountain is typical of Thomson's own life-course—at first flowing freely and joyously under the influences of love, then, by a sudden change, left silent and stagnant for years of loneliness and desolation, yet ever ready to leap forth afresh to the light in moments of rapturous resurrection and renewed vitality. The history of his life and poetry is faithfully rendered under this simple yet effective poetical figure, perhaps even more faithfully than the poet himself could at that time have realised or intended. In the latter portion of the poem Heine's influence is especially observable in the mixture of pathos and humour, tenderness and satire, and in the manner in which the story is brought down from the rapture of its spiritual altitude to its solid and realistic conclusion.

To discourse on the poetical merits of " Vane's Story " would be a superfluous task. The poem must be read to be appreciated, and it will only be rightly appreciated by those who have a natural sympathy with the feelings by which it was inspired. It is therefore not very surprising that puzzled critics should as a rule have missed the subtle and impalpable beauties which give to " Vane's Story," for those who rightly understand it, a peculiar and indescribable charm, and have concentrated their attention, with much satisfaction at their own acuteness, on certain obvious mannerisms and defects which lie on the very surface of the poem, such as its carelessness of diction, its indifference to all established literary canons, and the levity of the theological footnotes scattered over its pages. Some readers have also found a stumbling-block in the odd juxtaposition of the supernatural and commonplace, which often suggests a resemblance to Browning's " Christmas Eve and Easter Day," especially as the same octosyllabic metre is used in both poems.

The two Idylls of Cockaigne, "Sunday at Hampstead" and "Sunday up the River" (1865), consist of a series of idyllic pictures, by "a very humble member," as the author styles himself, "of the great and noble London mob." They indicate the high-tide of Thomson's spirits in holiday season, when he could escape for a time from his gloomy City to more cheerful companionship and more invigorating scenes; yet it would be a mistake to regard the descriptions as autobiographical, since they are in great measure dramatic.* Their charm lies not only in the beauty

---

* " These delightful poems must not be supposed to express the author's personal experiences. When I conveyed to him a lady's objection to the colour of the rower's costume in

of the poems themselves, which, with their varying metres, admirably portray the varying moods and fantasies of the holiday-maker's mind, but also in the conjunction of the most boisterous Bohemian humour with an undertone of true and deep feeling, which redeems the poems from the danger of lapsing into mere badinage and vulgarity, and gives them that element of reality which distinguishes true poetry from false. Some critics have rather unnecessarily stood aghast at Thomson's "boldness" in thus setting at naught all social and literary etiquette in his apotheosis of lower-class holiday-makers; let us rather feel that there is something very natural and exhilarating in his complete emancipation from the fetich-worship of Respectability—the Bumbleism which he so vigorously denounces in his satirical essays as the plague of all literary freedom. Of the beautiful lyrical pieces that are scattered through both these idylls, none, perhaps, is more perfect than the following from the "Sunday at Hampstead:"—

> As we rush, as we rush in the Train,
>   The trees and the houses go wheeling back,
> But the starry heavens above the plain
>   Come flying on our track.
>
> All the beautiful stars of the sky,
>   The silver doves of the forest of Night,
> Over the dull earth swarm and fly,
>   Companions of our flight.
>
> We will rush ever on without fear;
>   Let the goal be far, the flight be fleet!
> For we carry the Heavens with us, Dear.
>   While the Earth slips from our feet!

"Sunday up the River," he replied, with a slight sneer, "Do they think *I* ever went boating in that style? I write what I have seen."—G. W. FOOTE, in *Progress*.

On the whole, however, the "Sunday up the
River" is distinctly the finer of the two poems, both
in delicacy of thought and completeness of workmanship. When the poem was republished in the volume
issued in 1880, Thomson wisely restored the last
two stanzas, which had been omitted under editorial
pressure in *Fraser;* in these the reader is brought
back, as at the conclusion of "Vane's Story," from
the romance of a day-dream to the actualities of
ordinary life.

The transition from the blithesome and light-
hearted Idylls of Cockaigne to the grim, weird
fantasy of "In the Room" may seem at first sight to
be forced and unnatural; yet in truth the connection
between the two moods is closer than might be
supposed, since it is this very sense of capacity for
pleasure that is the greatest aggravation of pain, and,
as has been said of Schopenhauer, "to be on the
whole a believer in the misery of life, and yet to
be occasionally visited by a sense of its gleaming
gladness, is surely the worst of conceivable positions." "In the Room" is a relapse to that mood
of darkness and despondency which, at the date
when the poem was written (1867), must be considered to have become the normal condition of
the writer. In a room where a man is lying dead,
the various articles of furniture are represented
as conversing and speculating on his state, the
mirror, curtain, cupboard, table, and fire-grate in turn
discussing the meaning of the gloom and silence
around them, and wishing that the girl, their former
possessor, were back with them, instead of the
"dullard, glum and sour," who holds no social con-
verse with his fellow-creatures. The bed alone is

aware of the true fact, which it thus communicates
to the others :—

> This long tirade aroused the bed,
>   Who spoke in deep and ponderous bass
> Befitting that calm life he led,
>   As if firm-rooted in his place :
> In broad majestic bulk alone,
>   As in thrice venerable age,
> He stood at once the royal throne,
>   The monarch, the experienced sage :
>
> " I know what is and what has been ;
>   Not anything to me comes strange,
> Who in so many years have seen
>   And lived through every kind of change.
> I know when men are good or bad,
>   When well or ill," he slowly said ;
> " When sad or glad, when sane or mad,
>   And when they sleep alive or dead."

It then transpires, from the evidence of a little
phial which is lying empty on the chair, that the
man has committed suicide.   In addition to the high
poetical and artistic value of this strange and powerful poem, it resembles " Vane's Story " in possessing
a kind of autobiographical interest set off by fantastic
surroundings ; we feel " the room " to be none other
than that of the poet himself.   When the poem was
first published in the *National Reformer* in 1872,
Thomson remarked in a footnote—" This room is
believed to have been situate in Grub Street," adding
that the street was doubtless so called " on the well-
known ironical principle, because its inhabitants have
never much, and often nothing, to eat."

(3.) *Artistic and Narrative Poems.*—Leaving now
for a time those writings which are more or less
directly illustrative of Thomson's individual personality,

we come to a small group of poems, all dating from
1865 or 1866, which treat more generally of Nature
and Art. The relation of civilised man to uncivilised
Nature is the subject of "The Naked Goddess" and
"Life's Hebe," both of which are thrown into an
allegorical form, and written in the same swift and
sparkling trochaic metre, which Thomson well knew
how to use with grace and versatility. "The Naked
Goddess," whose apparition startles the inhabitants
of the city, and causes them to approach her in her
woodland solitudes with entreaties and expostulations, is typical of the spirit of Nature, indomitable
and unappeasable in its primeval wildness and
simplicity :—

> There she leant, the glorious form,
> Dazzling with its beauty warm,
> Naked as the sun of noon,
> Naked as the midnight moon :
> And around her, tame and mild,
> All the forest creatures wild.
>
> . , ...
>
> Naked as the midnight moon,
> Naked as the sun of noon,
> Burning too intensely bright,
> Clothed in its own dazzling light ;
> Seen less, thus, than in the shroud
> Of morning mist or evening cloud ;
> She stood terrible and proud
> O'er the pallid quivering crowd.

She rejects with contemptuous indignation the conventional phrases and stereotyped formalities of the
high priest and the arch-sage, as they proffer her
the garb of religion and philosophy, dismal brown
and sober grey respectively ; and her anger is proved
by the decay that falls thenceforth on the nation that

had offended her. Two little children alone, who had conversed with her fearlessly, are exempt from the curse; and to them, when in after years, as bridegroom and bride, they lead forth a colony of their fellow-citizens to a far western land, the goddess gives her blessing and protection. The poem is a satire on the sham respectability of modern civilisation, with perhaps a reference to the feebleness of all creeds and systems by which men attempt to shackle their natural instincts. " Such a creed or system," says Thomson in his essay on the " Worth of Metaphysical Systems," which essay is the prose equivalent of " The Naked Goddess," " is a little strait-waistcoat wrought by some little man, and in which he would fain confine Titanic Nature : she laughs with immense good-nature at the funny fellow at first, but if he seriously persists in attempting to force it on her, she inevitably makes him fit for a strait-waistcoat himself."

" Life's Hebe," a shorter and less important poem than " The Naked Goddess," has reference to the individual man rather than to collective society. Nature is here symbolised in the form of Hebe, the goddess of youth, who offers to every man the cup of life, which is baneful or beneficial in its effects according to the manner in which it is taken. Some dilute the nectar, and are poisoned; two only win praise for their wisdom—the philosopher, who refuses the cup altogether, and the poet, who fearlessly drinks it off without mixture and kisses the goddess on the lips. The lesson taught is, that the joys of life, if they are to be enjoyed at all, must be grasped boldly and without hesitation, and the poem seems to be an expansion of some lines in

the same style and metre which were interpolated in
" Vane's Story : "—

> Love a near maid, love a far maid,
> But let Hebe be your barmaid ;
> When she proffers you the cup,
> Never fear to drink it up ;
> Though you see her crush her wine
> From a belladonna vine,
> Drink it, pouring on the clods
> Prelibation to the gods.

The same doctrine had also been laid down in " A
Lady of Sorrow." " There is the cup of the wine of
life ; and scarcely one dares a deep draught of its
fiery intoxication, though scarcely one is willing to
have the unemptied and not-to-be-emptied cup with-
drawn. One short, trembling, rapturous sip in the
flushed fervour of youth; then you draw back frightened
at your own rash hardihood, and seek stupid safety
in soulless business and pleasureless pleasure."

Of the poems on " Art " and " Philosophy " it is
not necessary to say much. The moral of the former
is that real passion is too powerful and too direct for
artistic representation, and that art is the expression
of want rather than of satiety ; in Thomson's own
words :—

> Since he could not embrace it flush'd and warm,
> He has carved in stone the perfect form.

The lines on "Philosophy" convey a warning against
the philosophic tendency to sacrifice personal happiness by analysing outward appearances too minutely
—advice, however, which Thomson by no means put
into practice in his own most characteristic poems.

Three only of Thomson's poems can be called, in
the strict sense, narratives. The earliest written of

these * is " Ronald and Helen " (1861–1864), the bulk
of which has never yet been published, though ex-
cerpts were given in the *Secularist* and *Liberal* during
Thomson's lifetime, and some of the lyrics that are
scattered through the narrative were published in the
posthumous volume of poems issued in 1884. "Ronald
and Helen," which is written in *ottava rima*, is a most
unequal work, and must be pronounced to be a failure
when regarded as a whole, the narrative being dis-
jointed, ill-arranged, and almost devoid of action and
interest ; while the poetry, though exceedingly beautiful in parts, sinks occasionally into bathos and commonplace. Nevertheless " Ronald and Helen " contains
so many stanzas and passages worthy of Thomson's
best style that it is to be hoped it may some day be
published in full. It was conceived and partly written
in the isle of Jersey, and the descriptions of the island
scenery are distinctly the most valuable portions of
the poem.

The story opens with Helen's anxiety about her
lover Ronald, who has gone on a journey to the East,
while she is left without tidings. Her lamentations
and surmises as to his fate take up the greater portion
of the first of the four parts into which the narrative
is divided. In the second part, which is by far the
best of all, Helen narrates to her mother a dream of
the past night. A sudden, mysterious attraction to
the sea had drawn her, or had seemed to draw her,
to the very spot on the shore where she had sat with
her lover on the day before his departure ; coming

---

* It will be seen that I reserve the " Doom of a City,"
written in 1857, to be classed with the " City of Dreadful
Night," as being didactic rather than narrative.

now to the sands under a bright moon, she hears a voice singing sea-melodies, and discovers Glaucus, the sea-god, in the form of a benign old man, who comforts her in her sorrows and gives her an amulet, "a pure drop from the deep mid-sea," in which she descries the homeward-bound vessel of her lover. The following stanzas from the hitherto unpublished narrative can well bear quotation :—

> The sands, late flooded by the sounding tide,
>   Wore luminous silver spoil of its retreat ;
> But till I felt the glassy waters slide
>   With thin spent whispers round my naked feet
> (The gathering volume of the next wave wide
>   Nearing me fast with murmur full and sweet)
>   I could not raise my eyes to see indeed,
>   Being intent alone on my great need.
>
> I looked. I stood ; there never was a night
>   Of such heart-breaking beauty for despair;
> Our world's one dazzling and supreme delight,
>   Golden Beatitude—the moon—couched there
> 'Midst golden-tissued cloudlets : and her bright
>   Serene regard entranced the breathless air,
>   And dazzled her old slave, the fawning sea :
>   Oh, how the cruel splendour maddened me !
>
> Why linger here, where tireless ripples run
>   Enraptured in the glory of her gaze ?
> All lightsome creatures my dark sorrow shun,
>   No fiery wine a fiery thirst allays.
> But I must reach those low rock-ridges dun,
>   Where wrinkled shadows bar the silver rays ;
>   There shall I find some deep dark silent pool,
>   Dark as oblivion, deep as death, grave-cool.

The description of the amulet may compare, not altogether unfavourably, with that of the Beryl-stone in Rossetti's "Rose Mary," to which it offers some

o

striking points of resemblance, though written considerably earlier.

> Upon my open palm the jewel gleamed,
>   Faint, semi-lucid, almost colourless ;
> I gazed, gazed, turning slowly, till it seemed
>   Expanding by soft pulses in the stress
> Of my persistent gaze, whose full light streamed
>   Triumphant with prophetic consciousness ;
>   Pulse after pulse, wave after wave, poured still,
>   From eyes protending with imperious will.
>
> A golden star is kindled at its core,
>   The spherelet fills with the dissolving light ;
> Gather and shift and vanish shadows hoar ;
>   It is pervaded with miraculous might,
> Swelling in musical triumph more and more :
>   Behold ! within and yet beyond our night
>   Another heaven, star-blazoned, is unfurled,
>   Another vast horizon of our world.

In Part III., which does not much advance the
action of the story, Ronald's ship is seen entering the
harbour-mouth on a calm, delicious morning, and we
have an account of the thoughts and sensations that
occupy the minds of each of the two lovers at the
ending of their long separation.   The closing canto
describes the happiness of the reunited lovers, Helen
learning from Ronald that the cause of his return was
a vision which appeared to him on the same night
as that of her sea-dream.   Here the poem somewhat
abruptly ends, the poet moralising in the final stanzas
on the mystery of fate and the impossibility of fore-
seeing what good or evil destiny may await "the
fairest souls."   It must be confessed that the interest
of the story is by no means well sustained throughout
this long poem, which contains altogether nearly a
hundred and thirty stanzas, exclusive of lyrics.   The

characters of the lovers are not drawn with any accuracy or success ; that of Helen being vague and
undefined, while Ronald's is still less prepossessing,
owing to the unpleasant impression it conveys of
egoism and self-assertion.

"Weddah and Om-el-Bonain" (1866–1867), though
written only a few years later than "Ronald and
Helen," is notably and surprisingly superior to it at
every point. It is, indeed, unique among Thomson's
poems, as is "The Cenci" among Shelley's, in its
absolute directness of aim and subordination of all
minor interests to the general effect ; the narrative
being admirably chosen in the first place (since an Oriental story of love and destiny was exactly suited to
Thomson's genius), and then evolved with dignity,
swiftness, and self-control. The poem, which so far
resembles "Ronald and Helen" in being written in
ottava rima and arranged in four parts, is founded on
an Arabic story given in the "De l'Amour" of De
Stendhal ; but Thomson's modest remark that the
French original merits a better English "version"
than his own is likely to be somewhat misleading,
as it suggests the idea that he merely transcribed De
Stendhal's narrative, whereas the latter is comprised
within two pages of the "De l'Amour," and gives merely
the briefest outline of the events recorded. The full
development of the story, with the addition of many
new and important touches, is therefore entirely the
work of Thomson himself. It is worth noting, however, that there is a certain affinity of thought and
tone between "Weddah and Om-el-Bonain" and Keats's
"Isabella," not only in the use of the same metre, but
in the resemblance of occasional phrases and cadences,
where, under similar dramatic positions, we seem to

detect an unconscious echo of Keats.   As a rule,
however, Thomson's style in "Weddah and Om-el-
Bonain" is more rapid, vigorous, and incisive than
that of the dreamy, tender melodies of the "Isabella."

Of the three chief characters of the story, each
is felt from the outset, by a scarcely expressed yet
unerring presentiment, to be the victim of an inevitable doom.   Weddah and Om-el-Bonain, a noble
youth and beautiful maiden of the Azra, a tribe
famous for the passionate steadfastness of their love,
are cousins, betrothed from infancy, and destined to
love each other unalterably to the end ; while Walid,
a Syrian chieftain, whose alliance is indispensable
to the Azra warriors, is also smitten with passion
for Om-el-Bonain.   The doom of the plot commences
from the moment when Walid's strong, stern heart
first forms its resolve, as he chances to see Om-el-
Bonain during Weddah's absence on a foray :—

> But when one sunset flaming crimson-barred
> He saw a damsel like a shape of sleep,
> Who moved as moves in indolence the pard ;
> Above whose veil burned large eyes black and deep,
> The lairs of an intense and slow regard
> Which made all splendours of the broad world cheap,
>   And death and life thin dreams—fate-smitten there
>   He rested shuddering past the hour of prayer.

When Weddah returns he finds that Om-el-Bonain
has sacrificed her life's happiness for the welfare of
her father and the tribe, and has become the bride
of Walid, whose assistance, by which alone the Azra
could be saved from destruction, was only to be
gained on these terms.   At first he is wholly crushed
by sorrow, but by degrees learns silence and strength
in warfare, he and Walid being rivals in their exploits

against the enemies of the Azra. After the conclusion of the war he betakes himself to Walid's town, disguised as a merchant, and is introduced by Amine, Om-el-Bonain's favourite maiden, to the presence of her mistress. A large cedar chest is secretly prepared for his habitation in one of Om-el-Bonain's store-rooms, and here he dwells for some time in security, the lovers thus again finding happiness though encircled with the very toils of doom. In the following stanzas the influence of Keats is easily discernible :—

> Like bird above its young one in the nest
> Which cannot fly, he often heard her singing ;
> The thrill and swell of rapture from her breast
> In fountains of delightful music springing ;
> It seemed he had been borne among the blest,
> Whose quires around his darksome couch were ringing ;
>   Long after that celestial voice sank mute
>   His heart-strings kept sweet tremble like a lute.
>
> She heard his breathing like a muffled chime,
> She heard his tranquil heart-beats through the flow
> Of busy menials in the morning time ;
> Far-couched at night she felt a sudden glow,
> And straight her breathing answered rhyme for rhyme
> His softest furtive footsteps to and fro :
>   And none else heard ? She marvelled how the sense
>   Of living souls could be so dull and dense.

The secret is at last betrayed to Walid by a servant, and with the final crisis comes the most powerful part of the narrative. After bidding farewell to Om-el-Bonain, Weddah secretes himself for the last time within the chest, and Walid, entering with assumed carelessness, asks as a boon the gift of that particular coffer. Although "a clutch of iron fingers gript her heart," Om-el-Bonain holds out the key

unfalteringly, and for a moment Walid hesitates in
his conviction :——

> Swift as a double flash from thunder-skies
> The angel and the devil of his doubt
> Flamed from the sombre windows of his eyes :
> He went and took the key she thus held out,
> And turned as if he would unlock his prize.
> She breathed not ; all the air ran blood about
>   A swirl of terrors and wild hopes of guilt ;
>   Calm Weddah seized, then loosed, his dagger-hilt.

But Walid restrains his first impulse, and orders
his slaves to remove the coffer, and bury it under a
large cedar, after he has first challenged it with his
voice, leaning over the hollow chest when no witness
is present, and speaking words to the silent rival
whom he suspects to be within—a fine dramatic
incident borrowed by Thomson from the French of
De Stendhal. Seven days later Om-el-Bonain is
found dead on the grave of her lover ; and thus the
tragic story ends with an overpowering sense of the
" stringent cords of circumstance " with which Fate
entangles human lives. To those readers who are
not attracted by Thomson's pessimistic philosophy
and the idiosyncrasy that usually marks his poems,
" Weddah and Om-el-Bonain " will probably appear
his most successful work ; it is certainly superior to
all except the " City of Dreadful Night," and possibly
" Vane's Story."

" Two Lovers," a short narrative in elegiac stanzas,
written in 1867, is also based on a story told in De
Stendhal's " De l'Amour," concerning the love of a
Mahomedan youth and a Christian maiden. As their
difference in creed is an insurmountable barrier to
their union, they part, but only to die of grief. The

youth on his deathbed apostatises from his native faith and becomes a Christian, in order to dwell hereafter with the object of his love. A friend who is charged to carry the news to the maiden finds that she too is dead, but had just, for similar reasons, become an apostate from Christianity. Fate thus mocks the lovers to the last by endless separation.

> Yet both died happy in self-sacrifice ;
> A dolorous happiness, yet true and deep :
> And Gods and Fate and Hell and Paradise
> Perchance are one to their eternal sleep.

The inherent weakness of the story seems to have been felt by Thomson, for he turns aside at the end to moralise in the vein of his accustomed fatalism.

CHAPTER IX

THE POEMS—(continued).

THE POETRY OF PESSIMISM.

THOUGH it is difficult, as I have already hinted, to draw any exact boundary-line between Thomson's strictly pessimistic writings and others of a more general nature, there are two or three minor poems which have so much in common with the "City of Dreadful Night" that it seems best to class them under the same category. The earliest of these is the "Doom of a City," written in 1857, which has a special interest for the student of Thomson's writings as being a sort of first study for the "City of Dreadful Night," which it preceded by some fifteen years. Thomson himself calls it a Fantasia; a narrative it could hardly be called, since the thread of the story is even weaker than in "Ronald and Helen," and there is a still greater tendency to be discursive and allegorical. Written in the period of Thomson's early idealistic style, it is naturally lacking in the mature force and concentration of the "City of Dreadful Night;" nor is it steeped in the profound blackness of pessimistic thought which distinguishes the later poem. We see from several passages in the "Doom of a City" that its author still cherished, or tried to cherish, a belief in the guiding providence of God, in the immortality of the soul, and even in the possibility of the final triumph of good over evil in this present world—a faith which finds no place whatever in the "City of Dreadful Night." But though the "Doom of a City" is not distinguished by the stern consistency of thought or sustained power of description which belongs to its successor, it can at least claim the possession of many striking passages full of imagination, passion, and melody, and it is certainly nothing less than an extraordinary production for a youth of twenty-three.

It is an account of the discovery, by a solitary voyager, of a city in which all life has been turned to stone—an allegory of the stony insensibility of the human heart when numbed by destiny and despair. The idea is taken from Zobeide's story of the petrified city in the "Arabian Nights," a tale by which Thomson had been strongly impressed in boyhood, and to which a reference may be traced in more than one of his works. The variations of metre introduced in the "Doom of a City," as in most of Thomson's Fantasias, serve, here as elsewhere, to express the different phases of feeling through which the narrator passes, the continuity of the narrative being broken by the interpolation of several lyrical and rhetorical passages. The poem, as originally written, was in four parts, but in its published form * the first of these parts, entitled "The Voyage," was almost entirely omitted. The substance of the story in this unpublished portion is as follows. The poet relates how sleeplessness and sorrow drove him forth one

---

* In "A Voice from the Nile, and other Poems," 1884

night to pace the silent streets of the great city where
he dwelt lonely and despondent. He embarks in a
boat, and drifting down the marshy channels of the
river-mouth gains the open sea, where he encounters
a great storm, which is in turn succeeded by a morning of perfect calm :—

> I know not for what time I lay in trance,
> Nor in what course the tempest hurled us on.
> At length to scarce-believed deliverance
> I woke ; and saw a sweet slow silent dawn
> Upgrowing from the far dim grey abyss,—
> So slow it seemed like some celestial flower
> Unfolding perfect petals to its prime,
> And feeling in its secret soul of bliss
> Each leaf a loveliness for many an hour,
> With amaranthine queenship over time.

Again he is threatened with destruction through the
approach of a sea-monster, whose ghastly and loath-
some shape is apparently typical of some form of
mental horror—perhaps those fits of religious despondency and morbid self-condemnation hinted at
in a passage to be quoted later from " Vane's Story."
From this danger he unexpectedly escapes ; and here
the " Voyage " ends, and the " City," the first part of
the poem as published, begins. The boat arrives at
a strange harbour, which it enters under the glow of
the " saddest sunset ever seen."

> Who shall his own wild life-course understand ?
> From terror through great terrors I am brought
> To front my fate in this mysterious land.

Thus, half-expectant of some revelation from above,
he disembarks and makes his way towards the precincts of the city, first reaching a cemetery—" that
camp and city of the ancient dead "—in which he sees

a funeral train gathered round a maiden's bier, while
a youth, her bereaved lover, stands apart in silent
sorrow and despair. To his amazement and terror he
discovers that the mourners in the cemetery and all
the inhabitants of the city are a petrified people or
the dead.

> What found I in the City, then, which turned
> My deep and solemn hope to wild despair?
> What mystery of horror lay inurned
> Within the royal City great and fair?
> What found I?—Dead stone sentries stony-eyed,
> Erect, steel-sworded, brass-defended all,
> Guarding the sombrous gateway deep and wide
> Hewn like a cavern through the mighty wall;
> Stone statues all along the streets and squares,
> Grouped as in social converse or alone;
> Dim stony merchants holding forth rich wares
> To catch the choice of purchasers of stone.
>
> .   .   .   .
>
> The whole vast sea of life about me lay,
> The passionate heaving restless sounding life,
> With all its tides and billows, foam and spray,
> Arrested in full tumult of its strife
> Frozen into a nightmare's ghastly death,
> Struck silent from its laughter and its moan;
> The vigorous heart and brain and blood and breath
> Stark, strangled, coffined in eternal stone."

Then follows a rather lengthy and tedious description of the various characters encountered in the city
—the king and queen, the royal bodyguard, a young
mother and her child, a sage in his lofty turret. The
horror felt by the poet at this death-in-life is vividly
and powerfully described.

The ~~second~~ Third part of the poem, "The Judgments,"
gives an account of the doom pronounced by the
voice of God on the inhabitants of the city, as overheard and witnessed by the narrator. First there is

a series of condemnations of the wicked, reminding
the reader of Tennyson's "Vision of Sin;" some of
the statues sinking to dust at the thunder-crash of
each judgment.   Then is heard a voice "of infinite
love omnipotent," awarding eternal happiness to the
brave spirits "who had conquered life;" and the remainder of this part of the poem is chiefly a triumph-
song of the newly enfranchised souls, broken, however, by the interpolation of one remarkable lyric of
a wholly different note, in which the poet expresses
the sense of his own personal imperfection and despondency, even in the midst of these hymns of
rapturous exaltation.   Few of Thomson's poems could
surpass, for sheer splendour of conception and imagery,
the strange and pathetic stanzas from which the following are taken :—

As one who in the morning-shine
    Reels homeward, shameful, wan, adust,
From orgies wild with fiery wine
    And reckless sin and brutish lust;
And sees a doorway open wide,
    And then the grand Cathedral space;
And hurries in to crouch and hide
    His trembling frame, his branded face.

The organ-thunders surge and roll,
    And thrill the heights of branching stone;
They shake his mind, they crush his soul,
    His heart knells to them with a moan;
He hears the voice of holy prayer,
    The chanting of the fervent hymn;
They pierce his depths of sick despair,
    He trembles more, his eyes are dim.

He sees the world-wide morning flame
    Through windows where in glory shine
The saints who fought and overcame,
    The martyrs who made death divine;

He sees pure women bent in prayer,
Communing low with God above ;——
Too pure ! What right has *he* to share
Their silent feast of sacred love ?

The ~~third~~ ^{Fourth} and final part of the " Doom of a City "
describes the return of the poet to the city of the
living from which he had wandered forth, which we
feel to be meant for London. In some fine rhetorical
passages the moral of the story is then applied to
the present condition of English society ; the tyranny
and injustice of the rich and powerful are strongly
denounced ; while the concluding lines seem to hint
at a belief in future perfectibility. In spite of these
scattered indications of optimistic faith, the reader
cannot fail to see that the main tendency of the
" Doom of a City " is distinctly towards pessimism,
the most remarkable portion of the poem, both philosophically and poetically, being the description of
the " Mausolean loneliness " of the City of the dead,
which is in many respects a striking anticipation of
the sombre imagery of the " City of Dreadful Night."

The " Festival of Life," written in the same year
as the " Doom of a City," is also an expression of the
deepest despondency under a thin garb of religious
trustfulness. It cannot be ranked among the best of
the early poems, as the sentiment seems at times to
be rather over-wrought and the language too diffuse
for so gloomy and terrible a subject. " I fear you
will find the above very turgid throughout," wrote
Thomson in a copy of the " Festival of Life " which
he gave to a friend, " but the conception was so dithy-
rambic, and the stanza so long and elaborate, that I
have not been able to tone down the diction." The
poem is a vision of life as a wild Bacchanalian festival

whose masquers are sobered and startled from time
to time by the intrusion of two hooded and mysterious
strangers (personifications of Death in its two aspects
of gracious deliverer and malignant demon), who carry
off now one and now another of the unsuspecting
guests.   We have the same picture as in the " Doom
of a City " of the death of a young girl and the
bereavement of a lover ; and the whole poem seems
to imply a conflict in the mind of the writer between
a waning trust in immortality and a growing conviction of the certainty of annihilation.

   Such also is the purport of the " Poe-like verses,"
as they have rightly been called, of the " Mater Tenebrarum " (1859), a title borrowed from De Quincey,
the gloomiest and darkest of all Thomson's early
poems.   It is an anguished cry from one who even
now has not altogether passed beyond the border-
land that divides hope from despair ; even now he
cries in the sleepless night for one word of assurance
from his lost love that the soul does not die.   He
feels that she must indeed be dead, since she thus
leaves him unanswered ; yet still he cannot divest
himself of the last extreme hope.

In the endless nights on my bed, where sleeplessly brooding
     I lie,
I burden the heavy gloom with a bitter and weary sigh :
No hope in this worn-out world, no hope beyond the tomb;
No living and loving God, but blind and stony doom.
Anguish and grief and sin, terror, disease, and despair :
Why not throw off this life, this garment of torture I wear,
And go down to sleep in the grave in everlasting rest ?
What keeps me yet in this life, what spark in my frozen
     breast ?
A fire of dread, a light of hope, kindled, O Love, by thee,
For thy pure and gentle and beautiful soul, it must im-
     mortal be.

It is a relief to turn from this agonised outburst of the "Mater Tenebrarum" to the calmer and maturer thoughts and more solemn harmonies of the stanzas entitled "To our Ladies of Death" (1861), written at a time when its author had found at least some measure of comfort in the philosophic belief that the individual soul wins its immortality by being fused in the universal. "To our Ladies of Death" is one of Thomson's most beautiful and characteristic poems, closely prefiguring the "City of Dreadful Night" both in its tendency of thought and manner of expression. We have here for the first time the true poetry of pessimism, free from all the torturing disquietude of doubt and expectancy, and breathing a spirit of calm and passionless acquiescence in natural laws. The symbolism of the poem, as shown in the title and recorded by the author in a footnote, was suggested "by the sublime sisterhood of Our Ladies of Sorrow in the 'Suspiria de Profundis' of De Quincey," the three Ladies being here typical of various aspects not of Sorrow but of Death; while in its triple form and general affinity to De Quincey's writings, "To our Ladies of Death" bears a close resemblance to "Our Lady of Sorrow," the prose essay which was written a year or two later. Another influence which is very noticeable in the tone as well as the structure of "Our Ladies of Death" is that of Robert Browning. The seven-line stanza in which the poem is written was "moulded," as Thomson himself has recorded, "under the influence of 'The Guardian Angel' in Browning's 'Dramatic Lyrics;'" but those who compare the two poems will observe that Thomson has made two changes in the structure; first in making the final line rhyme with the fourth, instead

of with the third as in the "Guardian Angel;"
secondly, in not adopting the double-rhymes in the
fifth and sixth lines of the stanza. When we come
to speak of the "City of Dreadful Night," in which
this seven-line metre occupies every alternate section,
we shall note that these double-rhymes are rein-
troduced.

The three Ladies of Death represent the three
forms in which Death may be regarded by men ; first,
the "Lady of Beatitudes," the angel of personal and
conscious immortality ; secondly, the "Lady of Annihilation," the sorceress, "fraudful and malign;" thirdly,
the "Lady of Oblivion," who leads the weary individual soul to its peaceful fusion in the universal
world-spirit. Each of these deities is described at
some length, in language which, for power of poetic
vision and rhythmic melody, may compare with the
best sections of the "City of Dreadful Night." The
poet, weary of life with all its sorrows and disappointments, would fain call on the Lady of Beatitudes, the
youngest and gentlest of the three sisters whom he
has long known so well, but that he feels himself
unworthy to be gathered into her blissful rest. He
turns to the Lady of Annihilation, whose demoniac
form he has recognised through the mask of her fierce
beauty, but feels that, debased though he is, he can
yet defy her voluptuous enchantments. In the Lady
of Oblivion he finds the painless refuge of which
he is in need, and calls on her to lull him into perfect
sleep.

> Upgathered thus in thy divine embrace,
>   Upon mine eyes thy soft mesmeric hand,
> While wreaths of opiate odour interlace
>   About my pulseless brow ; babe-pure and bland,

Passionless, senseless, thoughtless, let me dream
Some ever-slumbrous, never-varying theme,
   Within the shadow of thy Timeless Land.

That when I thus have drunk my inmost fill
   Of perfect peace, I may arise renewed ;
In soul and body, intellect and will,
   Equal to cope with Life, whate'er its mood ;
To sway its storm and energise its calm ;
Through rhythmic years evolving like a psalm
   Of infinite love and faith and sanctitude.

But if this cannot be, no less I cry,
   Come, lead me with thy terrorless control
Down to our Mother's bosom, there to die
   By abdication of my separate soul :
So shall this single, self-impelling piece
Of mechanism from lone labour cease,
   Resolving into union with the Whole."

Under this allegorical description of the poet's
choice between the three Ladies of Death, we see
what is in fact a history of the several phases of
thought through which Thomson had passed regarding a future existence. He had at first been a
believer in a personal immortality ; then he had been
filled with horror as the doctrine of annihilation
threatened to force itself on his acceptance ; and
finally he had adopted the philosophical creed expressed in the stanzas just quoted. In a note prefixed to "Our Ladies of Death," when first published
in the *National Reformer*, there is an interesting
reference to the autobiographical aspects of the poem·
—"In my calmest and purest hours of contempla-
tion, my own verdict upon my own life attests this
poem to be genuine as the utterance of my individual
self ; whether it is true or not for others, themselves
must decide." He had now, in fact, become a con-

P

firmed pessimist in his views of life and death ; and though he did not yet give such exclusive utterance to the gospel of despair as in his crowning poem, he had already reached, as far as he himself was concerned, the complete and permanent form of his pessimistic faith.

The "City of Dreadful Night," written between 1870 and 1874, has been generally accepted as the masterpiece of its author—and rightly ; for if this poem does not take its place amidst the permanent works of English literature, it is difficult to believe that any of Thomson's writings will do so. It has not the rapturous idealism of "Bertram to the Lady Geraldine," nor the brilliant fantasy of "Vane's Story ; " but it has, in far greater measure than these poems, those two great qualities which George Eliot graphically described as "the distinct vision and grand utterance ; " we feel in reading the "City of Dreadful Night" that we are in the presence of one who has not only been profoundly moved by the mysteries of existence, but who has *seen* what he has felt, as only a great poet can see it ; and who, moreover, is gifted with the rare poetical faculty of translating his visions into words which impress themselves on the mind of the reader with all the vividness and intensity of a picture. The "City of Dreadful Night" is the full and final expression of that gloomy despair which, through year after year of suffering and disappointment, had been gradually but surely darkening on Thomson's life. It is an expansion and development of the "Doom of a City," all that was tedious and superfluous in the early narrative being now omitted, and replaced by a more poetical and more natural allegory. The city of *stone* now becomes a

city of *night*, an idea suggested possibly by Novalis's
" Hymns to Night ; " while the inhabitants, instead
of being represented as dead, stony statues, without
feelings, sympathies, or emotions, are now living men
and women, actuated by every sensation of pity,
horror, and despair.   It is obvious that a change of
this kind, which introduced into the poem a far more
subtle and spiritual element than any attainable in
the mere narration of a visit to a petrified city, must
give greater freedom to the imagination of the poet
and provide him with imagery at once more flexible
and more impressive.   All the awkward machinery
of the " Voyage " and the " Return," which makes
the first and fourth parts of the " Doom of a City "
so discursive and wearisome, is thus at once got rid
of in the " City of Dreadful Night ; " nor is the consistency of the poem ruined, as in the former case,
by the unnatural imposition of a weakly optimistic
conclusion on a narrative of an intensely pessimistic
tendency.   In short, the growth of artistic judgment
evidenced in the choice and treatment of the subject
in the " City of Dreadful Night," as compared with
the " Doom of a City," is still more noticeable than
the increased power of poetical expression acquired
by Thomson during the fifteen years that passed
between the writing of the two poems.   It will be
pointed out in a later chapter that much of the
imagery and even phraseology of the " City of
Dreadful Night " may be found in the prose phantasy,
" A Lady of Sorrow," written as early as 1864, the
third part of which, entitled " The Shadow," is in
fact scarcely less than a prose counterpart of the
poem.   How clearly Thomson had already realised
the conception of the gloomy. city and its doleful

inhabitants may be seen from the following passage :—
" And I wandered about the city, the vast metropolis,
which was become as a vast necropolis. . . . Desolate indeed I was, although ever and anon, here and
there, in wan haggard faces, in wrinkled brows, in
thin compressed lips, in drooping frames, in tremu-
lous gestures, in glassy hopeless eyes, I detected the
tokens of brotherhood, I recognised my brethren in
the great Freemasonry of Sorrow."

The object of the " City of Dreadful Night," as
stated in the Proem, is twofold ;—in the first place,
to set forth the " bitter old and wrinkled truth " of
pessimism ; and secondly, to speak a word of fellowship and comfort to the other wanderers in the city.
The idea of writing for the satisfaction of any except
those who are by nature in sympathy with his gospel
is foreign to Thomson's whole course of thought, and
is expressly disclaimed by him :—

> O sad Fraternity, do I unfold
>   Your dolorous mysteries shrouded from of yore ?
> Nay, be assured ; no secret can be told
>   To any who divined it not before :
> None uninitiate by many a presage
> Will comprehend the language of the message,
>   Although proclaimed aloud for evermore.

But although only the sad fraternity can wholly
understand the gospel of despair, it should be remembered that there are few thoughtful men who
at one time or another have not been to some extent
initiated into the " dolorous mysteries ; " so that
something of the true import of the poem may be
gathered by many other readers besides those to
whom it is primarily addressed. I think it may fairly
be said that the allegorical meaning of the " City of

Dreadful Night" is, in the main, sufficiently clear, though, as in most other allegories, the precise significance and inter-connection of some of the details may not admit of easy explanation. The City of Night is symbolic of the gloom of pessimistic thought; the dwellers in the city are they whose despondent mood has been so persistent as to become a second nature; who, having once found themselves within the "builded desolation" of the city, must pace its precincts to the end. Like Bunyan's pilgrims, they are the prisoners of Giant Despair, but they have no key of Promise by which to effect their liberation.

The first thing that attracts notice in the construction of the "City of Dreadful Night" is the interweaving of two independent threads of narrative, occupying alternate sections of different tone and metre. First there is a series of poems descriptive of the general appearance of the city and the condition of the inhabitants—in other words, of the rigid tyranny of that mysterious Fate which the poet makes it his chief object to describe. The rhythm of these sections is slow, stately, and impressive, the metre being invariably a seven-line stanza, identical with that used in "Our Ladies of Death," except that the fifth and sixth lines now end with a double rhyme-sound. Secondly, in every alternate section we have a picture of some particular incident or scene, which illustrates the characters of individual members of the fraternity of sorrow, and the various feelings with which they regard their common destiny. A six-line stanza, consisting of a quatrain and a couplet, is devoted to this series, broken, however, from time to time, by the interpolation of other

metres for the purpose of dialogue and dramatic
effect. These variations in the metrical arrangement
of the shorter stanzas, as compared with the severe
and uninterrupted regularity of the longer ones, may
perhaps be intended to represent the variableness of
the human moods therein depicted, in contrast with
that stern uniformity of Fate, which is the subject
of the other sections. The question whether the
transitions from the one style to the other are quite
successfully effected is one on which there will probably be a conflict of opinion. It seems to me that
on the whole the poem gains considerably in interest
and picturesqueness by the alternation of two distinct
tones ; but I think it must be admitted that at some
particular points of the narrative the variations are
somewhat abrupt, and that it would be difficult to
assign any clear reason for the juxtaposition of certain sections. This, however, is the exception, and
not the rule ; for there can be no doubt that the construction of the poem as a whole was the result of
deliberate forethought. Those who care to analyse it
more minutely will find traces of a carefully planned
proportion and balance between the opening and concluding sections, the first corresponding in the number
of its stanzas with the last, the second with the last
but one, and so forth.

In the first section the city is described as essentially a city of *night*, its darkness consisting in a
" distempered gloom of thought," a black dream,
which by its frequent recurrence has become a
present reality. Several stanzas are devoted to a
description of the site, surroundings, and appearance
of the city, of which it is easy to see that London
must have furnished the original conception, though

the outline is filled in with much that is poetical and visionary.

> The street-lamps burn amidst the baleful glooms,
>   Amidst the soundless solitudes immense
> Of rangèd mansions dark and still as tombs.
>   The silence which benumbs or strains the sense
> Fulfils with awe the soul's despair unweeping :
> Myriads of habitants are ever sleeping,
>   Or dead, or fled from nameless pestilence !

> Yet as in some necropolis you find
>   Perchance one mourner to a thousand dead,
> So there ; worn faces that look deaf and blind
>   Like tragic masks of stone.   With weary tread,
> Each wrapt in his own doom, they wander, wander,
> Or sit foredone and desolately ponder
>   Through sleepless hours with heavy drooping head.

With the second section commences the series of character-sketches running through alternate divisions of the poem, in all of which we may detect traits of Thomson's own personality in its different phases and moods.   The first figure whom the poet meets and accosts in the city is one whose life has lost all aim and purpose, though, like the works of a watch without a dial-face, it still continues its mechanical movement, as with slow and deliberate steps he revisits in perpetual recurrence the three scenes of his past life where Faith, Love, and Hope have successively perished.   To those who know the outlines of Thomson's history, it is needless to say that the first of these spots is the graveyard.

We are then told how the eye of the wanderer in the gloomy city acquires a new power of vision, seeing in darkness as before it saw in light; while, in a similar fashion, the ear hears through silence instead of through sound.   The sense of despair and awe still

remain as keen as ever, but the poet notes that all
sense of wonder is lost.   This serves to prepare the
reader's mind for the most mysterious and impressive episode in the whole poem—the account, given
by one of the inhabitants of the city, of a journey
through a desert, and of the fearful sights there witnessed.   I quote the first and last stanzas.

> As I came through the desert thus it was,
> As I came through the desert : All was black,
> In heaven no single star, on earth no track ;
> A brooding hush without a stir or note,
> The air so thick it clotted in my throat ;
> And thus for hours ; then some enormous things
> Swooped past with savage cries and clanking wings ;
>> But I strode on austere ;
>> No hope could have no fear.

He comes at last to a wild sea-shore, up which a
deep tide is thundering ; and here he sees advancing
a woman who bears in her hand a red lamp, which
proves to be "her own burning heart."   Then
suddenly he becomes as two separate selves; one
lying "stark in swoon," as the woman bends over
him with words of love and pity ; the other standing watchful apart, without power of speech or
movement.

> "As I came through the desert thus it was,
> As I came through the desert : When the tide
> Swept up to her there kneeling by my side,
> She clasped that corpse-like me, and they were borne
> Away, and this vile me was left forlorn ;
> I know the whole sea cannot quench that heart,
> Or cleanse that brow, or wash those two apart :
>> They love ; their doom is drear,
>> Yet they nor hope nor fear ;
>> But I, what do I here ?

In this weird and highly imaginative poem there appears to be a veiled reminiscence of the central sorrow of Thomson's career. He is himself the wanderer through the terrible desert of life; the woman that meets him by the fierce sea-tide of destiny being the phantom-figure of his lost love. His own self, as he is *now*, looks back powerless on his other self, as he was *then;* until at last the tide of time separates him for ever from his love and his better self, who remain, in spite of destiny, inseparable. Much of the tone and imagery seems to have been suggested by Robert Browning's " Childe Roland to the Dark Tower came ; " but even the wild track which led to the Dark Tower is less savage and spectre-haunted than the desert which forms the refrain of Thomson's poem.

Two powerful sections (vi., viii.) are devoted to recording the mysterious dialogues overheard by the poet as he wanders through the city. First is described the disappointment of two citizens who have failed to gain admission at the portal of death, because they have no means of paying the settled toll, which is the deposit of all remaining hope ; whereas all *their* hope has long been exhausted. The intermediate section (vii.) moralises on the shamelessness of these phantom-beings who observe no reticence in narrating the inmost secrets of their hearts. Then follows a dialogue between another couple, one of whom maintains that fate is malignant, the other that it is merely indifferent to mankind. In both these dialogues there is a marked resemblance in tone and metre to Tennyson's " Two Voices."

Then, in some stanzas full of sombre and sug-

gestive imagery, and showing a keen appreciation of
the gloomily-poetical aspects of London life, the poet
speculates on the meaning of the tide of traffic which
rolls through the streets of even this shadowy city.
Can it be that the merchandise thus borne away into
the darkness, as in a "fate-appointed hearse," consists of the joy and peace that might otherwise have
been man's portion in life?   From such meditation
we pass naturally to the picture of one whose life had
thus been laid desolate.   The poet enters an illu-
minated mansion in which he finds every room craped
with funeral pall, and adorned with images of one
self-same face—"a woman very young and very
fair."

> At length I heard a murmur as of lips,
>   And reached an open oratory hung
> With heaviest blackness of the whole eclipse ;
>   Beneath the dome a fuming censer swung ;
> And one lay there upon a low white bed,
> With tapers burning at the foot and head :
>
> The Lady of the images : supine,
>   Deathstill, lifesweet, with folded palms she lay :
> And kneeling there as at a sacred shrine
>   A young man wan and worn who seemed to pray :
> A crucifix of dim and ghostly white
> Surmounted the large altar left in night.

The tragedy is the one to which there are so many
allusions in Thomson's writings.   It is curious to
note that the particular form in which it is here expressed is borrowed from a passage in that story in
the "Arabian Nights" which has already been mentioned as the original of the "Doom of a City :"—
"About midnight I heard a voice, like that of a man,
reading the Alcoran, after the same manner and in

the same tone as we read it in our Mosques. . . .
Looking through a window, I found it to be an
oratory. I saw a little carpet laid down, and a
comely young man sat upon this carpet, reading the
Alcoran, which lay before him on a desk, with great
devotion."

In the next few sections the sequence of thought
is easily discernible. We are first told that the inhabitants of the city, however much they may differ
in rank, wealth, and intellect, have one essential bond
of union—the sense of despair. The following lines
lend weight to the idea that Thomson's melancholia
was constitutional and inherited :—

> They are most rational and yet insane :
>   An outward madness not to be controlled ;
> A perfect reason in the central brain,
>   Which has no power, but sitteth wan and cold,
> And sees the madness, and foresees as plainly
> The ruin in its path, and trieth vainly
>   To cheat itself refusing to behold.

The recognition of the unity of the sufferers leads
directly to the subject of the next section—the assem-
blage of citizens in the great cathedral, where each is
challenged at the entrance by a mysterious warder,
and responds with his countersign, the passport of
the freemasonry of sorrow. After an expression of
wonder and regret (xiii.) that men should look for
comfort to an eternity of life, instead of to an eternity
of rest, we come to one of the most powerful passages in the whole poem—the address given by the
atheist preacher to his "shadowy congregation," with
the final assurance that, however painful the present
life may be, there is at least nothing to fear in the
oblivion of the grave. The doctrine, it will be

observed, is the same as that conveyed in " Our
Ladies of Death."

> This little life is all we must endure,
> The grave's most holy peace is ever sure,
>   We fall asleep and never wake again ;
> Nothing is of us but the mouldering flesh,
> Whose elements dissolve and merge afresh
>   In earth, air, water, plants, and other men.

The effect produced on the congregation by the
preacher's eloquence leads the poet to moralise, in a
few intermediate stanzas, on the influences that are in
turn received and transmitted by the atmosphere of
every human gathering-place, as in this case the air is
rife with "infections of incurable despair." Accordingly (xvi.) there rises from the northern aisle of the
cathedral the " vehement voice " of one who refuses to
accept even such comfort as the preacher had offered,
and tells his own tale of a blank and inconsolable life.

The question of suicide, which has been touched
on once or twice in the foregoing sections, now comes
more fully into notice. When, in a lane adjoining a
northern suburb, the poet finds a half-human form,
searching on hands and knees for some long-lost clue
—a thread of gold which should lead him back from
dishonoured age to the innocence of infancy—the
thought that rises in his mind is, that it were far
wiser to press forward to death than backward to
birth. Then follows a description of the " River of
the Suicides," in which every night some sufferer
finds escape :—

> They perish from their suffering surely thus,
>   For none beholding them attempts to save,
> The while each thinks how soon, solicitous,
>   He may seek refuge in the self-same wave ;

Some hour when, tired of ever-vain endurance,
Impatience will outrun the sweet assurance
Of perfect peace eventual in the grave.

The concluding sections of the poem naturally bring us back to the main theme—the hopelessness of the struggle against Fate, and the dejection that results therefrom. The vision of the conflict between the Sphinx and the Angel,—the Sphinx typical of the blind, passionless immobility of nature, the Angel of the passionate intensity of the human intellect,—is one of the finest allegorical passages in the " City of Dreadful Night," and only to be surpassed by the final picture of the " Melencolia." The metamorphoses of the Sphinx's assailant, who is first a winged and sworded angel, then a sworded but wingless warrior, and lastly an unarmed man " with raised hands impotent," while the Sphinx for ever remains unchanged and unchangeable, may be taken to represent the three phases through which the poet's mind had passed in relation to the mysteries of existence ; first the exaltation of religious belief ; then the keen self-reliance of philosophy ; then the helplessness of complete despair.

Thus alike from the different scenes of the city, and from the various histories and dialogues of its inhabitants, one lesson, and one only, has been gathered and laid to heart—the old *vanitas vanitatum*, that all is vanity. One feeling is thus left dominant in the thoughtful mind, and to the personification and apotheosis of this feeling the last section is devoted.

Anear the centre of that northern crest
Stands out a level upland bleak and bare,
From which the city east and south and west
Sinks gently in long waves ; and thronèd there

> An image sits, stupendous, superhuman,
> The bronze colossus of a wingèd Woman,
>   Upon a graded granite base foursquare.

This figure, the idea of which is found also in "A Lady of Sorrow," is here identified with Albert Dürer's "Melencolia," which is faithfully transcribed in nine incomparable stanzas, full of that concentrated energy of which Thomson was so great a master. Then the "Melencolia" is finally recognised as the presiding genius of the mournful city :—

> Titanic from her high throne in the north,
>   That City's sombre Patroness and Queen,
> In bronze sublimity she gazes forth
>   Over her capital of teen and threne,
> Over the river with its isles and bridges,
> The marsh and moorland, to the stern rock-ridges,
>   Confronting them with a coeval mien.
>
> The moving moon and stars from east to west
>   Circle before her in the sea of air :
> Shadows and gleams glide round her solemn rest.
>   Her subjects often gaze up to her there :
> The strong to drink new strength of iron endurance,
> The weak new terrors ; all, renewed assurance
>   And confirmation of the old despair.

Thus Thomson's great poem characteristically ends with the word "despair," as Shelley's with the word "victory." The "City of Dreadful Night" is in many ways the exact antithesis of the "Prometheus Unbound;" yet it has also its points of similarity, for nowhere else in recent English literature do we note so clearly that tone of tender gravity and profound compassion for suffering humanity which is so essentially a Shelleyan attribute.

CHAPTER X.

THE POEMS—(concluded).

I. *Later Poems.*—We have seen that after the writing of the "City of Dreadful Night," and its publication in the *National Reformer* in 1874, there was a break of seven years in Thomson's poetical activity. Yet it was evident that his imaginative powers were only slumbering during this silent period; for we have a glimpse of the true poet in a beautiful lyric, "The Nightingale and the Rose," written in 1877, which seems to imply a consciousness on the part of the writer that the music lying dormant within him was still destined to be called forth, as the bird's song is called forth by the fragrance of the flower.

"A Voice from the Nile," though projected in notes ten years earlier, was written in 1881, and having appeared in the *Fortnightly Review* after Thomson's death in the following year, gave its title to the posthumous volume of poems issued in 1884. It is a blank-verse poem of about two hundred lines, the only piece of blank verse of any length to be found among Thomson's writings. The river Nile is represented as contrasting its own unaltered and unalterable destiny with the flux and change in the condition of the living creatures

that dwell by its banks ; man is especially a cause of
wonder and mystery to the great calm river, for
whereas the other animals are seen to live lives of
contented equality, man, " the admirable, the pitiable,"
is an alien and an outcast, unsatisfied with the present
life, and vexed with restless dreams of an eternity
hereafter.   Successive wars, tribes, creeds, empires,
and civilisations come and go, while the mighty
river flows on always the same.   Here is a typical
passage :—

> Dusk memories haunt me of an infinite past,
> Ages and cycles brood above my springs,
> Though I remember not my primal birth.
> So ancient is my being and august,
> I know not anything more venerable :
> Unless, perchance, the vaulting skies that hold
> The sun and moon and stars that shine on me ;
> The air that breathes upon me with delight ;
> And Earth, All-Mother, all-beneficent,
> Who held her mountains forth like opulent breasts
> To cradle me and feed me with their snows,
> And hollowed out the great sea to receive
> My overplus of flowing energy ;
> Blessèd for ever be our Mother Earth.

The influence of Browning is observable in a great
part of the " Voice from the Nile," especially in such
lines as the following :—

> The slant-sailed boats that flit before the wind
> Or up my rapids ropes hale heavily ;

And there is also a good deal that reminds one of
the cadence of Tennysonian blank verse, though perhaps Thomson would not have acknowledged any
conscious inspiration from that quarter.   The slow
and stately tone that breathes through the whole
poem seems to give it an affinity to Landor's " Gebir,"

and to the famous sonnet on the Nile which Leigh
Hunt wrote in his competition with Keats and Shelley.

We now come to three remarkable poems, all,
strange to say, full of as passionate an idealism and
as rapturous a melody as any which distinguished
Thomson's earliest period of authorship, and, stranger
still, marked by an element of hopefulness which
could not possibly have been expected from a poet
whose love had long been lost, and who was himself
about to die. " Richard Forest's Midsummer Night "
(1881) is a Fantasia consisting of a series of dramatic
lyrics like those in "Sunday up the River," to which
it is scarcely, if at all, inferior in tenderness of
thought and beauty of workmanship. The opening
sections describe a sunset by the sea-shore, followed
by a moonlit night of June, during which the youths
and maidens of the town (presumably a modern
"watering-place;" but the vulgarity of the idea is
redeemed by the same poetic touch as in the "Sunday
at Hampstead") are walking up and down on the
"shining sand" and "long curved pier." Meantime
Richard Forest is seeking his sweetheart Lucy in a
sequestered cottage in a neighbouring vale, a little
retired from the sea. The picture of Lucy's rustic
home, with the "good father" nodding in his arm-
chair, the "little mother" busily and watchfully
knitting, and Lucy herself with "white rose in her
hair, red rose in her fingers," is very vividly yet
delicately drawn ; the rest of the poem being devoted
to describing the bliss of the lovers' meeting :—

> As we gaze and gaze on the sleeping sea
> Beneath the moon's soft splendour,
> The wide expanse inspires a trance
> Most solemn and most tender.

Q

The heavens all silent with their stars,
    The sweet air hardly breathing,
The liquid light of ripples bright,
    Wreathing and interwreathing.

.   .   .   .   .

Deep as may be the deepest sea,
    Yet deeper is our love, dear ;
Our souls dilate with bliss as great
    As all the heavens above, dear.

We are the whole world yet ourself
    By some divine illusion ;
The I in Thee, and Thou in Me,
    By mystic interfusion.

In lyrics such as this we see the same resemblance
to Mrs. Browning's style which we noted in the
poems written twenty years earlier. Several passages
of " Richard Forest's Midsummer Night " also suggest a similarity to Tennyson's " Maud."

" He heard her Sing " (1882), a rhapsody in the
long sonorous anapæstic measure of Mr. Swinburne's
" Hymn to Proserpine," is one of the most passionate and imaginative of all Thomson's poems ; it
is conceived and written—to quote one of its own
couplets—

In a rapture of exultation made calm by its stress intense,
In a triumph of consecration and a jubilation immense.

In spite of the difference of names and times,
Alice being substituted for Lucy and " the midmost
Maytime " for a midsummer night, this poem may
be considered as in some measure a continuation of
" Richard Forest's Midsummer Night." There the
lovers say good-night at the close; here, after bidding farewell to his Alice at the cottage by the sea
(we somehow feel that it is the same cottage as in
" Richard Forest "), he goes down to the shore in the

broad moonlight, and there sees the vision which is the chief incident of the poem.

And thus all expectant abiding I waited not long, for soon
A boat came gliding and gliding out in the light of the moon,
Gliding with muffled oars, slowly, a thin dark line,
Round from the shadowing shores into the silver shine
Of the clear moon westering now, and still drew on and on,
While the water before its prow breaking and glistering shone,
Slowly in silence strange : and the rower rowed till it lay
Afloat within easy range deep in the curve of the bay.

In the stern of the boat sits a woman whom he recognises as a famous singer, and when she raises her voice in song the listener falls into a trance-like ecstasy of rapturous sympathy and exaltation.

And the Voice flowed on and on, and ever it swelled as it poured,
Till the stars that throbbed as they shone seemed throbbing with it in accord ;
Till the moon herself in my dream, still Empress of all the night,
Was only that voice supreme translated into pure light ;
And I lost all sense of the earth though I still had sense of the sea ;
And I saw the stupendous girth of a tree like the Norse World-Tree ;
And its branches filled all the sky, and the deep sea watered its root,
And the clouds were its leaves on high, and the stars were its silver fruit ;
Yet the stars were the notes of the singing, and the moon was the voice of the song
Through the vault of the firmament ringing and swelling resistlessly strong ;
And the whole vast night was a shell for that music of manifold might,
And was strained by the stress of the swell of the music yet vaster than night.

It is impossible to do justice to a rhapsody such as

this by the quotation of a few lines ; but it is safe to say that "He heard her Sing," with its sustained intensity of passion, its splendour of poetic imagery, and subtle recurrence of certain words and cadences which form the keynote of the melody, must be placed in the first rank of Thomson's shorter poems. At present it has not obtained from critics and reviewers one quarter of the notice which would have been accorded it had it been written by a more popular author.

The stanzas headed "At Belvoir" (January 1882) are the third portion, and from a personal point of view the most interesting, of this strange optimistic trilogy by the most confirmed of pessimists. They are a poetical record of the summer Sunday spent during the previous July at Belvoir Castle, near Leicester, in the company of hospitable friends ; and they are specially remarkable as indicating traces of a reviving hopefulness in Thomson's mind only a few months before the date of his death. Of the singular beauty of the poem from a literary standpoint there can be little question ; nothing more fresh and tender has been given us since Wordsworth's famous stanzas on "Yarrow," to which these seem to be poetically and spiritually akin.

> My thoughts go back to last July,
>   Sweet happy thoughts and tender ;—
> "The bridal of the earth and sky,"
>   A day of noble splendour ;
> A day to make the saddest heart
>   In joy a true believer ;
> When two true friends we roamed apart
>   The shady walks of Belvoir.
>
> A maiden like a budding rose,
>   Unconscious of the golden

And fragrant bliss of love that glows
　Deep in her heart infolden ;
A Poet old in years and thought,
　Yet not too old for pleasance,
Made young again and fancy-fraught
　By such a sweet friend's presence. . . .

The cattle standing in the mere,
　The swans upon it gliding,
The sunlight on the waters clear,
　The radiant clouds dividing ;
The solemn sapphire sky above
　The foliage lightly waving,
The soft air's Sabbath peace and love
　To satisfy all craving. . . .

My thoughts go on to next July,
　More happy thoughts, more tender ;
" The bridal of the earth and sky,"
　A day of perfect splendour ;
A day to make the saddest heart
　In bliss a firm believer ;
When two True Loves may roam apart
　The shadiest walks of Belvoir.

But, alas ! before the next July, this day-dream had
been broken by the death of the poet himself.

" The Sleeper " and "Modern Penelope," both written
in 1882, are short, graceful lyrics of a lighter and
less serious tone than those which I have just mentioned, yet showing similar traces of the revival of a
hopeful spirit. The same can scarcely be said of the
two or three remaining productions of this the last
year of Thomson's life ; for in these we find once more
a return to the sad thoughts and gloomy imaginings
of his usual style. "A Stranger," in several respects
unlike any other poem of Thomson's, is written in a
sort of *terza rima :* but here, as in Shelley's " Ode to
the West Wind," the metre is not continuous, being

broken up into stanzas of fourteen lines. The narrator describes how a mysterious lady, a "lady of all grace," had come in the early spring-time to the village where he dwelt. She was then accompanied by her little boy, "her only joy, her terrible dark grief," whose Christian name, with no surname to follow it, tells where he now lies in the village church-yard—a loss which had increased, rather than dimin-ished, the lady's benevolence to all around her :

Her sorrow flowed with blessings from above ;
　Her heart of joy and hope was in that tomb,
But not her heart of sympathy and love :

While her young flower was fading from its bloom
　She had been wonderfully sweet and kind ;
And now that it was buried in the gloom

Her own sore suffering did but closelier bind
　Her heart to other hearts in all distress ;
The little angel in her sad soul shrined

Was a true angel of pure gentleness
　And soft compassion and unwearying will
To soothe and aid and with all solace bless :

Our joys and sorrows take our nature still ;
Hers wrought bright good from her own darkest ill.

The pensive tone of the poem resembles that of "Bertram to the Lady Geraldine" and "Tasso to Leonora," except that the feeling here expressed is one of reverence rather than of love. The interest of the story is unfortunately slight, owing to the obscu-rity in which the subject is involved and the slender thread of narrative on which it depends ; but in its origin it is possibly connected with a prose story en-titled "Seen Thrice," published by Thomson in the *Secularist* several years earlier, in which a mother and child are described in somewhat similar terms.

Lastly, we come to two poems, closely connected in literary form, which furnish a clue to the understanding of much of the unhappiness of Thomson's latter years. "The Poet to his Muse" and "Insomnia" are the latest of Thomson's important poems, and though here classed for convenience with the other writings of the same date, might well be reckoned in the category of his pessimistic writings. They were written within a month of each other, in February and March respectively, and are both cast in the same gloomy tone, expressed in a ten-line stanza of great force and gravity. "The Poet to his Muse" is the exact opposite of "A Happy Poet," the early ideal poem of 1859, compared with which it affords significant proof of the change that had come over the mind of the writer during the twenty-three intervening years. Instead of felicitating himself on the lofty duties and catholic scope of the poetic calling, he now sadly and hesitatingly entreats his Muse to awake from her lethargy and aid him once more in singing some worthy song. But she replies that she too, like himself, is now weary and desolate, and can sing no songs either of life or death. There is a strange pathos both in the circumstances under which the poem was written and in the tone of the poetry itself; to which effect the refrain on the second line of each stanza (repeated as the commencement of the next) not a little contributes.

> I come unto thy sighing through the gloom
> My hair dishevelled dank with dews of night,
> Reluctantly compelled to leave my tomb;
> With eyes that have for ever lost their light;
> My vesture mouldering with deep death's disgrace,
> My heart as chill and bloodless as my face,
> My forehead like a stone;

My spirit sightless as my eyes are sightless,
My inmost being nerveless, soulless, lightless,
My joyous singing voice a harsh sepulchral moan.

My hair dishevelled dank with dews of night,
    From that far region of dim death I come,
With eyes and soul and spirit void of light,
    With lips more sad in speech than stark and dumb:
Lo, you have ravaged me with dolorous thought
Until my brain was wholly overwrought,
        Barren of flowers and fruit;
Until my heart was bloodless for all passion,
Until my trembling lips could no more fashion
Sweet words to fit sweet airs of trembling lyre and lute.

It is interesting to observe that, in the stanza just
quoted, the " dolorous thought" of pessimism is charged
with the extinction of the poetic fire; but it may
fairly be questioned how far this was really the case,
since Thomson's complaint as to the cause of his
own silence was already partly belied by his renewed
outburst of poetry in 1881 and 1882. " Not true
now, but true of seven songless years," was the note
appended by the author to the original draft of " The
Poet to his Muse."

" Insomnia " is in some respects the very darkest
and most terrible of all Thomson's writings. Its
expression of personal suffering is more poignant
and direct than anything in the " City of Dreadful
Night;" nor has it any of the comfort, if comfort it
can be called, which is there derived from a calm
and passionless system of philosophical resignation.
I have already remarked how important a part sleeplessness played in the physical and mental suffering
endured by Thomson throughout the greater part of
his life, and how much of his despondency and
morbid prostration may be traced to this origin; in

this poem the curse of insomnia is depicted with a ghastly and startling vividness which finds no counterpart in English literature, except in the work of the opium-eating brotherhood of De Quincey, Coleridge, and Poe.   There is a marked resemblance of tone between Thomson's " Insomnia " and Coleridge's Ode on " Dejection," with its bitter cry of—

'Tis midnight, but small thoughts have I of sleep ;

while in " Insomnia," as in the earlier " Mater Tenebrarum," there is also a strong admixture of the lurid intensity of sombre word-painting which is Poe's most remarkable characteristic.

The poet narrates how, while other men went one by one to rest in confident assurance of the blessing of sleep, *he*, haggard with many sleepless nights, could only lie down to a certainty of unspeakable torment. As he lies in silence he becomes aware that the dark presence of each hour watches in turn by his bed, while he, in a vision, is compelled to cross each period from " hour-ridge " to " hour-ridge " like one who struggles across a series of deep and gloomy ravines.

> Then went I down into that first ravine,
>   Wearily, slowly, blindly, and alone,
> Staggering, stumbling, sinking depths unseen,
>   Shaken and bruised and gashed by stub and stone ;
> And at the bottom paven with slipperiness,
> A torrent-brook rushed headlong with such stress
>   Against my feeble limbs,
> Such fury of wave and foam and icy bleakness
> Buffeting insupportably my weakness
> That when I would recall, dazed memory swirls and swims.
>
> How I got through I know not, faint as death ;
>   And then I had to climb the awful scarp,
> Creeping with many a pause for panting breath,
>   Clinging to tangled root and rock-jut sharp ;

Perspiring with faint chills instead of heat,
Trembling, and bleeding hands and knees and feet ;
   Falling, to rise anew ;
Until, with lamentable toil and travel
Upon the ridge of arid sand and gravel
I lay supine half-dead and heard the bells chime Two.

It is worth remarking that in one of the prose
essays, written in 1865, Thomson had already used
a similar metaphor of the abysses that divide the
hours. " It is only," he wrote, " in rare moments of
meditation that we can discern how black and profound are these abysses yawning between the successive hours of our life, and how impotent is our
reason to overleap or overbridge them. In some
manner or other, mysteriously, our being continues
across them, . . . until at length it plunges into the
abyss of death, not more profound and not more
mysterious than hundreds of abysses it has traversed
triumphing, not more wonderful than that gulf of
sleep through which it has passed from every night
to every morn."

The latter part of " Insomnia " contains some of
the most weirdly powerful stanzas that Thomson
ever wrote. He relates how, at last, in despair of
obtaining sleep, he rose from his bed and crept forth
into the silent city.

Constrained to move through the unmoving hours,
   Accurst from rest because the hours stood still,
Feeling the hands of the Infernal Powers
   Heavy upon me for enormous ill,
Inscrutable intolerable pain,
Against which mortal pleas and prayers are vain,
      Gastings of dying breath,
And human struggles, dying spasms yet vainer :
Renounce defence when Doom is the Arraigner ;
Let impotence of Life subside appeased in Death.

I paced the silent and deserted streets
  In cold dark shade and chillier moonlight grey;
Pondering a dolorous series of defeats
  And black disasters from life's opening day,
Invested with the shadow of a doom
That filled the spring and summer with a gloom
      Most wintry black and drear;
Gloom from within as from a sulphurous censer
Making the glooms without for ever denser,
To blight the buds and flowers and fruitage of my year.

That this terrible poem should have been written
by the author who only a few weeks before had produced " Richard Forest's Midsummer Night," " He
heard her Sing," and " At Belvoir" is worthy to be
recorded among the curiosities of literature.

II. *Political and Satirical Poems.*—In studying Thomson's political poems we find the earliest-written,
contrary to the usual rule, to be at once the longest
and most important. " The Dead Year," which was
published in the *National Reformer* early in 1861, but
is not included in the volumes of collected poems, was
written at the close of 1860, and is an idealised record
of the events of that year—a subject perhaps suggested by Dryden's " Annus Mirabilis." It is decidedly an interesting and characteristic poem, not
dealing merely with the passing politics of the day,
but giving a good insight into the general opinions
of its author; and being also of considerable value
from a literary point of view. In several ways it
is closely akin to the poem on " Shelley," * which
was presumably written about the same time, since
both have the same Chaucerian seven-line stanza,
both are highly ideal and allegorical in tone, and

* Cf. pp. 195, 196.

both are cast into the form of a vision of which the
poet is supposed to have been the spectator. The
same idea of an old-year and new-year vision on the
Eve of St. Sylvester was afterwards used by Thomson
in several of his prose fantasies.

Standing in a wild wood, at midnight, amid snow
and tempest, the poet sees "the weak Old Year"
descend from his chariot and yield his place to a
more vigorous and youthful successor who drives
proudly on his path, though not without a prescience
of the doom that must befall him also in his turn.
The poet in thought follows the exiled king to his
tomb in an icy cavern of the Southern Pole, where
his predecessors, a host of dim regal shadows throned
on icy thrones, await him in mournful expectation,
and question him as to the state of the world :—

> How tends the bitter fate-deciding war,
>   Constant between the Evil and the Good?
> Mankind—have they grown better than of yore,
>   Less steeped and brutalised in lust and blood,
>   Less fatally inconsequent of mood?
> More faithful, valiant, loving, and sincere?
> Is any hope that now the end draws near?

The rest of the poem is chiefly devoted to the
Year's reply. He informs them, in a spirit of pessimism scarcely less bitter than that of the "City of
Dreadful Night," that all is bloodshed, strife, and
selfishness, as of old; the temples are ruins; men
have no god but a pitiless and remorseless doom.

> Exiled from God and his paternal love,
>   Far, far from home men languish desolate;
> A dungeon-roof, instead of heaven above;
>   And constant vision through the iron gate
>   Of one stern Jailer, blind and stony Fate—

The stony heart unthrilled by wail or prayer,
The stony eyes that blench at no despair. . . .

The mass of traders full of lies and fraud,
  The mass of rulers cowardly and blind,
The mass of people without faith or God,
  The mass of teachers barren as the wind,
  The mass of laws unsuited to mankind :
What doom do these imperiously require,
But blood and death and ordeal as by fire ?

In reply to the question if there is no single "gleam of good" to brighten so dark a record, the old year tells the tale of Italian freedom as wrought out by "the thinker," Mazzini, and "the doer," Garibaldi ; and declares the "red shirt" to be the one happy symbol he bears. Thomson's reverence for Garibaldi is again expressed in some lines headed "Garibaldi revisiting England" (1864).

The poem on "A Polish Insurgent," written in 1863, at the time of the Polish rebellion, is not less powerful than pathetic. It describes the feelings of the exiled Polish patriot, who, in spite of the well-meant remonstrances of "Smith, your man of sense," the typical Englishman, leaves Smith-land and sets out eastward to join in the hopeless struggle against the oppressor of his country.

Must a man have *hope* to fight ?
Can a man not fight in despair ?
Must the soul cower down for the body's weakness,
And slaver the devil's hoof with meekness,
Nor care nor dare to share
Certain defeat with the right ?

They do not know us, my Mother !
They know not our love, our hate !
And how we would die with each other,
Embracing proud and elate,

> Rather than live apart
> In peace with shame at the heart. . . .

> O our Mother, thou art noble and fair !
> Fair and proud and chaste, thou Queen !
> Chained and stabbed in the breast,
> Thy throat with a foul clutch prest ;
> Yet around thee how coarse, how mean,
> Are these rich shopwives who stare !

It may be that the very hopelessness of Poland's insurrection against the Russian tyrant touched a kindred chord in the mind of a poet who had himself brooded so deeply on the disastrous struggle with "tremendous fate," and who knew by experience that one engaged in so desperate a warfare can get but little true sympathy from the inhabitants of Smithland, "kindly—but dense, but dense."

The only other political poems that call for special mention are "L'Ancien Régime; or, The Good Old Rule" (1867), and "Despotism Tempered by Dynamite" (1882). The former has been described by one of the critics as "a scathing denunciation of the old Continental monarchical system;" though one may shrewdly suspect that Thomson intended the application to be considerably nearer home and of somewhat more modern date.

> Who has a thing to bring
> For a gift to our lord the king ?

is the bitter refrain that runs through the poem ; the moral being that "our lord the king" usually undervalues such gifts as love, justice, truth, and loyalty ; those which he most appreciates being servility, war, harlotry, and lies ; while from the subjects' point of view the best of all gifts for him is—a tomb. "Despotism and Dynamite," written in May 1882, and

published in the *Weekly Dispatch* on the day after its
author's death, is the last poem that Thomson wrote.
Each of its seven stanzas consists of six unrhymed
lines, with a refrain on the last; the subject being
the terror with which the all-powerful Tsar looked
forward to the date of his own coronation :—

> My peasants rise to their unvarying toil,
> And go to sleep outwearied by their toil,
> Without the hope of any better life.
> But with no hope they have no deadly fear.
> They sleep and eat their scanty food in peace—
>   I look with terror to my crowning day.
>
> My palaces are prisons to myself;
> I taste no food that may not poison me ;
> I plant no footstep sure it will not stir
> Instant destruction of explosive fire ;
> I look with terror to each day and night—
>   With tenfold terror to my crowning day.

Thomson's satirical and humorous poems are not
many in number, as he usually made prose his vehicle
for satire ; but there are several which show that he
might have made his mark in this kind of writing,
had he chosen to cultivate it further. One of the
earliest and most notable is "A Real Vision of Sin,"
written in 1859, and published in *Progress* after
Thomson's death. A pencil note on the original
MS. records that it was "written in disgust at Tennyson's ("Vision of Sin"?) which is very pretty and
clever and silly and truthless." Thomson's poem is a
bitter retort, or perhaps it should be called burlesque,
on that cheap optimism, as he considered it, which pro-
fesses to demonstrate to satisfaction that man has no
cause to find fault with any of the laws of existence.
It takes the form of a conversation between a man
and woman, an old and wicked pair of degraded and

hardened sinners ; the man being cruel, timorous, and
half-hearted, hating this life, yet afraid of entering
the next ; the woman possessing at least the courage
of despair to end the life they had found so wretched,
and showing traces of humanity in her reminiscences
of the "child-dream" of a "murdered brat" apparently killed by the man in years that had long gone
by.   The imagery of the poem is terrible in its re-
morselessly sombre realism ; the sky is spongy and
lax over the head of the wretched couple, the trees
loom dimly around them in the drizzling rain ; at
their feet is a slushy hollow by the bank of a noisome
canal :—

> They cowered together, the man and crone,
> Two old bags of carious bone ;
> They and a mangy cur alone.
>
> Ragged, haggard, filthy both ;
> Viewing each the other loath ;
> Growling now and then an oath.

The woman proposes that they should put an end to
their misery by plunging into the "green scum" of
the water, but the man cannot muster the requisite
courage :—

> He sat still, nipping spiteful blows
> On the snarling cur's amorphous nose,
> Relishing faintly her propose.
>
> " This here damned life is bad enough,
> But say we smother in that stuff,
> Our next life's only worse; you muff."

So the argument goes on, point by point, till at last
the woman plunges in and disappears, while the man
rushes to his gin-bottle, in the hope of at least nerv-
ing himself to die dead-drunk, though he dare not
die sober.   A *deus ex machinâ* is now provided in

the shape of the dog, who opportunely goes mad, and, seizing his master, causes him to take the step at which he had so long hesitated, thus bringing the controversy to a decisive conclusion :—

> It haled him to the festering dike,
> So all sank dead in its calm alike,
> The Man, the Woman, the virtuous Tyke.

Grotesque as the subject may sound when thus briefly stated, the poem, when studied in full, will impress the reader as a very singular production for a youth of twenty-five, and as showing quite another phase of Thomson's genius. The most puzzling thing about it is, to my mind, the title ; for there does not seem to be any valid reason why it should be called a "Vision of Sin," nor does it bear any obvious relation to Tennyson's poem of that name. On the other hand, it *is* closely connected with Tennyson's "Two Voices," the metre being the same throughout, as also is the subject of the two poems, which is in both cases a dialogue on the right and wrong of suicide, the conclusions arrived at being of course diametrically opposite. I cannot help thinking that Thomson's poem was in reality meant as a burlesque on Tennyson's "Two Voices," to which the expression "very pretty and clever and silly and truthless," as used by a pessimist, is far more applicable than to the "Vision of Sin." This view is further strengthened by the fact that in the "City of Dreadful Night" (section viii.) there are five or six stanzas in the same metre, which are certainly inspired by Tennyson's "Two Voices." May we not therefore surmise that the present title of "A Real Vision of Sin" was given to it by a slip of mind, which was the more

R

likely to pass uncorrected as the poem remained in
manuscript till after the author's death ?

In the *London Investigator* of 1858 there are some
characteristic lines by Thomson satirising that pseudo-
religious spirit. (always particularly odious to him)
which groans over the sinfulness of unregenerate
human nature and leaves the hard work of life to
other hands. " Mr. Save-his-soul-alive-o " is the hero
of the poem, which is " dedicated without permission
to the Rev. Ebenezer Grimes and the Rev. Habakkuk
Sinfulman, of Little Bethel." Life is represented as
a storm-tossed vessel drifting on a savage sea, and
the poet remonstrates with "Mr. Save-his-soul-alive-o"
for idly croaking and crying while the rest of those
on board are putting forth their utmost strength :—

> Are sighs and groanings needed to swell
>   This great dead wind, whose pitiless blasts
> With enormous swoop and savage yell
>   Come clutching our poor thin masts ?

" Virtue and Vice " (1865), included by Thomson
in his first volume of poems, is a piece of keen and
sparkling satire on a particular form of female conventional piety. It describes two characters, that of
a godless husband and that of an over-godly wife :—

> She was so good and he was so bad :
> A very pretty time they had !
> A pretty time, and it lasted long :
> Which of the two was more in the wrong ?
> He befouled in the slough of sin ;
> Or she whose piety pushed him in ? . . .
> So she grew holier day by day,
> While he grew all the other way.
> She left him ; she had done her part
> To wean from sin his sinful heart,
> But all in vain ; her presence might
> Make him a murderer some mad night.

> Her family took her back, pure saint,
> Serene in soul, above complaint ;
> The narrow path she strictly trod,
> And went in triumph home to God :
> While he into the Union fell,
> Our half-way house on the road to Hell.
> With which would you rather pass your life,
> The wicked husband or saintly wife ?

This same idea of anxiety to save one's own soul is yet again satirised by Thomson, though this time from a somewhat different standpoint, in an epigram quoted in Mr. Dobell's *Memoir* :—

> Once in a saintly passion
>   I cried with desperate grief,
> " O Lord, my heart is black with guile,
>   Of sinners I am chief."
> Then stooped my guardian angel,
>   And whispered from behind,
> " Vanity, my little man,
>   You're nothing of the kind."

Last, but not least, among the humorous poems, there remains to be noticed the " Pilgrimage to St. Nicotine of the Holy Herb " (1878), a burlesque of some seven hundred lines in mock-Chaucerian style, written to accompany and explain a large coloured plate published in connection with *Cope's Tobacco Plant*. This plate is a parody on Stothard's " Canterbury Pilgrims," and represents various well-known characters of the day, whether politicians, churchmen, artists, or poets, thronging in pilgrimage to the shrine of the saint of tobacco. To write a poetical commentary on this picture was a task for which Thomson, himself a poet, humorist, and inveterate smoker, was excellently qualified.

The poem is divided into two parts, the first of

which describes and characterises each of the pilgrims
in a few brief and picturesque touches, while the
second relates at some length the story of the martyrdom of the saintly Nicotine.   This narrative, though
partly a burlesque on ecclesiastical martyrology, is
told in poetical style, with much felicity of expression,
and deserves to be known by heart by all devoted
smokers.   The process of martyrdom is an idealised
description of the preparation of the tobacco-plant,
—an idea doubtless suggested by Burns's "John
Barleycorn."

> They first exposed him in the open air
> To stand long days and nights unmoving there ;
> Then scalped him as their Indian custom was,
> And pinced out pieces from his sides, alas !
> And still he smiled with more benignitie
> Upon these cruel men, ah, woe is me !
> They cut his legs from under him the while
> He stood regarding them with that sweet smile ;
> Then he was hanged, immitigable Fates !
> Then taken down and crushed with monstrous weights ;
> And when the body was all mummy-dry
> They cut the backbone out, oh fie ! oh fie !
> Then shred down all the flesh as we may shred
> A salted ox-tongue, poor dear body dead !
> And of the morsels some they ground to dust,
> And snuffed it with an eager savage lust ;
> And some they put in censers to consume
> To ashes, and inhaled with joy the fume ;
> And some these horrid cannibals did bite
> And chew and savour with a wild delight :
> Such were some tortures of this sweetest Saint,
> Whose mere recital makes us sick and faint.

Before his death the martyr foretells to his
destroyers how the "Herb of Holy Grace" shall
spring from the scene of his martyrdom and become
a boon and blessing to men of every nation.   At first

his words are discredited and forgotten, but when they are seen to be realised in the virtues of tobacco, then the canonisation of Nicotine is universally accepted.

> But when they found his marvellous prophecy,
> Incredible for gloriousness, no lie,
> But in its every word the solid truth ;
> Then joy and sorrow, then delight and ruth,
> Then love and anguish, triumph and remorse,
> Then wailings for the unexistent corse :
> For it is verily a law of Fate
> Repentance evermore must come too late ;
> Since what is done may never be undone
> Till backward on his pathway rolls the sun ;
> Since that which hath been as it was must last,
> Nor gods themselves have power upon the Past.
> Then they adored his Name as one divine,
> And eke the Plant his symbol and his sign ;
> And evermore its fragrant incense rose
> In mild propitiation for his woes.

I have now said enough about this class of Thomson's poems to show that he at any rate possessed a keen sense of humour, and could write, when he was so minded, with no lack of satirical and incisive severity—a quality of which we shall have further proof when we examine the prose essays.

III. *Translations.* Before closing this chapter, it remains to say a few words about the translations. Many of Thomson's versions from Heine's "Buch der Lieder" appeared originally in the *Secularist*, and several of these were collected and reprinted, under the title of "Attempts at Translation from Heine," in the volume which contained the "City of Dreadful Night;" while a few others may be found scattered among the other writings. The following extracts from Thomson's own opinions on the subject of poetical translation, as recorded by him in some MS. notes, are interesting as showing the principle on which he worked.

I hold that while adequate translation of any long poem is impossible, some short poems may be adequately translated. In attempting to translate various short poems it is not wise to confine oneself throughout to any one system; some admit of almost literal translation, others may be reproduced faithfully as to the spirit, with free disregard of the letter. If a lover of poetry who is ignorant of the original does not care for the translation, the translation is certainly a failure, whether necessarily or by the incompetence of the translator. He, however skilful, who sets out to translate each and every poem of a long collection will assuredly do many of them badly. If each translator would attempt only his chief favourites in the collection, and of these only such as favour him beforehand with glimpses of a happy version, all the best pieces in the collection would get well translated in time. . . . From the well-chosen attempts of various translators, a really valuable anthology might be collected by a gardener who did not fear to engraft and prune and transplant. The system, based upon jealousy and selfishness, by which each translator must make the version of any piece wholly his own, even when fully conscious that some predecessor has given the best possible rendering of certain portions thereof, makes consummate translations far more rare than they ought to be. . . . I consider it a rule with very rare exceptions that a translation, to avoid utter failure, must conform to the metre of the original, and run stanza for stanza with it. A paraphrase or dilution of the original is worse than nothing at all, sacred to noodles, a graft from the "Tree of Knowledge" in the "Paradise of Fools."

As a translator of poems of which the essential charm and grace must be regarded as well-nigh

untranslatable, Thomson has fared better than others
who have attempted the same task; though his
translations, viewed solely as English poems, cannot,
I think, be compared for brilliancy and power with
his own original productions.   In a letter addressed
to Thomson, shortly after the publication of his first
volume, Dr. Karl Marx expressed his delight at the
versions from Heine, which he described as "no
translation, but a reproduction of the original, such
as Heine himself, if master of the English language,
would have given."   Here is a fairly typical specimen
—the well-known " Loreley :"—

I know not what *evil is coming*,
 But my heart feels sad and cold ;
A song in my head keeps humming,
 A tale from the times of old.

The air is fresh and it darkles,
 And smoothly flows the Rhine ;
The peak of the mountain sparkles
 In the fading sunset-shine.

The loveliest wonderful Maiden
 On high is sitting there,
With golden jewels *braiden*,
 And she combs her golden hair.

With a golden comb sits combing,
 And ever the while sings she
A marvellous song *through the gloaming*
 Of magical melody.

It hath caught the boatman, and bound him
 In the spell of a wild sad *love ;*
He sees not the rocks around him,
 He sees only her above.

The waves through the pass *sweep swinging*,
 But boatman or boat is none ;
And this with her mighty singing
 The Loreley hath done.

If these stanzas be compared with the German they will be found to be a tolerably faithful rendering both of sense and rhythm, except in the words I have italicised, where a new idea has been substituted for the original, or an addition made in order to get the required length of line.

In addition to his poetical versions from Heine, Thomson translated Novalis's " Hymns to Night " (still in MS.), and most of the " Dialogues " of Leopardi, some of which appeared in the *National Reformer* during 1867 and 1868, while the rest, which are partly rough drafts, are as yet unpublished.   A well-known critic and accomplished Italian scholar has spoken of Thomson's published translations from Leopardi as executed " with extraordinary felicity," * and as worthy of republication in more permanent form.

---

* *Encyclopædia Britannica ; art.* " Leopardi."

CHAPTER XI.

PROSE WRITINGS:

ESSAYS, SATIRES, CRITICISM.

It is my intention in this chapter to study a few of
the most important and characteristic of Thomson's
essays, satires, and literary critiques ; to deal at all
fully with the bulk of his prose writings would be
beyond the scope of the present work, since, in
addition to the collected essays, there are a great
many prose pieces of various kinds lying temporarily
hidden in the columns of the journals where they first
appeared. These uncollected articles are to a considerable extent merely biographical notices written for
journalistic purposes, reviews of new books, political
jottings, and the like ; but even in Thomson's most
ephemeral work there is generally something that
renders it worthy of preservation. It is a noticeable
fact that the period of Thomson's best prose corresponds with that of his best poetry, the majority of his
first-class essays and satires bearing dates between
1862 and 1875. The "seven songless years" that
followed this period, though marked by the production
of much useful and graceful literary writing, were for
the most part destitute, in prose as in poetry, of any
works of high creative effort or striking originality.
Let us now proceed to a consideration of the prose

writings, which can be conveniently grouped under three heads, as essays, satires, and criticism.

I. The essays may be subdivided, according to the nomenclature which Thomson himself adopted in the prose volume issued by him in 1881, into Essays and Phantasies. Of the essays proper, the first which claims attention is that on " Open Secret Societies " (1865). The "open-secret" societies are those natural and spiritual affinities which bind together kindred souls in a voluntary and self-made confraternity, as contrasted with the artificial secret-societies organised by human ingenuity. The leading idea of the essay is that belief in the immutability of nature which was an integral part of Thomson's philosophy, resulting partly from his necessitarian creed, and partly from his intense love of individuality—the only "societies" for which he could feel the slightest respect being those which are intuitive, natural, and self-constituted.

After touching briefly on the necessary and inevitable failure, according to his judgment, of all such artificial associations as are secretly framed from time to time in order to further some special object in religion, politics, or warfare (this part of the argument is perhaps not very cogent, but serves its purpose in acting as a foil to the rest), he proceeds to speak of the genuine secret societies, which are the main subject of the essay. They are shown to be *open*, since there is no ceremonial of admission ; they are *secret*, since none but those who are foreordained can ever obtain admission to their mysteries.

Their members are affiliated for life and death in the instant of being born ; without ceremonies of initiation,

without sponsorial oaths of fidelity. Their bond of union
is a natural affinity, quite mysterious in its principles and
elements, precise and assured in its results as the combina-
tion and proportion of oxygen and hydrogen in water, or
oxygen and nitrogen in air. No spy or traitor, no unworthy
or uncongenial brother, can obtain entrance among them,
any more than a hemlock or a lily can be adopted into the
family of the roses, any more than an ape or a tiger can
pass as one of a herd of elephants. Their esoteric doctrines are the most spontaneous and independent thoughts
of each and every of their members ; their secret watch-
words are the most free and public expressions of their
members ; their mysterious signals are telegraphed in the
most careless gestures which all eyes can see. The watch-
words and symbols change from generation to generation,
the supreme secrets are immutable from the beginning to
the end of Time.

Having thus defined the general nature of the
" open-secret societies," the essayist deals with five
particular classes—those of the Heroes, Saints, Philosophers, Poets, Mystics—and with their respective
parodies or counterfeits. The true-born Heroes
are they who feel, by a natural instinct, that in the
whole range of the universe there is nothing, out of
himself, that a man need fear ; the pseudo-heroes
are " the armies of the nations, those elaborate
artificial organisations or aggregations, whose spirit
and tradition are popularly supposed to be heroism."
The Saints are they who know, and live up to the
knowledge, that love is the one supreme duty and
good ; of which saintly societies the Churches, with
their canonised pontiffs and patriarchs, are the "solemn
artificial burlesques." The Philosophers are the few
men who have realised that " silent and pure and

eternal, above the fleeting noisy world, with its agitation of action and passion, rests the sphere of intellect, the realm of ideas ; " the sham-philosophers are the noisy sophists and self-seeking professors, who, in our universities and colleges and schools, win themselves high reputations and big salaries by building up complicated systems of philosophical rubbish. The Poets are they who, listening to the music of Nature, "are able partially to reproduce its rhythms and cadences in the language of men ; " and the parodists of this class are the subtle rhymesters who win worldly honour and renown by their clever imitation of the true poetic melody. Thomson's remarks on this subject are particularly interesting, as showing that, in his heart of hearts, he felt himself to belong to the genuine brotherhood of poets. There is much significance in the contrast he draws between the poetaster and poet, especially in the words I have italicised :—

For many of them can copy with marvellous adroitness the rhythm and rhymes and melodious phrases which are much loved by the true brotherhood, so that not only by others, but also by themselves, they are believed to be genuine bards. But when one who is initiate hears or reads their productions, he discerns that they are as fair bodies without souls ; for the music and splendour of infinity are not within them, and they are utterly unrelated to eternity. Many, however, who are not learned and who are quite without profitable talents, shepherd youths and farm maidens, *men in great cities who will never get on in the world*, rude mountaineers familiar with sounding storms, sailors with the rhythm of the ocean-tides in their blood, can hear this undertone of the cosmic harmony, and see this light transfiguring the world, and enter with these true Poets into the mysterious trance; and are thus, even though they know it not, real members of this high confraternity.

Finally, the members of the society of the Mystics, which is less liable to be parodied than the rest, are declared to be " the very flower and crown of the four already touched upon, Saints of Saints, Heroes of Heroes, Philosophers of Philosophers, Poets of Poets." The whole of this essay on " Open Secret Societies" is remarkable, not only for its literary beauty, but also for the insight it gives us into Thomson's philosophical creed. The supremacy of natural law and the consequent folly of proselytism were two of his most cherished tenets.

The essay on " Sympathy," also written in 1865, is another of Thomson's most powerful prose writings, and full of subtle analysis of certain mental phenomena. Its general purport is to show that true sympathy, which cannot exist without intense and comprehensive imagination, is much more rare than is commonly supposed ; since to *feel with* another person, in the sense of realising *his* emotions as if they were one's own, is a quality which only the greatest of men possess. It is argued that this quality is seldom discoverable in acts of charity or acts of friendship, however commendable these may be, and that it is for this reason that the people who are most energetic in charitable works are, from lack of imagination, often very unsympathetic. Their practical beneficence may shame the common sentimentalists ; yet nevertheless the uncommon sentimentalists, the men and women who are really sympathetic, are judged to be of a still higher type. The further question is then raised—how far a man can really sympathise with his past self; and this leads to an inquiry whether there is, in any true sense, a continuity of the *ego*. Amidst the varying moods and creeds of a lifetime, how far can a man's personal identity be said to be maintained? No definite conclusion is arrived at, but the idea suggested is, that the conviction of continuous personality is not a necessary or obvious truth.

It is true that the interior personal memory is not continually continuous. At one time, when we look along the line, many of the beads are out of sight; there seem great gaps. At another time these gaps are glittering with jewels, and there are gaps where before gleamed beads. Hence we all feel that the seeming gaps are but loops and festoons; and that if the line be drawn tense enough, every one of the thick-strung beads will be ranged visible on its straightness. Just so we feel that the moods and phases of our being for which we do not care at the present moment, will have their turn of domination as they have had many turns before, will be really ourselves in their time. As our so-called sympathy with others is mainly not a *feeling with* them, but the result of an intellectual algebraic process; so our sympathy with our past selves is mainly not an identical *feeling with* the various past phases of our being, but a result of a complicated personal experience and memory, the most striking fact in the domain of the association of ideas.

It may be said, therefore, that this essay, like the last-mentioned, is inspired by Thomson's intense individuality of temperament. As in "Open Secret Societies," he insisted on the unalterable distinction of species, so in "Sympathy" he insists on the equally marked distinction of the individual, existing independently in each successive mood.

"Indolence, a Moral Essay," (1867), is yet another illustration of Thomson's hatred of that spirit of busybodyism and proselytism which would interfere with the natural bent of the individual mind. It is a eulogy of Indolence, in the sense of pure spiritual quietude, as opposed to restlessness and the gospel of work for the mere sake of self-occupation. He first gives definitions of various types of idlers, some, as he admits, blameworthy; others, as he claims, commendable; this leads to what is really the vital part of the essay, viz., the justification of the seventh class, the "idlers by faith." These are they who look with sorrowing pity on the fussiness of fads and missions, themselves content to enjoy life and leave the world in the hands of the Providence or Nature that rules it. We feel that these "idlers by faith" are the class to which Thomson himself, as the author of the "Lord of the Castle of Indolence," undoubtedly belongs; and it is therefore interesting to find him making a direct reference, under this head, to his own pessimistic philosophy :—

Let me note that the faith which is the root of indolence in this class may be of despair instead of assurance, of pessimism instead of optimism. It may be a profound and immutable belief in the absolute tyranny of blind fate, in the utter vanity of all efforts to assuage or divert the operation of the inexorable laws of the universe. The difference, however, as regards our subject, is intellectual merely, not essential. The spiritual root is the same in both, though the one bears blossoms of mystical ravishment under the heaven of Providence, and the other dark leaves of oracular Stoicism under the iron vault of Destiny.

In this essay Thomson teaches with equal force

and delicacy a truth which is too apt to be overlooked
in these busy times ; a truth on which Sydney Smith
insisted many years ago, and which was the keynote
of Thoreau's gospel.   "Except in those rare cases,"
he says, "where sudden supreme emergencies demand
supreme raptures of uncalculated toil, I admire the
work of no man who is not working within himself,
superior to his work."   In other words, work for the
sake of work is not a good but an evil ; it is as great
an error to ignore the claims of leisure as to ignore
the claims of business ; and we should think twice
before either condemning or praising any man on the
score of indolence.

His indolence may be worthy of condemnation (if indeed
anything in any man can be worthy of condemnation by
any other man or by himself) ; or it may be the quietude
of a spirit cherishing profound thought, supreme faith, ideal
beauty.   Speaking down to our common tea-table level of
morality, since on no other level is the world likely to
heed or hear a word one says, and leaving aside the
drudgery for daily bread, I would put it that on the one
hand no indolence is to be praised which involves conscious
shirking and sneaking, with fear more or less definite of
the consequences ; and, on the other hand, no industry is to
be praised which involves fussing and fuming, and usurps
dominion over the general nature of the worker.

With this essay on " Indolence " may be compared
"A National Reformer in the Dog Days" (1869),
which repeats the same doctrines in a lighter and
more humorous form.

Turning now to the Phantasies, we find that the
longest and most important of these is "A Lady of
Sorrow" (1862–1864), to the third part of which I
have already alluded as being almost the prose

counterpart of the "City of Dreadful Night," though it was written ten years earlier. "The triune Lady of Sorrow," says Thomson, in his Introductory Note, "must have been derived from De Quincey, whose influence is obvious in other respects." The reference is, of course, to the three Ladies of Sorrow in De Quincey's "Suspiria de Profundis;" and this common origin accounts for the close resemblance between the prose "Lady of Sorrow" and the poem "To our Ladies of Death," which bears almost the same date.

"A Lady of Sorrow" is the most elaborate and stately of all Thomson's prose writings; it is indeed rather a prose-poem than a mere essay, being full of sublime symbolism and sombre imagery, and not unworthy to be classed with the most impressive of De Quincey's dream-fugues, to which it is closely related in tone and expression. I have already quoted several passages from the Introductory Note, which is full of autobiographical interest; "my friend Vane," to whom the essay is attributed, being, of course, identical with the author of "Vane's Story." The three successive stages of grief, which are described in the three parts of "A Lady of Sorrow," are also an allegorical record of Thomson's own sufferings, and should be carefully studied by those readers who wish to understand the course of his pessimistic thought. The first form which his sorrow takes is that of "The Angel," typical of a pensive and hallowed grief—a grief transfigured into the image of his lost love.

For she was simply the image in beatitude of her who died so young. The pure girl was become the angel; the sheathed wings had unfolded in the favourable clime, the vesture was radiantly white with the whiteness of her soul,

S

the long hair was a dazzling golden glory round the ever-young head, the blue eyes had absorbed celestial light in the cloudless empyrean ; but still, thus developed and beatified, she was only the more intensely and supremely herself; more perfectly revealed to me, more intimately known and more passionately loved by me, than when she had walked the earth in the guise of a mortal.   She would take me by the hand, sometimes impressing a kiss, which was an ample anodyne, upon my world-weary brow, and lead me away floating calmly through the infinite height and depth and breadth, from galaxy to galaxy, from silver star to star.

This rhapsody of trust in God and glorified sorrow is succeeded by the domination of " the Siren," representative of a cynical, voluptuous, ignoble grief, which, instead of soaring through the heavens, sinks into unknown depths, and learns gradually to distrust both God and man.

Such was the enchantment now wrought upon me by my spell-bound Enchantress.   For she was always with me, though she assumed now rarely, and ever more rarely until never, the holy guise of an angel.   When fresh from the consecration of bereavement I was found worthy to be comforted with angelic communion ; but as in the course of time the virtue of that consecration from without was exhausted, while yet I had not by its blessing attained inward self-consecration, my ignoble heart found ignobler companionship. . . . And this Siren sorrow was the saddest I have ever known ; for she affected—nay, frantically endeavoured—to renounce, to defy, to ignore her own essential sorrowfulness, expressing a wine of mad intoxication from the berries of her deadly night-shade.

It will not escape notice that these two phases of grief, the Angel and the Siren, correspond respectively to the two first aspects of death in "Our Ladies of Death," viz., our Lady of Beatitudes and our Lady of Annihilation. As in that poem the final form of Thomson's creed was represented by our Lady of Oblivion, who, in her complete freedom from either hope or terror, stands midway between her two predecessors; so in this prose phantasy the third and final shape assumed by sorrow is that of "the Shadow," less comforting than the Angel, but also less terrible than the Siren. The Shadow is in fact the symbol of the calm, hopeless, passionless gloom of confirmed pessimism; and this third part of "A Lady of Sorrow" is therefore the key to the right understanding of the "City of Dreadful Night," which it anticipates not only in its general conception, but also in its detailed pictures of the great and terrible City, with multitudes of doleful inhabitants, gloomy streets, twinkling lamps, and din of endless vehicles; and still further in its strange notion of the colossal statue of the Melencolia, "a vast black shape dwarfing the Cyclopean rock-wall behind it." *

At first she used to lead me, and still she often leads me, hour after hour of dusk and night, through the interminable streets of this great and terrible city. The ever-streaming multitudes of men and women and children, mysterious fellow-creatures of whom I know only that they *are* my fellow-creatures—and even this knowledge is sometimes darkened and dubious—overtake and pass me, meet and pass me; the inexhaustible processions of vehicles rattle and roar in the midst; lamp beyond lamp, and far clusters of lamps burn yellow above the paler cross-shimmer from brilliant shops, or funereally measure the long vistas of still streets, or portentously surround the black gulphs of

---

* *Cf.* Page 227-228.

squares and graveyards silent; lofty churches uplift themselves, blank, soulless, sepulchral, the pyramids of this
mournful desert, each conserving the mummy of a great
king in its heart; the sky overhead lowers vague and
obscure; the moon and stars, when visible, shine with alien
coldness, or are as wan earthly spectres, not radiant rejoicing spheres whose home is in the heavens beyond the
firmament. The continuous thunders, swelling, subsiding,
resurgent, the innumerable processions, confound and over-
whelm my spirit, until, as of old, I cannot believe myself
walking awake in a substantial city among real persons.

The poet and his companion Sorrow, who has now
become a "formless shadow," no longer soar or sink,
but wander slowly about the world and note the
mortality of all things, all the tribes of men being
seen in perpetual motion, but moving only towards
death. The rest of the Phantasy is taken up with a
quotation of some of the "anthem-words" of sorrow,
consisting of pessimistic passages from great poets
and prose-writers, and with the sermon addressed by
the Shadow to her worshippers, which may be regarded as a kind of panegyric of pessimism, similar
to that uttered by the Preacher in the cathedral, in
one of the most powerful sections of the "City of
Dreadful Night."

The three remaining Phantasies are all concerned
with the eve of the New Year, a time which possessed
a peculiar attraction for Thomson, being, as he described it, a night "potent with sleeping visions as
with waking reveries; a night that looks back to the
past and forward to the future; a night pregnant with
phantasy." These Old and New Year visions are
somewhat similar, in form and method of narration, to
that which has already been mentioned as the subject

of one of the political poems, " The Dead Year." The
earliest of the three, " A Walk Abroad " (1866), which
describes an imaginary visit to Mercury and the other
planets, after the manner of some of Edgar Poe's fantastic tales, is comparatively trifling and unimportant ;
but the two later pieces are written in Thomson's
best style, and are full of real feeling. " The Fair of
St. Sylvester " (1875) is a sort of prose reproduction
of " Vane's Story," which it resembles both in the
outline of the narrative and in the tone of mingled
humour and pathos by which it is pervaded. The
poet, sitting in a reverie by his fireside on the last
evening of the year, is surprised by the appearance of
a spirit-visitor, " the beautiful "—so he describes her
—" the ever-young, who is so gracious and loving
when it pleases her to visit me, who is so capricious
and cruel in keeping away altogether for weeks and
months, however sorely I need and earnestly suppli-
cate her presence." This Lady of the vision seems
to be the personification partly of the Muse, the
patroness of the poet, and partly of that same lost love
who plays so important a part in " Vane's Story."
She chides him for his drowsiness in thus sleeping
by the fire ; and going forth together into the cold
clear night, they enter a sleigh and drive to the scene
of the Fair. Thomson has drawn many charming
pictures of summer scenes by lake, river, and sea-
shore, but scarcely anything more magically picturesque
than this weird wintry drive.

In an instant we were in the open air. There attended
us a sleigh, curved like a sea-shell for grace, poised like a
butterfly for lightness, heaped with thick skins barred and
starred, the robes of the hot fierce life of the tropics to
envelop us in the frigid north ; with two small fleet horses,

full of fire, whose champing kept their multitude of bells
in continual silver chime. Mounting, we sank and muffled
ourselves in the furs; my Lady took the reins, and we sped
away ringing through the night. . . . Ere long I found that
we were racing down the broad clear aisle of a pine-forest,
the firm snow crunching under us, and the keen stars
racing with us over the black-rushing trees, whose snows
freely powdered us as we passed. Nor were we alone. To
right and left, behind and before, sleigh-bells were merrily
ringing; down all the parallel glades these cars of the snow
were gliding; we outstripped hundreds on either hand, we
outstripped scores on our own pathway: none could keep
up with us, so gallantly we flew. Coming to the broad
arm of a lake, we skimmed across it, one of many; and the
stars, which had been flying with us, glimpsed through the
vanishing hair of the pine-trees, now fell back from us;
rolled rearward with their deep blue immensity of sky.
Then again we ran among the pines, all resonant with
bells as other woods are resonant with birds in June; and
sweetlier resonant with clear young voices and laughter,
so that never were woods so vocal even in leafy June.

Coming to an open space where St. Sylvester's
Fair is being celebrated, they dismount from the
sleigh, and stroll among the crowds of barterers and
pleasure-seekers. Then follows a rather mystical
description of two colossal figures, the symbols apparently of Fate and Hope; the one "a great calm
Oriental figure, serenely smoking an enormous pipe,
the clouds from its lips flowing forth grey and dim
against the surrounding light;" the other "a great
serene child, thoughtfully blowing bubbles from such
another pipe, and they floated off large and splendid
as luminous balloons against the surrounding light."
The advent of the New Year having been proclaimed
by sound of trumpets, the poet and his Lady exchange

gifts, she giving him the Pipe of Peace, with great store of Tobacco of Content, and he purchasing for her "a golden bracelet, a Serpent of Eternity, with carbuncle eyes, and a certain Name enamelled within." They re-enter the sleigh and start on their homeward drive, the poet waking to find himself alone in his study.

And that the visit of my Lady and our travel and the Fair were not a dream, I have proof positive ; for here on the table is the Pipe of Peace she gave me, together with the sweet Tobacco of Content, even such as is never found in earthly jars ; while it is clear that I bought for her the bracelet, since of the money I had by a rare miracle in my pocket, there are but a few shillings left.

"In our Forest of the Past" (1877), which differs from the preceding Phantasies in dealing not with personal subjects, but with the universal sorrows of mankind, is full of evidence of the depth and tenderness of Thomson's compassion for human suffering. The poet, falling into a trance on New Year's Eve, dreams that he visits a gloomy forest, "even the forest of the past which is dead," led by a mysterious guide, "tall and stately, and muffled in darkness." In this forest they see various classes of sufferers, the ghosts of those who have led a life of suffering — young children, bereaved lovers ; the halt, the maimed, the insane ; the victims of poverty, tyranny, and war : the dupes of asceticism, superstition, money-making, ambition, and power. As they go forward continually "from moaning to moaning," the poet inquires and learns of his guide the causes of the various scenes of misery they see before them, the answer in each case concluding with the reiterated words, "they moan

their frustrate lives." Then follows the other side of
the vision, a brief picture of the Elysium of happy
souls ; a blissful oblivion contrasted with a sorrowful
reminiscence.

And we turned to the right and went down through the
wood, leaving the moanings behind us ; and we came to a
broad valley through which a calm stream rippled toward
the moon, now risen on our left hand large and golden in a
dim emerald sky, dim with transfusion of splendour ; and
her light fell and overflowed a level underledge of softest
yellow cloud, and filled all the valley with a luminous mist,
warm as mild sunshine, and quivered golden on the far
river-reaches ; and elsewhere above us the immense sweep
of pale azure sky throbbed with golden stars ; and a wonderful mystical peace as of trance and enchantment possessed
all the place. And in the meadows of deep grass, where
the perfume of violets mingled with the magical moonlight,
by the river, whose slow sway and lapse might lull their
repose, we found tranquil sleepers, all with a light on their
faces, all with a smile on their lips. And my leader said :
Their wine was pure, and the goblet full ; they drank it
and were content ; . . . and therefore they now sleep placidly
the sleep that is eternal ; and the smile upon their lips, and
the light in shadow from beneath their eyelids, tell that they
dream for ever some calm, happy dream ; they enjoy unre-
membering the fruit of their perfect lives.

The close of " In our Forest of the Past " is remarkable as containing almost the only passage in
Thomson's writings where a belief in the possibility
of human progress is distinctly hinted at, and where,
in direct contradiction to the general drift of his doctrine, Man, and not Nature, is declared to be responsible for the burden of human suffering.

And I said : How few are these in their quiet bliss

to all the countless moaning multitudes we have seen
on our way! And my companion answered: They are
very few. And I sighed: Must it be always so? And
he responded: Did Nature destroy all those infants?
did Nature breed all those defects and deformities? did
Nature bring forth all those idiocies and lunacies? or,
was not rather their chief destroyer and producer the
ignorance of Man outraging Nature? And the poor, the
prisoners, the soldiery, the ascetics, the priests, the nobles,
the kings; were these the work of Nature, or of the perversity of Man? And I asked: Were not the very ignorance
and perversity of Man also from Nature? And he replied:
Yea; yet perchance, putting himself childlike to school, he
may gradually learn from Nature herself to enlighten the
one and control the other.

II. The most considerable, though hardly the most
brilliant, of Thomson's Satires is the " Proposals for
the Speedy Extinction of Evil and Misery " (1868–
1871), a burlesque on the Utopian views of those
sanguine philanthropists who contemplate the speedy
reformation of the world. The Satire reminds the
reader in several ways of the style of Swift, being
expressed with the same remorseless, caustic humour
and sustained irony, and entering into the same
deliberate minuteness of detail in the elaboration of
the schemes proposed, even to the extent of becoming at times overdrawn and wearisome. The idea
that animates the whole work is Thomson's cardinal
belief in the immutability of natural laws, and the
consequent absurdity of attempting to improve away
defects of race and character which are innate and
organic ; but in order to give freer play to his irony,
he affects to be treating the question from the contrary
standpoint, and writes as if with the enthusiasm of

one who believes himself to be possessed of a solution of the great mystery of evil. The " proposal " which he makes is " simply a universal change to perfection of nature and human nature." A committee of three persons is to be appointed, as a nucleus of the " Universal Perfection Company, Unlimited ; " and this Company will proceed to the reformation, first of mankind, then of Nature ; the details of which process are set forth and explained with much precision of statement. The objections that might possibly be raised against this scheme are then considered and answered, especially the important one that we cannot extirpate evil until we know the cause. We here recognise the very essence of Thomson's agnostic creed.

This great river of human Time which comes flowing down thick with filth and blood from the immemorial past, surely cannot be thoroughly cleansed by any purifying process applied to it here in the present; for the pollution, if not at its very source (supposing it has a source) or deriving from unimaginable remotenesses of eternity indefinitely beyond its source, at any rate interfused with it countless ages back, and is perennial as the river itself. This immense poison-tree of Life, with its leaves of illusion, blossoms of delirium, apples of destruction, surely cannot be made wholesome and sweet by anything we may do to the branchlets and twigs on which, poor insects, we find ourselves crawling, or to the leaves and fruit on which we must fain feed ; for the venom is drawn up in the sap by the tap-roots plunged in abysmal depths of the past. This toppling and sinking house wherein we dwell cannot be firmly re-established, save by re-establishing from its lowest foundation upwards. In fine, *to thoroughly reform the present and the future we must thoroughly reform the past.*

After ironically suggesting a method for surmounting this difficulty which he believed to be insurmountable, Thomson concludes by giving some humorous reasons to account for his not practising this "simple perfecting process" on *himself.*

"Bumble, Bumbledom, Bumbleism" (1865) is Thomson's fullest and most vigorous protest against a power with which he was in conflict from the beginning to the end of his career, and to which he owed not a little of his obscurity and ill-fortune. Bumble is identified in Thomson's Satire not merely with Officialism, but with all the respectability, orthodoxy, and comfortable self-seeking worldliness of English life. Here is Bumble's portrait, drawn by one who had studied his features with unusual attention :—

His carriage is erect, and he moves with a slow pomp, for well he knoweth that he is a chief pillar of the State, and that there is not an institution in the realm more ancient and honourable than he. For he is more truly essential to the sanctity of the cathedral than the Dean himself, more necessary to the stability of the bank than are the chairman and all the other directors. His reverence for the rich and powerful is in exact ratio to his scorn for the poor and mean. . . . He reverences the rich because they *are* rich, and because people get rich by leading model lives, by being through many years frugal, industrious, sober, discreet, and orthodox. He scorns the poor because they *are* poor, because poverty is odious in itself; and because, if indeed it is not a crime in itself, it is at any rate the fruit and symbol of vice, the outward and visible sign of an inward and spiritual disgrace ; for people get poor by being reckless, improvident, lazy, dissolute, enthusiastic, heterodox, and generally by flying in the face of the world.

Bumble is further identified with that dulness at which Pope struck in his "Dunciad." He is described as not naturally malignant, but stirred to exceeding wrath by one thing above all others—the promulgation of a new opinion. For this reason he is careful to hold the Press and Literature (which by a strange fallacy are regarded as being "free") under the heavy and depressing dominion of his purse, the power of *not buying* giving him a more than imperial authority. He may thus be regarded as a kind of Fate, a rock on which the waves of thought break vainly year by year. Finally, the author avows himself one of those literary desperadoes and free-lances who alone may venture to speak disrespectfully of Bumble, simply because, having nothing to hope from him, they have also nothing to fear.

One is very free, with no name to lose; and one is freer still, with such a name that it cannot possibly be lost for a worse; and, between us, we possess both these happy freedoms. Thus have I written my own condemnation, immolating myself, as well it behoves me, beneath the irresistible Triumphal Car of our great, our divine Juggernaut—Bumble.

In his burlesques on what he considered the "aggressive absurdities of theology" (some of which have been collected and published in a posthumous volume entitled "Satires and Profanities") Thomson made a still more daring inroad into the enemies' camp, and "immolated himself" still more ungrudgingly on behalf of the principles he held dear. It is not my intention to quote passages from these Lucianic satires, these "outbursts of Rabelasian laughter,"

as Thomson called them ; because, while the bulk
of his poetry and prose may be appreciated by men
holding every variety of opinion, these particular
writings were primarily intended for a special class
of readers, and would certainly be misunderstood by
the rest.   But as these Heine-like productions are
full of keen literary and satirical power, and as they
have been used, and may again be used, by hostile
critics to create prejudice against their author, it
may not be amiss to quote the justification which
Thomson himself advanced for the employment of
this style of satire.   In a spirited article on the
Saturday Review, parts of which were republished in
" Satires and Profanities " under the title of " A Word
on Blasphemy," he insists that Christians have no right
to claim for their religion a special immunity from
ridicule while they themselves deliberately mock at
the old pagan mythology and at the agnostic philo-
sophies of modern times.   Again, in a remarkable
passage in the essay on " Open Secret Societies,"
he shows beyond a doubt that in satirising the
orthodox theology he was attacking only what he
believed to be fraudulent and base, while he still
preserved a deep reverence for all essential piety
and real holiness :—

Sometimes when one, being full of scorn and indignation,
seeks relief in riant mockery of this Established State Church
of ours, a keen pang pierces one's breast, and the gloom of
past time is filled with reproachful eyes, as the gloom of
night with pale stars.   Full of sad reproach, and of love
whose sweetness is the worst gall and wormwood of reproach,
they gaze down upon him, these eyes of holy bliss and
sorrow, these faces worn with suffering and fasting and
self-renunciation, yet shining with ineffable beatitude, the

eyes and the lineaments of true brothers and sisters of this
Sacred Order, who being Christians were yet also indeed
Saints. And in every pale regard one reads the sad question: Did I, O my friend, live and die thus and thus that
you should laugh and fleer? And at first one is smitten
with pain and remorse, but when he has reflected a little
he replies humbly: Beloved and pure and beautiful souls,
these whom I was mocking are not of you, though indeed
they assume your name; they are of the fraternities of
those who in your lifetimes mocked and hated and perse-
cuted and killed you; they have caught up your solemn
passwords because these are now passwords to wealth and
worldly honour, which for you were passwords to the prison
and the scaffold and the stake. . . . Even I, poor heathen
and cynic, am nearer to you, ye holy ones, than are ninety-
nine in a hundred of these.

This is not the tone of one who would indulge in
wanton or vulgar insult; and an unprejudiced study
of such satirical pieces as "The Story of a Famous
Old Jewish Firm," "Christmas Eve in the Upper
Circles," or "Religion in the Rocky Mountains"
will convince the reader that thay are the work of
a man who, sincerely believing certain theological
doctrines to be false and mischievous, did not hesitate
to ridicule and burlesque them, in order as far as
possible to weaken their authority. Heine's "Gods
of Greece" and "Gods in Exile" furnished Thomson
with a model for this style of satire; whether he
was acquainted with Lucian's "Dialogues of the
Gods," the prototype of all such writings, is not
equally apparent.

III. Thomson's critical writings give evidence of
his wide literary sympathies, catholicity of taste, and

natural insight into what is best in contemporary literature, as well as in that of past periods. It is true that there is little direct mention of Shakspere and Dante in his essays, but this silence was certainly owing to no lack of esteem. For Dante he is said to have expressed unbounded reverence, in private talk; accepting as correct and true Mr. Ruskin's statement that Dante is "the central intellect" of the world. Shakspere he only quoted rarely, and when deeply moved. His love of the Elizabethan poets is shown in his delightful essay entitled "An Evening with Spenser," where he declares Spenser and his fellows to be "peers of the noblest men that have existed since the human race was born;" for Milton he seems to have felt a less hearty admiration, if it is fair to judge by a few scattered references to parts of "Lycidas" and "Paradise Lost." I will now proceed to mention the most noticeable of Thomson's critical writings, omitting those which are biographical rather than critical, as in the case of the articles on Marcus Antoninus, Rabelais, Jonson, Leopardi, Heine, Schopenhauer, Wilson, Hogg, and several others. These essays originally appeared in the pages of the *London Investigator, National Reformer, Secularist, Tobacco Plant,* or *Liberal*; and very few of them have found a place as yet in the collected volumes of Thomson's prose.

"A Few Words about Burns" (1859) is one of the finest of the short essays. Burns's "large sweet nature, full of generous vitality and joyous humour," as he calls it elsewhere, was one with which Thomson was in hearty sympathy, being indeed the exact contrary of the self-seeking pseudo-religious spirit which he so often satirised. He speaks of Burns as "the

most genial of our great men," endowed with "vigorous strength and intense human or earthly sympathies." "His love-poems," he tells us, "are differen-
tiated from most others by their dew-fresh simplicity
and directness, their intense reality. . . . He is the
supreme representative man of his nation in literature.
Scott was a good archer, but he never bent so mighty
a bow, nor sped a shaft so true to the centre." It
is interesting to see what Thomson says respecting
Burns's excesses :—"No wealthy life, fearless and
free, will suffer itself to be pitied. . . . Let not the
ordinary cabman despise Phaeton because he could
not control the sun-steeds." There is also a trace in
this essay of Thomson's half-serious leaning towards
the doctrine of metempsychosis, for he expresses his
belief that Burns, before his appearance as we know
him, "had been working vehemently for some half-a-
dozen lives at statesmanship, philosophy, war, divinity,
and what not; whereof we find dim reminiscences in
the papers left behind him here." The concluding
passage of the essay remains to be quoted,[*] as an
instance of Thomson's early tendency to pessimism.

In "The Poems of William Blake," an article
written and published in 1865, before the appearance
of Mr. Swinburne's essay on the same subject, Thomson recognised Blake as the true herald and fore-
runner, even more than Cowper or Burns, of the
nineteenth-century poetry; he is "a reincarnation
of the mighty Elizabethan spirit," on the one hand ;
while, on the other, his mixture of mysticism and
simplicity marks the earliest growth of a new school
of thought.

---

[*] Page 309.

The essence of this poetry is mysticism, and the essence of this mysticism is simplicity. The two meanings in which this last word is commonly used—the one reverential, the other kindly contemptuous — are severally appropriate to the most wise and the least wise manifestations of this spirit of mysticism. It sees, and is continually rapturous with seeing, everywhere correspondence, kindred, identity, not only in the things and creatures of earth, but in all things and creatures and beings of hell and earth and heaven, up to the one father of all. It thus ignores or pays little heed to the countless complexities and distinctions of our modern civilisation and science, a knowledge of which is generally esteemed the most useful information and most valuable learning. . . . Its supreme tendency is to remain or to become again child-like, its supreme aspiration is not virtue, but innocence or guilelessness : so that we may say with truth of those whom it possesses, that the longer they live the younger they grow, as if " passing out to God by the gate of birth, not death."

In the latter part of the essay, which deals with the relations between Blake and the principal subsequent poets, there are some interesting indications of Thomson's own critical estimate of the merits of Wordsworth, Coleridge, Scott, Byron, Keats, Shelley, the Brownings, and Tennyson. Of the last-named he here and elsewhere expresses a depreciatory opinion, regarding him as " an exquisite carver of luxuries in ivory," but as living on " scanty revenues of thought." " Nothing," he adds, " gives one a keener insight into the want of robustness in the educated English intellect of the age than the fact that nine-tenths of our best-known literary men look upon him as a profound philosopher." Robert Browning, on the contrary, is described as " a really great thinker, a true and splendid genius, though his

T

vigorous and restless talents often overpower and run away with his genius, so that some of his creations are but half redeemed from chaos."

Thomson's writings on Shelley, together with the poem which has been already noticed, have been collected in a volume privately printed in 1884. The chief essay, which is dated 1860, is full of that profound insight which cannot be acquired without true sympathy between the critic and the subject of his study ; and Thomson was the first writer who, recognising in Shelley the teacher as well as the singer, ventured to drop the tone of timid apology which even the most favourable reviewers had previously considered indispensable. Here is a suggestive and striking piece of criticism, written, be it remembered, long before the time when Shelley's poems became in any sense popular.

In musicalness, in free and, as it were, living melody, the poems of Shelley are unsurpassed, and on the whole, I think, unequalled by any others in our literature. Compared with that of most others his language is as a river to a canal,—a river ever flowing " at its own sweet will," and whose music is the unpurposed result of its flowing. So subtly sweet and rich are the tones, so wonderfully are developed the perfect cadences, that the meaning of the words of the singing is lost and dissolved in the overwhelming rapture of the impression. I have often fancied, while reading them, that his words were really transparent, or that they throbbed with living lustres. Meaning is therein, firm and distinct, but "scarce visible through extreme loveliness ; " so that the mind is often dazzled from the perception of the surpassing grandeur and power of his creations. I doubt not that Apollo was mightier than Hercules, though his divine strength was veiled in the splendour of his symmetry and beauty more divine.

"Mr. Kingsley's Convertites" (1865) is a brilliant and witty arraignment of the doctrine of "muscular Christianity," which Thomson demonstrates, by illustrations drawn from Kingsley's novels, to be sickly and unnatural rather than healthy and robust. After dwelling on the absurdity of the various conversions to which Kingsley subjected the heroes of his stories, he concludes as follows :—

It is believed that "muscular Christianity" has added the gospel of the body and this life to the primitive gospel of the soul and the next life ; and yet the most popular and vigorous writer of this new school, after exhausting a very fertile imagination in the suggestions of methods and modes by which godless sinners may be converted to godliness, has absolutely found no other process effectual than this of showering upon them misfortunes, humiliations, afflictions, calamities (such as do not in real life fall upon one human being in a thousand, and working results such as they would not work in one real human being out of ten thousand); until health and hope, self-respect and the capacity for sane joy, are altogether destroyed in them, the manhood and womanhood overwhelmed and crushed out of them ; after which he brings in these miserable wrecks and relics of what were once men and women, as all that he can contribute to the extension of the Church, which ought to be the cheerful congregation of wholesome men and women throughout the world, the richest flower and ripest fruit of humanity.

In his "Notes on the Genius of Robert Browning," a paper written in 1881, and read before the Browning Society in January 1882, he pays a fit tribute of admiration to a poet of whose writings he had been a zealous student for over twenty-five years.

I look up to Browning as one of the very few men
known to me by their works who, with most cordial
energy and indomitable resolution, have lived thoroughly
throughout the whole of their being, to the uttermost verge
of all their capacities, in his case truly colossal; lived and
wrought thoroughly in sense and soul and intellect; lived
at home in all realms of Nature and Human Nature, Art
and Literature : whereas nearly all of us are really alive in
but a small portion of our so much smaller beings, and
drag wearily toward the grave our for the most part dead
selves, dead from the suicidal poison of misuse and atrophy
of disuse. Confident and rejoicing in the storm and stress
of the struggle, he has conquered Life instead of being
conquered by it ; a victory so rare as to be almost unique,
especially among poets in these latter days.

The four contemporary writers of English prose
whom Thomson most valued were Ruskin, George
Eliot, Garth Wilkinson, and George Meredith. The
"Note on George Meredith" (1876) is one of his
finest pieces of criticism, a splendid testimony to the
high qualities of a great novelist whose name at that
time was comparatively unknown. The leading features of Meredith's genius are caught and reproduced
with rare insight.

He loves to suggest by flying touches rather than
slowly elaborate. To those who are quick to follow his
suggestions he gives in a few winged words the very spirit
of a scene, the inmost secret of a mood or passion, as no
other living writer I am acquainted with can. His name
and various passages in his works reveal Welsh blood, more
swift and fiery and imaginative than the English. . . . So
with his conversations. The speeches do not follow one
another mechanically adjusted like a smooth pavement for
easy walking ; they leap and break, resilient and resurgent.
like running foam-crested sea-waves, impelled and repelled

and crossed by under-currents and great tides and broad
breezes; in their restless agitations you must divine the
immense life abounding beneath and around and above
them; and the Mudie novice, accustomed to saunter the
level pavements, finds that the heaving and falling are sea-
sickness to a queasy stomach. Moreover, he delights in the
elaborate analysis of abstruse problems, whose solutions
when reached are scarcely less difficult to ordinary appre-
hension than are the problems themselves; discriminating
countless shades where the common eye sees but one
gloom or glare; pursuing countless distinct movements
where the common eye sees only a whirling perplexity.

Meredith is further described as "the Robert Browning of our novelists," whose day is bound to come
at last. Elsewhere, also, Thomson declares himself
"a most devout admirer, who had been watching
through a quarter of a century for the dayspring,
confounded by its prodigious delay."

Lastly, we find Thomson, in a double series of
articles on Walt Whitman contributed to the *National
Reformer* and *Tobacco Plant* (1874-1876), paying an
equally warm tribute of reverence to the great poet
of American democracy. His appreciation of Whitman, as a man of healthy physique, in contrast with
Heine, Leopardi, and other instances of blighted happiness, to whom he himself was so closely akin, is a
proof of the breadth of his sympathies. "I, for one,"
he says, "cannot remember these (*i.e.*, Heine and
similar writers), with others only less illustrious,
and yet contemplate without joy and admiration a
poet supremely embodied "—a sentiment which may
be paralleled by a remark in his "Evening with
Spenser " about the poets of the Elizabethan era, that
" intense and fecund vitality is mysteriously identical

with the purest morality and the profoundest truth ; and that when and where they appear to clash, it is all the worse for the morality and the truth, not for the vitality." Again, he declares Whitman's poems on the Civil War to be "immeasurably greater and deeper and nobler than anything I have seen by Emerson, or Lowell, or any other American, on the same subject;" while he compares him favourably with the Boston literary school. "Their prose," he says, "which includes a large part of their 'poetry,' may be more compact and scholarly than his, but their sectarian and local narrowness makes a very poor figure in contrast with his continental breadth and freedom."

CHAPTER XII.

GENERAL CHARACTERISTICS.

HAVING now traced the course of Thomson's life, and studied his chief works in verse and prose, we may conclude by taking a general view of his position as thinker and writer, pessimist and poet, examining first his philosophical opinions, and then his literary characteristics.

He had been brought up, as we have seen, in the strictest Presbyterian doctrines, and in the opening period of his authorship he had not altogether lost belief in the tenets of Christianity, though his keen and trenchant intellect, sharpened by early misfortunes, had cut him adrift from much to which he had previously clung. Two distinct phases of religious opinion are therefore observable in his writings. We see him, at the outset of his literary career, in that painful state of hesitation and doubt, through which so many powerful thinkers have had to pass with labour and misgiving of mind, before emerging into the comparative calm of affirmative or negative conviction. In some lines written in 1855, "suggested by Matthew Arnold's stanzas from the ' Grande Chartreuse,'" he gives expression to the regret which he still felt at the parting, inevitable though he saw it to be, from the central doctrine of Christianity ; while in the

"Doom of a City," written two years later, and even
in the gloomy "Mater Tenebrarum" of 1859, there
are still signs of a belief, or half-belief, in the immortality of the soul and the benevolence of an overruling
Deity.   Apparently connected with this change of
religious faith was that period of hesitation between
alternate moods of self-reproach and self-confidence
of which, and of his final deliverance, Thomson has
left a record in "Vane's Story:"—

> I half remember, years ago,
> Fits of despair that maddened woe,
> Frantic remorse, intense self-scorn,
> And yearnings harder to be borne
> Of utter loneliness forlorn;
> What passionate secret prayers I prayed!
> What futile firm resolves I made!
> As well a thorn might pray to be
> Transformed into an olive-tree. . . .
> My penitence was honest guile;
> My inmost being all the while
> Was laughing in a patient mood
> At this externe solicitude,
> Was waiting laughing till once more
> I should be sane as heretofore.

The second phase, which, roughly speaking, covers
the period of his life in London—that is, the greater
and more important part of his career—was one of
negative conviction.   Of all external influences, the
writings of Shelley seem to have had most share in
thus transforming Thomson's religious opinions; but
the change was, of course, chiefly due to the development of his own intellect, and once adopted, was
carried out fearlessly and honestly to what appeared
to be its full and necessary conclusion.   In an article
on "Conversions, Sudden and Gradual," which he

wrote in 1876,* there is a passage which looks very
like a personal reminiscence. " The gradual convert,"
he says, " was not easy to transplant because he had
struck deep root, and his root strikes deeper yet in the
new soil when transplanted. He clung with love and
reverence to the past, rich for him in hallowed and
tender associations, resigning reluctantly belief after
belief as he found them incompatible with honest truth.
He has thus comprehension and sympathy for all who
are at the intermediate stages ; their position now was
his position once. He has not hurried and excited
himself to change, but has followed the direction in
which the currents of his intellect and character
slowly but surely set. He cannot be pert and self-
sufficient ; he has suffered too much in rending himself from the things he was taught to revere, and in
alienating loved ones who continue to revere them ;
his life has been a slow painful learning and unlearning, and the long process has profoundly impressed
him with the assurance that he must still, and while
life lasts, go on learning and unlearning."

Acting on these principles Thomson became now
a declared atheist, disbelieving the doctrine of personal
immortality, and looking to death as the final comfort
and recompense for the misery of life. But the am-
biguity that attaches to the terms *theist, pantheist*, and
atheist has so often, as in the case of Shelley, been a
cause of injustice and misunderstanding, that it will
be safer to quote Thomson's own words on the subject
of his creed. In the introductory note to his " Lady
of Sorrow " (1864) he thus alludes to himself under
the title of " my friend Vane :"—" He was at that

---

* *The Secularist*, September 16, 1876.

time wont to declare that he believed in the soul's immortality as a materialist believes in the immortality of matter : he believed that the universal soul subsists for ever, just as a materialist believes that universal matter subsists for ever, without increase or decrease, growth or decay : he no more believed in the immortality of any particular soul than the materialist believes in the immortality of any particular body. The one substance is eternal, the various forms are ever varying."

Seventeen years later, towards the close of his life, we find him thus expressing his view of the Secular creed :—

We gaze into the Living World and mark
Infinite Mysteries for ever dark :
And if there *is* a God beyond our thought
(How could He be within its compass brought ?),
He will not blame the eyes He made so dim
That they cannot discern a trace of Him ;
He must approve the pure sincerity
Which, seeing not, declares it cannot see :
He cannot love the blasphemous pretence
Of puny mannikins with purblind sense
To see Him thoroughly, to know Him well,
His secret purposes, His Heaven and Hell,
His inmost nature—formulating this
With calmest chemical analysis,
Or vivisecting it, as if it were
Some compound gas, or dog with brain laid bare.
And if we *have* a life beyond our death,
A life of nobler aims and ampler breath,
What better preparation for such bliss
Than honest work to make the best of this ? *

It will be seen from these passages that if the term *atheist* be used (as it should not be used) in an op-

---

* Address for the opening of the Leicester Secular Hall, 1881.

probrious sense, it is not applicable to Thomson. Nor
was he a Secularist in any narrow and literal meaning
of the word; on the contrary, his writings are full of
intense spirituality, and he did not hesitate to declare
that "a Free-thinker who continues a mere negationist
has gained nothing by his conversion from Christianity, and is worse than no gain to the cause of
Secularism." * "He cannot fulfil his duty," he continues, "to himself, his party, and his cause without
assiduous study, meditation, and work. The only
effectual substitute for faith is thought; for theological dogma, well-reasoned principle; for the religion
of God, the religion of Humanity. It is evident that
the mere detection and exposure of Bible mistakes
and contradictions are but very short first steps in
the long journey; and a sensible person will quickly
leave off wasting his time on these, except when
challenged by the unemancipated orthodox, whom he
may hope to assist to freedom. Soon satisfied and
sated by the negative, he must set himself to learn
something positive. He must study the great works
of our literature and of other literatures, in so far as
his talents and opportunities allow. . . . Large numbers who call themselves and account themselves Free-
thinkers appear to limit their reading not merely to
anti-Christian books and pamphlets, but to the most
commonplace and uninstructive of these. The intelligent Free-thinker will certainly study for himself the
writings of our great champions, but he will by no
means limit himself to these. Though there have
already been some avowed sceptics of loftiest genius,
they are as yet far outnumbered by the writers of

* *The Secularist*, September 23, 1876.

genius who have, at least outwardly, conformed to the Christianity so long dominant We must admit, with regret, that there is far more to be learnt from these than from all save a very few of our own apologists."

It must be understood, therefore, that while Thomson thoroughly identified himself with the party of Free-thought, he never degenerated into the mere partisan.   In his bitterest jests at conventional piety there is still a tenderness for all unselfish devotion to the welfare of mankind and a reverence for all genuine religious feeling.   What he most keenly detested and satirised in so-called religious life was the self-seeking, self-conscious spirit, which, under the guise of piety, is intent on the saving of its own soul and the securing of its own immortality.   It was the total absence of these "feverish raptures and hypochondriac remorses" which gave to the characters of such men as Burns and Blake a strong hold on Thomson's admiration.   "As to his soul's salvation," he wrote of Blake, "I do not believe that he ever gave it a thought."   "Immortality!" he exclaims in another of his prose essays; "why, the most of us don't know what to do with this one little personal life, and might well wonder how we came to be promoted to the dignity thereof; the claim to immortality is the claim to be trusted with millions of pounds because one has shown himself unfit to be trusted with sixpence."

As in religious questions, so too it was in social and moral; for here also Thomson was unable to take any but a despondent view of the destiny of mankind. The sense of a Doom—mysterious, incalculable, immitigable—broods darkly over his genius almost from

the first, and makes him perforce a necessitarian in
his philosophical creed.

> I find no hint throughout the Universe
> Of good or ill, of blessing or of curse ;
> I find alone Necessity Supreme.

So he wrote in a notable section of the " City of Dreadful Night," and the same doctrine of necessity dominates
the greater part of his writings. He admitted, it is
true, that this theory is not, and cannot be, consis-
tently carried out in the ordinary practical conduct of
life, since he saw that necessitarians were no better able
than other people to avoid expressions implying moral
praise or blame. Yet he was so far consistent in his
belief in necessity as to accept the conclusion that it
is useless and irrational to confide in any schemes for
the improvement of the human race ; and he laughs
at the incongruity of those necessitarians who, after
premising that man is the creature of circumstances,
proceed to lay down the strange corollary that circumstances may in their turn be improved by man.
Thomson himself was a disbeliever in all human progress, and, ardent admirer though he was of Shelley's
character and writings, he could not subscribe to the
cardinal doctrine of Shelley's faith—the perfectibility
of man, since it seemed to him that if there is any
advance in intellectual well-being, it is an advance in
a circle, with the result that after centuries of earnest
labour, and seemingly forward movement, the latest
condition of the civilised race is much the same as
the earliest. It is evident that one who held this
belief could not but be convinced at heart of the
futility of all social reform ; and though by natural
sympathy and predilection he was led to range him-

self among the reformers, he always looked with
suspicion and dislike on anything approaching to
propagandism or asceticism. "Were I required," he
says, "to draw a practical moral, I should say that
all proselytism is useless and absurd. Every human
being belongs naturally, organically, unalterably, to a
certain species or society; and by no amount of re-
peating strange formulas, ejaculations, or syllogisms
can he really apostatise from himself so as to become
a genuine member of a society to which these are
not strange but natural." In a similar vein he defines
sin as being the violation of one's own nature, the
striving after some forbidden object not through
natural desire, but through mere vanity or fashion.
"The iniquity which a man draws and tugs painfully
to him, that is the abomination; not the iniquity
which itself draws him." The notion of *repentance*
finds no place in Thomson's ethical doctrine, which
may be summed up in three lines of "Vane's Story:"—

> Oh what can Saadi have to do
> With penitence? And what can you?
> Are Shiraz roses wreathed with rue?

Of the question of the right relation of the sexes
there is little direct mention in Thomson's writings,
but in one passage he avows himself a follower of
Shelley on this point. Throughout all his poems he
maintains a high ideal of woman's innocence and
purity, regarding her especially as the source of comfort and solace to suffering mankind.

> When too, too conscious of its solitude,
> My heart plains weakly as a widowed dove,
> The forms of certain women sweet and good,
> Whom I have known and love with reverent love,
> Rise up before me.

Such is the feeling expressed in the series of unpublished sonnets addressed to the friends of his early days ; and, again, in his essay on " Sympathy," he speaks of a woman's " wealth of cordial sympathy," as contrasted with the more laboured and self-conscious benevolence of men. Of the purely intellectual capacity of women he formed but a low estimate, on the ground that they have the intense but not the comprehensive imagination. He asserts that he never knew a woman with " even the most elementary idea of truth and justice ; . . . the best woman would overthrow the equilibrium of the universe for the sake of her lover, her child, or her husband."

In politics Thomson's sympathies were entirely with the popular cause, his keen pity for the downtrodden victims of all social injustice being attested by several indignant passages, especially in the "Doom of a City," written in 1857, and the prose essay " In our Forest of the Past," which is dated twenty years later. In the satirical essay on " Bumbleism " it is pointed out that though there is more liberty in England than on the Continent in matters affecting political discussion and private life, the reverse is true as regards questions of morals and sociology, for there the power of Bumble's purse rules our so-called free press and free institutions with a hand heavier than that of any Continental despot. Thomson saw clearly that true democracy must be quit of other things besides political inequalities ; since religious intolerance, backed up by plutocratic influence, is absolutely fatal to the existence of a free community. " Imperialism imposes fines, imprisonment, banishment ; Bumble simply imposes death by starvation."

Equally firm was Thomson's sympathy with all

struggling nationalities, such as the Italy and Poland of that day; his lines on "A Polish Insurgent" are full of intense spirit and pathos. He could also be just (a rarer gift) to those national aspirations or prejudices which ran counter to the policy which he personally approved; we find him, for instance, speaking favourably of the Basques, who had supported the Carlist cause in 1873. In his "Carlist Reminiscences" he states his opinion, in reference to the Basque nation, that "the adherents of obsolete causes are usually so by virtue of noble qualities, not by vice of bad ones; very commonly they are more simple and elevated in character than the adherents of the more modern cause by whom they are doomed to be conquered." He further contrasts the simple devotion of these Basques with the so-called English loyalty. "Such was the loyalty of these people; far more noble than ours; for they were giving freely of their substance and their lives, whereas we give chiefly snobbish cringing and insincere adulation, and our rich give the money of the nation, in large part wrung from the poor." It hardly needs to be said that Thomson heartily despised and detested the bellicose spirit of certain modern statesmanship. He graphically describes the Crimean war as "a mere selfish haggle for the adjustment of the balance of power, badly begun and meanly finished," and refers to the more recent exploits of Jingoism as "brutally iniquitous battue-wars against tribes of ill-armed savages."

Yet, unswerving as was Thomson's devotion to the cause of the people, and strong as was his indignation against every form of privilege and self-aggrandisement, he was devoid, in politics as in other matters

of the hopefulness and confidence which are essential
to success. For, in addition to his general disbelief
in the possibility of substantial progress, he had little
or no trust in particular political combinations as
a means of attaining any desired end; so uncompromising was his individualism that he considered
a society to be "a maimed, mutilated, semi-vital com-
promise," and a meeting to be "always less wise than
a man." In the prose piece entitled "The Sayings
of Sigvat," which may, in fact, be considered as a
record of Thomson's own opinions, he imagines an
interlocutor asking him why, if he has no faith in the
improvability of man by man, he himself works hard
in that very direction. The answer given is, that he
is simply following the dictates of his own nature;
"one works, and cannot but work, as his being
ordains." But, apart from this philosophical reference
of all personal conduct to the law of necessity, the
immediate and practical motive of morality should
rather be sought, as he himself admits, in the sense
of brotherhood and pity excited by the spectacle
of human ignorance and suffering. "Though no
word of mine," he says, "will ever convert any
one from being himself into being another me, my
word may bring cheer and comfort and self-know-
ledge to others who are more or less like myself,
and who may have thought themselves peculiar and
outcast."

Thomson's views on art and literature were pervaded by the same tinge of melancholy and despon-
dence. His strong natural yearning for action in
preference to thought led him to regard art as a mere
substitute and makeshift for the fuller and truer life
of reality that is so often denied us by destiny; art

U

was to him the outcome of want rather than fruition, of disappointment rather than success, of mortality rather than vitality. Shakspere is instanced by him as the supreme and typical example of the wise man who will practise art only so long as he is compelled to do so by circumstances, and will return to actual life from the mere study of life on the earliest opportunity; since no man "of opulent vitality" will deliberately and finally commit himself to the "imprisonment with hard labour of a great work." This pessimistic view of literature is further illustrated by another passage, much in the style and sentiment of Poe, in which Thomson speaks of *despair* as a valuable auxiliary of art, admitting that it is a sign of "interior death and mouldering," but adding that "this mouldering has manured some of the fairest flowers of Art and Literature." His whole position on this subject is briefly summed up in some introductory remarks prefixed to "A Lady of Sorrow." "The night-side of nature," he says, "has been the theme of literature more often than the day-side, simply because literature, as a rule, is the refuge of the miserable; I mean genuine, thoughtful, earnest literature; literature as an end in and for itself, not merely as a weapon to fight with, a ware to sell, a luxury to enjoy. The happy seldom write for writing's sake; they are fully employed in living." The above limitation in the definition of what is meant by literature is connected with Thomson's disgust at the present rule of Bumbleism, which at every point checks and thwarts the production of thoughtful and outspoken writings, while encouraging much that is trivial and valueless. "The condition of our literature in these days," he remarks elsewhere, "is disgraceful to a nation of men; Bumble has drugged all its higher powers."

Such is the pessimistic line of thought that everywhere runs like a dark thread across the web of Thomson's philosophy; let us now proceed to consider his pessimism as a whole, as set forth in his writings and exemplified in his life. One of Thomson's admirers * has questioned the applicability of the name *pessimist* to him at all, on the grounds that he was a believer in the law of *nature* rather than of pessimism; yet I cannot but think that in his case a belief in natural law and a belief in pessimism were identical. Able exponent though he was of the gospel of despair, it was no new doctrine that he taught, but merely a new and more powerful presentment of the *vanitas vanitatum* that has had its Preacher in every age and every literature of the world. Leopardi was the modern pessimistic writer by whom Thomson was most strongly and most directly inspired; but if it be true, as an essayist in the "Encyclopædia Britannica" has assured us, that a page of "Sartor Resartus" scatters Leopardi's sophistry to the winds, then I think we must conclude that Thomson's philosophy is less vulnerable than that of his master, for the pessimism he preaches could hardly be so expeditiously disposed of. Critics are too apt to assume that the phase of thought which we call pessimism must be absolutely true or false, right or wrong; for in reality we are not driven to the dilemma of any such alternative. Pessimism, at any rate as advanced by Thomson, is the expression

---

* "B. E.," in Preface to "Leek Bijou Free-thought Reprints," No. VI.

of a mood, not of an invariable principle—a mood
with which all thinking men must be acquainted at
times, but which is felt by some far more often
and more strongly than by others.] That this was
Thomson's doctrine may be placed beyond doubt by
the quotation of his own words. " I wish," he says,
in his essay on Sympathy, "to draw into clear light
the facts that, in two moods of two several hours
not a day asunder, a man's relations to the most
serious problems of life may be, and often are,
essentially opposite; that the one may burn with
hope and faith, and the other lour black with doubt
and despair; and that there is no possibility of
conciliating (philosophically) this antagonism, since
the two are mutually unintelligible." In the same
essay he asserts that there are cases, though not
frequent ones, in which "a dark mood has dominated
a whole life," in which remark we may doubtless see
a reference to his own personality. But though the
dark mood was the one with which Thomson was
specially familiar, and though in the " City of Dreadful Night " and similar writings he was never weary
of dilating and insisting on this mood to the exclusion
of the other, yet he was himself well aware that it
was a half-truth and not the whole truth to which
he was then giving expression. " Is it true," he asks
of his own pessimistic doctrine in the Introduction
to " A Lady of Sorrow," " is it true in relation to the
world and general life ? I think true, but not the
whole truth. There is truth of winter and black
night, there is truth of summer and dazzling noonday.
On the one side of the great medal are stamped the
glory and triumph of life, on the other side are
stamped the glory and triumph of death; but which

is the obverse and which the reverse none of us surely knows. It is certain that both are inseparably united in every coin doled out to us from the universal mintage."

It might perhaps be objected that the words just quoted were written some ten years before the "City of Dreadful Night," and so possibly before the time of Thomson's entry into the final gloom of pessimism; yet, on the other hand, where could one find a fuller confession of the pessimistic faith than in the following remarkable passage taken from a still earlier essay of 1859?—"Fate stands impassive—a Sphinx in the desert of life. The rigid lips will not wreath into smiles for all your abounding humour, the stark blind eyes will not moisten with tears for all your lamentable dirges, the stony heart will never throb responsive to your yearning, your passion, your enthusiasm. However rich in gifts and graces, you shall not front this fate unvanquishable, unless they be grounded on a stony prudence, armed with an iron resolution, fortified with an adamantine self-control. . . . In the meanwhile to love our fellow-prisoners, helping and serving them as we can, is the sanctitude and piety of our miserable existence."

This sense of "sanctitude and piety," finding action in services of gentleness and tenderness to suffering fellow-beings, is a most important and characteristic feature of Thomson's pessimism, relieving it altogether from any suspicion of misanthropic churlishness, and allying it not only with the most valuable part of Schopenhauer's philosophy, in which compassion is made the principle of moral action, but also with the tender and benevolent sadness of Buddha. In an essay on Schopenhauer he expresses a strong dislike for the

tinge of sullenness and vanity that disturbed the
philosophic composure of the great German pessimist,
while he refers to Buddhism as " the venerable, the
august, the benign, so tender, so mystic, so profound,
so solemnly supernal." This frank human sympathy
is the one ray of light that relieves the deepening
gloom of his despondency. If we regard Leopardi as
the source of Thomson's most pessimistic inspiration,
so in like manner must we attribute to Shelley's example much of the gentleness and humanity that per-
vade even his most sombre productions ; and we note
that while the " City of Dreadful Night " was appro-
priately dedicated to Leopardi, the " younger brother
of Dante," " Vane's Story," which is conceived in a
somewhat more tender spirit, was dedicated to Shelley,
the " poet of poets, and purest of men." Next to
these two literary sponsors, Heine and Novalis must
by no means be overlooked as having strongly affected
Thomson's imagination and line of thought ; Novalis
perhaps in a minor degree, and more by a sense of
spiritual relationship and the similarity between their
lives than by direct force of teaching, whereas Heine's
influence is very noticeable in all his mature thoughts
and writings. In a series of essays on Heine published in the *Secularist* in 1876, Thomson himself
remarked on the affinity existing between the characters and the destinies of such men as Heine, Shelley,
and Leopardi (and he might well have added his own
name and that of Novalis to the list), in whom a
capacity for full enjoyment of life went side by side
with a prescience of early decay or death. " In all
moods," he wrote of Heine, in words that are to a
singular degree applicable also to himself, " tender,
imaginative, fantastic, humorous, ironical, cynical ; in

anguish and horror, in weariness and revulsion, longing backward to enjoyment, and longing forward to
painless rest ; through the doleful days, and the
dreadful immeasurable sleepless nights, this intense
and luminous spirit was enchained and constrained to
look down into the vast black void which undermines
our seemingly solid existence. . . . And the power
of the spell on him, as the power of his spell on us,
is increased by the fact that he thus in Death-in-Life
brooding on Death and Life, was no ascetic spiri-
tualist, no self-torturing eremite or hypochondriac
monk, but by nature a joyous heathen of richest
blood, a Greek, a Persian, as he often proudly proclaimed, a lusty lover of this world and life, an enthusiastic apostle of the rehabilitation of the flesh."

But if Thomson owed much to Leopardi and
Shelley and Heine—a debt which he himself openly
and gratefully avowed—he was none the less perfectly
independent and original in his methods of thought
and in the conclusions at which he arrived. Both
by nature and conviction he was far too jealous an
upholder of the freedom of private judgment to be
in danger of blindly following any intellectual lead ;
indeed, he was more likely, if he erred at all, to err
in the opposite direction, "obstinately individual"
being the description applied to him by one of his
friends. Nor does he betray the least tendency to
preach his pessimistic gospel in an over-positive or
dogmatic spirit, exhibiting it, as I have already said,
simply as that side of the great medal of life which
most men would gladly overlook, but which had pre-
sented itself to him as the more important and significant one. The insolubility of the mystery of
existence is the chief point in Thomson's pessimistic

creed, from which he deduces the entire worthlessness of all metaphysical systems, and mercilessly satirises those theologians and philosophers who expatiate on the origin of the universe. He compares such metaphysicians to a colony of mice in a great cathedral getting "a poor livelihood out of communion-crumbs and taper-droppings," and speculating confidently on "the meaning of the altar, the significance of the ritual, the clashing of the bells, the ringing of the chants, and the thunderous trepidations of the organ."

Some of Thomson's critics have raised the question, in rather a casuistical spirit, as it seems to me, why, if he found life so bitter and looked forward so longingly to death, he did not himself cut the knot of his perplexity by having recourse to the suicide which he several times mentions with approbation as a justifiable means of escape from the sorrows of existence. This is a sort of *argumentum ad hominem* which it seems scarcely fair to use, though probably Thomson would have been the first to admit that it would be impossible to give it a perfectly logical answer. In several passages of the "City of Dreadful Night" suicide is directly commended, as also in the following lines taken from "In the Room," a poem devoted specially to this subject :—

> The drear path crawls on drearier still
>   To wounded feet and hopeless breast ?
> Well, he can lie down when he will,
>   And straight all ends in endless rest.

It may be observed that in one or two of his poems Thomson himself anticipates the personal application of this argument, and gives reasons to account for his own continuance in living. In the

" Mater Tenebrarum " of 1859 his action is attributed
to the spark of hope still kindled in his mind by his
lingering belief in the immortality of his lost love;
but in the unpublished lines of 1878, at which time
all belief in immortality had left him, he refers to
the poet's passion for creative art as the one prop
of life.   It will be seen from this that Thomson was
not careful to give consistent reasons for what, after
all, scarcely calls for explanation.

> Songs in the Desert! songs of husky breath
>   And undivine Despair;
> Songs that are Dirges, but for Life, not Death,
>   Songs that infect the air :
> Have sweetened bitterly my food and wine,
> The heart corroded and the Dead Sea brine.
>
> So potent is the Word, the Lord of Life,
>   And so tenacious Art,
> Whose instinct urges to perpetual strife
>   With Death, Love's counterpart;
> The magic of their music might and light
> Can keep one living in his own despite.

Turning now to the consideration of Thomson's
qualities as poet and essayist, we find that the
essential characteristic of his genius, and that which
differentiates him from all other writers, among his
predecessors and contemporaries, is his singular com-
bination of the logical and imaginative faculties, of
the analytic element and the constructive.   Something of this dual quality is, of course, observable in
other poets, ancient and modern, as, for instance—to
name two to whom Thomson is closely akin—in
Shelley and Browning; but whereas we see that in
Shelley the imaginative faculty is often more powerful
than the intellectual, and in Browning the intellectual

than the imaginative, we note in Thomson's case an
almost faultless balance between the two opposing
tendencies; he is at one and the same time the
sternest and most logical of realists and the most
imaginative of poets. The richness of his nature
shows itself very clearly in the largeness of conception
and thought, in the rhythmic melody of language and
versification, and in the remarkable beauty and fulness of imagery which characterise most of his poems.
Those written in the earlier part of his life, and
before the commencement of his work in London, are
especially distinguished by their strong idealistic tendency, and passionate, almost rhapsodic, wealth of
metaphor and allegory; but in the more mature poems
we are struck by the stern brevity and conciseness of
expression, which, without any apparent sacrifice of
poetic quality, go straight to their mark and produce
a powerful effect on the mind of the reader.

Speaking of the poems as a whole, we may say that
they all, more or less, bear evidence of Thomson's capacity for full, rich life; of his oriental love of repose,
coupled with an ever-present sense of the mystery of
existence; and finally, of his growing conviction that all
labour is useless, and all progress impossible, in face
of the stony and impenetrable destiny by which all
mortals are confronted. The metaphors in which he
most delights are those of wine and the wine-cup; of
the raptures of the dance, of the rose's rich scents,
and the nightingale's sweetness of voice; of sunshine
warmth and moonlight purity; of the sea, the sky,
and all the opulence that nature seems to lavish on
man; but side by side with these is the strong, stern
mathematical grasp of facts, which, in its determined
and deliberate realism, does not scruple to borrow a

simile from a piece of mechanism or even from an algebraic formula. Then, again, there is the strange contrast, yet no sense of discord, between Thomson's allegorical, visionary, and symbolic tendencies and his logical, practical habit of thought; in the highest heaven of his most spiritual flights he is still the keen, calm reasoner, while in his coldest speculations he retains something of the impassioned poet. Like De Quincey, he possesses the gift of distinct mental vision finding utterance in sublime imagery; those who read the "City of Dreadful Night," "Insomnia," and many others of his poems cannot doubt that the forms there described were actually existent to the eye of the poet. He himself tells us how, during his sojourn in London with his "Lady of Sorrow,"—the life-long grief that is thus allegorically represented,— he lived in a spiritual world of his own, not less real than the actual world around him. "She annihilated from me the huge city, and all its inhabitants; they, with their thoughts, passions, labours, struggles, victories, defeats, were nothing to me; I was nothing to them. As I passed daily through the streets, my eyes must have pictured the buildings and the people, my ear must have vibrated to the roar of the vehicles; but my inward vision was fixed the while on her, my inward ear was attentive to her voice alone. She annihilated so utterly from me the dark metropolis, whose citizens are counted by millions, that the whole did not even form a dark background for the spiritual scenes and personages her spells continually evoked." Yet this same mystic visionary was also one of the shrewdest logicians, one of the keenest critics, and one of the most trenchant satirists of the age in which he lived !

At the time when Thomson first entered on his literary career the most prominent representatives of English poetry were Tennyson, Arnold, and the Brownings, Landor's star having already practically set, and the names of Swinburne, Morris, and Rossetti being as yet unknown. The influences most discernible in Thomson's early writings are those of Shelley and Mrs. Browning; but as his style matured it became Dantesque rather than Shelleyan in the gravity and conciseness of its imagery and expression, and it is evident that Dante, whom Thomson had studied till he knew him almost by heart, had made a profound impression on his mind. Heine, too, became before long a very potent influence, as is proved by the affinity of thought and tone, the numerous references to his writings that are scattered through Thomson's works, and the "attempts at translations," as he modestly called them. Thomson has been charged by some critics with a lack of originality, an accusation which is certainly a mistaken and misleading one, though it is by no means difficult to see how it arose. One of his most marked features as a student and writer was what may be called his receptivity; he absorbed and assimilated in a most singular manner the essence of what he read, so that in his own references to some kindred and favourite poet (Shelley, perhaps, or Blake, or Burns, or Robert Browning, or Fitzgerald's "Omar Khayyam," "with that supreme Dantesque intensity of his," as Thomson himself expressed it) he seems at times to write unconsciously in the very tone and spirit of the author whom he had in mind. The following couplet in the memorial lines on the death of Mrs. Browning—

Italy, you hold in trust
Very sacred English dust,

seems to belong to Mrs. Browning herself; and the
stanzas commencing—

He came to the desert of London town
Grey miles long;
He wandered up and he wandered down,
Singing a quiet song,

might almost pass as written by Blake, the poet to
whom they refer. But such receptivity is perfectly
compatible with complete originality; and original
Thomson undoubtedly was, if ever poet was so. The
strong, clear impression of his very marked personality
is stamped ineffaceably alike on the thought, style,
and diction of every poem he ever wrote; and there
are probably few writers whose work could be so
easily distinguished and identified by those readers
who are familiar with its chief characteristics. He
has, of course, something in common with those contemporary writers who rose to fame and celebrity
while he was still condemned to struggle with obscurity and neglect, but the similarity, where any
similarity exists, is only such as must necessarily be
found between all poets of the same social and
political epoch; the dates, moreover, which are in most
cases prefixed to Thomson's poems, often show that,
though published later, they were in reality written
earlier than those to which a resemblance may be
fancied or traced.

This mention of dates leads naturally to the subject of Thomson's method of composition and publication. It was not his habit to write down anything,
either in the shape of verse or prose, until it had

been to some extent shaped and perfected in his mind, and the work once written underwent but few corrections, some of the original manuscripts being almost untouched. Thus the " Voice from the Nile," which was published in the *Fortnightly Review* in 1882, was projected ten years before that date ; while in the case of other poems there elapsed a considerable interval of time between the writing and the publication. Several of Thomson's critics have noticed the fact that there is a striking resemblance between the " City of Dreadful Night " and the prose piece entitled " A Lady of Sorrow," the latter being indeed the prose counterpart of the former. But I do not think it has been sufficiently noted that the " Lady of Sorrow " was written ten years earlier than the " City of Dreadful Night," so that during all that time Thomson had been carrying in his mind the sombre imagery, and even actual phrases, which he afterwards converted with such effect into a poetical form. In this patient workmanship and conscientious elaboration of the details of his art we see the secret of much of his success in the creation of vivid word-pictures which fix themselves indelibly on the minds of his readers.

Like all other writers possessed of a strongly-marked individuality, Thomson had his own peculiarities of diction, rhyme, and phraseology. His style, excellent as it is in its general effect, is by no means free from minor blemishes and lapses, and some of his mannerisms have been severely, and justly, censured by indignant critics, who perhaps have relished the task of correction all the more on account of their dislike of the culprit's religious and social heterodoxy. He is apt to use strange or

antique words, such as *rauque, sain, amort, lown ;* or
odd forms, such as *lucenter, benedictive, tenĕbrous, tenĕ-
briously, sombrous ;* while he exhibits an excessive
partiality for certain nouns and verbs which occur
repeatedly in his writings ; for example, *riant, boon*
(adjectives), *ruth, shine, dole, mirk* (substantives), and
lamp, voice, glimpse (verbs). Careful readers of the
poems will not fail to notice his liking for words of
Latin origin, such as the adjectives *fulgent, fervent,
regnant,* of which many examples might readily be
found ; also for such words as *crystalline, hyaline,
vastitude ;* and especially for those Latin terminations
which often furnish material for the double rhyme-
endings which he so frequently introduced. Such a
couplet as the following—

> Whose curtain raised, whose hush of expectation
> Foretold a solemn drama's celebration,

is characteristic of much of Thomson's work ; as also
is the formation of compound words, *star-sweet, sky-
pure, dove-quick, dim-steadfast,* and the like, and even
triple forms, as *sweet-sleep-like* and *all-day-drooping.*
It should be stated, however, that it is chiefly in the
early poems, which are more passionately conceived
and executed, that the above-mentioned tendencies
are indulged ; where any license is taken in the later
writings, it is generally taken sparingly, deliberately,
and with good effect, as in the use in the "City
of Dreadful Night" of such archaisms as *teen and
threne* and *enorm.* Less pardonable than these verbal
blemishes, if blemishes they be, is the looseness of
expression which sometimes, though very rarely, mars
the natural grace and purity of Thomson's sentences ;
as, for instance, in the awkward and prosaic inter-

change of the pronouns *thou* and *you*, a beautiful sonnet being spoilt by the line—

> Thou gracious presence wheresoe'er you go;

or, again, in such faulty rhymes as *war* and *more*, a vulgarism which grates harshly on a sensitive ear in listening to the stately harmonies of the "City of Dreadful Night." There is also, perhaps, too much easy-going repetition of certain common epithets and of too obvious rhyme-sounds, such as *calm, balm, truth, ruth,* and a few others which need not be enumerated; while it must be admitted that some few of the pieces included in the published volumes fall altogether below the standard of true poetry, and ought never to have been set side by side with the rest.

But if Thomson is not free from such mannerisms and blemishes in his style and expression, little fault, I think, can be found even by the most fastidious critic in the rhythm and melody of his verse. It would scarcely be possible to give him higher praise —and yet to give him less would be to deprive him of his due—than to say that of all Victorian poets he comes at his best nearest to Shelley in the sonorous harmony and subtle sweetness of his language. He has caught one great Shelleyan quality in which his contemporaries are deficient—that inexpressible gentleness of tone, which may be heard almost as clearly in the sublime dirges of the "City of Dreadful Night" as in the sublime triumph-song of the "Prometheus Unbound." Nor must it be supposed that the stern repression and Dantesque severity of style which are characteristic of the central period of Thomson's career indicate any lack of that passionate feeling by which the true lyrist is usually inspired; on the contrary, a white heat of passionate intensity everywhere underlies the deliberate and measured calmness of the language.

Most of Thomson's writings, whether belonging to his early or his late period of authorship, are subjective in a high degree, being full of a marked and easily discernible individuality. Through the medium of his poems, grave or gay, as the case may be, we see him as he was actually seen in his lifetime; now overshadowed by the profound gloom of pessimistic thought, as in the "City of Dreadful Night;" now forgetting his sorrows for a time, in some interval of hearty and almost boisterous merriment, as in the "Sunday at Hampstead" or "Sunday up the River;" and now in the intermediate mood, half pensive, half playful —the mood of "Vane's Story"—in which he was most familiar to his friends. Yet the scope of his genius was perhaps wider than would be supposed by those who know him only by his published volumes of poems, for his prose works and scattered pieces show that he was also gifted with a very keen power as satirist, critic, and journalist—a power which would certainly have brought him to the fore, if it had been enlisted in a more popular cause, and exerted under less depressing circumstances.

Of dramatic talent there is little trace in his writings, and his success in the way of prolonged narrative is limited to "Weddah and Om-el-Bonain," which is a model throughout of severe concentration and artistic finish; but his power of strong, vivid description is made evident in many scattered passages, of which the most notable is the poetical reproduction, in the closing section of the "City of Dreadful Night,"

x

of Albert Dürer's " Melencolia "—a piece of descriptive writing certainly not surpassed by anything of its kind in contemporary literature. This feature of Thomson's style is rightly insisted on by Mr. Bertram Dobell. In comparing the " Doom of a City " with the " City of Dreadful Night " he says :—" Both display the same power of picturesque description ; a power that invests the scenes and events described with extraordinary vividness. A painter would find in both many incidents inviting him to transfer them to his canvas, and he might do so almost without introducing a single detail that he did not find described in the poet's verses." *

In addition to this quality of picturesque insight, Thomson was gifted with a remarkable faculty of clear and lucid expression. His love of allegory may occasionally lead him in a few of his earlier writings into something approaching to mysticism, but otherwise I doubt if there is a single passage in his works which is not perfectly plain, intelligible, and perspicuous. His pure, racy, idiomatic English is free on the one side from any trace of academic fastidiousness or artificial elaboration ; yet at the same time he possessed the cultured taste of a man who is a master of several languages. But the main power which underlay all his literary qualifications, and enabled him to use them with real and lasting effect, was the absolute genuineness of feeling which lends to his word-pictures an intensity which could not have been supplied by any external culture. Poe has been accused not infrequently of indulging in poetic exaggeration and darkening the shadow of

---

* Memoir of Thomson.

his gloomy imaginings for the sake of artistic effect; I do not think the accusation is a just one, but there is at least some ground for the suspicion. With Thomson it is quite different; his absolute sincerity of conviction is writ very plainly for those who give his writings the attention they deserve. In the record of the extraordinary errors into which even first-rate critics have sometimes fallen when estimating the qualities of new poets, a place should certainly be reserved for the discovery made by one of Thomson's reviewers, that "he has simply written dreadful poetry just because now it is the fashion to be dreadful." *

As regards literary form, the bulk of the poems may be roughly classed under two heads, as Fantasias (to use his own word) and Lyrics. The precise meaning of the former term may be seen from Thomson's note appended to the "Doom of a City." "I call it a Fantasia, because (lacking the knowledge and power to deal with the theme in its epical integrity) I have made it but an episode in a human life, instead of a chapter in the history of Fate. Thus it is throughout alloyed with the feelings and thoughts, the fantasies of the supposed narrator, and the verse has all the variableness and abrupt transitions of a man's moods, instead of the solemn uniformity of the laws of Fate." This description is applicable not only to the "Doom of a City," but to many others of the longer poems, such as "Vane's Story," "Sunday up the River," "Richard Forest," and, in a modified degree, the "City of Dreadful Night;" it is noticeable, also, that "Phantasies" was

---

* *Athenæum,* May 1, 1880.

the title which Thomson himself gave to the more imaginative of his prose works. It is his prevailing method in these Fantasias to give a series of pictures of the varying moods by which the human mind is dominated in its conception of the laws of existence; the final result pointing usually in the direction of pessimism.

Concerning Thomson's lyrical genius little need be said, except that his best lyrics, many of which are to be found scattered among the Fantasias, are informed by very true and deep feeling, which finds fit expression in words of consummate grace and tenderness. Such poems as those entitled "The Three that shall be One," "A Song of Sighing," "Withered Leaves," "The Fire that filled my Heart of Old," and many others that might be mentioned, are not merely "good poetry," as judged by an easygoing contemporary standard, but masterpieces of lyrical construction. Nothing is more indicative of Thomson's right to be numbered among true and real poets than his faculty of swift and certain selection of the subjects most suited to his pen.

> As surely as a very precious stone
>   Finds out that jeweller who doth excel,
> So surely to the bard becometh known
>   The tale which only he can fitly tell.

So Thomson wrote in "Weddah and Om-el-Bonain;" and his words are true not only of the origin of that narrative, but also of the keen instinctive insight which guided him in the choice of his lyrics. In the notes of Fitzgerald's "Omar Kháyyám" he lights on a chance sentence quoted from the diary of a traveller in Persia, concerning the date of the commencement of the nightingale's song ; and this is forthwith adapted to be the key-note of a beautiful piece of lyrical harmony, entitled "The Nightingale and the Rose." Again, in a list of the titles of some old Scottish songs, he chances to see "this most pathetic one," "Allace ! that samyn sweit face !" and to this chance we owe the production of the following exquisite and moving lines :—

I.

"Allace ! that samyn sweit face !"
    Bitter tears have drowned the shine
    Wont to laugh in azure eyne ;
    Fear hath blanched the laughing lips,
      And they tremble trying to speak :
    Pain hath cast a wan eclipse
      On the round and rosy cheek ;
    Grief has greyed the locks ; and how
    Care hath wrinkled that smooth brow !
"Allace ! that samyn sweit face !"
    Sweet then, yet sweeter now !

II.

"Allace ! that samyn sweit face !"
    Eyes have lost the light of youth,
    But have kept their loving truth :
    Lips that tremble while they speak,
      Speak the words that ravish me ;
    And the forpined hollow cheek,
      Oh, it breaks my heart to see !
    Hair yet witnesseth a vow ;
    Loyalty is on the brow :
"Allace ! that samyn sweit face !"
    Sweet then, yet sweetest now !

III.

"Allace ! that samyn sweit face !"
    Could one kindle up those eyes,
    Think you, with a love-surprise ?

> Could a rain of kisses turn
> 　Those poor lips to bloom once more?
> Would those wan cheeks swell and burn,
> 　Fed with joys of heretofore?
> Would caressing hands allow
> Not a furrow on that brow?
> "Allace! that samyn sweit face!"
> Dear then, yet dearest now!

Both in the lyrics and fantasias a considerable variety of metres is employed by Thomson, and generally with good effect, his originality appearing in their choice, treatment, and arrangement rather than in their actual form. Blank verse and the Spenserian stanza are used by him only once or twice, a measure for which he shows more liking in his narratives being the *ottava rima*, which is handled with entire mastery in "Weddah and Om-el-Bonain," and with much beauty, but less uniform power, in the earlier "Ronald and Helen." The seven-line stanza is, as we have seen, a still greater favourite with him, being found in the poems on "Shelley" and "The Dead Year" (not included in the published volumes) in the shape in which Chaucer used it, consisting of *ottava rima* wanting the fifth line; while in "Our Ladies of Death" and alternate sections of the "City of Dreadful Night" he adopted another form of the seven-line stanza, nearly identical with that of the "Guardian Angel" in Browning's "Dramatic Lyrics." The double rhymes of the fifth and sixth lines of this stanza, as used in the "City of Dreadful Night," form one of its most striking features, and are introduced with rare delicacy and skill. In proportion to the total amount of the poetry, the number of sonnets is very small; and their quality is certainly unequal to that of the best of the lyrics.

Thomson's prose writings are scarcely less excellent than his poems, though they have attracted far less attention in the literary world. Here, too, the juxtaposition of the imaginative and logical faculties is seen to stand him in good stead, and we might say of his best essays what he himself has said of Shelley's, that "with the enthusiasm and ornate beauty of an ode, they preserve throughout the logical precision and directness of an elegant mathematical demonstration." His style is light, simple, and perspicuous, yet inspired by the same latent passion and intensity of feeling that have been noted in his poetry. In the prose "Phantasies," which are in reality prose-poems, and closely akin to the imaginative studies of De Quincey, there is a certain amount of deliberate word-structure and carefully balanced melody; but even here his sentences are quite free from unnecessary tropes and superfluous ornament, his manner being that of a writer who knows exactly what is to be said and the most effective way of saying it. Owing to his affinity to De Quincey some critics have been over hasty in mistaking Thomson's unconscious receptivity for conscious plagiarism; but in reality there is as much distinction in his prose as in his poems, the same strong-minded thinker speaking unmistakably through both. A parallel might be established between some of Thomson's "Phantasies" and Edgar Poe's imaginative tales, such as "Ligeia" or "Eleonora;" but as a rule we feel that the former, sombre as they are, have, like Thomson's poetry, a more intense reality of feeling, with less consciousness of deliberate effort.

As an essayist pure and simple, Thomson is seen at his best in such pieces as those I have already

noticed, on " Indolence," " Sympathy," and " Open
Secret Societies." It has been well remarked that a
really fine essayist is one of the rarest of literary
phenomena, because the mere suspicion of any
didactic tendency or ulterior purpose is often sufficient to destroy the peculiar charm and indefinable
aroma of the literary essay. Thomson, though too
much of a metaphysician and revolutionist to be quite
a model essayist, was endowed nevertheless with a
considerable portion of the genuine Addisonian faculty
of lambent humour and gentle raillery of human
foibles, as appears to a marked extent in the essays
just mentioned. In letter-writing, where somewhat
similar qualities are indispensable to success, he was
also a proficient ; his letters, as may be judged from
the examples given in this volume, being remarkable
for their ease, directness, versatility of style, and
incisive vigour of expression. Serious or humorous,
descriptive or critical, these letters seldom fail to
wield the charm of high artistic finish united with
perfect freshness and spontaneity ; even in Shelley's
famous " Letters from Abroad " it would be difficult,
I think, to find many finer pieces of descriptive
writing than Thomson's long letter to Mr. W. M.
Rossetti from Central City, Colorado.

Again, in his satirical and critical writings, Thomson is in relationship with Swift and Heine ; his
satires giving evidence of that trenchant and occasionally merciless intellectual power of which Swift
is the great master, together with something of
Heine's half - tender, half - cynical fantasy. Thomson's nature, as has been sufficiently shown, was
eminently gentle and considerate, and a kindly tone
predominates largely in his critical essays. Yet how

severe he could be in his literary judgments and polemical satires is shown by one or two scathing reviews of books which he felt to be aggressively pretentious and slovenly, and by his Lucianic burlesques on certain theological tenets which seemed to him to be so superstitious and degrading as to deserve no quarter.

In conclusion, it cannot be doubted that Thomson's literary style, in poetry and prose alike, with its singular prevalence of gloomy thoughtfulness, broken only to be enhanced and confirmed by occasional flashes of sprightliness and merriment, is closely and inseparably connected with the whole bent of his character and opinions; the writings can as little be understood apart from the man, as the man apart from the writings. His "poetry of pessimism" is no doubt partly akin to the despondency which may be detected in other poets of the last quarter of a century, such as Arnold and Swinburne and Rossetti; but whereas with them it is only an undertone, seldom emphasised though never wholly forgotten, it is with Thomson the very keynote of the harmony, the central theme on which he dwells with strange and powerful persistence. This intensity of vision and, in a certain sense, narrowness of scope serve to connect him, on the one hand, with Coleridge and Poe, the only poets who have possessed the same faculty of producing by sombre imagery and sonorous music the same weird and haunting effect of darkness and desolation; while, in another direction, as I have said, he breathes the freer atmosphere and more gentle spirit of Shelley, of whom, in spite of their difference of creed, he always regarded himself as a follower. But, after all has been said regarding

Thomson's resemblances to other writers, the fact remains that his position in English literature is unique; a special niche will have to be set apart for him in the gallery of poets.

When we take into consideration Thomson's whole body of work, poetry and prose together, I think it must in justice be said that he possesses the two prime qualities that are essential to the making of a great writer. In the first place, he has that strong sense of humanity which lies at the back of all really memorable and permanent literature; pessimist though he may be, his sympathies are entirely human; the subject, in one shape or another, of all his writings being that great struggle between Love and Death, the pessimistic view of which must present itself, in certain moods and at certain times, to the mind of every thoughtful person. Secondly, he is gifted with the not less indispensable faculty of poetic and artistic expression—the rich tone, the subtle melody, the strength, speed, and exquisite flexibility of his language will scarcely be denied by those who have made it their study. Popular he perhaps can never be, in the ordinary sense, since his doctrines all point to a conclusion which is eminently disagreeable to the popular taste; but when once his claim to literary immortality is deliberately and impartially considered by those who are qualified to judge, it will be impossible for posterity to deny him his place among the true and sacred poets of his own generation.

INDEX.

THE END.

PRINTED BY BALLANTYNE, HANSON AND CO.
EDINBURGH AND LONDON.